A
RAKE
OF
HIS
OWN

A RAKE OF HIS OWN

OF

HIS

OWN

A STARIEL NOVEL

A.J. LANCASTER

Published by Camberion Press, Wellington, New Zealand

Printed by KDP.

A CIP record for this book is available from the National Library of New Zealand

ISBN 978-0-473-62479-8 (paperback)
ISBN 978-0-473-62480-4 (Kindle)

Cover design © Jennifer Zemanek / Seedlings Design Studio

ajlancaster.com

CONTENTS

For the anxious ones.

CONTENT ADVISORY

This story contains:
- period-typical homophobia
- references to past sexual assault
- mind-altering drugs
- coercive magic

A FRUSTRATING PROLOGUE

They kissed in the shadows. It felt like the exhalation of a breath held for too long, an inevitability, as his shoulders hit wood panelling behind him. A voice at the back of his mind murmured that perhaps this wasn't wise, that he'd made terrible mistakes before and didn't think he could survive making them again. He wasn't sure whether he even liked this man. This fae.

But tonight, he was past caring. The muted sounds of merrymaking hummed in the distance, but here there was only the thunder of his heart and their harsh breaths comingling. They kissed feverishly, hands moving and bodies hard. He was so tired of being alone, and he didn't want to think anymore. It had been building for months, this magnetic push-pull between them. Why not finally give in and let the sensation drag him under for a while?

"My room," he gasped when they broke apart.

Rakken's eyes were molten, his lips flushed scarlet. He stared at Marius for a long, long moment, and then desire slid from his face, leaving only a cold hardness.

He gave a soft, contemptuous laugh. "No. No, I think not. This was sufficient. Let us not repeat it."

He pushed Marius away as if burned and stalked out without a backwards glance, leaving Marius open-mouthed and aching, too shocked at the sudden reversal to call after him.

1

THREE MONTHS LATER

MARIUS HAD TAKEN only two steps inside the make-shift pub before deciding he was going to strangle his cousin.

"Oh, come on, Em," Caro had wheedled last week. "It'll be fun—just a casual get-together with a few friends. You've been hiding in that greenhouse for too long; you'll start growing roots yourself soon!"

Her resigned expression was what had done for him. In it, he'd seen that she took his refusal as a foregone conclusion. He never did anything fun anymore; he'd been moping about for months now for reasons she didn't know. She was worried about him.

Not that she'd said any of that aloud.

But he'd heard her thinking it, so of course he'd said, yes, actually, he *would* come along, thank you very much for asking, and damn the probably dire telepathic consequences. Also, he had *not* been moping; he'd just been keeping busy and certainly not avoiding anything. Or anyone.

Not that he'd said that aloud either.

"You just going to stand there, mate?"

With a start, Marius got out of the doorway, mumbling an apology. The noise of the packed rooms engulfed him. Someone had hired an illusionist to make coloured dancing lights hover above the dance floor, and raucous laughter and conversation mingled with the music from the phonograph.

A few friends, eh, Caro? he thought wryly.

It was certainly a casual get-together, though, in this rabbit warren writhing with people mostly younger than him. He felt himself withering into dust at the grand old age of twenty-nine.

Where was Caro? He began to search the teeming mass for a glimpse of his cousin's distinctive red curls. Several minutes and no successes later, he washed up against the bar.

A woman perched on a stool next to the bar was dressed like a man, hair cut short, wearing exposed braces over her loose linen shirt. She wasn't the only woman here dressed so. Students from the sole women's college in Knoxbridge? They had a certain reputation. As he watched, she laughed uproariously at something the woman next to her was saying. Yearning stabbed through him. How did you live that comfortably in your own skin?

He ordered a drink. The beer was cheap and the publican suspiciously fresh-faced. Not great omens. His head gave a warning twinge, an even worse omen. He ignored it. He was determined to stick it out, at least until he found Caro. That would show her.

Is it really her you're trying to show, though? his relentless inner voice piped up. *Or is it yourself?*

I'm showing... someone, he retorted. So there.

Taking his drink, he retreated through the crowd. The building was probably five hundred years old, and the layout suggested it had been built as a family home rather than a public house. Some of the walls between rooms had been knocked out, and the overall effect was an endless series of alcoves. He had to keep ducking to avoid the wooden beams. By the tenth time, he was swearing under his breath. He might be taller than average, but this was ridiculous. Either people five hundred years ago had been substantially shorter, or the building had been originally occupied by dwarves.

Do dwarves exist? he couldn't help wondering on the heels of that thought. *After all, the fae turned out to be real. Could dwarves be just another type of fae?* The re-connection of the Faerie and Mortal realms after a three-century separation was still so new that it was hard to know which bits of folklore remained only that.

He stepped out of the way of a merry couple and narrowly avoided banging his head again. Time for a new strategy. Diving for the safety of the nearest free seat, he found himself on a bit of bench along the wall, in a no-man's land between two other tables.

He felt as out of place as a tussock in a flower bed, although now that he'd reduced the risk of braining himself, he began to warm to the atmosphere. The cheapness of the drinks had put Caro's hundred or so friends in good spirits. Loud conversations clamoured with opinions and politics. People wore devil-may-care personal fashions, and men and women mixed with complete disregard for convention.

At the table to his left, three girls were arguing about the merits of some poet. From the group on his right, he caught the edge of a more worrying conversation.

"—said she saw them in Meridon, at some palace function. Ambassadors from different fairy courts."

"Do they really have wings?"

Marius could have told them that fae varied greatly in appearances. Greater fae were shapeshifters besides, so that even those who had wings didn't have them all the time.

"Some of them did." The first speaker laughed. "Bunty waxed rather lyrical in her descriptions. 'Tall, dark, and handsome as sin, with eyes like cut emeralds and wings of beaten bronze.' I told her she'd been at the gothic novels too long."

Everything in Marius went quiet and cool. Then he shifted deliberately away along the bench. He didn't want to think about the fae prince who met that description, who he hadn't seen hide nor hair of since Hetta's wedding but who apparently had had time to swan about to soirées or whatever it was Rakken had been doing at the palace.

Not that he cared.

He focused on the crowd, checking faces in case Caro had slipped in. His head gave another twinge. A sensible man ought to leave now, before the worst could happen, but a flicker of rebelliousness curled in his stomach. He fixed his gaze on his drink. Maybe it would help?

Why would a substance known to make people lose control help you keep yours? his inner logician pointed out.

We don't know that it doesn't, he returned. Alcohol interfered with coordination and perception. Maybe it turned off magical abilities too.

Right—that logic definitely held up to scrutiny.

You have a nine o'clock tutorial to give tomorrow, remember? his sense of responsibility reminded him.

The restless, uncomfortable parts of himself currently in the majority voted strongly for inebriation.

Someone brushed past him on their way towards the bar, a large fellow with rugby shoulders, and Marius heard his thoughts clear as a clarion bell. Rugby-shoulders was wondering what were the chances of getting his oar in later that night with a large-breasted woman.

Marius put his glass down and strongly considered placing his forehead beside it. *If you're hearing other people's thoughts, it's time to leave.* But maybe he hadn't heard anything; maybe it was all his imagination. He lived in a state of interminable uncertainty now. His own head was tangled enough that it was always possible he'd simply projected his own thoughts onto reality.

Besides, he still had to find Caro. He pinched the bridge of his nose, pushing up his spectacles, and imagined a wall around his brain. Wall, wall, wall. If only he knew where the bloody off-switch was for this telepathy business.

"Valstar?" *Found him!*

Marius found himself being surveyed by a short, vaguely familiar young man with dark eyes, ruddy-brown skin, and rolled-up shirtsleeves displaying the sort of muscular forearms that had no business belonging to an academic. The stranger smiled down at Marius as if he expected to be recognised, and Marius tried hurriedly to place him. A touch too young to be one of his old classmates from before his years of enforced absence from university life; a touch too old to be one of the undergrads he tutored now. Another post-grad from the college? Yes, that was it; he'd seen this fellow in the dining hall of Shakif College on occasion. Now, what was the chap's name? He didn't think they'd ever spoken. Had they? The name was on the tip of his tongue. Come on, come on—now would be a *great* time for telepathy—

"Thomas Bakir," the man said, correctly divining the problem. He had a trace of a Dumnonic accent, from the southernmost tip of Prydein. "Floor above you. Literature."

"Botany," Marius said reflexively.

Bakir cocked his head. "I don't think we met at the time, but I started off reading law. I knew John Tidwell. You used to be… friends, didn't you?" The deliberate pause held a world of meaning.

Anxiety pulsed through him. Bakir knew. The knowing came with a spike of pain in his temples. Bakir knew what John had been to him, and more than that, Bakir was… like Marius. And wanted him to know it. Which meant… he didn't dare speculate.

He'd known there were others like him out there, a casual network of lovers, dark alleys, private rooms, coded phrases and implications. Knoxbridge wasn't the more conservative North where he'd grown up. If such things weren't exactly accepted here, a lot more of a blind eye was turned. But Marius had never been part of those networks, unable to find his way in and too anxious to take the risk of being wrong.

What were the chances that he'd stumbled on them now? But this *was* an unconventional gathering if ever he'd seen one—and just why had Caro invited him to it? As far as Caro knew, Marius was as conventional as they came.

Bakir watched him with dark eyes, still waiting for a response.

"He and I are not friends anymore," he said shortly, gripping his glass so tightly he had to force his fingers to relax. Of all the sodding luck, running into one of John's friends—but Bakir was already shaking his head.

"Oh good, that means I can admit I never cared for Tidwell either." Bakir gestured at the space on the bench next to Marius.

Marius shuffled back out of instinctual politeness. "No?" he asked warily as Bakir sat down.

"Always got the impression I wasn't useful enough to be worth bothering with." Bakir gave a self-deprecating shrug. "Scholarship student, you know. No money or connections to speak of."

"I—" *wasn't useful enough to him either, as it turned out.* John had cut things off the moment Marius had failed to inherit his father's estate, and then, feeling aggrieved at being denied such rewards, he'd tried to blackmail Marius's family. And *then*, when that hadn't worked, he'd tried to ruin the Valstars in other ways.

It had taught him not to trust a pretty face. Rakken had merely been a small remedial lesson after the major course of study, since he was apparently a slow learner. *Never again, though.*

"So… from law to literature? How did that happen?" he asked.

"A bit of a switch, yes." Bakir took the change of subject gracefully. "It was the chance to pursue professional obscurity, unreliable employment, and bore people senseless at parties that appealed, naturally. You?"

Marius smiled. "Oh, the same, naturally."

Bakir returned the expression. He had a pleasant smile, white against dark skin. "Though as to that, times are changing. I'm specialising in folk tales, which my parents had originally despaired of, but now I look like a veritable genius of foresight."

All Marius's muscles locked up. "Folk tales," he repeated. "Fairy stories." His younger sister Hetta had recently married a fae prince, the first such union since the Iron Law had been revoked. Creatures living under rocks now knew the Valstar name and their association with fae.

His reaction didn't go unnoticed, but Bakir didn't stop smiling. "Not the same thing, actually. For those not keen to read an 800-page monograph on the difference, all fairy stories are folk tales, but not all folk tales are fairy stories. Of course, nuances aside, I thought of shamelessly cosying up to you for information, but my professor doesn't think it's an admissible form of literary analysis." Bakir gave a deep, put-upon sigh. "Into each life some rain must fall."

Marius gave a grudging laugh but didn't entirely relax. People had tried to use him too many times before for him to treat it as much of a joke.

Bakir eyed him speculatively. "If only there were some *other* comfort to be had from cosying up to you."

Marius nearly knocked his glass over. *Honestly!* he thought with internal exasperation. *You'd think a telepath wouldn't be so easily shocked!* Heat rose in his cheeks. Fear spiked in a disorienting counterpoint, freezing his limbs and heart with an ice-cold anxiety on the edge of nausea.

What was wrong with him? What was he afraid of? Wasn't this what he should want? Bakir was perfectly nice to look at, had enough confidence for both of them, and, and... why did Bakir even want him, anyway? Did he see the same weakness that John had? The same thing that had made Rakken curl away from him too, when it came to it?

He'd taken too long to respond, and he heard Bakir's frisson of anxiety: *I haven't misjudged, have I?*

The instinct to reassure was so ingrained that he acted without thought, resting a hand lightly on Bakir's knee where it was hidden beneath the table. Bakir smiled again like the sun had come up. Marius snatched his hand back, belatedly realising he hadn't just soothed Bakir's anxiety but indicated he welcomed his advances. And now it seemed horribly awkward to clarify matters. How did he get himself into these tangles?

Maybe he *did* welcome Bakir's advances? He was sick of his

own company, of the spinning anxiety of his brain, of the ache of loneliness sitting lump-like in his stomach. Maybe this was the way to erase the sense-memory of the last person to touch him, which he kept returning to even though he'd rather not think of it.

Memories assaulted him: heat, citrus, sweat, and the brush of feathers... *Not helpful,* he told himself. *Say something normal!* "Er, I've an interest in folklore myself. With plants. Plants and folklore," he said hurriedly.

"'Rowan tree and red thread'?" Bakir quoted from the old rhyme.

"Er, yes, well, no, not that specifically, but that sort of thing, yes. There's been very little research into the potential magical properties of plants, and mostly it's been considered superstition rather than science. But now, with fae magic seeming to behave so differently from the human sort..." He found himself launching into the talk he hadn't worked up the courage to have with his supervisor.

"And have you found them? Magical plants?" Bakir asked after politely letting him run on for a few minutes. To his credit, he managed to look interested.

Marius nearly said: *I figured out how to use them to see through minor fae glamour and resist compulsion, with the reluctant help of a fae prince,* but just stopped himself. "It's all hypothetical thus far. Though there is some interest in the department." *From someone who isn't my supervisor. Who I have been having off-campus meetings with. Because my life isn't complicated enough.*

"Fascinating stuff, though, isn't it? All those stories filed under 'fiction' that turned out to be true. I might have to reclassify myself as a sociologist," Bakir said in disgust, and Marius laughed.

"Another drink?" Bakir shifted closer, his thigh pressing against Marius's. The physical contact increased the already-disorienting sweep of Bakir's thoughts into a tornado. *I've always liked long legs on a man. Wonder what it would take to get them wrapped around me? Tidwell was a shit, but he had good taste in men, I'll give him that.*

Marius tried to jerk his mind away, but his thoughts caught in a whirl that expanded out from Bakir to include the girls at the poetry table, out and out and out and—

Wonder if she's single?

Andeus certainly wasn't the premier architect of his day, fuck you!

Woah, floor, steady on...

What's that line again?

A hundred petty musings, half-ends of conversations, and inebriated feelings washed over him.

"Marius?" *He came! Who's that he's talking to? Oh, Thomas Bakir!*

Marius started, surfacing from the chaos with a gasp. "Caro!"

His cousin beamed down at him. She was a few years younger than him, prettily plump, and as primly dressed as ever, though for tonight's revelries she'd worn a feathered band to tie back her red hair. "You came!" she said. *I didn't think you would; you've been such a shut-in lately. Everyone's been so worried. Oh no, he looks cross. He's going to make an excuse and leave, isn't he?*

"I—" Which bit had she said aloud?

Thoughts were coming at Marius from every direction now. He stood too quickly, barely hearing Bakir's concerned query. Dark liquid spread across the table, reflecting the yellow lights. He stared at it a moment before righting his glass with shaking hands.

"Sorry. Have to go. Sudden migraine coming on."

Caro's face fell. "Oh. Oh, of course. Is there anything I can do?" *But you only just got here! Does he hate it so much? Maybe I shouldn't have invited him. But he does look grey. Why did he come, if he was feeling poorly? Is he all right? Hetta did say he was still recovering from that fae attack.*

"Marius?"

Oh, wait, had there been a verbal question in there somewhere? He couldn't separate it out. "Sorry," he said again, shaking his head. "I'm fine."

He pushed his way through the crowd, his head ringing. His telepathy spooled outwards, bringing streamers of chatter and emotions, and he stumbled against the doorframe, misjudging the depth of the step.

He shuddered in relief as he hit the cool night air and the emptiness of the streets. His telepathy circled, uncontrolled and hungry as a wolf, but the streamers of thoughts were thinner out here with fewer people around. Shoving his hands in his pockets, he walked, blindly seeking the path that took him furthest from other minds.

The telepathy had been a growing problem for the last year, sparked by an attack that Wyn, his new brother-in-law, thought had probably triggered a latent psychic ability. Marius still didn't know how or why his telepathy worked. He'd hoped it would just... either fade away or he'd figure out how to turn it off.

But instead, it was getting worse. Was it getting worse? Crowds always seemed to exacerbate things. Maybe it was just that and the half a drink he'd had tonight.

No, it *was* getting worse, and he knew it. There was a reason he'd been practically a hermit these past few months.

He strode through the lamp-lit darkness and tried to

imagine a wall rising around his mind, narrowing his focus to the breeze on the back of his neck, the sound of his shoes on the cobblestones. Each footstep rang out, a beat driving back the other minds. It would've been quicker to walk through the streets of Knoxbridge, but he headed down to the towpath instead. There were fewer people down there.

Gods. What an absolute mess. The moon hung full and low in the sky, casting an orange glow. Riverboats knocked gently against each other, the wind just high enough to ruffle the water.

He shoved his hands deeper into his coat pockets. His fingers closed on the modified quizzing glass that he'd made into a glamour-detector when painted with the right herbal mixture. Briefly, he considered checking the river for lowfae but decided against it.

He walked past the Botanical Gardens, the greenhouses dark and silent at this hour, and turned into the street that held Shakif College. The night porter wondered if he'd been troubled by insomnia again, this late-night walking of his was getting to be such a habit, though not so late tonight as usual, and Marius nearly responded before realising the man hadn't spoken.

"Er, good night, Carter," Marius said, recovering himself in time.

"Night, Mr Valstar." *Too much time spent indoors; not good for a young man. Wonder what the Missus will have on for us tonight? I hope it's not the meatloaf again.*

Marius breathed, in, out, trying to find the line between himself and the world as he made his way upstairs and let himself into his room. Reflected lamplight gleamed in the bay windows at the far end. The geometric lines of the panes were interrupted by stacks of books piled on his desk and along the shallow windowseat.

He navigated through the piles to draw closed the curtains. Turning away from the windows, he contemplated his rumpled bed. A better person than he would've made it before he'd left this morning, but he'd been in a mad scramble to get to a lecture in time.

The thought of hot running water tempted him briefly out of his room to the shared bathrooms. It was late enough that he had the showers to himself, thank the gods. For long moments he stood with his head immersed in the spray, hot water running down his body in streams that utterly failed to wash away anything that mattered. Closing his eyes, he rested his forehead against the cool shower tiles and said, eloquently, "Fuck."

Then he turned off the taps and took refuge in the small comforts of cleanliness, fresh towels, and his cosy, deep-pocketed dressing gown, and returned to his room feeling somewhat cheered. Now, where had he left that book he'd been reading earlier?

On the windowseat, of course, for his sins. He was about to pick his way back through the fire hazard when the scent of citrus and storms rolled over him. He froze. He knew that signature.

He was imagining it.

He was *not* imagining it, and all he could do was clutch his dressing gown to his chest like a startled rabbit as a portal opened between desk and dresser and a naked, bloody fae prince stumbled through.

2

HIS HIGHNESS RAKKEN TEMPESTREN

I F ONE DISTILLED all the qualities that Marius found most aggravating into a single man, that man would be His Highness Rakken Tempestren, prince of the fae Court of Ten Thousand Spires.

You couldn't trust anything he said. His words might be technically true, but there was always a hidden current beneath them, an agenda known only to Rakken. He'd been the one to convince Hetta and Wyn to conceal Marius's awakening telepathic powers from him. For the best, of course, and not at *all* to avoid Rakken losing the upper hand.

You couldn't trust his actions either. He had once kissed Marius while seemingly overcome with desire (flattering), only for it to turn out that what he actually wanted was an emotional boost to fuel his flagging magical reserves (not flattering). He'd refused to help with Marius's anti-glamour experiments right up until the moment he'd needed something from those same experiments for his own spellcasting. Even when he did something useful—such as the time he'd acted as Marius's bodyguard—it was always driven by his need to discharge his obligations in the complicated and maddening system of fae debts.

He was fascinating in the same way that tigers and deadly poisonous snakes were. Yet people *flocked* to him. He became the centre of attention the moment he walked into a room. Partly because he was so shockingly handsome (and knew it, damn him) but mostly because of his insufferable air of self-assurance and, if that failed, his questionable use of mind magic. Marius had seen Rakken command an entire crowd more than once, bending them to his will with his compulsion.

In conclusion, Rakken was utterly, immeasurably terrible, and Marius was *delighted* that he hadn't had to deal with him for months.

Except now, here he was.

Naked.

Rakken's dark hair spilled wild and unkempt over his bare shoulders. Blood spattered one of his horns and the miles and miles of muscular brown skin that wasn't nearly hidden enough by his great bronze-and-green wings. He looked dreadful. He looked glorious.

Marius gaped at him.

Rakken gaped back, as if *Marius* were the one who'd sprung unexpectedly and nakedly from nowhere.

Under other circumstances, it would have been gratifying to see Rakken so taken aback. As it was, Marius's brain wouldn't stop repeating the word NAKED at the top of its lungs. His gaze drew inexorably downwards. Right. Yes. Of course. He wrenched his gaze back up.

"What are you doing here? *How* are you here?" Because fae

couldn't open portals just anywhere, or so he'd thought. Before the portal snapped out, he glimpsed cavernous darkness.

"Marius Rufus Valstar," Rakken said. His green eyes were deep enough to drown in. *Like a swamp full of crocodiles*, Marius told himself. "I—" Rakken swayed, and Marius grabbed his arm to steady him out of sheer reflex, and Rakken got his wing caught on the edge of the desk, and they both went down in a pile of feathers and nudity and tangled limbs and Marius was only wearing his nightshirt under his dressing gown and oh gods there was more blood on Rakken than he'd realised.

And now he was lying on top of Rakken. Rakken blinked up at him from two inches away, his expression almost dreamy. One hand came up and brushed against Marius's cheek. *You're really here.* The single thought came through before Rakken's mental shields snapped up.

Or at least, Marius thought it had been Rakken's thought. Maybe it had been his own. He disentangled himself, getting to his feet and backing away. Rakken sat up more slowly, propping himself up against the dresser and continuing to stare at Marius in an unfocused way.

"Are you injured? You're covered in blood," Marius added, gesturing when Rakken continued to do nothing but blink dreamily at him.

Rakken followed the motion and looked foggily at his own thigh as if this was news to him. "So I am," he said, sounding surprised. He began to take inventory of himself, fingertips ghosting over his body. His extremely naked and sculpted body.

Mighty Pyrania and all the little gods.

"Here," Marius said, scrambling for the nearest scrap of fabric, which turned out to be the damp towel from the shower he'd just taken. He threw it at Rakken, who caught it with uncharacteristic clumsiness and stared at the towel for a bit before feebly starting to wipe at the blood.

"No, I mean, yes. It's—hang on, I'll get some water and a cloth for you to clean yourself up. Just, just cover yourself, all right?" Marius turned his back and went to the tiny recessed sink in the wall. He put the heatstone on. His heartbeat thundered in his ears to the rhythm of *naked, naked, naked. Which you should not be ogling because he is hurt and possibly drugged and also because you should not be ogling him at all, because you dislike him.* Marius grabbed his spectacles off the shelf, the world coming into crisp focus.

"Cover… myself?" Rakken's voice had an odd slowness to it, but then he chuckled, sharpness rushing back. "Oh, your mortal mores. Am I *bothering* you?"

"Good to see your ego hasn't been dented by whatever scratched you up," Marius said. "What did scratch you up?"

Rakken's chuckle filled the room, warm and touchable. "Oh, Marius Valstar, you are so easy to provoke." But when Marius turned back, Rakken had draped the towel around his waist, though not without adding: "Nudity doesn't *always* lead to fucking, you know. Surely this is true even for mortals?"

Marius choked, heat swarming over him. "It's—that's not— what are you doing here, Mouse?"

Using the pet-name from Rakken's twin sister seemed to snap him further back to himself. "Don't call me that, Marius Valstar."

"Don't call me that, then," he said evenly. It was an old argument. Using someone's full name was a bit of fae dominance posturing, Wyn had told him. Wyn was Rakken's younger brother. Marius's extended family had gotten rather complicated.

Rakken got unsteadily to his feet. The change in position threatened to release the towel, but Rakken rolled his eyes at Marius's expression and tied it back in place.

Rakken wouldn't have fit easily into his rooms in his fae form even under normal circumstances, but wobbling and absent all his normal grace, he took up the entire room and all its oxygen. His feathers sent a pile of papers sliding across the floor. Rakken pulled in his wings, but the motion only sent his hip knocking against the desk, making the pens clatter across it.

"Ah, stormwinds take it," Rakken muttered and changed.

In his mortal form, there was less of him, but he still moved like a drunken cat.

"Sit down before you fall down," Marius said, waving at his solitary armchair.

It was a measure of how Rakken was feeling that he obeyed without protest, collapsing into the worn chair with a muttered curse. Marius approached with the damp cloth and went to wash some of the blood off Rakken's shoulder.

Rakken shifted away, holding out a hand for the cloth just in case the unsubtle message not to touch hadn't been received. Marius stepped back and passed him the cloth. Why did he feel hurt by Rakken's action? It wasn't as if he *wanted* to touch him.

That wasn't a very convincing lie even in his own head. Of *course* he wanted to touch Rakken. He wasn't a monk-druid. But he *shouldn't*, was the point. He knew what came of tangling with unprincipled, beautiful men, and Rakken was the most beautiful man he had ever seen.

He swallowed. "What's wrong with you?" he tried asking again. "Were you attacked? Has something gone wrong in the Spires?"

Rakken shook his head as if he were trying to clear it. "Cat is fine. The Spires are fine." He scowled at the bloodied cloth in his hand as if it were an impenetrable logic puzzle. Marius had never seen Rakken and the word 'vulnerable' in the same room together, but that was the descriptor that now rose to mind. Rakken sat stiffly, trying to both focus and hide the fact that he was worried by his own inability to do so.

"Oh, for goodness' sake." Marius plucked the cloth out of Rakken's hand. "This is going to take all night if we wait for you to do it." When Rakken looked as if he was still going to refuse, Marius hissed: "No debt for this. Now sit still."

Rakken huffed. "That is not how obligation works, mortal."

"Don't 'mortal' me, and yes, right here it does. I don't have to work to your stupid fairy rules. I'm not patching you up out of a sense of obligation; I'm doing it because I would do the same for anyone in this situation. Because it's the decent thing to do." Even if Marius remained angry with him for a long list of past offences. And even if Rakken was currently adding to said list by being his typical secretive self.

"Even your enemies?" A half-teasing note snuck into Rakken's voice, but Marius could feel the tension under his hands.

"We're not enemies, Prince Melodramatic. We're just… I don't know, antagonistic acquaintances."

"Now, why does that feel like a demotion?" Rakken said, but he didn't shift away when Marius went to dab at the nearest wound.

Marius bit his tongue. He *could* show some degree of maturity, damn it. To his relief, after cleaning the worst of the blood away, he discovered that the reason for Rakken's alarming appearance was the quantity of wounds rather than their individual severity. He was covered in small, shallow cuts with neat edges. Most of them had already begun to scab over. Fae had abnormal healing powers.

"You look like you've been attacked by a hundred angry razor blades," he said quietly, making a question of it.

Rakken said nothing, and Marius wiped one of the deeper cuts on his back with more force than necessary. Rakken didn't flinch. Not that Marius had expected him to; he'd once seen Rakken trading quips after nearly being cleaved in two.

"Is this the true reason you're helping me? For the chance to poke my open wounds?" Rakken asked.

"That's just a happy bonus."

Rakken chuckled, and it made Marius irrationally furious. How dare Rakken turn up flirtatious and bleeding, without a breath of apology or explanation? Stroking the cloth over his skin made Marius remember things he'd rather forget. How Rakken had looked at him the last time he'd seen him. The low growl he'd made when Marius had pressed his mouth to the clean line of his throat, the sound a vibration against his lips. The sheer heat of him, so close.

Was Rakken remembering that too?

Why in the hells was *Marius* thinking of it? It had been a mistake, and one he wouldn't have made if not for the circumstances leading up to it. Happy as he'd been for his sister and best friend, weddings were the sort of occasion that left one feeling the empty spaces of one's own life more so than usual. He ought to have expected the overindulgence and subsequent melancholia-driven bad decisions.

So it's a good thing Rakken didn't want you then, isn't it? his helpful inner commentary piped up. *That you never slept together. Saved you both the regret.*

Yes, Marius returned. *Because I don't want him either. A few moments of madness notwithstanding, he is the absolute last person in the world I would choose. If I were choosing anyone. Which I'm not. Better to keep out of entanglements entirely.*

"Far be it from me to criticise your work," Rakken said, a burr of amusement in his voice. "But I think my shoulder is quite clean now."

Marius jolted back to find he'd been making furious repetitive circles in the same spot for who knew how long. Rakken's skin glistened with moisture. Marius's cheeks burned.

Unable to think of a rejoinder, he went back to the sink. Took a deep, steadying breath as he rinsed out the cloth. Stared at the wall above the sink for a moment. *Get it together, Marius.*

"Have you come from ThousandSpire, then?" he asked as he turned back. "Is that where you've been since—since Cat ascended?"

What he wanted to say was, *three months, Rakken.* Three months since the bickering between them had boiled over into that fraught moment of unfulfilled heat at Hetta's wedding. Three months since Rakken had walked away without a word of apology or farewell. Three months in which he knew Rakken had visited Mortal, had visited Stariel, had apparently even visited Meridon, only an hour's train ride away and less than that flying, and yet had made no effort to speak to him.

Except that would imply that Marius cared that Rakken had been avoiding him. Which he did not.

"For much of the time, yes." Rakken was watching him closely. His eyes had an odd glitter to them, almost feverish.

"Except when you've been in Mortal."

"Yes," Rakken said without further elaboration.

"I take it you've been involved in the treaty talks."

"You did not ask my brother?"

"No." He hadn't wanted to face the concern he knew such a query would provoke. Wyn was already far too concerned about him, and Marius couldn't bear the weight of any more. "Lean forward so I can get at this one."

Rakken did so, but his gaze had turned inwards, a frown forming between his brows. There remained an off-balance sense to him that made Marius worry, despite everything. Rakken clearly wasn't all right and just as clearly had no intention of admitting to it.

"Are you going to explain what you're doing here if I ask enough times?" Marius put the cloth back in the sink for the final time. "And do you have any clothes, or do you want me to lend you something?" He'd seen Rakken store small objects around his person before with magic, but he didn't know how far that ability extended.

"You are curiously obsessed with covering me up, Marius Valstar." Rakken rose, steadier on his feet than before but lacking his usual grace.

A cursory knock sounded on the door before it pressed open.

"Valstar? I saw your light was on and thought I'd check—" Bakir broke off at the sight of Rakken.

Rakken was so very naked, and the crisp white of the towel wrapped around the brown skin of his midriff only accentuated that fact. He was also glistening with a sheen of what Marius knew was water but which might have looked, to an uninformed observer, like sweat.

Well, damn, he heard, a low whistle of a thought. *I can see why I batted out, then.*

"Marius is busy," Rakken purred, putting every bit of his not-inconsiderable sensuality into those three words. Magic, too, Marius was pretty sure. "You may leave us."

Marius was too frozen in absolute mortification to say anything about this piece of high-handedness. Bakir gave him an impressed look. "Right. Right. Glad you're all right, then. Maybe lock the door, though? Careless of you." Bakir shut the door before Marius could respond.

"You—you—" Marius spluttered in Rakken's direction. His heart pounded. Gods, what if it had been someone other than Bakir? And Bakir now thought— "You made him think we're, we're…"

Rakken gave a tigerish grin. "Yes?"

He hated the heat that rose to his cheeks. "Did you compel him?"

Rakken rolled his eyes. "Oh no, those were entirely organic conclusions he drew. It's more fun that way."

Marius pinched the bridge of his nose. "I'm going to leave now, and when I come back, you'd better be either gone or fully dressed and full of explanations."

"I—" Rakken swivelled like a pointer catching a scent. His gaze lost focus, brow furrowing in a way that Marius recognised. It was called leysight, a fae ability to see magic in the world. Marius followed Rakken's attention, but as he was staring straight at the wall, this didn't tell him much.

Wouldn't it be wonderful if he could read minds? But Rakken had himself under wraps, his mind only smooth darkness, and Marius couldn't guess what he was thinking except he wasn't enjoying it much from his expression.

"What is it?" he asked.

Rakken's eyes snapped back into focus. All his lazy sensuality had snuffed out, replaced with something cold and wary. He looked at Marius as if he were a stranger. "Someone is performing magic near your greenhouse. Fae magic. *Dark* fae magic. What exactly have you been doing there? Who are you working with?"

"No one! And nothing!" He would've accused Rakken of changing the subject, but fae couldn't lie, so he must've sensed something. It seemed much less important right now than getting to the bottom of Rakken's inexplicable appearance.

Rakken gave himself a loose shake, as if struggling to ground himself. "You were experimenting with plants known for their anti-fae properties, before—are you still?"

"Which turned out to be extremely beneficial to you, remember? There's nothing in my greenhouse you haven't already seen. And I don't even know what dark magic *is*."

Ignorance is dangerous, Marius.

Marius's temper snapped. "Yes, tell me how dangerous ignorance is when you refuse to tell me what you're doing here! And when it was your idea not to tell me I was a telepath in the first place! And you who refused to help with my research until you suddenly needed me!" That was Rakken; always scheming, using people and discarding them when their use ran out. Just like John had.

Rakken raised an eyebrow. "I do not regret my actions, and I will not apologise." He strode towards the door, somewhat unsteadily.

"Where are you going?" Marius half-yelped when Rakken would have pressed past him.

"To your greenhouse. That flare was no casual thing. I wish to know who cast it, and to what purpose, and, if you are not working with them, what exactly a fae was doing in your greenhouse at this time of night."

Marius thought about arguing that Rakken was in no fit

state to go anywhere but in the end just sighed. "Give me a minute to change."

"I do not require your company."

Marius ignored this and started pulling drawers open. "And you'd better as well—you can't go waltzing through Knoxbridge in a towel." Gods save both him and the citizenry from the world's most aggravating fairy.

3

FULL MOON RISING

RAKKEN *HAD* HAD spare clothing with him, as it turned out. Marius got briefly distracted with wondering how much Rakken could store in his pocket dimensions. Was weight or volume the restriction? Or was he making mini-portals to a closet in Faerie somehow? But how could that work? Marius had thought greater fae could only build portals between two locations that shared a resonance, and then only if the fae building the portal was familiar with each place. Which raised the question of how Rakken had portalled to Marius's room in the first place since he'd never been in here before.

He tried asking Rakken this last question as he fastened his cuffs and got a less-than-satisfactory answer.

Rakken frowned. He had pulled his hair into a long tail, exposing the clean lines of his cheekbones. "It is possible to portal blind, if one has the skill—which I do."

"Blind portalling means you don't know where you're going to come out beforehand? Isn't that risky?"

"Yes," Rakken said. "Come. We have lost enough time." He swept out of the room.

Marius followed, worried about what it meant that Rakken had taken such a risk. Trouble in ThousandSpire? Trouble somewhere else, wherever that cave-like darkness had been that he'd stumbled out of? Trouble for Hetta and Wyn?

"You can make the night porter not notice us, can't you?" he asked as they descended the stairs at the end of his corridor. He didn't want to explain Rakken to anyone they might meet along the way. Bakir's expression kept rising in his mind's eye, the wide-eyed fascination that Rakken always provoked whenever he wasn't actively trying not to. It was called 'allure', which was an aggravating name for an aggravating phenomenon.

"I thought you were opposed to my using magic on unsuspecting mortals."

"Compulsion, yes. Glamour, sometimes, depending on the ethics of the situation." Compulsion could make people do things against their will; glamour altered people's perceptions, the fae equivalent to human illusion magic, though they worked on different principles.

"Is it ethical to hide un-logged visitors from your door-guard? Or does it become so merely when weighed against your personal convenience?"

Marius knew Rakken was trying to rile him, but he answered seriously anyway. "If I thought you were here intending harm to the college, then, yes, it would be unethical to smuggle you in. As it is, no. Half the residents smuggle people in for far less reason. Besides, technically I'm smuggling you *out*."

"It is my magic, so technically *I* am smuggling *you*. Do you wish to bargain for the favour?"

"I promise not to strangle you until we're outside."

Rakken threw back his head and laughed. Marius had
almost forgotten the impact of that laugh, rolling out rich
as velvet, Rakken becoming the most vivid part of a world
centred on him.

Marius looked away, forgetting what he'd been about to say
and only remembering when the first person they passed in the
corridor paid them no attention. Rakken *had* glamoured them,
then. Sometimes Marius could see through glamour unaided
and sometimes he couldn't, but since he was inside this particular spell, he wouldn't have noticed it in either case.

They emerged onto the town's dark streets without arousing
the night porter's interest. Despite his earlier words, it made
Marius squirm a bit. What *was* ethical when it came to magic
that interfered with people's minds? He'd been so sure before
his own telepathy had come to light and crumbled his high
ground to pieces.

He walked beside Rakken, mulling over that. The streets
weren't busy, but they weren't deserted either. Every now and
then there was a roar of light and voices as they passed one of
Knoxbridge's many taverns.

"You're right; I have changed my stance on fae magic,"
Marius said eventually. "I mean, not completely—I still think
the compulsion is wrong—but I can see there was more nuance
in the rest of it than I thought."

Rakken's stride faltered before smoothing out again. *I
thought you were still angry with me.*

"Oh, I am," Marius agreed. "You should've told me about
the telepathy. You owe me an apology for that at the very least."
It was the least of the things he was angry about, but also the
safest. He'd blundered about for months wondering whether
he was going mad before finding out the truth by accident.

"I will not apologise for that choice, Marius Valstar. It was for your own good. I judged you likely to lose control once you lost the subconscious instinct protecting you. Can you say that I was wrong, with your face shadowed from lack of sleep, and the fact that you have responded to my thoughts at least five times since my arrival without realising you have done so?"

Had he? "You still had no right to decide for me. And for all you know, knowing has nothing to do with it. My powers might have grown regardless. Not knowing what was happening to me would have been worse."

Rakken's face was smooth of emotion as they passed beneath a streetlamp. "Regardless, it is done, and it cannot be undone."

"Can you… no, you can't take the mind-reading away, can you, because you can't compel me," Marius answered himself. He was naturally immune to compulsion. Discovering this fact had thankfully not involved Rakken. Small mercies.

"I cannot. I'm not sure I could even if you weren't resistant to compulsion. Some things go bone-deep, and magic is frequently one of them."

"Is that what you're doing for Cat, now? Compelling for queen and court?"

Rakken's stride didn't falter this time, but somehow Marius knew he'd struck deeper than intended. Rakken and his twin were fiercely loyal to each other, but Marius also knew Cat's recent ascension had changed the dynamic between them.

"She is my queen," Rakken said quietly.

"I actually know quite a lot about one's younger sibling being unexpectedly elevated above you, you know." The estate Marius had grown up on—Stariel—had chosen his younger sister Hetta to rule, to everyone's surprise. Marius, as the old lord's eldest son, would have been a much more expected choice.

"I'd ask how you know that Cat is the younger, but it merely demonstrates my earlier point: You are not in control of your powers, Marius Valstar."

"Well, feel free to tell me how I control them, then. I'm all ears. But you don't know anything more than what Wyn's already told me, do you? So it's all very well to tell me I need more control, but until Wyn finds someone who can teach me, I'm on my own."

Rakken made a dismissive sound, a general commentary on his younger brother's competence. They turned down a cobbled alley between two main streets. Rakken walked now with no sign of injury, though there was a tightness to him, as if he were having to concentrate hard to achieve the effect. "Tell me about your experiments," he said.

"I promise I haven't been experimenting with dark fae magic or whatever it was you sensed earlier," Marius said testily.

"What have you been experimenting with, then?"

Marius slid him a look. He couldn't read Rakken's expression in the shadows. He might have been out for a casual stroll but for the restless movements of his fingers. Was he testing the night air for traces of magic?

Marius sighed. "Many and various things for my supervisor. Sunflower movement in response to light. Flower inheritance patterns in snapdragons. I haven't settled on my own topic yet."

"What happened to your work on plants with anti-fae properties?"

"My chief experimental subject wandered off," Marius said acidly, making Rakken chuckle. "I have been doing some related work, still, though my supervisor would be appalled if he found out about it."

"I find myself suddenly in charity with your supervisor."

"Of course you do." Marius scuffed a loose cobble.

"What related work?" Rakken asked, and it struck him that Rakken was seeking distraction, something mundane to anchor him amidst the disorientation he wasn't quite managing to hide. Marius wished Rakken would just *say* what had happened rather than keeping up this facade of stoicism. He wasn't sure how worried to be; the injuries had seemed minor, but what if Rakken had lost more blood than he'd thought? What if he'd suffered some sort of head injury and that was the reason for his confusing manner tonight? Did fae get concussion?

"All right," Marius said and proceeded to tell Rakken what he'd been working on, making his explanation more involved than it needed to be. Serve Rakken right for being secretive.

This cunning plan backfired as he got caught up in his own explanation, and a quarter of an hour later he was somehow neck-deep in speculating on why moon phases should matter when it came to plants and magic without quite remembering how he'd got there.

"It's symbolism again, isn't it? A time caught between two states: full and new," he said, waving at the full moon shining above the jagged rooflines of the terraced houses. "I'd say that's why all the more alarming-sounding magic in folk tales gets linked to 'dark of moon', but Faerie has different connotations about that, doesn't it?"

"If you're referring to the mortal love for the binary of equating black with villainy and white with moral purity, no," Rakken said, because it was impossible for him not to add a dig at mortals when presented with an opportunity. Marius was too interested in having his theory confirmed to mind as much as usual. "Darkness is an aspect of natural cycles, marking a change in emphasis rather than an opposing force—"

"—such as winter and night?" he interjected.

"Yes, and new moon as both death and rebirth. A nadir. Full moon, in contrast, marks a zenith; it's why it is sometimes used when spellcasting to provide an additional spark of power."

"Is the actual physical quantity of light received by a plant at, say, midsummer versus midwinter, a factor in its magical properties or is it just the symbolism?"

Rakken frowned. "How would you propose to test one without the other? Artificially extend the days?" He waved at the streetlights.

That was an idea, and Marius's thoughts ran ahead of him. "Yes, but I don't know how you'd get the funding. Although—I know someone trying for a grant to study the possible magical properties of plants as they relate to folklore. Dr Vane." Oh, in for a penny as for a pound. "I'm, ah, considering requesting to change to his supervision for my thesis."

He found the words spilling out of him before he could stop them, about how his current supervisor was highly regarded but held no interest in this new line of research. It was madness to ask Rakken for advice on this, since Rakken not only had no understanding of university processes but also opposed experimenting with plants inimical to fae magic on principle.

"But you dislike this Vane, even though your research interests align," Rakken said, after listening to Marius's rather incoherent account on how things stood.

"I don't *dislike* him," he began to argue. "It's just a bit awkward, is all, because he was an undergrad at the same time as me, and now he's—"

"—unexpectedly elevated above you," Rakken said drily.

"Well, not unexpectedly," Marius said, feeling defensive at having his own words tossed back at him. "Vane just had all those years here to progress while I was stuck back at Stariel. It's not surprising he's a lecturer now." Even if it was awkward. Marius was neither fish nor fowl. Too old to fit in with the other new post-grads, yet not truly part of the staff.

"Which he seems to have been at pains to emphasise when you spoke. Were you rivals, before?"

Marius glared at Rakken, feeling ruffled at having somehow revealed more than intended.

"I did not ask you to lay this problem at my feet, Marius Valstar, but seeing as you have—" Rakken pulled up short, and Marius blinked back to some awareness of his surroundings. He'd almost forgotten why they'd come.

They'd reached the private gate to the gardens, for staff rather than the public. The gate looked much the same as it always did, signposted with a chain and an 'authorised access only'. There was nothing to stop members of the public ignoring the sign and using this entrance except the fact that this area of the gardens held none of the attractions of the public areas, being sheds, composting, and garden beds arranged for ease of data collection rather than aesthetics.

Of the Tempestren twins, it was usually Cat who put Marius in mind of a hunting falcon, but Rakken was doing a good impression of one now in her absence. His attention had narrowed, his features sharpening, though he remained in his human form.

"What is it?" Marius asked.

"The flare of magic from earlier has faded but…" Rakken trailed off.

"But what?"

"Nothing good. Don't chide me for vagueness; I don't know precisely what yet." Rakken undid the latch and began to move unerringly in the direction of Marius's own greenhouse.

Well, not technically Marius's greenhouse; the gardens belonged to the university, the greenhouses to the botany department. Marius merely had a claim on part of one under the aegis of his supervisor, Professor Greenbriars. Greenbriars, fortunately, wasn't interested in micro-managing his post-grads, or he'd have had conniptions at the extracurricular uses Marius had put the space towards. Oh, Marius was still duti-fully growing the endless crosses of snapdragons that no longer held his attention, but in every spare corner were the plants he'd read about not in scientific journals but folklorists' compi-lations, old wives' cookery books, and tales from his childhood.

It was darker in the gardens, away from the streetlights, with the trees bordering the gardens and the buildings deepening the shadows. He wished he'd brought a torch.

The greenhouses varied in size and style, from historic archi-tecture to the large modern building that took pride of place nearest the department to the rickety slapdash jobs put togeth-er as 'temporary' shelter decades ago and patched up through the subsequent years.

His greenhouse was one of the older historic buildings, which meant it was both picturesque and cramped. Enclosed by glass windows on three sides, the third wall was solid brick and connected the greenhouse to the large potting shed behind it, where the fireplace would've been when it had been built. Nowadays they used heatstones, of course; they were cleaner and had a lower fire risk, though they were also more expensive.

A thin strip of light shone from within the building, making strange shadows of his plants against the wrought-iron bones of the glass house. He frowned, realising that the shed light must be on, the interior door left ajar. Unease shivered down his spine.

"There shouldn't be anyone in there at this time of night," he said in a low tone. He walked them around to unlock the shed door, but there was no need. It was unlocked.

He pushed open the door and was over the threshold before Rakken could do more than growl a warning. "Marius—"

Marius gasped. Distantly he was aware of Rakken behind him, muttering a curse. Marius couldn't make sense of what he was seeing, his mind absorbing it in slow drips.

Blood, lots of it. Shapes in unfamiliar attitudes. More blood. Torn stems. Wilting plants and broken terracotta. Shattered glass.

A body.

4

THERE'S BEEN A MURDER

"OH GODS, VANE!" Marius stumbled towards him, recognising the tweed jacket. Dr Vane was lying on his side on the floor next to one of the work-benches, fallen at a broken angle amidst the debris of plants and soil. Black hair and unnaturally pale skin, his eyes open and staring. His chest a red, wet ruin. There was so much blood. More blood than a human being could lose and be among the living, but it didn't stop Marius from stepping over a fallen rake and kneeling next to Vane. He shook his shoulder.

"Marius—" Rakken repeated.

Marius ignored him and kept shaking. "Martin! Martin, are you all right?"

Dr Martin Vane was not all right. The way his shoulder moved at Marius's touch felt wrong in a way that made him want to immediately recoil, but instead he shook Vane harder. Vane's head lolled back. For a split second, Marius mistook it for a sign of life. But it was only gravity and Marius's shaking, exposing the mess of Vane's throat. Marius flinched. That's where all the blood had come from. Gods. The man's throat had been cut.

A clinical part of him logged the sight: this is what a man looks like with his throat cut. This man is Dr Martin Vane, who you saw alive on Tuesday. You remember his throat intact when he spoke in that careless, confident way he has—had—that always irritated you even when you were undergrads together and isn't—wasn't—any less irritating now, with you a lowly post-grad trying to curry his favour. He loved it, too, you could tell from the way his mouth curved in that little self-congratulatory smirk. Which he'll never make again. Because his throat is cut. Why in the hells are you thinking about this right now?

"He's dead," Marius said, trying out the word. He felt like a player in a pantomime, waiting for the audience to shout ritualised denial.

"Throat slit. Stab wounds on his upper body too. A bladed weapon. Short dagger, at a guess." Rakken sounded coolly disinterested, as if he discovered dead bodies every day. "No ripples along the leylines, though. Either whoever did this has left, or they are shielding their presence from me."

"Do you think he was killed by whoever made that burst of fae magic you sensed before?" Marius said slowly, feeling as if the words were coming from outside himself. Vane lay so still.

"Dark magic, and a mortal stabbed to death under the full moon? I doubt that's coincidence." Rakken sounded so calm and unaffected. What would it take to shake him?

Rakken made a thoughtful sound in the back of his throat and moved past Marius to the workbench. He stepped lightly, like a cat trying to avoid getting its paws wet. Soil and a few empty crates were strewn across the bench, none of which had been there when Marius had closed up earlier. Put there by Vane? Why had he been shifting plants about at this time of night? And why here in Marius's space rather than his own?

Rakken tapped the edge of one of the empty crates. "Something of Faerie was here recently, I think. There is a residue, though the trace is faint and nearly overpowered by the violence. This man collected rare specimens, I think you said, and he had an interest in Faerie?"

Marius stared at the empty crates and mess of wilting plant matter. His mind moved sluggishly. "Are you saying that Vane was taking delivery of fairy plants?" Was that what Vane had meant when he'd spoken cagily of his and Marius's common interests earlier this week? If Vane *had* been taking delivery of fairy plants, where were they now? Impossible to say if there was anything unfamiliar strewn amongst the debris of his own projects.

"If he was, I am interested to know how he came by them, for there are no open trade terms agreed for such, not yet." Rakken narrowed his eyes at the empty crates.

The damage to Marius's own plants itched at him in a way he found hard to ignore. The neat lines of specific crossbreeds were muddled, with labels torn loose; a nightmare for his records. He could re-pot seedlings and take cuttings of larger specimens if necessary where stems had been torn from their roots, but the sooner the better. A hysterical laugh croaked its way out. What sort of inappropriate thought was that? Vane was *dead*; he ought not to be thinking of rescuing plants at such a time! How could he be thinking of his experiments with Vane lying here with his throat cut?

Rakken made an odd growl and moved. He was suddenly at Marius's side and reaching past him. Ignoring Marius's half-formed protest, Rakken turned Vane over, making his head flop again in that abhorrent way. Marius swallowed and looked away. When he looked back, there were glass shards glittering beneath Vane's coat, wet with blood, and Rakken was reaching into Vane's pocket.

When Rakken withdrew his hand, his long fingers were smeared with blood. He held a tiny pale pink creature, smaller than the palm of his hand and crushed out of shape. It took a moment for the sight to make sense. A frog? No, it was the wrong colour, its limbs too oddly proportioned. A type of lowfae, Marius realised with dull horror. Also dead, crushed by the weight of Vane falling on it.

There was a beat of silent thunder, but when Rakken spoke, all he said was, "Interesting," in that same unaffected way. He pulled out a square of silk cloth and carefully folded the lowfae inside. A flourish, and both the cloth and its contents disappeared. Rakken removed another handkerchief and began wiping his hands clean.

"Interesting? How can you stand there and say *interesting*?!" Marius's voice went up. He looked down at Vane's lifeless face, the skin oddly waxy when only two days ago it had been tanned and alive with vigour. And now Vane's blood was all over the greenhouse and soaking into his trousers and on his hands and under his fingernails and, and… he scrambled to his feet, away from it, but his legs didn't work properly and oh god if he fell on Vane that would be—

Rakken caught his weight as his knees gave out, arm across his back. Half-dragging him over to the back wall, he forced him down into the seat there. Marius turned his face into Rakken's shoulder and took deep shuddering breaths, struggling against the sudden urge to vomit. The smell of Rakken's magic increased, rain-drenched citrus, strong enough to block out the smell of blood.

The surge of panic began to subside, shame curling in its place. What kind of man was he that he couldn't seem to stop shaking? "Sorry, I'm sorry," he said, pulling away.

"You haven't seen violent death before. It hits hardest the first time." Rakken's voice was oddly gentle. Of course. Rakken had seen war in Faerie. Rakken had killed people. Like someone had killed Vane. Murder. That was the word. It all felt unreal.

Rakken's arm was still around his waist. Marius shrugged away from it and stared down at his own hands, which were smeared with blood from when he'd touched Vane. He swallowed.

Rakken matter-of-factly took his own handkerchief and began to wipe Marius's fingers clean.

Marius sat numbly and let him. His hands were shaking too badly to do the job himself. "Thank you," he said quietly. There were bloody marks on Rakken's shirt where Marius had gripped him. "I've got blood on you."

"Then we are even for tonight."

Marius gave a croak of laughter. He was angry, he realised, beneath the shock. This was—this was his sanctuary, and he was angry not just at whoever had done such a terrible thing but at Vane for coming here with his illicit plant trade or whatever those crates had been about. Especially given his and Vane's recent discussions. He felt hopelessly naïve. How dare Vane have pretended to only a tidy theoretical interest in Faerie?

Am I really getting angry at a man who's just been murdered? It felt impolite, and he pushed down a hysterical urge to laugh. Closing his eyes, he tried to pull himself together.

He took a deep breath before opening his eyes. "We should…

the city watch. And we shouldn't have moved things—the crime scene." Because this was a crime scene, wasn't it? "We need to tell someone."

"I am less interested in mortal authorities than in whatever caused that flare of dark magic earlier, but a tracking spell will be useless here and now, with so much violence muddying the leylines."

Marius took another steadying breath. "Vane is a mortal and he's been murdered. There are rules about that. The watch have procedures and things to find out who did it." Didn't they? He didn't have the foggiest notion. He stared blankly at a tray of snapdragon seedlings and frowned. Amongst the crushed stems, something glittered. He got unsteadily to his feet.

Rakken's head snapped up, following his line of attention. "Don't touch it!"

Marius leaned closer to inspect his find. It was a dagger with a leaf-shaped blade and a plain handle, all one smooth piece. It looked as if it were made of wood, and it was coated in splatters of what he feared very much was blood.

"I think I found the murder weapon," he said faintly. "But you're right. The police probably wouldn't want me to move it."

"Storms take your police—that is a dryad blade, and it may hold some trace of whoever made it." Rakken was beside him, frowning intensely at the dagger where it lay on the dark potting soil. His fingertips ghosted over it without touching, and his frown deepened. "Damn. Blood and death are the most effective ways to destroy any pre-existing sympathies, and this is saturated with both."

"What is a dryad blade?"

"A weapon made by a dryad's magic. Light and durable. They're not uncommon in Faerie."

"Vane was killed by a *dryad*? After bringing him fairy plants and then... taking them away again?" None of this made any sense to him.

"Anyone can wield a dryad blade after it is made; they are often traded by dryad clans in bulk." Rakken's eyes began to glow, a sure sign that he was leaning hard on his leysight. He cursed again. "No, there is too much violence here muddying the leylines—but someone comes. A mortal."

They both turned towards the shed door.

"Mr Valstar, are you still working?" a young woman's voice called out, and Marius hurried to stop her because the last thing his supervisor's daughter needed to see was, well, any of this but—

—too late.

Miss Greenbriars froze on the threshold, her mouth falling open, and Marius saw the whole awful mess again through her eyes. She made a cut-off shriek of a sound as her gaze fell on Vane.

"Martin!" She darted forward, much as Marius had, drawn by that same instinct to help what was clearly beyond helping.

He moved to block her path. "Miss Greenbriars, don't. You can't do anything for him. He's dead, stabbed; you don't need to see it." But his words didn't seem to register, and he had to catch her wrists and then her shoulders to stop her.

She struggled to get past him, bones thin as a bird's and full of the same wild-creature panic that had gripped him so recently, but she was a slight woman. A myriad of thought-feelings hit him, denial strongest amongst them, a ragged scream of it. *Nonononono. I'm sorry; I did everything I could.*

"He's dead, Miss Greenbriars—Jenny—you can't help him. I'm so sorry." He gave her a little shake. What was the tactful way to deal with this sort of thing? *Was* there a tactful way to deal with it? He didn't know how well she'd known Vane. Vane had been something of a flirt, but women tended—had tended—to like him despite or perhaps because of it. But Vane had also been at odds with her father. The past tense kept queasily slipping in and out of his thoughts.

She gulped but stopped struggling, her eyes flicking up to meet his. "Mr Valstar." He could see the whites all around her eyes. "You—you found him?"

He let go of her wrists, took a breath. "Just now. It looks like someone broke in."

"Are you sure? He wasn't—he wasn't still alive when you found him?" Miss Greenbriars asked. Behind her huge, frightened eyes lay a silent roar of anguish that made him flinch.

He shook his head. "No. I'm sorry."

He steered them both out of the greenhouse, needing to be away from that thick, metallic atmosphere. Once they were outside, Miss Greenbriars shook him off but made no attempt to go back in. She stood staring blankly into the shadows, breaths coming harshly. "He's dead," she said helplessly.

"Yes." He felt entirely useless. He'd been on cordial but carefully distant terms with Miss Greenbriars since his return to Knoxbridge this year. She was nearly ten years his junior and officially her father's assistant, which would not have been a problem except that she and her father had differing ideas about her future at the university. Miss Greenbriars hungered to pursue her own research; the professor assumed that she would sooner or later find a nice young man to settle down with. Marius sympathised with her but had been mainly concerned with conveying to the professor that that nice young man would not be him.

Right now, as the two of them stood next to each other in the shadows of the gardens, it felt as if they were strangers. His head ached. At least he wasn't getting flashes of Miss Greenbriar's thoughts now that he was no longer touching her.

He felt rather than heard Rakken follow them out. He wasn't sure whether Miss Greenbriars had met Rakken the last time he'd been in Knoxbridge. On that occasion, Rakken had passed himself off as human royalty from an unnamed faraway country, visiting incognito and hinting at a delicious but mysterious backstory that had left everyone speculating, much to Marius's disgust.

"This is Miss Greenbriars, Rake," Marius said, feeling some introduction was called for. "My supervisor's daughter. Miss Greenbriars, this is—"

Miss Greenbriars broke out of her frozen attitude, whirling to face Rakken but directing her words to Marius. "He's a fairy, isn't he?"

"Yes," said Marius, since there didn't seem much point in denying it now. "He's my brother-in-law's brother, Prince Rakken Tempestren." Everyone knew about Marius's sister and Wyn now, though Miss Greenbriars and her father were generally good about not bringing it up unprompted. Not that Marius was ashamed of Hetta, but as public awareness had grown, a distressing number of people who ought to have known better wanted to talk to him about gossip or politics rather than plants.

"What were you doing here?" Miss Greenbriars demanded of Rakken.

Marius was vaguely impressed that she was eyeing him with such hostility. Perhaps Rakken was damping his allure, or perhaps the shock of the situation had cut through it.

"I was showing him what I'm working on. I don't know what Vane was doing here; we found him like this when we came in," he said.

Why had he said that? He didn't need to justify his presence here. It sounded like something a guilty person would say, and he hadn't done anything to feel guilty about, and now she might think that he had. Sometimes his whole life felt like one big pre-emptive justification.

Miss Greenbriars gave a shuddering breath. "He's been stabbed, you said?"

"Yes," said Rakken. "What were you doing out here at this time of night, Jennifer Greenbriars?"

Miss Greenbriars bristled. "Working late. I was walking home from the department and saw a light had been left on."

An uncomfortable beat of silence in which they all thought of the brutally murdered man lying so close.

"We should report this to the police," Marius said.

Rakken sighed. "I suppose such things are necessary."

Miss Greenbriars narrowed her eyes. "Why wouldn't they be necessary?"

"He's just not used to how things work in this world," Marius said quickly, for he could tell Miss Greenbriars was wound too tight for Rakken's levity. "There's a phoneline in the department."

They each looked in that direction. Darkness, made into ominous shadows by the lights cast from isolated lamps. It was only a five minute or so walk, but it felt like an eternity.

"We shouldn't leave him alone, should we?" she said aloud, soft. The whirling sorrow of her had either gone quiet, or he had managed to turn his telepathy off. He wished he knew which.

"You are right. Go; I will stay and watch over him," Rakken

said to Miss Greenbriars with great gentleness, apparently having realised his earlier error. Everything about him conveyed how deeply he sympathised with Miss Greenbriars, a hint of tragedy lurking in his eyes. Marius didn't trust a whit of it; he knew Rakken wanted to stay so he could investigate further before he must deal with the complication of additional mortals. He wished to see if he could find any trace of who had done this, or what the dead man had been doing with fae plants in Marius Valstar's greenhouse.

Telepathy not off then, Marius supposed. Possibly he ought not to leave Rakken unsupervised with a crime scene, but he could hardly ask Miss Greenbriars to walk by herself with a murderer potentially loose on the grounds.

"Let's go together," he said, offering her his arm.

Rakken's eyes glowed briefly as they left, like a cat caught by a streetlamp.

5

OFFICIAL INQUIRIES

THE NEXT MORNING found Marius caught in an endless bureaucratic web, kicking his heels in one of the labs of the botany department. The city watch had taken over the greater part of the building, since it was closest to the crime scene. Rakken had disappeared at some point after the watch had turned up and before they'd decamped to the department. Typical.

His head throbbed, as it had been doing for some hours. Normally classes and labs would be starting soon, but they'd cancelled today's. Which meant if he could just get through this last bit of bureaucracy, he could go back to his room and collapse into bed. *Bed*, he thought longingly. He'd already spoken to one officer, but they'd asked him to wait. So here he was, perched on an uncomfortable lab stool and drinking yet another cup of over-brewed coffee.

He put his head down on one of the long wooden benches and then sat back up because he could feel himself nodding off. How much coffee was too much? He thought he might have had that much; all his muscles were jittery, an uncomfortable counterpoint to the bone-deep fatigue threatening to pull him under on every blink.

The lab's double doors swung open, and Professor Greenbriars came in, awash with distress. He was a stout, pale-skinned, snowy-haired man in his late sixties, a good bit shorter than Marius. Greenbriars had been with the university forever, and if his research wasn't the sort that got anyone outside botanical circles excited, he was widely respected within the community.

Usually Greenbriars embodied the word 'jovial', but today he was all to pieces. Marius suspected it stemmed less from grief and more from a sense of outrage at Vane for involving the department in such a messy business. Greenbriars had never liked Vane, ruffled partly by his youth but mostly by the fact that Vane had had a knack for choosing research topics that drew both interest and more importantly funding from non-traditional sources. Greenbriars might appear in respected scholarly journals with meticulous statistical analyses, but Vane gave dashing interviews in popular publications about Kebulyn jungles and collected fascinatingly exotic specimens.

Yet the same distaste for what Greenbriars called 'flash-in-the-pan' nonsense had made him back Marius's application to re-join the university where he had earlier received only lukewarm responses. Greenbriars didn't care that Marius's family name might be appearing in the press all too often or about the long gap in his career. He cared only that Marius had interest and ability.

"Horrible, just horrible. Just what the department doesn't need," Greenbriars was saying. "And for Jenny to see that! I sent her home to lie down and told her she must take a restorative. She's had quite a shock. Thank goodness you were with her; I know Jenny appreciated it. A woman needs a responsible man to lean on at these times."

Marius made a non-committal sound, bitterly envious. *He* was the one who'd found the body, not Miss Greenbriars; why couldn't *he* go and have a nice lie-down and restorative?

The professor was half-babbling his stream of consciousness. "Vane was supposed to lecture the second years this morning; obviously they're cancelled today, but how can we find a substitute at this point in the year? I certainly don't have time!" He looked at Marius accusingly and then hastily added: "Poor chap. A terrible business. Just terrible. I suppose it must have been a vagrant, hoping to steal his valuables, no doubt."

A tragedy, of course, but still—for the best, isn't it? Vane had had far too much influence with the board, using shallow dazzle to distract from shoddy science, and his most recent proposal had drawn more attention than it deserved. But at least now his latest funding application was no threat at all, was it?

Marius wished very much he hadn't heard that last bit, which he didn't think the professor had spoken aloud. He mumbled something non-committal in case it hadn't been.

He was swept into another police interview, with a different officer than last time. Or perhaps the same one—his memory had blurred.

How would he describe Vane?

He tried to think of how to put it in a way that wouldn't incriminate him. That ought to be easy since he hadn't done anything wrong, except that his head was pounding.

"He was brilliant and energetic," he said eventually. "Everyone knew he was going places."

Why had Marius come to the greenhouse so late? Did he know what Vane had been doing there? When had he last seen Vane alive?

He wondered how Rakken had answered these questions—
or if he had. He rather suspected Rakken would've considered
the exercise a waste of time and used whatever compulsive
magic necessary to extract himself. He was too tired to feel
angry about that and only wished vaguely that Rakken had
extracted him as well.

His thoughts felt sluggish, like clotting blood. He shuddered. They'd let him wash up, but he was still in last night's
clothes, and there were dark stains on his trouser legs where
he'd knelt and pinkish discolouration at his cuffs. Vane's blood.

Why had Rakken arrived last night covered in blood?

There had been so much blood in the greenhouse.

Marius didn't think the two facts were related. *But you know
Rakken is capable of killing*, Marius thought uneasily. He didn't
know the details, but he knew Rakken had killed at least one
person before, the crown prince of an enemy court, many years
ago. More recently, Rakken had also planned the assassination
of his own father, even if that plan had never come to fruition.

But Marius couldn't believe Rakken had had anything to
do with Vane. Rakken had been too surprised by what they'd
found last night, and his prior dark deeds had been highly
strategic. He didn't seem likely to start murdering random
botanists.

A fact for which I should be grateful, Marius supposed. But
he wasn't going to mention it to the police in any case. Rakken
might have left him for the wolves, but it wasn't in him to do
the same. *What if I'm wrong, though?*

"I don't know," he found himself saying over and over,
rubbing at his temples. It felt like tacks were being pushed
out of his brain from the inside. "It looked like he might have
been unpacking a delivery of new specimens, maybe. Those

empty crates."

He immediately regretted making this observation, for it sprouted an entire field of new questions.

Why would Vane have been receiving a delivery at that time? And why in that greenhouse?

"I don't know. Perhaps it was simply most convenient." Or most secluded. Marius's greenhouse was far more hidden from casual observation than the larger, more modern buildings closer to the gates.

What had Marius been talking to Vane about when they'd last spoken, anyway?

"We were discussing potential research pathways," Marius said. He hesitated, but it *was* relevant, so he couldn't omit it. A man had been murdered, after all. How could he not do his best to help? "But he was interested in pursuing a new subject recently—plants that might have magical properties. Perhaps that's why he was taking delivery so late, if it involved, er, unusual specimens. Especially if they came from Faerie. I don't know where they are now though, if that's what was in the crates."

The two officers interviewing him exchanged glances. The skinny toff had to have done it, right? Maybe he'd lured Vane there with talk of these fairy plants. Maybe it was about money; maybe a girl. That Miss Greenbriars wasn't much to look at, but you never knew. After all, it was Valstar's greenhouse and he'd been found with the body, covered in blood.

Marius's head pounded. Great; so he was their prime suspect, was he?

Where in the hells was Rakken? He was the one who'd got them into this mess in the first place, speaking of dark magic and a whiff of Faerie about those crates. Why was Marius the one having to answer awkward questions about it?

The officer who'd left the room returned escorting a middle-aged, fair-skinned, dark-haired woman in plain clothes.

"Miss Dauntry, our sniffer," he introduced her. The man didn't know what to make of this fae-magic angle, but this was the closest they had to an expert.

"Mage consultant," Miss Dauntry corrected. "I'm an illusion-ist." She looked Marius over curiously. "I have some questions about this fairy business."

Marius knew a bit about illusionists—Hetta was one—but the main thing it seemed important to convey was that this wasn't human magic they were dealing with. He spared another fleeting thought to curse Rakken's absence. Fae magic was *his* area of expertise.

Miss Dauntry listened to Marius's garbled explanation with interest. Her thoughts were like birds, curious and sifting bits of information back and forth. This was the new world, wasn't it, this talk of fae plants and fae magic? And no one with the least idea of what to do about it or who to call in, including the tired young man in front of her.

Her sentiment was generally shared. The city guard Did Not Like the fairy angle. Fairy plants and fairy politics, they felt, did not fall within their remit, and whatever Rakken had said to them before disappearing had left them with the strong impression that he had something akin to diplomatic immuni-ty, or at least a worryingly close connection to the royal palace. A great stinking heap of complications, in other words.

Marius was dismayed to realise that they were hoping his suggestion of black-market fae plants was his attempt at a red herring. His only comfort was that the officers weren't happy with their theory either, since if Marius Valstar had murdered

Vane, that was only one step removed from things Getting Political, his family being who they were. Much better if this turned out to be a garden-variety murder with a garden-variety motive involving, ideally, known mundane criminals who would be apprehended and confess as quickly as possible.

Had Marius taken anything from the scene? Could the now-empty crates have been unpacked inside the greenhouse—were there any new plants there?

"No! I didn't take anything. They were empty when we arrived. I didn't get a chance to see whether there was anything new there, under all the debris. It didn't look like it."

They'd get the old professor to tell them whether there was anything unexpected in the greenhouse after they'd taken the body away.

Marius stared hard at the officer's lips. Had they moved?

The old professor was Professor Greenbriars. Who didn't normally pay much attention to the minutiae of day-to-day experiments but who would certainly notice how many odd plants Marius was growing beyond those that were supposed to be the subject of his research, even if none of them were magical or illegal. His stomach twisted.

By this time, the police's speculation and that of everyone else in the building was starting to meld into a single hammer with Marius as the anvil. He squeezed his eyes closed. "Can I go now? I've a migraine starting."

"Soon," someone promised him. "Just a few more questions."

It was at this moment that Rakken decided to grace them with his presence. He came like he had every right to walk wherever he pleased, the eye of a hurricane about which everything else oriented itself.

Marius had never been more relieved to see anyone.

"Have you discovered who killed the mortal yet?" Rakken demanded of the officers, as if they had arrayed themselves for his personal convenience.

The lead officer's mouth hung half-open, as if he'd been about to object to Rakken's sudden appearance but had forgotten what he was about to say. Miss Dauntry's hand rose to press dreamily against her lips. She blushed.

Rakken repeated his question, and Marius felt the full force of his allure rise. It wasn't compulsion, quite, but if Marius's head hadn't been aching he would've still objected to Rakken using it like that. Allure was something between magic and charisma, not glamour but a metaphorical shininess that distracted and charmed and made everyone around want to please its source. Rakken could dampen it, if he wanted. He wasn't damping it now, and everyone began to fall over themselves to be as helpful as possible.

On Rakken's part, he smiled and flattered, perfectly understanding the awkwardness of the situation. He praised their work and the expertise of their consultants and sympathised with how frustrating it was that they hadn't been briefed on how to deal with this sort of thing. Of course he could offer his own expertise in the matter of fae magic. Things could get Political, otherwise, and they all wanted to avoid that, didn't they? What a fortunate chance that he was here.

If Marius hadn't been losing his grip on the line between speech and thought, he might have admired the ruthless way Rakken steered them between threat and flattery until they gave him what he wanted.

"And now I must take Marius Valstar with me."

"We haven't finished interviewing him—"

Rakken said something persuasive, or at least Marius had

to assume it was persuasive because the next thing he was aware of, Rakken was grasping his elbow and directing him out of the room.

"Did you compel them?" Marius asked. It came out more curious than disapproving, but Rakken shook his head.

"My brother, in his wisdom, has decreed no compulsion is to be used on mortal authorities unless life or limb is at risk." A sharp smile. "I merely dazzled them with my charm and wit. Also, I told them you were helping me with an important fae matter last night when they asked if you had an alibi."

The police *really* needed training on how to deal with fae and their approach to truth, but Marius was grateful for the lack in this case.

"Right. Thanks," he said vaguely, missing a step, distracted by the whirl of thoughts. He stumbled, and Rakken steadied him.

"You are unwell."

Marius shook his head and immediately regretted the movement. "Just—my head. Need to get away, get some sleep. I'll be all right." The world spun in dips and eddies, like saplings bending in strong winds, stems threatening to break.

The light hurt his eyes as they went out the front entrance. Out on the street, everyone seemed to be whispering, words just beyond the edge of hearing. He spun, trying to see where the voices were coming from, but the footpath was empty this early in the morning, only the odd cyclist passing on the street. A burst of starlings took flight from the nearby plane tree, and Marius flinched at their loud cries.

He could hear the police officers speculating, theories and images and Vane lying in a pool of his own blood, and the reaction of the undergrad who'd come in early, and the officer cleaning the scene, and the deliveryman, and the first reporter to hear the news trying to sweet-talk the guard. In the terraced houses across the street, people were waking for the day. A man was kissing his wife farewell. A woman spoke sharply to a child to pick that up before someone breaks their neck. Strange minglings of domestic wakings fought with the darker, more officious tone of the police and those who knew of Vane's murder.

—and so I told him, seven pounds for the lot—

—If I take the coach to Evenberry at 10, that should give me a good twenty minutes to catch the number seven—

—not again, Davey, love, come on now—

It felt like his tie to his body had been lost amidst the cacophony. He was left without gravity, a bulb in air, sending roots out without finding soil. Thoughts cut at him, laced with splinters of images and sounds and emotions not his own. Or at least, he didn't think they were his own, but his own were currently quite messy, so it was hard to be sure. It was hard to be sure of anything except—

—a physical hardness and a rush of heat.

He came back to himself with a start and found his back pressed against a stone wall. Pressed by Rakken, who was invading his personal space with no compunction.

"Marius Valstar." A command from only inches away.

Marius was more often than not the tallest person in any group, but at this intimate distance, he was disconcertingly aware of having to tilt his head slightly.

Neither of them moved. His heart thudded against his ribs. Rakken's pupils had blown wide, his lips parting. He had such a sensuous mouth, as persuasive on skin as with words, Marius knew. They stood for an eternity as the world dropped away and went quiet but for the potential humming between them.

A glimmer of wickedness in Rakken's expression said that he was considering kissing him, but more than that, a deeper yearning that he had to be imagining.

"No," he breathed, a hoarse whisper. He brought his palms up to rest against Rakken's chest, exerting no pressure. Warmth, and the rapid thud of Rakken's heartbeat under his hands. Or maybe it was only the thunder of his own pulse he felt. "No, Rake."

Rakken's expression smoothed out. "Welcome back," he said drily. He stepped back, and Marius felt the loss like a punch to the gut.

"Marius!"

Marius turned towards the familiar voice, his head and heart pounding. It was his cousin Caro, wheeling a bicycle.

"I heard about Dr Vane. Have you been here all night?" she asked rather breathlessly. She frowned at Rakken. "I didn't know you were in Knoxbridge, Your Highness."

"Temporarily," Rakken said.

"Are you all right, Em?" Caro thought he looked dreadful, and he'd worried her last night, rushing off like that.

"Sorry," he said tiredly, only realising he'd responded to her thoughts and not her words when she looked confused.

Maybe he ought to tell her about the telepathy. Ethics said that if he couldn't control it, he should tell anyone whose mind he might accidentally read, or at least those he could trust not to burn him at the stake. People ought to get the choice of whether to subject themselves to having their minds read. He would have hated for anyone to do it to him, after all.

But if he could figure out how to turn his powers off, the fewer people he'd told about it, the better. He didn't want anyone to treat him as damaged or difficult, as so many people in his life were already inclined to do. So long as Caro didn't know, there existed a version of him that wasn't cursed.

"He hasn't slept since last night," said Rakken, tugging Marius's elbow. "He is going to sleep now if I have to dose him with peacerose myself."

"Peacerose?" Caro asked.

"A plant in Faerie used in common sleep spells."

"We do actually have non-magical sedatives, you know." Caro sounded amused. "But I take your point. Marius?"

She was asking him if he was all right letting Rakken shepherd him around like this. She'd never been quite sure of the relationship between the two of them. Rakken could be perfectly amiable, and he *was* Wyn's brother, but she also didn't entirely trust him.

It was a good question, but his head pounded far too much to consider it. "It's fine. I'll talk to you later."

He let Rakken lead him away in a daze, the world blurring into white noise. "Why are you helping me?"

"You helped me last night, Marius Valstar."

"Right." That made sense. Didn't it? Fae hated debts, and Rakken was very fae in that.

Bits were missing of his journey home, and he ended up leaning on Rakken's shoulder. No one said anything when they got back to the college. Glamour. Right.

"Sleep, Marius Valstar," Rakken told him. "I will set the wards."

It was only as Marius was tumbling headlong into darkness that he thought to wonder what Rakken was setting wards against.

6

AFTERNOON ACTIVITIES

H E WOKE OVERHEATED, the room stuffy and filled with that glow it only got in the afternoon. Though he was facing the wall rather than the windows, he could tell he'd not quite managed to close his curtains from the bright line cutting across his bed, painting the wallpaper into two different shades of pale blue. He ought to get up and open a window. *Soon*, he told himself. Soon, he'd do it.

He felt groggy, as if he'd overindulged. Had he overslept? He began to struggle upright. What was on at which time today, and had he missed any meetings? But memory arrived with full consciousness, and he fell back with a sigh. It didn't matter what time it was. Classes were cancelled for today. Thank Almighty Pyrania.

For the cancelled classes, not his murdered colleague.

He didn't know how to feel about Vane. Probably he ought to feel something more sombre than his current overwhelming relief at the prospect of a lie-in. He burrowed back into the pillow. He'd find the appropriate sentiment later.

His gaze followed the bright stripe up the wallpaper, stopping at a tear in the paper that formed an odd indentation. How long had that been there? Admittedly, he didn't usually spend time examining his walls, but the damage looked new—and something about the shape nagged at him. Almost deliberate. He sat up to take a closer look. The blanket pooled in his lap, the coolness on his bare skin welcome.

There was a symbol scratched into the wall, freshly cut. He frowned at it, and something slipped into focus for a moment, a flare of green. He blinked. The green had gone, just a scratch in the wallpaper again. He squinted. It couldn't be *glamour*, could it?

"Awake, little scholar?"

Marius scrambled around, attempting to pull the bedclothes over himself, but got them tangled around his knees and so ended up with only a sad triangle of sheet stretched taut, covering not much above the waistline.

"You and your human notions of modesty. Really." Rakken lounged in the windowseat, holding a book in one hand. He didn't look up.

Rakken was right; it was nonsense to be prudish with a fellow who'd had his tongue halfway down your throat and his hands halfway down your... Well, and no further, Rakken having cut things short at that point. Alas. No, *not* alas. *Good.*

He still didn't lower his pitiful notion of modesty.

Rakken sat in profile, and Marius's gaze caught on his features, following the line of his jaw down to his throat. His loose unbuttoned collar lay sharply white against the bronze of his skin, exposing a hint of collarbones. He held a slender volume in one hand, turning a page as Marius watched, his strong, long-fingered hands moving with lazy grace. Strands of dark hair had fallen free of their tie so that they caressed his cheekbones.

He looked like one of those classical paintings, chaste on the surface and seething with dark meanings and hidden eroticism underneath, temptation personified. Marius had never been much good at understanding art, and he felt the same way now as he had when faced with said paintings: fascinated, stupid, and unable to tear his eyes away.

He swallowed. "Have you been here all day? And are you reading *poetry*?" His stepmother had given him a slim volume of collected verse several Wintersols past; he hadn't realised he'd packed it. Must have been hiding amidst his other books.

"I'm furthering my acquaintance with mortal culture. Truths and untruths mingled together."

"You're finding the common ground with fae culture, then?"

Rakken's lips curved. "That is the job of an ambassador." He shut the book with a snap and set it aside, finally looking up.

Marius tried not to fidget at Rakken's scrutiny or to make another grab for more of the bedclothes.

"You've lost weight," Rakken said after completing his assessment.

"Hardly. We can't all be overgrown barbarians." He hunched his shoulders and got the sheet untangled enough that he could wrap it around his waist while he stood and fished around for his dressing gown.

"I was not trying to insult you. I was merely expressing concern."

That made Marius whirl back, now protected by dressing-gown armour. Ah yes, that most seduction-proof of materials.

"Concern? You're pretending you care now? Pity for a lesser creature?" Rakken had called humans that before, more than once.

Rakken got up in a decidedly predatory manner. Marius stood his ground as he stalked closer. Too close. Slowly, he reached out, found the gap at the top of the dressing gown, and laid two fingers just above his sternum. Marius inhaled.

Neither of them moved.

He let out the breath, shakily. "That's not actually an answer."

"Pity isn't what stirs me when it comes to you, Marius Valstar. It never has been, storms help me." All his careless sensuality had sharpened, nothing lazy about it now. The air between them felt like a live thing, slippery and elektric.

Marius stepped back. He could feel the imprint of Rakken's fingers, a brand beating against his skin. "That's not the impression you gave last time."

Why in blazes had he said that? He didn't want Rakken to think he'd been *dwelling* on that incident from months ago, on the night of their respective siblings' wedding, when the wine had been flowing for hours and the fires had burned low and hot.

Rakken didn't ask for clarification on what 'last time' meant. The moment shivered between them again now, drawing all Marius's wounded anger back to the surface. It wasn't as if it had been *Marius* who'd been the main aggressor in this thing between them; Rakken had pursued *him*. And then when Marius had finally given in, Rakken had rejected him in the most cutting manner possible.

The humiliation had stung. Had left him wondering if that had been the entire point, to punish Marius for the sin of resisting in the first place. Maybe Rakken's flirtations had always been only for the thrill of winding him up. And now here Rakken was trying to play the exact same game. He wouldn't fall for it again.

Rakken frowned. "You were inebriated."

"I was not," he said, incredulous. He ran over his memories, just to double check. No—he'd been tipsy enough to loosen inhibitions but not so far gone as to be repellent.

"Sometimes I feel the human ability to lie is wasted on mortals, you spend it so frivolously."

Marius narrowed his eyes. "Because fae are so straightforward in their dealings. I'd had a couple of drinks, which isn't the same thing as inebriated. I knew what I was doing, gods help me. So did you. Why did you really leave that night?"

"Do you wish I had not?" Rakken asked archly.

"No. I just want to know why you were such a bastard about it."

Rakken's eyes were mirrors, all reflection and giving nothing away of the mind behind them. As if he could hear Marius's thoughts, he said softly, "And will you try to take the thoughts from my mind? Who was it who told me a man's mind was sacrosanct?"

"I'm not going to try to read your mind, but you're also avoiding the question."

Rakken's expression didn't change as he spoke. "You are human; I am fae. Our interests lie with different courts. You seemed likely to regret matters later, and that would have made things potentially difficult for Cat, given your family's connections. Lovers are an easy enough commodity to come by; I prefer mine without regrets."

Marius remembered the heat of that night, and it was difficult to believe that Rakken had run such a cold-blooded calculation in the midst of it. Or perhaps it wasn't that difficult. That was who Rakken was, wasn't it? The sort of person who thought of fucking as a commodity. Which was why he was glad nothing had really happened between them. Even if part of him was simultaneously irked that he hadn't been permitted to bear the consequences of his own poor decisions; that Rakken had unilaterally decided Marius wouldn't be able to *cope*.

"Good to know you think I'd regret sleeping with you, you're that bad at it."

Rakken laughed. "Oh, the mortal has teeth."

Honestly, how had no one strangled the man yet? Marius pinched the bridge of his nose, taking another step further away.

"Why are you here?" he asked for what felt like the thousandth time, though he wasn't sure which 'here' he meant. Here, giving sexually charged mixed signals? Here, tumbling through a portal covered in blood? Still here in Marius's room despite him being asleep most of the day? He glanced at his watch, lying on the nightstand: nearly three o'clock. When was the last time he'd slept so many hours straight? His head felt surprisingly clear and pain-free.

"You do remember the murder we discovered last night?" Rakken asked drily. "One fae and one mortal dead by a dryad blade. Strong suggestion of black-market trade with Faerie. I am not purely decorative, Marius Valstar. I am my queen's Second, and Faerie and Mortal are in the middle of highly delicate negotiations. I cannot in good conscience leave without making some attempt to unravel this, and I have little faith in your mortal authorities."

"So why have you been sitting in my room all day, then?"

Rakken canted his head. "This Vane was a mortal botanist of similar age to you, dark haired, pretty, according to those who knew him, and he was found dead in your greenhouse surrounded by fae magic. Even your names have some superficial similarity."

Marius sat down on the bed. Hard. "You think someone was trying to murder *me*? And Vane was, what, a mistake?"

Wait, had Rakken called him *pretty*?

An indignant thrill went through him. It was such a damned *feminine* word, and Marius had had enough of that sort of thing to bristle instinctively. But it also meant Rakken found him attractive, didn't it?

No, he told himself, exasperated. Because he didn't care what Rakken thought of him. And it was so very beside the point right now regardless. A man was dead; it mattered not a whit what Rakken thought of him.

"Perhaps. I do not like the coincidence," said Rakken.

Marius hugged his arms around himself. "If it was a case of mistaken identity, then I'm the reason Vane's dead." Nausea roiled in his stomach.

"No. You did not kill him, and moreover, if this was someone from Faerie, I doubt you motivated anyone to kill you for yourself."

Marius's eyes narrowed. "Why do you think someone would target *me* to get at *you*? Not everything is about you."

Rakken shifted his weight. "I have my own enemies, who may have observed our... previous collaboration and wished to send a message. But perhaps you are right. I hope I *am* being egotistical in this instance."

"Collaboration," Marius repeated. The word sat oddly.

"We made a new spell together," Rakken pointed out. "That is no small thing." That had been more than six months ago now, long before Hetta's wedding. Marius's contribution had grown out of a series of experiments with plants with anti-fae properties that Rakken had disapproved of—up until the point they became useful to him, of course. "In any case, since you are now awake, I'm minded to see if there is anything else to be found of fae magic in your Botanical Gardens."

THEY LEFT THE COLLEGE. The streets were bright and jarringly normal, as if Marius hadn't just found out his colleague might have been murdered instead of him in a case of mistaken identity. Gods, Vane. It was difficult not to feel horribly guilty about it, whatever Rakken said.

His thoughts whirled as they walked. Just who were these unspecified enemies of Rakken's? Had they thought *Marius* was trading in fae plants?

"Are all plants in Faerie magical?"

"It would depend how you define such things. But some more than others, certainly."

"You didn't mention there were magical fairy plants when I asked you about plants with anti-fae properties." He felt incredibly slow not to have considered that while he'd been so intent on plants from *this* realm, there existed a whole *other* realm of plant possibilities. The biggest ecological discovery ever, possibly. And Vane had realised it before him.

"You did not ask."

And of course Rakken never went out of his way to be helpful if there wasn't something in it for him.

Marius wished the plants hadn't been taken from the

scene—and by who? The murderer, presumably. The dryad who'd made that blade? Was Rakken enemies with any dryads? Or could the murderer have been human? But, no, that didn't explain the fae magic Rakken had sensed—or the fae plants Vane might have been receiving.

He was so absorbed in his thoughts that he'd taken several strides alone before realising Rakken had stopped outside a pub. He turned back to him, frowning. "What happened to being in a rush to sort this out?"

Rakken waved a hand at the pub. "It will be highly inconvenient for me if you expire of mortal weakness."

"Would it kill you to utter normal phrases like, 'Let's grab something to eat'?"

Rakken chuckled. "It wouldn't be nearly as amusing. But very well, then; I hunger, and you ought to also, given the power you recently expended."

Marius rolled his eyes but followed him into the pub anyway. He didn't much fancy the headache that would undoubtedly result from being close to this many people, but he was starving, now that he'd had his attention drawn to the fact. And he hadn't heard anyone's thoughts since he'd woken up, had he? Huh.

The blissful silence of his own mind continued as they went inside, and Marius perked up. It had been ages since he'd been out without at least a few twinges.

Rakken seemed to know his way around the place. Had he come here last time he'd been in Knoxbridge? Without Marius? For all Rakken's talk of 'mortal weakness', Marius knew fae lived much like everyone else, but it still felt incongruous, thinking of the high-and-mighty fae prince ordering a pie and chips.

Not that Rakken was being haughty right now. No, this was

Rakken at his most charming, making waitstaff trip over themselves with helpfulness. Other patrons cast admiring glances as he walked so that they moved through a tunnel of attention on the way to the table. Charming only to other people, obviously; Rakken had never once made the effort to adopt the Prince of the People persona towards Marius. He didn't know what he'd done to deserve Rakken in only his most acerbic guise.

"Are you going to tell me anything about these ominous enemies of yours who might have murdered Vane?" he asked in a low voice after they sat down.

Rakken grimaced. "I am sure of nothing. I did not recognise the magic I sensed last night, but there are ways to mask one's signature. Do you know how your Vane might have made contact with someone from Faerie?"

Marius shook his head. "I was thinking the same thing—how did he get hold of fae plants, and why did the murderer take them? Has it come up at all, in the negotiations?"

"Trade terms for plants? No, it had not been discussed; I expect that will speedily change."

"Is there a… a court of dryads? A king of the dryads?" Faerie was broken into many courts, though Marius's knowledge of them was limited to the one Rakken came from (ThousandSpire) and ThousandSpire's mortal enemies (DuskRose), both of which had caused various issues for Stariel.

Rakken shook his head. "There are courts where dryads are more common, and many among the wyldfae—those of no court allegiance—but there is no single leader of dryads. If it was a dryad who sold Vane the fae plants, I would assume them to be unaffiliated with a court, or at least undertaking it without the knowledge of their ruler. I do not think any of the greater courts would risk the treaty negotiations over this. My brother could use it as a reason to ban any court showing such blatant disregard for the negotiations from the Mortal Realm entirely, and they know that." Rakken grimaced. Wyn had been appointed as the High King's ambassador, with the power to enforce decrees over all Faerie regarding the Mortal Realm. Marius didn't have to be telepathic to know he resented it.

Their food arrived. Marius picked at it, marvelling at the fact he was sitting here without the smallest twinge in his mind.

"Can you use up telepathy? You said I expended a lot of power yesterday, and I'm not picking up anything so far today."

Rakken didn't look pleased. "With all magic, one can over-extend oneself and flame out. It's a condition best avoided; it pushes the walls of one's power in odd ways and can make it less predictable if it returns. Flameout leaves one defenceless for a time until the mind and body recover." He waved at Marius's plate. "Fuel will help. Inadequate sleep and food will affect even the most practised of mages; it is no great wonder that your control has been struggling of late given a lack of both."

Marius paused in stabbing a chip. "It's not like I *wanted* to go without sleep. *If* it returns, you said. So it's possible to burn the power out of yourself?"

There was no amusement in Rakken. "Flameout is not a condition to be sought. You don't appear to have burnt out your mind, so yes, your power will return."

Burning his mind out didn't sound good, but, "Is there a way to make my current state permanent?"

"Even if it meant I could reach into your mind at will?"

"Can you?" Marius was familiar enough with fae wordplay to treat that sort of statement as highly suspicious.

"I suspect not. But compulsion is not the only mind magic, Marius Valstar; there are others." Rakken's voice was low and sensuous, and when Marius looked up, all the hairs on the back of his neck stood on end.

Rakken's eyes were fathomless, forbidden depths. His lips curved into a mocking smile, a promise of sin. Marius's breath caught. Desire jerked through him, and he was abruptly so hard it was painful. He swayed forwards before he realised what he was doing, desperate to touch. The warmth of Rakken's arm against his fingertips shocked him awake. He snatched his hand back, head ringing like distant bells.

Rakken reared back in the same moment, his eyes wide. The pressure of his magic ceased so abruptly that Marius sagged and had to put his hands on the table for balance. Desire still pulsed through him, but it was only his own, hot but less jagged, and combated by rising anger. Thank the gods for the table between them.

"What in the hells was that?"

"Allure. I…" Rakken swallowed, and it occurred to Marius that this was the first time he'd seen Rakken flustered. "I was making a point. I did not intend it to—I am sorry." He stood. "Eat. I will wait outside."

"You're *sorry*?"

Rakken's lips curved, a bit of hauteur coming back into his features. "It does occasionally happen."

He left whilst Marius was still struggling with outrage. He furtively adjusted himself and reached for his coffee with shaking hands, feeling hot with anger—he told himself it was anger—and willing the unwanted arousal to subside. *Did you really need that demonstration to know he's not to be trusted?*

He ate mechanically, trying to calm down and think this through. All right, so he hadn't been prepared for Rakken's sudden re-entrance into his life on top of the shock of Vane's death. He could be excused some temporary idiocy.

But now he had a moment to think, he needed to make sure he didn't get distracted into forgetting again what Rakken was: ruthless, prone to playing games, amoral. Marius refused to get tangled up in that sort of mess again, no matter how much he might be tempted. And it *would* be a mess; he knew himself too well to have any illusions about his ability to keep the emotional and physical separate. No fleeting physical satisfaction would be worth it.

How can you be sure without testing that theory at least once, though?

He told his libido that it did not get a vote and got up. Emerging from the pub, he half expected to find Rakken had already continued on to the gardens without him, but Rakken was leaning against a lamp post, watching the world go by. He straightened at Marius's reappearance.

Marius narrowed his eyes. The sharpness of the earlier arousal had faded, but he could feel the echo of it, making his heart pound. "That was… you can't all do that at will, can you?" He knew Rakken's mind-magic abilities were unusually strong, even among greater fae.

"Not unless it's someone particularly susceptible. I did not expect you to be. I should not be able to influence you so strongly if your normal shields were in place. You *did* break free of the influence unaided, but not as quickly as I had expected. I am sorry."

"You shouldn't have been trying to influence me in the first place! I'm not a bloody wind-up toy for your amusement!"

Rakken continued as if he hadn't spoken, as if he were talking himself out of his earlier agitation. "I told you that you may be the target of other interests from Faerie. What if one of them had caught you in their lure?"

"That doesn't make you messing about right!"

Rakken's eyes narrowed. "I am not messing about."

"You could've fooled me. Look, whatever happened before, whatever this thing is between us…" He gestured vaguely—

"—it's called lust, Marius Valstar."

Marius pushed on, even though he could feel his cheeks heating. "Yes, *thank you*, I know. Anyway, nothing's going to come of it, you understand? You were right to think it was a bad idea. And you can stop doing that name-thing."

Rakken's face was expressionless. "Quite. Come." He turned and began to walk towards the gardens.

After a moment, Marius followed.

7

THE HEDGEHOG FAE

A LOW APPREHENSION FILLED him as he unlatched the gate to the gardens, even though the worst had surely already happened. But the gnawing sense of unease only grew as they approached his greenhouse. Vane's body had been removed, but the scene remained cordoned off. The smashed window was more obvious in daylight, and through it he could see that even the plants that hadn't been damaged looked as if they were sulking.

"How long until we can get back in?" he asked the officer standing guard. "I need to do what I can to salvage my work."

The man gave him a long look that reminded Marius someone had been murdered here and perhaps plants ought to be secondary to justice?

"Right," Marius said, and shuffled off. That.

"You have life and limb intact; plants can be regrown," Rakken said, undercutting his attempt to be comforting by adding, "Besides, this location is useless to me, muddied as it is by violence. Is there somewhere on these grounds where we are unlikely to be interrupted?"

Marius led them to the Ernest Azalea Garden, which was nothing much to look at this time of year and off the main track besides. Shrubby azaleas fringed the private patch of grass. A few of the deciduous varieties sported brilliant orange and yellow leaves, with the evergreens in more muted greens. Marius sometimes came here to read in the height of summer; in autumn, it tended to bog up and was too cool for him to sit still for long. *You were born with cold bones*, his grandmother always said.

Rakken's expression was sober as he withdrew a folded bundle of silk from nowhere. He bent to lay it on the dewy grass.

Oh. Marius had forgotten that tiny death, preoccupied with Vane. Was Marius responsible for this one too, if he'd been the intended target all along?

The dead lowfae's pale pink hair spread in a fan, its long frog-limbs splayed bonelessly. There was something unutterably sad about the sight, a sense of fragile vivacity stilled. Rakken stepped back, moving a little distance away before kneeling gracefully on the soggy lawn.

He gestured for Marius to join him. "They won't come if you are outside the circle."

Marius moved to stand beside him. He'd never seen him like this before, solemn without subterfuge or mockery.

Rakken shook his head and patted the ground next to where he knelt. Marius considered pointing out that it was damp, but how could he be concerned about such trivialities under the circumstances? He sank down onto the grass, crossed his legs, and looked at Rakken expectantly.

Rakken made a curt gesture, and a sharp burst of air cut around the two of them, leaving a fine circle in the grass and the smell of tangerines and rain in the air.

"There's probably a charge for damaging university grounds," Marius said, attempting lightheartedness even though his heart felt anything but.

Rakken's mouth curved but he did not respond. Instead, he placed his palms face up on his knees.

"What now?"

"We wait," Rakken said, his lips curving again. "Quietly."

"For how long?"

"I do not know." He looked towards the lowfae, stark against the white silk. "Not too long, I expect. They will want to take her back. But we will wait for however long it takes."

The damp seeped through the seat of his trousers, and as the minutes stretched, pins and needles began to prickle in his left foot, folded under. He shifted, trying to get more comfortable. Rakken frowned at him, and he subsided. Rakken was somehow managing to sit comfortably, his eyes half closed, breathing slow and deep.

We're not all fae sorcerers accustomed to meditating or whatever it is you're doing, Marius thought but didn't say. Not with the dead lowfae so near. Something—some*one*—had died, and if this was how fae showed respect for such things, then so be it. So long as no one expected him to stand up in a hurry afterwards.

He was so preoccupied with manfully ignoring the discomfort that he didn't notice the lowfae until it had crept halfway across the lawn. He sat up straighter.

Rakken shot him another warning look before speaking. "I am Rakken Tempestren, prince of Ten Thousand Spires." A hint of thunder and citrus flared as he dipped his head in acknowledgement. The gesture was oddly dignified, even whilst kneeling on the lawn.

The lowfae sat back on its haunches and considered them. It wasn't the same sort as the dead one. This one had a black button nose, a squat, plump body and a back covered with long quills, almost like a hedgehog. It glanced warily at Marius before fixing its attention back on Rakken.

"Greater fae," it whispered.

Rakken nodded at the square of silk. "I have brought you this one to return to her kin. She was killed last night alongside a mortal."

The lowfae hissed, its quills puffing out. "Vane," it said, showing a row of pointed teeth.

"Yes," said Rakken. He held out a hand, and a glow of magic appeared in his palm. Marius had seen him summon a small ball of charge before, but this was different, a hovering sphere of green-gold with a softer appearance than his usual lightning.

The lowfae's eyes widened. It took an involuntary step forwards, drawn like a moth to a flame.

"Tell me about Vane." Was Rakken going to compel the fae to answer? But no—he merely extended a hand. "I offer payment for the information."

The hedgehog fae sidled closer to the dead lowfae. One small paw reached out to touch the silk handkerchief, the expression on its face fearful.

"Where are the others?" it asked.

"Others?" Rakken's voice remained low and persuasive, but Marius felt his sudden tension.

"He takes us. We don't come back."

Glass shards, Marius recalled, feeling extremely thick. The dead lowfae had been in a specimen jar—trapped. Vane had been trapping lowfae. He felt sick.

Rakken continued to question the hedgehog fae, his tone

tightly controlled, and the details gradually filled in. The way the fae spoke of time was odd, but if Marius was interpreting correctly, Vane had been trapping lowfae for at least a month, maybe longer. A *lot* of lowfae had disappeared.

Bile rose in his throat. What had Vane been doing with them? Marius didn't have much stomach even for the animal experiments they did in the medical research laboratories, but this was worse; lowfae weren't animals. He knew not all of them could speak, but they were clearly sapient in a way that the average mouse wasn't.

"Do you know who killed Vane last night?" Rakken asked the lowfae.

The lowfae shook its head. They avoided Vane, but they had felt a burst of portal magic disturb the leylines in the garden after he went into the greenhouse. That had been followed by the shockwaves of violence and death—and dark magic. It had not made them wish to venture closer.

Rakken coaxed information from the lowfae with surprising patience. Had Vane entered the gardens with anyone else? Had anyone followed him or left afterwards?

"A different mortal left. After the dark magic."

Marius straightened. "Who? Did they go in with Vane?"

The lowfae shied at the sound of his voice. Rakken frowned at him.

"Sorry," he mumbled.

Rakken repeated the question, but the lowfae had no answer to give. Rakken's frown deepened, but he dismissed his circle and extended out his palm, glowing with magic. "I will find out what happened to your kin," he said. Not idle words. Fae were bound by their promises; if they broke them, they lost part of their power.

The hedgehog fae approached tentatively. Reaching out with a paw, it touched Rakken's glowing orb. A pulse of light washed through its body, and it was still glowing as it gathered up the dead lowfae. Some kind of energy transfer? It bowed low before scampering away. It had gone only a few steps before Marius could no longer see it, though he wasn't sure if that was glamour or the camouflage of the bushes.

"Is that—was that a member of the dead one's family?" he asked.

Rakken shook his head. "The dead one was a sylf. They are shy, and they do not speak in the way you or I do. Hurchyon are more robust, which is undoubtedly why her family chose one to speak with me."

Rakken got up. For a moment, his mask fell away, revealing a primal anger, something that spoke of blood and storms, of a nature at odds with the careful cultivation of the gardens. The rage of a hurricane or a forest fire.

One owes a duty of responsibility to lesser creatures, Rakken had said once. Marius had objected to that at the time, since Rakken seemed to file 'humans' under that label too, but he thought now that he hadn't quite understood what Rakken meant by it.

Rakken's lips pressed together. "Humans," he said. "Humans and your experiments."

Marius got gingerly to his feet, wincing as the pins and needles kicked in. "We should check Vane's office. I don't know if he would have kept the trapped lowfae there, but it's a start."

Something hardened in Rakken's expression, and Marius had the sense that he was shoring himself up, intentionally stoking his own anger. "You wanted to work with him. This mortal trapping lowfae."

"I didn't know what Vane was doing! Do you really think

I'd be part of something like that? I knew he was interested in magic and plants—that's all!" Gods, it put his and Vane's conversation earlier in the week in a different light, though, didn't it? His stomach twisted. What if he'd put in his transfer request before discovering this? "You know I wouldn't be involved in something like this!"

Rakken's fingers flexed in and out of fists. "My brother is naïve, believing Mortal can be only good for Faerie, and this, here, is the proof of his flawed judgement."

Should he remind Rakken that fae hadn't exactly caused no harm to the mortal realm? But he refrained. It would be a game of one-upmanship with no winner.

"What Vane did is horrible, but this is one man, Rake. One *dead* man, whose death is most likely related to his own poor choices regarding Faerie. Which means this probably isn't a case of mistaken identity at all—or the enemies you're being so vague about," he realised with guilty relief.

Rakken stared at him for a long, long moment. "Take me to Vane's office."

VANE HAD AN OFFICE on the second floor of the department. During the few minutes it took to get there, Rakken's anger transformed to icy civility, and his allure—gods, how Marius hated that term—inverted. It made it rather like walking next to a contained snowstorm.

The office was locked. No doubt Rakken could do something magically helpful here, but in his current mood, Marius didn't trust him not to blow the door off its hinges.

"If you wouldn't mind making us uninteresting if anyone comes past in the next few minutes?" He fished about his coat for his key ring and began to uncurl the wire of it.

Rakken's brows rose. "You pick locks?" He sounded surprised, which Marius knew was because he wasn't the sort of person who had mysterious depths from which interesting skills like lock-picking might emerge.

He pulled himself straighter. Perhaps he wasn't a terribly exciting person, but he did have *some* mysterious depths. "Locks in general, no, but in this specific case, yes. The locks on these doors aren't exactly high security, and I've had to fight with my own enough times to know the trick of it." He knelt and began fiddling. "I learnt at school, actually. There was a boy there who... well, he did get expelled eventually, but that was after he showed me. I like puzzles." Charles had been... Well, it wasn't so unusual for schoolboys to fool around in the dark, stolen moments and awkward hands, bringing each other off. It had meant more to him than it had to Charles. *Story of my life. Perhaps I've always had terrible taste*, he thought helplessly.

He wondered where Charles was now and then flicked the thought away, focusing instead on the lock, the sound of the metal. The lock clicked, and a tiny thrill shot through him. There was something pure about the sound of tumblers turning, everything in its place for once. He stepped back with a flourish. *Call me boring now, why don't you?*

Except Rakken had never called him that—that had been John. A chill swept over him. Then the import of what he'd just done hit him. He'd broken into a *murdered man's office*. In broad daylight. He stared at the door, a sort of awed horror holding him in place. What was *happening* to him? What if someone *found* them here? Half of those police officers already thought him guilty of something, and this would only be taken as confirmation.

Weren't you supposed to leave this sort of investigating to professionals? What if he wrecked their investigation by interfering like this? What if the murderer got away with it because of him? What if they murdered someone else because of him? What if they found something here? What if they didn't?

An ever-increasing puffball of what-ifs grew, releasing spores of anxiety with every extrapolation. "We shouldn't be doing this," he said.

"The others didn't come back." Rakken echoed the hedgehog fae's words, and Marius sucked in a breath. Yes. That was it, wasn't it? That was the why.

He pushed open the door.

It was a perfectly ordinary office, even by the standards of the botany department. Some of the far-voyaging field biologists' offices were adventures in and of themselves. But Vane was neat. Only one proper plant: a tropical *Scindapsus* trailing from the shelf under the single multi-paned window. North-facing; unsuitable for a lot of plants. Shelves containing books, propped up with a few jars of various dried mosses. Filing cabinets.

Marius hadn't met with Vane here; he'd been worried about the possibility of Professor Greenbriars finding out. The department was a leaky sieve when it came to comings and goings. Which reminded him.

"Shut the door, if you don't mind. I'd rather you didn't glamour anyone if you don't have to."

"Magnanimous of you," Rakken said drily but complied.

Marius walked over to inspect the jars of mosses. None

looked like they contained any lowfae, even when he squinted in case there was glamour involved. He could pretty reliably detect lowfae glamour these days if he tried, even unaided. A good thing too, because when he put a hand to his coat pocket to double check, he realised he'd left his modified quizzing glass back at the college.

"It doesn't look like he kept lowfae here," he said, picking a glass jar up and bringing it to eye level. Some species of sphagnum moss; impossible to tell which at a glance.

"No," Rakken said slowly, his gaze unfocused. He was using leysight. "There are no lowfae here, and no active wards, but…" He frowned.

"But what?" Marius prompted.

"A trace of something fae. As if something was here recently."

"How recently? And what are we looking for?"

Rakken shook his head. "Within the past few days, at a guess. And I do not know." He made a disgusted sound.

Marius looked helplessly at the shelves and desk. "I suppose we… see what we find, then? If Vane *was* experimenting on lowfae, he will have made notes." His insides curdled, but he leaned down and pulled open the top drawer of Vane's desk. It opened to reveal several pens, notebooks, a ball of string, and a set of labels. He picked up the notebooks, feeling squeamish. How would he feel if someone rifled through his own desk—which was far less orderly than Vane's? But the memory of the dead lowfae rose again, so small and pitiful, and his resolve hardened.

The notebooks were blank, and he slid them back into place. Were they in the same position as they'd been when he'd opened the drawer? He adjusted them by a hair.

Rakken was far less fastidious, systematically pulling books

from the shelf and holding them up to his nose before carelessly returning them.

"Does fae magic actually smell?" Marius wondered aloud,
watching him.

Rakken paused mid-sniff and gave him an incredulous look.

Marius expanded: "I mean, is it a physical property in the
air that one detects olfactorily? Because whilst some of you
seem to have wholly scent-based magic, Irokoi's signature has
a texture as well—which doesn't seem physically possible. And
so does yours, come to think of it. It makes me think of rain on
leaves, not just the smell but the sensation. And—"

He broke off, because Rakken's expression had started
twitching, as if he were trying and failing to maintain his earlier
icy composure. After a moment, he began to laugh, helplessly. It transformed him, softening the hard angles of his face,
filling the room with warmth, drawing attention inexorably to
his mouth.

Marius jerked his gaze away. "What exactly is so amusing?"
he demanded.

"You *are* aware that we are currently furtively ransacking a
dead man's private belongings?"

"Ah. Right." He ducked his head and pulled out the next
drawer. Spare ink, a letter opener, copies of the Royal Society's
latest periodical. Pulling one out, he held it upside down and
riffled the pages in case something fell out. Nothing did. He
moved on to the next.

"Yes," Rakken said suddenly. "A magical signature is not a
true scent, and you are correct that many signatures include
sense elements other than smell. There are small differences
in how individuals perceive the same signature; I have heard
various theories as to why, though none wholly convinced me."

"Why are you smelling the books with your nose, then?"

Rakken's smile grew sheepish. It made him seem dangerously approachable. "Habit, I suppose. I may not truly use my nose to detect signatures, but… it *feels* as if I do."

"And beliefs are powerful, with fae magic," Marius thought aloud.

Rakken canted his head to the side. "Yes, they are." He paused. "Little scholar." He set the pet name out knowing it would annoy Marius.

Marius rolled his eyes. "Now who's distracting who from the task at hand, Mouse?"

Rakken huffed and returned to pulling out books.

It felt invasive, going through Vane's things. And yet, the man was not to be found here, in the arrangement of stationery and artefacts. Everything was curiously impersonal; it might have belonged to any of the faculty.

"He must have kept his real notes somewhere else," he concluded after sorting through the filing cabinet. "He always kept meticulous notes when I knew him; they're missing."

Rakken was eyeing the desk suspiciously. He began to pull out drawers, though Marius had already checked them.

"A secret compartment?" Marius asked, and then wondered if that had been telepathy or just deduction. He'd been enjoying the mental quiet.

"The dimensions do not add up." Rakken tapped a finger on the desk. He pulled the lower drawer all the way out. It was shallower than its counterparts; a false bottom.

Marius swallowed, dread of what they might find making all his muscles tense. But when Rakken opened the secret compartment, it revealed not the notebooks or—worse—more dead lowfae, but something unexpected: a letter, composed using text cut out from a newspaper.

Rakken scanned it. "It looks like a threat as prelude to blackmail, if I'm any judge. '*I know the briars you're tramping in*'," he quoted aloud.

Blackmail. Marius swallowed. He'd been the target of a blackmail attempt before, and even knowing this one had nothing to do with him didn't stop his stomach twisting. "We should tell the police," he said, though it came out as half question.

Rakken shrugged. "If you like. They have quite sensibly agreed to my pursuing the fae aspect of this, since they have no expertise in the matter." So that was what Rakken's discussion with them had entailed. He wondered if the police understood what they had agreed to. "I am not overly concerned with them, so long as they do not obstruct me."

"I suspect they might say the same of you. What if it's a mortal who killed Vane? A threatening note hidden in his desk is a mundane sort of thing, though I hate to say it. And that lowfae before—the hurchyon—it said another mortal visited the greenhouse before we arrived."

Rakken shrugged. "Then your authorities are welcome to them, but I still wish to know how they came to be wielding a dryad blade and if they knew of Vane trapping lowfae. And what caused that burst of dark magic."

"It does seem unlikely that Vane's murder wasn't connected to Faerie somehow, even if it was a mortal," Marius agreed. His mind picked at what the lowfae had said. Could Vane have had an assistant who knew about his Faerie connections? What if they'd stumbled across the scene just before Rakken and Marius and taken fright? Or maybe they'd been the one to stab him and then… stolen the plants for themself?

The two of them continued sorting. It was quite hard not

to get distracted. There was a pile of the latest *Royal Societys* that Marius hadn't yet read, and Dr Baltimus from Serenna had sent Vane an unpublished draft of his latest research on lichens. Would anyone mind if he took it? But no, that would be stealing. Which was wrong.

More or less wrong than breaking into a dead man's office, though?

That was different; that was in aid of a noble and defensible goal. Pilfering fascinating lichen papers to assuage his own curiosity was not.

Marius had just managed to resist the temptation of a lovely set of mycelium prints when a sound came from the door. A key turned in the lock. He and Rakken both froze.

The door opened.

He and Miss Jenny Greenbriars stared at each other.

"Mr Valstar," she said blankly before suspicion began to sharpen her features. "What are you doing here?"

"Why do you have a key?" he asked.

Miss Greenbriars paled and began to splutter. "That's—I borrowed it from the—how did *you* get in here?"

Rakken moved, quick and silent as a shadow, and pushed the door shut. The sound of it closing broke Miss Greenbriars out of her fluster. She rounded on him: "You!"

"Do you know where Vane kept his work?" Rakken said without preamble, magic thick and sudden. Miss Greenbriars answered without hesitation.

"He has a flat in Meridon." She blinked, drawing in on herself, looking as off-balance as Marius felt.

"How do you know that, Jenny? And why do you have a key to his office?" Marius paused, incredulous at the answer. "Really? You and Vane?"

Miss Greenbriars gave an angry laugh. "Is that so hard to believe? Just because you're not interested, no one else can be?" Martin had loved her! He had seen her, in ways no one else ever had.

He flushed. He'd hoped that her father's matchmaking was one of those things they'd silently agreed to ignore together. "I meant, isn't—wasn't—Vane engaged?"

He'd never met Vane's fiancée, but he had some vague notion that she came from a well-off aristocratic family and that it was one of those big society affairs. Someone had told him—or had he heard it accidentally?—that she was currently out of the country. He supposed someone must have contacted her by now. What a horrible thing to learn at such a distance.

"He was going to break it off!" Jenny said. Martin's fiancée could never have understood him like she did! That woman wasn't a scientist, not like her! Martin loved that she understood his research, that she could help him. Martin hadn't cared for his fiancée at all! He'd only agreed to the match in the first place because he'd felt obligated to, and that was before he'd met Jenny. He was going to break it off with that woman as soon as she was back in Prydein, he'd promised. He'd *promised!*

"Oh, Jenny," Marius sighed, because not even Jenny really believed that. *And flameout over, I suppose.*

Jenny didn't want his sympathy. Her expression hardened in a way that he'd never seen before. "You've no right to judge me! Not when you're a, a homosexual!"

The word hit like a slap. He'd always half-suspected Jenny knew or at least guessed, but it didn't lessen the shock of hearing her say it aloud. Gods, Professor Greenbriars didn't know, did he? No, he couldn't; he wouldn't keep pushing his daughter on Marius if he knew. Or perhaps that was exactly why, he thought, feeling sick.

The red in Jenny's cheeks had faded a fraction. She searched his face, regret already worming its way through her anger and grief. Marius wasn't a bad sort, better than the men who 'accidentally' rubbed up against her in the close confines of the greenhouses and spoke only to her breasts. What business of hers was it if he was bent? But how dare he look at *her* with pity!

He'd given himself away, he realised distantly. He ought not to have frozen; he ought to have protested immediately. It seemed a bit late for it now. Still, "I'm not…" he began weakly, a beat too late, but Rakken was already speaking, voice low and menacing.

"And do you know the nature of your lover's experiments?"

Jenny curled up again, but Rakken grew tall and frightening, and she gasped out, in real terror: "It's just plants! Magic plants, and why shouldn't he be interested in that! He was a scientist! You think you're the only one interested in fae!" she said to Marius. "Everyone's interested."

"Not your father," he felt bound to point out.

Jenny jerked her head like a horse getting rid of a fly. "He just doesn't like change; he would've come round eventually. You were talking to Martin too, don't pretend you weren't. You knew Martin is—was—brilliant. The department would have granted him funding in the end, and it would all have been above board." Her voice gave a little quaver.

Marius put a hand on Rakken's arm when he seemed about to terrify Jenny again. "You didn't know about the lowfae. This flat of his in the city—you never went there, did you? He never let you."

Rakken relaxed under his grip. "Ah."

"Martin said it would draw too much attention to us," she

said defensively. "He was just trying to protect me. Why do you care, anyway?"

"Because, Jennifer Greenbriars, there are dead fae involved in this, and I gave my word to their kin that I would find out why they were killed."

"And who killed Martin," Marius added hastily. "Do you know the address of his flat?"

Jenny looked between them and shook her head.

Rakken didn't seem concerned. "That will not be a problem."

MARIUS DIDN'T REALISE HOW shaken he was until after they'd left the department. It was dusk, and murmurations of starlings wheeled and turned, their cries deafening.

He took gasping breaths, finding the nearest lamp post (safely out of reach of the starlings' roosting trees) and clinging to it. His legs felt like they might give way. Gods. Gods. His head pounded. What else had he been oblivious to? How could he be so oblivious whilst being bombarded with people's thoughts against his will? It all seemed horribly unfair.

"Marius," Rakken said, soft and... worried? The sound of only his first name, unadorned, had a peculiar intimacy. He put a hand on Marius's arm.

He shook off the touch, the lie of comfort it presented. He had to remember that. Everything about Rakken was false.

"It's—I'm fine." He swallowed and hurried on. "So, someone opens a portal, and then Vane enters the gardens, and the lowfae all scatter for fear of him. Followed by your dark magic pulse, Vane being murdered, and another human fleeing the scene. So was that other human there all along—Vane's assistant, perhaps? Or did they come through the portal? Humans can't make portals, can they—that's fae magic, isn't it?"

"Yes." Rakken was still frowning at him.

"So it had to be a fae who opened the portal. But where did the portal open from? I thought my greenhouse resonated with the one at Stariel?"

Rakken shook his head. "It does, or at least it *did* for me. The violent death will have changed the resonance. But resonance is a subtle, complex magic and is not wholly about the connection between two places. It's also about the person making the portal. Multiple resonances in the same location are rare but possible." He stared at Marius, an odd expression in his eyes. "Conventional wisdom is that individuals are too fleeting to make much impression upon the world, magically speaking, but I am beginning to suspect that you are an exception to this. I do not think it is coincidence that it is *your* greenhouse that resonates for multiple magic-users in Faerie. Or that it was your room I came to last night, portalling blind." He grimaced.

"I wish you weren't being so secretive about that."

"I'm sure you do."

Marius glared at him. "You know, since you bring it up, *you* have opened a portal into my greenhouse before, and you did turn up on the night of Vane's murder covered in blood." And Rakken had been furious on discovering Vane's experiments—furious enough to kill?

Rakken inspected his hands. "Are you accusing me? I admit I am not grieved at Vane's death, given what the hurchyon told me."

Anyone else might have been fooled by Rakken's nonchalance.

Marius wasn't. He gave him a long, unimpressed look. "No. I don't think you killed Vane, though you could help by being less ominously mysterious about everything. Why do you always want me to think as badly of you as possible? Most people would think it a *good* thing that I wasn't suspecting them of murder!"

"Perhaps you are too trusting."

Marius gave an exasperated huff. "I'm not being trusting. I don't believe you killed Vane because you didn't know he was kidnapping lowfae until after he was already dead, so I can't think what would have motivated you. And if you had killed him, for some as-yet-unknown reason, you wouldn't have made such a mess of it."

Rakken almost smiled. "I did not kill Vane. I never met the man."

"Which you could have just said!"

"I take it you did not kill him either, since we're having this little chat on the subject."

Marius glared at him. "I've never killed anyone!"

Rakken sobered. "I am aware."

Because Rakken *had* killed people, Marius knew. Or at least, he'd killed one person—Marius desperately hoped it wasn't more. Rakken and his sister had murdered the crown prince of another fae court, years ago. Marius had asked Rakken about it before, and Rakken had both owned the crime and refused to explain his motivations. Not that there could be a justifiable explanation, could there?

He rubbed the bridge of his nose, shifting his spectacles. The starlings continued to flock, dark specks against the sky. There was something soothing in their movements, in the way each individual bird somehow knew where to fly. He wondered if birds could be telepathic and if that might explain it.

At least he was no longer feeling panicky about the confrontation with Miss Greenbriars, thanks to Rakken providing such an aggravating distraction.

"That threatening note we found," he remembered with a start. "It was about Miss Greenbriars."

"The briars he was trampling in." Rakken pulled the offending paper from his pocket and offered it to Marius. "Go on, then. Take that note to your mortal authorities. You can tell them who it relates to for good measure."

Marius hesitated. "It would ruin Miss Greenbriars. And likely her father's reputation too."

"From what I have gleaned of mortal culture, quite possibly, though it is all a great foolishness to me. Mortals. You're all so curiously obsessed with each other's various sexual escapades or the lack thereof."

"But the person who sent this note might have been the murderer! Oh. That's why you took it. Can you trace it back to whoever sent it, magically? How strong a link would this sort of thing even have, since it's not even hand-written?"

Rakken looked surprised at how quickly Marius had grasped the principles of fae magic. "A weak one at best, but something to try, nonetheless. But it is not my present priority."

The missing lowfae. His stomach twisted. "I assume you can find this flat of Vane's somehow, even without an address?"

"Yes. I have taken a sufficient number of things from his office to use as a base for the spell."

Of course he had.

"—and if that fails, I shall work my way through this department of yours until someone tells me what I wish to know."

That pulled Marius up short. "No, you will not!"

Rakken's eyes glittered. "You seem to labour under the belief that you get some sort of say in this, Marius Valstar. I will do as I see fit."

"Does Wyn know you're proposing to compel people willy-nilly?"

"Oh, what a fate to be threatened with, my little brother disapproving of me. However shall I cope." Rakken's mocking tone grew edged. "And if you are so high-minded about me compelling people to tell me what they know, perhaps you should accompany me and take it directly from their minds instead."

8

TRULY APPALLING METHODS OF TRANSPORTATION

THE NEXT MORNING, there was still a prickling atmosphere between them when they took the train up to Meridon. It was only an hour's journey, a trip Marius had made often enough. Back when Hetta had lived in the capital and he'd been doing his undergrad, he'd gone up to visit her on weekends. That had been before his father had ordered him home; a degree was well enough for a man of his class, but the lord's eldest son pursue a career in scholarship? No.

A bolder, more independent man would have found a way around his father's dictate, lack of funds and threat of disowning notwithstanding. Or a more independent woman—Hetta had done it, after all. But Marius wasn't like Hetta. He hadn't been able to stop trying to please his father or risk losing the tie to his home and family, most especially to his younger half-siblings. He couldn't imagine leaving them or his stepmother to face his father's displeasure alone. At the time, he'd told himself it was merely a temporary compromise; he'd find some other way to pursue his dreams.

Which turned out to be Father dying unexpectedly and Hetta inheriting over everyone, Marius thought with black humour as they bought their train tickets. Rakken was giving off an aura of hostility such that the only other person in their carriage got up and moved after a few minutes. Marius wondered if he could reverse his allure in other ways, or if it was a simple binary of either attraction or repulsion.

No one else came in. He ought to call Rakken on it, but it was bad enough being up this early without adding a headache from too many nearby people. It also felt safer. Rakken didn't seem at all worried that whoever had bloodied him up might come for him again, but Marius couldn't help fretting. He wasn't sure how worried to be for himself, if Vane's murderer really had meant to target him. What if Vane's murderer was the *same* person who'd attacked Rakken?

He put this idea to Rakken as the train drew out of the station.

Rakken shook his head. "The two incidents are not related." He turned back to the windows, apparently finding the passing scenery fascinating.

"It would help if you told me why you think that."

"I cannot lie, Marius Valstar."

"Yes, but you can be massively and unjustifiably over-confident."

Rakken's mouth curved, but he did not respond or look away from the view.

Marius huffed and pulled out the stack of marking he'd brought with him. A terribly mundane task, but he knew he'd be too distracted to read, and he'd learnt to take advantage of small bursts of uninterrupted time. Yesterday's cancelled tutorials had given him a few days' grace. This lot ought to have been done already, but since it was now Saturday, he figured that meant no one would be expecting it to be done until after the weekend.

However, he had only begun on the top-most essay when Rakken demanded an explanation. This required a significant digression into the reasons lichen was important to an understanding of ecology.

("Interrelationships; a lichen is made up of two organisms—an algae and a fungus—working together for mutual benefit. Or that's the current theory, anyway; the lichenologists are somewhat divided on which one benefits more."

"Whether one party exploits the other," Rakken summarised.

"Are you going to force political parallels into everything?" Marius complained.

"What else was I trained for if not this?" Rakken said, so drily that Marius laughed despite himself.)

And then once he'd explained lichen, he had to defend the essays themselves and Rakken's scathing opinions of their writers' intelligence—and, yes, Rakken wasn't *wrong* about the quality, but these were first years, and what could you expect, really?

"I can't fail half the class," he said reasonably. "They get the hang of it, eventually. The stuff they were writing earlier in the year was much worse. They're... a work in progress."

"Like so many things," Rakken said, his head tilted to one side, and Marius couldn't read him at all.

And so no marking had occurred by the time the train pulled into the station. Ah, well. Marius found himself in an oddly good mood anyway as he tucked the papers away again.

The crowds in Pickering Station parted easily around them,

exhibiting a respect he'd never experienced from the average Meridonian. Rakken, of course, strode through as if it didn't occur to him to expect anything less.

They stepped out of the station into a pleasant morning, the sun promising a fine, clear day. Marius had seen Rakken perform a tracking spell in Meridon once before, so he wasn't surprised when he made for the nearby park.

They stopped beneath the sheltering arms of a majestic copper beech. Their fellow park-goers paid them no attention, including a large poodle chasing after a ball, which diverted at a wide angle around them though the ball sailed directly past the beech.

"If iron interferes with your leysight, how can you still track things within the greater city?" Marius asked.

Rakken settled into place cross-legged in the dirt before answering. Only he could manage to make this position somehow dignified. "The iron interference is why I am casting the spell here; once the link is forged, it is easier to hold it through that. Though of course one of lesser ability might have difficulty."

Marius snorted. Rakken cast a circle about himself and plucked several objects from the air, holding them in his open palm: a letter opener and—

"—is that Vane's hair? Where did you get that?"

"His office," Rakken said absently. The smell of rain and citrus began to seep beneath the beech tree, somehow conjuring the feel of rain-drenched leaves against skin. The sense of wind stirred without movement, and feathers rustled, just beyond the edge of hearing.

Layered through Rakken's signature was something else. The bit of Vane's essence he was using for the tracking spell, trying to connect like with like? He caught little flashes of sense-images: Vane's laugh, a faintly familiar cologne, and—blood.

Rakken's eyes snapped open, his irises a more brilliant green than usual. A small light hovered above his palm, glowing a soft peach. Rakken's fingers curled, holding the light in the manner of a ball about to be thrown. He stood, changing to his fae form as he did so. Great bronze-and-green wings unfurled. The bronze filaments in his feathers caught the morning light, glittering like the crushed carapaces of rare beetles.

Rakken threw out his spare hand in invitation. "Come here," he commanded.

Marius's mouth dropped open. "I beg your pardon?"

Rakken looked impatient. "When I loose this trace, we may need to follow it some distance. I have no intention of inefficiently traipsing about this city on foot, and you have no wings of your own."

That was… extremely logical. Marius stayed where he was.

Rakken rolled his eyes. "If you are concerned I shall take the opportunity to fondle you, be assured I shall not do so without invitation. This is merely a practical matter. Unless you wish to be left behind?"

Right. Of course. Practical.

"Fine." He stepped closer.

Framing this as pure practicality did not change the intimate reality one iota. *But it means nothing*, he told himself.

Stormdancer feathers had a unique scent. A sort of spicy-sweet musk, overlain with Rakken's own signature, magic and mundane both. It made Marius's heart race, made blood rush towards places it should not. Made one think in intensely unhelpful directions. It was all so horribly awkward. Yes, that was the word.

Having now crossed the distance between them, he stood helplessly, unsure what to do with his limbs or hands or, well, anything. It wasn't as if there were an obviously dignified way to proceed. Hesitantly, he placed one hand on Rakken's shoulder, holding his briefcase between them as a shield.

Rakken gave a soft huff of laughter and took the case from him, disappearing it with a snap of his fingers.

"I'm going to want that back, you know."

"It's safe." Rakken put a hand around his waist and drew him in. "I won't bite, starling."

"Starling?" Marius asked, not sure if this new moniker was better or worse than the usual overly formal address.

"Put your hands behind my neck," Rakken instructed. A few awkward moments later, Marius was being held, bridal-style (and *there* was a comparison that was helping with his feelings of emasculation). Rakken held him without any apparent effort, which was almost as humiliating.

With a powerful sweep of his wings, Rakken took off. Marius clutched at him with an undignified sound that was certainly not a cut-off shriek. He squeezed his eyes shut as they rose in swift, dizzying wing beats.

After a few moments, he dared to open his eyes and found the city had receded into a series of geometric shapes, the park flattened to a green rectangle as they rose with impossible swiftness. He swallowed and fixed his gaze on Rakken's shoulder. Even beneath the fabric, the bunching of muscle was visible with each wingbeat. He could feel it, the power of the thrusts.

Bad word choice.

Really, it was unfair that Rakken should be so bloody *physical*. It made you speculate.

Risking another glance down, he was suddenly glad he'd

kept his spectacles on. He'd once climbed the tower of the oldest temple in Meridon to take in the view. It had given a fascinating new perspective on the city. From a height, the details of individual shop fronts and lamp posts disappeared but you could suddenly appreciate the whole, the proverbial wood that all those brick-and-mortar trees made up.

This was even better than that, without the restrictions of a fixed viewing platform. A curious thrill went through him. Only he and Rakken could see the city in this way. Well, and presumably Wyn and Catsmere had also seen it from this perspective when they had last been here. Plus however many more winged fae had visited the city since. But still—it was an uncommon privilege.

Rakken, having reached a satisfactory height, threw the tracking spell with a flare of magic. It shot off like a bird released from a snare. Hard to say how quickly it was moving, but if they'd been on the ground, Marius suspected they would have needed to run to keep up.

They flew, following the tracer's pale light. Below, the great city sprawled, a peculiar mix of organic patterns and man-made geometries battling for supremacy. There was the silvery curve of the river, casting its irregular shape across the city blocks as the streets tried to meet it at right angles. The bridges spanning the river looked strangely rigid against its curves.

The tracer eventually led them to the older suburbs, near one in particular that Marius knew. It wasn't the height of fashion or riches but a respectable enough area. Stariel Estate owned a dilapidated townhouse here, which had only survived sale through an entail.

Rakken's trace sank down between buildings and flitted towards a block of flats, where it attached itself to the top floor windows and spread out. The entire level began to glow softly with that same peach light. Rakken made a satisfied sound and landed on the roof.

Marius hurriedly released his grip and scrambled back to his own two feet. He looked around. The roof was framed by a knee-high lip. Within its bare confines lay a squat A-frame glass, which covered a raised bed in the lee of the stairwell exit. The makeshift greenhouse contained some sort of flowering annual he didn't know, with clusters of oval leaves and large globe-shaped magenta blooms, lurid in colour. He wandered over to the glass and found the mechanism to open it.

Instinct made him turn. Rakken had gone deadly still, eyeing the flowers as if they might explode. He had taken several steps backward from where they'd landed, so that he now stood hard up against the edge of the roof and as far away from the flowers as possible.

"Faerie plants? Are they dangerous?" Marius asked.

"Bloodlock," Rakken said grimly. "It's a highly controlled plant, outlawed in most Faerie courts."

"Why?"

"The flowers affect greater fae. Make us"—his lips pulled back in distaste—"biddable."

Marius looked down at the row of brightly coloured flowers. "Do you mean like how compulsion affects mortals?"

"No. Do not try to make some point here, Marius Valstar. You forget that compulsion affects fae as well as mortals. Bloodlock is highly addictive."

"A drug," Marius murmured. "Does it work on contact, or do you have to consume it? Will it harm me?"

Rakken looked extremely irritable, and Marius knew why; he hated admitting to weakness.

"I promise not to rub you down with it," Marius added.

"It does not affect mortals, or even all fae. Only greater fae, and I have heard that royal fae react to it strongest of all. It can work via simple skin contact, but it is stronger when imbibed in concentrated form. Being found carrying such a concoction would be a death sentence in ThousandSpire."

"It's not the only plant in here," Marius said, lifting the cover frame free. "Do you recognise the others?"

Rakken edged closer, as if the bloodlock might leap out at him. His eyes narrowed at the other plants. "Sleeping glory invokes paralysis, death lily is a highly dangerous poison. Sensophorium." Rakken gave a dark chuckle, expression turning wry for a moment. "An aphrodisiac that is pleasurable in small quantities, excruciatingly painful in large ones. All highly dangerous plants that incapacitate fae in various ways. All tightly controlled in most faelands."

Marius knelt to better examine them. "Do any of them affect humans? Where would Vane have gotten them from? Someone from Faerie would have had to supply them, wouldn't they, and if they're as illegal as you say... We need to tell Wyn about this, don't we? This is definitive proof that Vane was engaging in black-market trade to collect plants known for anti-fae properties."

"Like you yourself have been attempting."

"Not the black-market trade, and not fae plants," Marius pointed out. "If I'm not allowed to make parallels to compulsion, you're not allowed to keep drawing parallels between my work and Vane's."

Rakken's eyes narrowed. "Get out of the way."

He didn't move. "What are you going to do?"

"Destroy them."

"You know, there are plants in our world that affect humans just as strongly as these ones affect fae, our own poisons and stimulants. Things aren't innately evil just because we're vulnerable to them. We're all vulnerable to something. Besides, you shouldn't destroy something that might be needed as evidence. Have you forgotten Vane was murdered? Or about the dead lowfae?"

"I have not forgotten," Rakken said. "Move, or I will move you."

Marius threw his hands up and got to his feet. He backed away from the plants. "Fine. On your own head be it when this comes back to bite us."

Rakken made an elegant curve of a gesture. The winds struck like an adder, sweeping the glasshouse and its contents up in a controlled hurricane. Glass shattered, wood thudding against the stairwell as the ball of broken plants rose. Marius had just enough time to squawk and shut his eyes before the lightning struck, blinding, the heat of it sizzling even at a distance. The sharp smell of ozone and burnt wood assaulted his nose.

When he opened his eyes, ash was falling silently in a dark snow around him. It didn't touch him, falling so as to leave a clear hollow in the air around his body. Rakken had put up an air shield for Marius as well as himself.

On the other side of the roof, Rakken's hair had come loose. It billowed around him with odd grace, like the dark tendrils of an underwater kelp forest. His eyes burned. Too bright, too green. Outstretched wings emphasised the breadth of his shoulders, the power of that chest that Marius had been pressed against so recently. Rakken looked carved out of time, too primal for the cityscape, dangerous and mesmerising as sharp rocks beneath a high, sheer cliff, and Marius couldn't breathe with the urge to step closer to the edge. It wasn't allure, wasn't magic. It was—

—sheer idiocy, that's what, he told himself sharply.

Rakken snapped his wings shut and gestured curtly at the stairwell. "Let us see what else our enterprising mortal has in store."

They went downstairs. Vane's flat contained everything his office had lacked and more besides, being closer to a laboratory than the slick bachelor's pad Marius had half-expected of the man. There was a small, neat bedroom with the usual personal effects, but the greater part of the space had been given over to scientific equipment: microscope, distillery glassware, and technomantic lamps.

Why had Vane bothered with this private setup? No one at the university would have recognised the rooftop plants as Faerie imports, and even if they had, would they have cared? Marius himself wasn't sure. Importing new species was supposed to be regulated, but everyone knew that was rarely enforced. The politics of the department were such that no one liked to inquire too closely into just where, exactly, things came from. Jenny Greenbriars had been right about that.

Then they found the other door, and it became immediately apparent why Vane had wanted to be sure of his privacy.

9

THE THISTLEDOWN CREATURE

RAKKEN HISSED, AND Marius swore the temperature dropped several degrees. He too stood horror-struck at the room they'd found. The walls were lined with shelf upon shelf of specimen jars. Trays of lifeless forms covered a central bench, with lowfae pinned like beetles. The memory of the crushed sylf rose along with his gorge. And then he realised that many of the shelves' contents were still alive, and the relief was so strong he staggered.

The lowfae began to stir, paws, claws, and hands tapping against their confines. They were organised by size, with the bottom shelf holding cages rather than jars. The smallest of the lowfae was the size of his thumbnail. The largest, on the lowest shelf, was a ferret-like creature with fur resembling thistledown. The thistledown creature had been sleeping, but it got to its feet, blinking in the light, and gave a muted mew. Its eyes were the same purple as thistle flowers, and its ears were disproportionately large.

Rakken and the room full of fairies eyed each other up and

down, and then he said, "You will owe me a debt of my choosing for taking you to safety."

"What!" Marius whirled on him.

The lowfae murmured agreement, a series of mews, chirps, and small, pitiful words.

"That is how things are done, Marius Valstar," Rakken said. He stepped into the room and began with the top-most shelf, pulling off jars and unscrewing lids. The first lowfae to emerge was a bright blue creature rather like a stick insect. It scuttled up Rakken's arm with nervous energy.

Marius crouched and opened the cage on the bottom shelf. "Well, that doesn't apply to me. You don't owe me anything."

The thistledown fae blinked at him, ear tufts twitching. He got the strong sense that it was having trouble reconciling his presence next to Rakken's.

"Yes, I'm a human," he told it. "Not like the one who put you in here, though." The creature appeared to accept this, stepping daintily out of its enclosure and sniffing his hand. "See, it's safe—ow!"

It gave him a disconcerting smile, its mouth too wide and showing teeth more needle-like than a ferret's. He nursed his finger, where a few drops of blood welled from the bite. "I understand the sentiment, but I really am trying to help."

The creature settled down on its haunches without taking its eyes off him, tilting its head this way and that.

"Biting me isn't much of a thank you," he told it.

Its ear tufts spread, a trio on each side of its head. Each one twitched independently as he and it took each other's measure. After a beat, it licked its lips without breaking eye contact.

Bugger it all. Why was he having a staring competition with a lowfae? He looked away and heard the creature make a small, smug sound as if it had won something.

Rakken had finished freeing the rest of the lowfae while Marius had been busy with the thistle creature. The other lowfae were more subdued than he'd expected, and he caught a shimmer of something as Rakken freed the last. It looked like the same kind of green-gold magic he'd offered the hedge-hog-fae back in Knoxbridge.

"You're giving them energy?" he hazarded.

Rakken shrugged. "Of course; I said I would see them to safety, and they have been diminished by their time here." His attention caught on the cabinet beside Marius. Marius turned, but Rakken had already stalked across to pick something up and opened his hand to reveal a modified quizzing glass. A very *familiar* modified quizzing glass.

Marius held out a hand for it, too horrified to speak.

Rakken passed it to him, the line of his mouth thinning. "I suppose this explains how Vane was able to trap lowfae so easily. I had assumed he had the Sight, but it seems not."

Marius felt sick. There was a dried greenish film over the lens. He had only gotten his devices to work on quite low-level glamour. Exactly like the don't-see-me misdirection glamour that a lot of lowfae used.

He swallowed, his throat tight. "This isn't one of mine, though it looks like it's designed on similar principles." This felt like no defence at all.

"Did you tell Vane of your experiments?" Rakken's face was unreadable.

"I… mentioned them. I didn't show him anything, but I talked about experimenting with anti-glamour mixtures. I'm sorry. I shouldn't have told him—I wouldn't have told him if I'd known this was what he was doing with it!"

Rakken said nothing, but his eyes were hard.

"I—"

"He was manipulating you," Rakken said. Marius flinched. "You think, because you are good, that everyone else must be also, you—" He cut himself off with a snarl and turned to the assembled lowfae. Marius realised he had also collected up the dead, disappearing them with a snap of his fingers. "This place is not safe, but there is a waypoint to Faerie nearby. I will take you." Marius assumed he meant Malvern Place, the dilapidated townhouse that housed a Gate to Stariel and from thence to the Spires.

But before any of them could move, there came a sound from the main part of the flat. A door being unlatched.

They exchanged glances. *Vane's assistant?* Marius mouthed.

Rakken went... other, was the only word for it. He was already in his fae form, but it was as if he had been maintaining a skin of normality up until this moment, when he shed it. He went through the door into the main room of the flat with the speed of a viper striking. By the time Marius had followed him out, he already had the intruder by the throat and pressed up against the wall. The room was so thick with his signature that it was like walking into a thunderstorm.

Marius jerked, recognising the man.

"Wait, I know him! He's from my college. His name is Thomas Bakir." He had no idea what Bakir was doing here, but a cold suspicion began to curl up, alongside a kind of resigned despair. He'd thought it was mere coincidence that Bakir, with his interest in folklore, had introduced himself at that pub. Had he been played for a fool *again?* Gods, Rakken was *right*. He'd been stupidly, unforgivably naïve. Again.

Rakken threw Bakir into the nearby armchair. He let out

a stunned groan, but he had sense enough to stay put with Rakken emanating all the ominousness of an enraged death god.

"Did you kill any of the lowfae here?" Rakken asked.

"The lowfae?" Bakir repeated. His eyes widened. "The little fairy creatures? No!"

"Tell me the truth, Thomas Bakir." Outright compulsion, such as Marius had never seen Rakken wield so mercilessly. His face was hard, a queer light glittering in his eyes.

"I am telling the truth! I came here to release them!" Words spilled out of Bakir, his knuckles white on the chair arms, as if he could not stop himself. Because he couldn't. "Vane wanted to sell them off to collectors or some such, and the gods know I could do with the money, but after I saw them, I started to think they weren't just animals. I told Vane it didn't seem right—couldn't he be content with the plants? He wouldn't be persuaded. And then, I heard he was dead, and I knew I couldn't just leave them here. So I came to let them out!"

"You were working with Vane," Marius said, coming to stand in front of him.

Bakir gave a convulsive start, as if he'd forgotten Marius was here. Or—no—as if Marius had disrupted the compulsion. Bakir's gaze swung between him and Rakken, eyes widening as he recognised Rakken as the man from Marius's room.

"Tell us," Rakken said, and there was a relentless thread of iron in his voice that made the hair on the back of Marius's neck stand on end.

And Bakir told them. Without hesitation.

He told them how Vane had approached him at the start of term, knowing of Bakir's interest in folklore and his willingness to take on paid research commissions. "He said he'd come by some unusual specimens, actual fairy plants. I didn't believe him at first, but he was willing to pay for my time, so I thought, what the hells. What do I have to lose? If he wanted to pay me for stories about fairy plants, I wasn't going to say no. But he really did have a source, it turned out. A fairy he'd met somewhere—he wouldn't tell me how, and I never met them myself. I don't know the fairy's name. I helped Vane shift the plants, sometimes, but he was always careful to make sure that by the time I arrived, the fairy had gone.

"He had a deal going with them. Vane was supposed to grow certain plants in large quantities, and the fairy would turn up each month to collect each batch as they matured. In exchange, the fellow supplied Vane with new plants each time. The fairy wouldn't tell Vane what he wanted the plants batch grown for—that was what Vane wanted me to find out for him. He wanted to know why they were valuable."

"And did you find out?" Rakken asked softly. No part of him moved except the tips of his wings, which flexed.

"Only one of them, so far. In the account I found, it was called sleeping glory. There was a tale of a prince who slept for a hundred years." Bakir swallowed.

Rakken's wings relaxed a fraction, but his voice remained dangerously soft. "The lowfae," he prompted. "What part do they play in this?"

Bakir kept talking, helpless to resist. The whites showed around his eyes. Marius knew Rakken could make the compulsion easier on him—he'd seen Rakken use it before in such a way that people didn't even realise they were being compelled. Clearly, he was choosing not to do so in this case. The walls seemed to shiver with the force of his anger.

Bakir's voice was hoarse with terror. "Vane started trapping them about a month ago. He'd gotten hold of some device that meant he could see them more easily. The creatures have a kind of magic that hides them—like illusion, except that a regular quizzing glass doesn't work on it; you need a particular mix of herbs. But you can learn to see through their magic after a while, once you know they're there, even without the device.

"At first I thought they were just animals, but some of them can talk. Vane was testing to see if the plants did anything to them. I told him I wasn't happy with what he was doing. We argued. He told me he didn't need my help with the exchange this month; usually I would help him move things afterwards. I know that's what he must have been doing the night he was murdered. Whatever happened with his fairy supplier must have gone wrong. Maybe they found out about the creatures."

Something eased, and Bakir's near-frantic recitation came to a shuddering halt. He hunched in on himself, pressing the back of his fist to his mouth.

Rakken withdrew across the room, wings folded tightly against his spine. His expression was as cold as Marius had ever seen it, and he was every inch the superior prince regarding a mere mortal. The lines of his face had shifted to their most alien arrangement, almost painfully beautiful.

Bakir shuddered, his eyes flicking to the door. Marius knew he considered whether to make a break for it before deciding it wasn't worth the risk of provoking the terrible fairy man. The fellow had moved so fast before, inhumanly fast. Bakir didn't understand what had just happened—had that been fae magic? Was he losing his mind? He gathered the threads of himself up with visible effort.

"Did… did he kill Vane?" Bakir asked Marius in a small voice, giving a sharp jerk of his head towards Rakken, as if he were too afraid to look at him directly.

Marius started. "No! He's not a killer."

"I am," Rakken disagreed. "Though I did not kill your mortal." He sounded as if he wished otherwise.

Marius glared at Rakken. "Must you make unnecessarily terrifying announcements?" He turned back to find Bakir staring at him with a kind of awed horror.

How are you not afraid of him? he heard Bakir wonder.

Marius thought about trying to explain that Rakken wasn't frightening, reflected on the last few minutes, and discarded the idea. Bakir wasn't being irrational in his fear, even if Marius had never been afraid of Rakken. How could he explain that Rakken was both exactly as terrible as Bakir thought and nothing like it? That the masks Rakken wore were so numerous and well-worn that even Rakken believed they were true sometimes? That fae, although they could not lie, were inclined towards making everything sound much more dramatic and/or ominous than it needed to be?

Bakir swallowed again. "I'm sorry. I didn't—I thought you might be Vane's contact to Faerie," he admitted. "But then you were out on the night I knew he was meeting his contact, so you couldn't be. But then Vane turned up dead, and you had a fae with you, and I feared…"

"Is that why you propositioned me? To find out if I was involved?" He felt hollow. That night at the pub had been such a nice *normal* interaction, for all its awkwardness, and now it was tainted in hindsight. Rakken looked up sharply.

Bakir straightened. "What?!" Anger gave him new life, his eyes flashing. "A nice idea you have of me. I don't pimp myself out, not even for you, Valstar."

Marius winced.

Rakken spread his wings, and Bakir flinched away, his anger

deflating in an instant. "You may go now," Rakken told him. Bakir scrambled out of the chair but caught himself mid-step. "What about the lowfae?"

Rakken bared his teeth, and the storm flared in his eyes. "*I* will take responsibility for their welfare."

Bakir cringed and hurried out of the room. The door slammed, and Marius heard running footsteps echoing in the stairwell as Bakir fled.

Marius rounded on Rakken. "Did you have to be so, so…"

"So what, Marius Valstar?" Rakken hissed, opening his wings. His fists were clenched, but the queer hard light had drained from his face. He looked shaken, and it struck Marius that he'd enjoyed what had just passed even less than Bakir.

"So intent on making yourself a monster in other people's eyes."

A blankness in Rakken's eyes for a moment, a tiny hint of vulnerability, before he folded it under yet another of those damn masks. His feathers settled neatly against his back. "I said I would see justice done for the dead lowfae. I did not say it would be *nice*, and we now know far more than we did."

Marius put a hand on his arm, distressed. "Rake—"

Rakken gave a sharp jerk of his head and pulled away. He raised his voice and spoke to the lowfae huddling behind the door. "You may come out now."

10

YET MORE TRAIPSING BACK AND FORTH

Escorting a swarm of lowfae through the Meridon streets was certainly an experience. There was no sign of Bakir, though Marius wasn't surprised. He hadn't needed telepathy to know that the man had planned to get as far away from Rakken in as short a space of time as possible.

Some of the lowfae could fly, and they hovered around them like dragonflies. Others trotted alongside. The smallest ones perched on Rakken, sitting on his shoulders and in his breast pocket. A frog-like one sat on his head, clutching a bronze horn for balance. Still others had arrayed themselves along his wingbones, putting Marius in mind of sparrows on an icy day, huddling together on a single branch. It was the least dignified he'd ever seen Rakken look.

"I can carry some of you too," Marius had tried offering, which statement went ignored by all of them except the this-tledown creature, who blinked and then scrambled its way up his clothing in a ferret-like blur. It had wound itself into his scarf before he could do more than let out a startled sound. Its

A RAKE OF HIS OWN

fur brushed the back of his neck, coarser than he'd expected from its appearance.

Rakken watched the interaction with sardonic amusement but didn't comment as they set off. The fae that had chosen to walk or fly stayed close to Rakken—so close that Marius kept almost stumbling, fearing he'd crash into one or another. He got the strong sense that they wanted the reassurance of proximity to a greater fae. In other circumstances, it would have been amusing to see Rakken treated in the same light as a parent to a flock of nervous toddlers. As it was, Marius didn't blame them for needing reassurance, not after their time in captivity.

The human city clearly alarmed the lowfae too, and they started at each strange noise and passer-by. Passers-by who not only ignored the entire parade but actively diverted around them, which he knew was Rakken's doing. Lowfae glamour wasn't powerful enough to achieve that sort of effect.

The day was blustery, and the lowfae about Rakken's feet skittered sideways as a stray bit of litter scuttled across the pavement. Rakken didn't break stride, walking as if he had no fear of tripping or squashing anyone underfoot. Amazingly, this approach worked more effectively than Marius's. He startled an annoyed squawk out of a snake-like lowfae as he trod on its tail.

"Sorry," he apologised. The lowfae gave him a dark look and slithered closer to Rakken. *He's much less trustworthy than I am!* Marius wanted to object, but he couldn't really blame them under the circumstances.

Even with the bubble of pedestrian-avoidance around them, his head began to throb. He wondered if anyone had categorised the different kinds and strengths of fae glamour.

"Are there universities in Faerie?" he asked Rakken.

"Not like humans, with your oh-so-civilised funding pro-grams—or not so civilised."

"There's a reason Vane was hiding this away from the uni-versity. It wouldn't have gotten ethics approval." He hoped. He reached to touch the tail of the thistledown ferret where it poked out beneath his scarf. The creature withdrew its tail with a chittering objection. "Are you going to claim Faerie is a happy utopia of unproblematic learning?"

Rakken acknowledged the hit. "No. I have seen worse than this there."

Marius shuddered. "That doesn't excuse Vane."

"No."

Malvern Place was a narrow two-storey townhouse in a row of similar buildings, though decidedly worn in comparison to its neighbours. Faded white guard rails ran along the front-age, the window boxes overflowing with weeds. The front door might once have been blue under the peeling paint.

Marius fished about for a key. Hetta had given him one with the admonition that he was to use it to avail himself of the Gate between Malvern Place and Stariel if he needed it. "Maybe you could come home more often," she'd said, grey eyes searching his face, a worried expression in them.

"I'm fine, I don't need to be fussed over," he'd snapped, and then felt like a cad. "Sorry." You shouldn't snap at heavily preg-nant women.

Hetta had smiled. "I haven't actually become made of glass, you know. And I didn't invite you just to fuss. We enjoy your company, astonishing though it seems at this precise moment, brother mine."

The door opened without a creak—someone had oiled it

since last time, then—and greeted them with the overwhelming smell of dust edged with cleaning products. Someone had swept the floor and washed the windows since he'd last set foot here, but the latter had only made the decay easier to see. Half the panes were smashed, and the wallpaper was peeling. A water stain was slowly eating its way down the hallway ceiling from the front door. The place hadn't been maintained for years, not since Marius's father had been a young man, probably. There was no money to repair it now.

It felt… Marius blinked as he stepped over the threshold. His land-sense had always been weak, but he still felt it whenever he crossed the borders to Stariel Estate, the connection to the silent land guardian flaring to life, a pulse that said *home*. This wasn't quite that, but it was somewhere in the vicinity of it, a tickling familiarity that went deeper than bone.

He turned to hold open the door and found both Rakken and assorted lowfae hesitating on the threshold.

"Is this a faeland? Part of Stariel?" he asked. "Do you need me to invite you in?" He wasn't sure he even could—that sort of thing usually fell in Hetta's domain, as lord.

Rakken looked beyond him, examining leylines. "No," he said after a long pause. "This is not a faeland, not yet." He stepped over the threshold and relaxed a fraction as he did so.

"Hetta hasn't given you blanket permission to come and go as you like, then?" Marius couldn't help observing. Greater fae could enter faelands without permission, but it stripped them of their powers if they did.

Rakken gave him a cutting look. "She would be a fool to do so."

"Why? Are you intending harm to Stariel?"

"It is not my court."

"Your brother is married to its ruler. Your nieces or nephews will be born there." And whatever Rakken liked to pretend, Marius knew that he cared about family.

"And I should like very much to know that my niephlings' parents will not be so careless of their safety as to let such as me in without warning."

"'Such as you'," Marius repeated, unimpressed. "You would no more endanger them than you would Cat, and Hetta knows that as well as I." So why would Rakken put up with the inconvenience of forgoing his full powers whenever he entered Stariel? Oh. "You told Hetta that if she extended such a sign of favour to you, she would have all the other courts demanding she do the same with their representatives," he guessed.

"It was a stroke of brilliance on my brother's part to install Gates to the most powerful Faerie courts to Stariel and get them to agree to travel from there to the wider Mortal Realm. It increases his legitimacy in speaking for Faerie," Rakken admitted, then grimaced. "Don't tell him I said so."

Marius laughed. "I think he already knows. But doesn't he already have such legitimacy from the High King himself? I thought that was the whole point of that adventure he and Hetta went on."

Rakken's face darkened. "Even my brother is not such a fool as to think force more effective than persuasion for this sort of thing. The combination of carrot and stick is as ever a powerful one."

Marius became aware of the crowd of lowfae loitering on the doorstep, watching the two of them interestedly. Rakken seemed to remember them in the same moment, giving himself a shake.

"Perhaps this is not the moment to discuss politics." Rakken gestured at the lowfae to follow him into the house.

The lowfae drew closer to Rakken's feet as Marius led them down the long hallway. The townhouse was a narrow building, the kitchen, sitting and dining rooms on the ground floor, the bedrooms on the upper. The hallway led in a straight line between back and front doors and was the only part of the house that showed any sign of use. Marius led them straight to the back door and pushed open into the garden.

Like the house itself, the back garden showed the signs of many years of neglect. The Gate Hetta and Wyn had built to Stariel was set into the brick wall at the back of the garden, and the path between it and the door had been cleared. Otherwise, the garden was a tumble of cut-back weeds, strewn with crumbling relics from when the house had last been inhabited. The broken bones of an aged conservatory could be seen through a mass of ivy.

The lowfae cautiously spread out across the overgrown lawn. Rakken went to the back wall. Inactive, the Gate looked as if someone had carved an abstract pattern into the bricks between a lichen-covered trellis. Gates were more reliable than portals, being fixed in a single location and permanently connecting two points. Unlike portals, they could be used by non-magic users. They were complicated to build; Wyn had tried to explain the theory to Marius but had had to admit he didn't fully understand how they worked either. It wasn't entirely Wyn's fault; his magical education had been cut short as a boy, when he'd fled Faerie for Stariel.

Rakken traced a line in the pattern that reminded Marius of the ridgeline of the Indigo Mountains at home. The lines sprang to life. Light flared, and the brick wall opened, revealing a view into the battered receiving room of the Dower House.

There was a stir amongst the lowfae.

"You can cross to Faerie here," Rakken told them. "Or you may remain. This property belongs to the Lord of FallingStar, though it is not yet part of her faeland. If any of you wish to return to the place where you were originally taken from, I will take you when I return."

Marius looked at him sharply. "What?"

"I must report this incident to my queen. It will affect the ongoing negotiations with Mortal, especially if Vane's killer was fae." Rakken said it so smoothly, as if he weren't talking of his twin. As if there were nothing left of Cat-and-Mouse, the pet names the twins had for each other. Was it true?

"You're not worried I was the target anymore?"

Rakken shook his head. "No. I agree with your assessment. Vane clearly had his own ties to Faerie; that takes the use of fae magic surrounding his death past coincidence or mistaken identity. I will find the supplier of the plants in Faerie and deal with them."

"And if they're who killed Vane?"

An elegant shrug. "I find myself in sympathy with them, but they will face justice for the bloodlock."

Rakken waved again at the lowfae, most of whom went to inspect the Gate, sniffing it warily. Rakken rolled his eyes and stepped through to demonstrate its safety. Marius hurried to follow.

Stepping through a Gate was a bit like falling off something, a sickening drop that ended as he found himself inside the Dower House. His land-sense flared to life, the sense of home-coming sliding into place. Stariel was unique, a mortal estate that was also part of Faerie, magically connected to a mortal bloodline: the Valstars. It was always an odd moment, adjusting to that primitive *homecoming*, which swept over him no matter his own opinions on the matter or all the evidence to the contrary. Stariel might be where Valstars were supposed to belong, but Marius had always been a half-step out of rhythm with it.

At least it was a less fraught feeling now that his father no longer ruled here—now that Marius was no longer trapped here being a perpetual disappointment. Look at his cousin Jack—why couldn't Marius be more like him, eh? For gods' sake, Marius, pay attention. Away with the bloody fairies. Moody as a girl. Put that book down! No one likes a know-it-all. Real men don't cry, boy; stop snivelling!

He gave himself a little shake, letting the memories disperse. Father was dead, in the ground for more than a year now.

For a few moments, the lowfae blinked at them from the other side of the Gate, which on this end was framed by decorative plasterwork. Reassured by Marius and Rakken's safe arrival, they began to stream through into the receiving room. Marius went to the door and opened it. Rakken followed, and they led the lowfae through the unoccupied house, past rooms filled with sheet-covered furniture until they reached the front door and the lowfae spilled onto the steps outside. He and Rakken watched the lowfae disappear into the landscape, whether by glamour or stealth.

Marius sighed. "I suppose I ought to tell Hetta why I'm sending a packload of lowfae her way."

"I shall leave that task to you, then. Farewell, Marius Valstar."

Marius frowned, something in Rakken's voice catching at him. "What do you mean? You're coming back, aren't you?" he burst out before he could stop himself.

"It's flattering to know you pine for me in my absence, but I do have other commitments." A wicked flash of teeth, and

Marius couldn't help thinking of how Rakken had said lovers were an easy enough commodity to find. Why was he thinking about that now?

"You're the one who said you couldn't leave this business alone! What if Vane's killer *wasn't* the fae who was trading plants with him? Or what if you can't find them in Faerie? I'd like to know who murdered my colleague, too, you know. And you promised to liaise with the police." He ought to be celebrating the end of this temporary alliance between them, but instead it felt like a rug had been jerked from under his feet. He thought of Vane's modified quizzing glass and the lowfae they'd been too late to save. His resolve hardened. He needed to see this through, to make some small part of this right.

Rakken gave a long-suffering sigh. "Perhaps you are right. I shall return to tie up loose ends when I have discharged my immediate duty, since you desire my company so greatly. You may await me here."

"I didn't mean—" But Marius's indignant protest was lost in the rush of wings as Rakken took flight. "I have to get back to Knoxbridge for classes! I'm not just sitting here indefinitely waiting for you!" he shouted into the wind. Rakken gave no sign of having heard him.

Marius grumpily watched him become a smaller and smaller bronze-and-green speck against the grey of the sky, winging towards the Standing Stones, where the Gate to ThousandSpire stood.

"Oh, fuck you," he muttered and started walking up to the main house.

11

ONE ANGSTY FAE PRINCE

RAKKEN STEPPED THROUGH the Gate and fanned his wings in and out a few times to let the Spires-sense sink in. Always bittersweet, that sense of homecoming. He was not ThousandSpire's ruler; the faeland had looked deep into his soul and found him wanting. He did not blame it. How could he, when it had passed him over in favour of the person he loved most? But it was nonetheless an unpleasant truth, to be reminded that one was lacking in some crucial aspect.

Still, it was good to be back in Faerie. The Mortal Realm fascinated and threw him off balance in equal measure, and no one embodied that combination more than the man he'd just left. His hand tightened on the stone arch of the gate.

Why was he still so affected by this one mortal? An image of said mortal stirred in his mind, of narrow shoulders, lean torso, and a hint of flank and long legs as he'd risen from his bedclothes. His black hair had been wildly disarrayed, jawline shadowed, grey eyes wide, and mouth soft. Marius's face had perfectly mirrored his emotions, as it so often did, the blush sweeping over his cheeks and down his throat as he'd held

Rakken's gaze, trying for defiance and landing in fluster instead. Rakken grimaced. He'd thought the pull would fade in the absence of proximity, given sufficient distraction. He'd certainly tried the latter, bedding a veritable flock of lovers in the past few months. Until two days ago, he'd been convinced he'd exorcised every last remnant of his fixation.

Ah yes, so well exorcised. His lips pulled back in a snarl. This storms-tossed… *thing* had roared to life at full strength the moment he'd tumbled out of his ill-advised portal and met a pair of startled grey eyes. Unfaded by time, intervening orgies, or, as it turned out, murder.

It was aggravating.

He tipped his head back to assess the weather through the translucent circular roof. The sky was clear, promising easy flying so long as the winds were not too high. He did not care much if they were; though there were non-aerial paths through the city, he would take them only should the weather turn cataclysmic.

This Gate room was located on the lowest level of the palace complex. A higher location and an open roof would have been more convenient, but that would have made it too vulnerable to attack. There were other Gates throughout the palace, some more publicly accessible than others, but none had been positioned without consideration for how to defend them.

This Gate was not yet open to ThousandSpire's general citizens. One day there would be freer travel between the realms, exchanges of goods and ideas alongside all their fraught costs and benefits. Despite the events of this past day, he still believed it would ultimately be to ThousandSpire's benefit. He would hardly have wasted so much time in committee meetings with mortal diplomats otherwise.

The discovery of Vane's activities had not shocked him; he had known fae to do worse, and he'd always assumed the mortals were just as capable. It had only been a matter of time before such issues began to arise. It was *why* the negotiations with the Mortal Realm were so crucial. His brother Hallowyn held a touching faith in people's inner goodness, in a vague, happy utopia where fae and mortals all worked for mutual benefit, untouched by darker motivations. Hallowyn had a tendency to see mortals as the more innocent party in the negotiations, as if they were less capable of deceit. Ironic, that.

Rakken held no such illusions about the innate goodness of either fae or mortals. He would not rely on optimism to protect his people, and he would not let Hallowyn make wide-ranging decrees without forcing him to consider their impact. The potential for failure in any system always rested in its fine points.

Tucking his wings, he shook off his ruminations and prepared to sally forth. He could not appear anything less than self-assured in public. Cat might have the power of the faeland behind her, but by fae standards she was considered young and inexperienced. The court was a well-trained pit of vipers, waiting to strike at the first sign of weakness, and that was to say nothing of ThousandSpire's enemies. Cat needed to appear unassailable, and he was her right hand.

People paused as he strode through the labyrinthine stone corridors, wanting to bask in the glory of his presence and absorb some of its brilliance if they could. Power was always attractive, and he represented a direct line to the throne. He bestowed smiles and doled out misdirection and morsels of gossip, all designed to subtly bolster Cat's position whilst giving nothing of value away.

The rulership of ThousandSpire had not changed hands in an exceedingly long time. His father had been one of the ancient fae, so old no one was quite sure what had come before. Power came with age, for most fae, and so had been the case with King Aeros. His magic had seeped into every part of the Spires, large and small.

And now it was almost all gone. Magic could be cast to outlast the caster's death, but it was fiendishly difficult, and King Aeros's arrogance had been such that he had not planned for such an eventuality. It was almost enough to make Rakken regret his father's death. Almost.

"We have missed you, Your Highness," a high-ranking courtier with long pink hair purred in one of the many brief interactions he had whilst making his way through the palace. "More time spent in Mortal?" She fished for information on where he had been.

"You flatter me," he said with a wide smile, and dodged the question with a barbed riposte. "And slight Emyranthus, if you've been pining for others whilst you've been in her company." He knew this courtier was Emyr's latest bit of bed sport, though he doubted she'd last long there with such a clumsy lack of subtlety. She was pretty enough, but Emyr had no taste for fools.

The courtier stuttered, unsure whether agreeing or disagreeing would be worse. Her companions watched her dilemma with hungry eyes, waiting to tear her to pieces if she judged wrongly. She swallowed, the colour draining from her face. "I—"

Abruptly, Rakken took pity on her. "But I must take my leave of you; my queen calls," he said and strode away. It was in his interest for Emyr to keep her distractions, anyway; it might save him from another ugly scene between them.

When he finally reached the audience chambers, they were empty.

"The audience ended earlier than expected. It's not like you to miss one." A thin stormdancer, Wetherbel, spoke from the doorway. Their eyes picked him over, wondering what had caused his absence, but they were not bold enough to ask. "I suppose you are looking for Her Majesty?"

"No." He knew where Cat would be, after such.

He found his twin in her private training salle. The space was a vast cavern on the lower levels of her tower, lined with mirrors on one side and a wall of weapons on the other. Light streamed in through the floor-to-ceiling windows.

Queen Catsmere Tempestren. She moved like the warrior she was, fluid as a summer breeze, deadliness and grace. As he came in, she was practising with a glaive, the long pole an extension of her body, the bladed head glinting. He knew she'd noticed his entrance, but her form did not falter.

He took up a matching weapon and joined her, finding his place in the pattern so that he mirrored her movements. For several minutes neither of them spoke. He fell into the familiar rhythm, his muscles warming.

Cat struck with no warning, moving from the solitary forms to catch his weapon with her own as if that had always been the next step in the dance.

He adjusted just as smoothly, grinning at her as he blocked the blow. "In a temper, then? My, what did the elders say to you?"

She rolled her eyes, and he didn't need Marius's telepathy to know her thought: *Don't waste breath in combat, Mouse.* But all she said was, "No magic." Setting the terms of the bout.

After that, he could not have found breath to say more even if he'd wanted to. Strike, block, dodge, a frantic back and forth.

They knew each other too well, had danced this dance too many times. His reach was slightly greater than hers, but her skill ran deeper. His skill was a rational result of time invested, but Catsmere loved the warrior arts in a way that he did not. It gave her the edge, an instinct for timing and angles that was unmatchable unless he used magic, in which case he would usually win about one bout in three. Or at least, he used to. Nowadays, with Cat's magic amplified by the faeland…

He struck when she was at the point of greatest vulnerability, her body extended in a strike. His lightning snapped out as he dodged, only to discharge harmlessly on her shield, which had come up a touch too quickly to be her instinct alone. It had been the faeland, acting to protect its ruler.

Unsurprisingly, the fight ended with blinding speed after that. She used her shield for momentum, swept his feet out from under him in a rather beautiful piece of timing, knocking his wing with a powerful blow at the same moment so he lost his balance. He landed on the sand of the salle, winded, the point of the glaive at his throat. Cat glared down at him, her green eyes the exact shade of his own. One of the most annoying things about her was that anger did not make her more prone to mistakes. It just made her strike harder.

Her eyes blazed. "What part of 'no magic' did you fail to understand?"

The echoes of past arguments hung in the air.

Since she'd inherited, she'd forbidden either of them to use magic in bouts against the other. Her magic was too strong now, she'd argued. Her bond with the faeland wasn't yet mature enough to mitigate the risk to him if it thought him a danger to her; what if it lashed out at him before she could stop it?

Rakken repeated his own argument aloud. "If someone

comes for you, they will not be so fastidious. I will not allow you to indulge in weakness out of sentimentality. You would not allow a novice to discard their best weapon, nor fail to practice with it."

Cat huffed and turned away, deciding not to re-open her side. Because he was *right*, and she knew it. "A noble sentiment, from someone who just *lost*."

"It hardly counts, since you cheated," he said loftily. "That was the faeland in your last strike."

"It counts, since we *both* cheated." Offering him a hand, she helped pull him to his feet.

He brushed dust off his shirt. "What has put you in such a mood? I saw no blood in the audience chamber."

"The audience was sadly lacking in bloodshed," Cat agreed, wrinkling her nose. "Though perhaps not figuratively. You know how it is."

He searched her face. "I do. Cat—"

She waved his concern away. "Just more court politics. I dealt with it. What of your errand? Did you find what you hoped?"

"I found them, but it will not serve. I was forced to make a rather awkward retreat and found myself unexpectedly in Mortal." He hesitated. "In Marius Valstar's lodgings."

"I see now why you were delayed," Cat said, her eyes gleaming with sudden amusement.

He ignored this bait, though he felt the feathers at his neck fluff up in irritation. He forced them flat with an effort.

"Shortly after I arrived, I sensed a disturbance along the leylines. Dark fae magic." He told her what had passed since he'd last seen her.

She put her weapon away and began to stretch, but he knew she was listening intently. When he reached the part with the bloodlock and the other black-market plants, she swore.

"Yes," he agreed. "I intend to hunt down the supplier, though if it were they who killed the mortal, I find myself in some sympathy with them, after what I saw of Vane's experiments. I may need to attend the Goblin Market, if my networks cannot find the source."

"Speaking of mortals…" Cat cocked her head at him.

He gave her a quelling look.

"You're still obsessing over him, then."

"Hardly. This is the first I have seen of him for several months."

"Yes," she agreed placidly.

Rakken waved his hand irritably. "There are some loose ends to tie up in Knoxbridge, but I expect it shall not keep me there long."

"One bespectacled, grey-eyed loose end, is it?" she said, and only smiled wider when he flicked a wing at her. "It's not like you to choose avoidance over indulgence. Why not get it out of your system? I've never seen you be so"—another sly grin—"*fastidious.*"

He frowned. "Do you truly wish me to speak explicitly?" They were usually careful to keep clear of the details of each other's love lives.

She arched an eyebrow. "Is the answer that explicit?"

"Sadly not. He does not want me." He waved away her objection. "Oh, of course he desires me, but he hates that he does."

"Is that *why* you can't leave it alone?" She knew him too well.

"Perhaps." *Storms, I hope that's why.* A tangling sensation clawed at his wings. Curse the mortal; he *refused* to be made ridiculous over this. There had to be some way to rid himself of it. Perhaps a change of tactics? He was irritated enough to needle Cat in return. "If we are being explicit, what of you?"

Cat was balanced on one leg, a wing extended, stretching her other limb with casual grace. She didn't even wobble at his question. "I have never aimed to copy your excesses."

He laughed. "You've never been willingly celibate, either, and you have been alone more oft than not, of late. Is it the crown?"

Being part of the royal family had always meant a share of sycophants and power-hungry beauties wishing to bed a royalfae for reasons other than simple attraction. It had never bothered Rakken; so long as they desired him, what did he care if they also coveted his power? They would learn soon enough that he did not share anything beyond bodily pleasures.

Cat had always taken much the same approach, but that had been before. It was not the same now. She was no longer one of King Aeros's many children; she was Queen Catsmere, the throne itself.

Cat finished her stretch and put her foot down. He could tell she was about to say something he wouldn't like.

"I met with Princess Sunnika," she said.

Rakken almost dropped the weapon he'd been holding. Princess Sunnika, heir presumptive of the Court of Dusken Roses, ThousandSpire's sworn enemy. The courts were no longer in open warfare, thanks largely to their mutual alliance with Stariel, but Queen Tayarenn still sat on a throne ornamented with stormdancer horns, and there was a personal bloodfeud between her and ThousandSpire's crown. For good reason.

"The boon you so foolishly promised her," he guessed. Cat had made the gesture as thanks for saving their wretched little brother's neck. She'd done it for political reasons, an attempt to soften the enmity between their families. He couldn't fault her logic; Princess Sunnika appeared to be by far the most open-minded member of her house. It didn't change the fact that he wanted nothing to do with that court. He wanted *Cat* to have nothing to do with that court.

"Yes. Although we have agreed no terms but to meet again."

Rakken stilled, reading the unspoken sentiment. "You admire her," he accused. "More than that. You like her."

"Of course I admire her. She is acknowledged as one of Faerie's great beauties, and I'm not blind," she said drily.

Rakken's eyes narrowed.

Cat gave a huff. "Oh, very well, then. I confess: I did not expect to find common ground with a shadowcat, but Sunnika is... interesting."

"And Sunnika? Has she forgotten I killed her cousin, or is she cosying up to you to further her own agenda?"

"*We* killed her cousin, and neither of us forgets it. But I do not think she mourned him overmuch." Cat's gaze saw straight through him. "I have not told her, and I will not, unless you say I might, but I think she suspects something of what happened. She knows what Prince Orenn was."

"So did Queen Tayarenn, and I would not trust Sunnika's life in her hands if Tayarenn thinks her involved with her son's murderers. I wouldn't trust Sunnika not to be playing some deeper game, either. This is beyond foolishness, Cat."

"Perhaps; or perhaps good politics. Or perhaps it is nothing at all. But I do not think Sunnika has told her aunt that we have spoken."

"And you did not tell me." Once, he'd thought there were no secrets between them. "Where did you meet her? Who guarded your back, Cat?" And why had it not been him?

"Neutral ground. Unclaimed lands."

Rakken hissed. "Outside the Spires. Outside the protections of the faeland. Did you at least take bodyguards? Don't give me that look—if I had done such a thing, you would flay me for carelessness."

"I wanted…" Cat trailed off. "I am trying to be a good queen, but sometimes, one needs something for oneself. To be alone in one's self."

He moved towards her, feeling her distress as his own. ThousandSpire was in his soul too, but it was not the same now. He could not bridge this divide between them; she had left him the day that ThousandSpire had chosen her, flying to a height where he could never follow.

Cat wrapped her wings around him in a rare show of sentimentality. Her colours were the same as his; bronze limned with green at her primaries. The signature of her magic had changed, subtly strange since her ascension in a way that unsettled him. It still held its usual cinnamon and the sea in storm, but they were joined now by other less familiar notes drawn from ThousandSpire.

"Oh, Mouse," she sighed. "Do not feel *too* sorry for me. No bird was fledged in a single day, but there is still more good than bad in this, for me." She released him and stepped back, searching his face. "I wish I could be as sure the same was true for you."

Wishes are for children. He knew she heard the echo of their father's words too.

He shook his head, discarding the thought. "Enough. Now tell me of what I have missed at court, Cat, and what you need me to do."

12

A MISSHAPEN WOOLLEN HAT OF LOVE

A s Marius began to walk from the Dower House down towards the lake, something shifted on his person. He yelped and then realised the thistledown creature was still wrapped about his neck.

"You can come down now," he told it, reaching up. It only retreated further into his scarf. "Have it your way, then. I'm going up to the main house."

It was one of those vivid autumn days, the sky a piercing blue and the landscape painted shades of gold, with Starwater a perfect reflection. His headache eased as he walked. It was Stariel—Hetta had gotten the faeland to do something that didn't completely block his telepathy but helped greatly.

The main house lay on the other side of Starwater, the largest of the many lakes dotting the estate. The Dower House, a smaller and more modern building, had lain empty for a long time now. Hetta's plans to refurbish it and see it leased out were now on hold thanks to the Gate in one of its drawing rooms. Presumably prospective tenants weren't thrilled at the notion of fae traipsing through their living spaces.

As if thinking of his sister had summoned her, he rounded a stand of willows and met her coming towards him on the lake path. Hetta was four years his junior and, like him, a child of Lord Henry's first marriage. The two of them had always been closest, significantly older than the three half-siblings who'd resulted from their father's second marriage to Lady Phoebe. They both took after their father in their narrow features, though Hetta had auburn hair to Marius's (still mostly) black. Lord Henry had gone entirely grey by the time he was thirty. Marius devoutly hoped not to follow in his footsteps.

Hetta wore a narrow-brimmed yellow hat set jauntily on her cropped locks, the hat matching her coat. Usually, Hetta's stride was recognisable for the same brisk confidence that characterised her personality, but there was no denying her gait had lately become something he wasn't foolish enough to call a waddle in her hearing. The sight of her heavily pregnant was still strange. He was happy for her, truly, but some part of him continued to see her as his reckless little sister in need of his protection. Not that he'd ever been especially successful at that.

She smiled as he approached, tilting her head so that the sun fell on her face, and he saw she was wearing a vibrant pink shade of lipstick. "I felt you coming."

"Should you be out walking alone? Shouldn't you be, I don't know, lying about indolently with Wyn waiting on you hand and foot and feeding you grapes?" Waddle aside, she looked well enough, her cheeks a little flushed from the exercise and her eyes bright. But he couldn't help but think of their mother more and more now. Lady Edith had died in childbirth.

Hetta's grey eyes sparkled. "Well, Wyn would if I let him, but I should like my husband to survive this pregnancy and not force me to strangle him. Don't fuss, brother mine. I'm perfectly well. You arrived with Rakken?" A question in her eyes. "Or do you want me to pretend I didn't feel him cross the bounds with you?"

He stiffened. "Of course not! There's nothing—we weren't—I mean, why would I want to pretend anything about him at all?"

Her mouth curved. "You tell me."

He spluttered. "Just because I am... what I am and he flirts with anything that moves, it doesn't follow that there would be anything more between us." Part of him marvelled that they were touching on the subject at all. Only a year ago, even the thought would have made him curdle. It still made him curdle, but it was also... good that he didn't have to hide this part of himself from her, even if it simultaneously made him want to leap into a hole in the ground and bury himself.

Her amusement dimmed, taking on a more sober edge. "I can't say I'm not relieved to hear it. He's not... well, you know."

Nettled despite having long since come to the same conclusions, he couldn't help protesting: "You don't have any high ground; you *married* a fae!"

"I married *Wyn*," she said. And Wyn was different, they both knew. Marius wasn't sure if it was the ten years he'd spent as a servant or some essential difference of personality, but there was no arguing it. There was a softness to Wyn, an open compassion that he wielded ruthlessly because he was still a manipulative sod, but nonetheless. No one could accuse Rakken of sentimentality.

"Did I poke my nose into your affairs?" he asked. Oh no, why had he thought that was a good argument to make, because—

Hetta gave a tinkling laugh. "Yes, you very much did! Consider this turnabout." She was truly worried about him, he saw by her earnest expression. "You know you're—what is *that*?" she broke off, pointing at his neck.

Oh, thank the gods. He felt a rush of affection for the lowfae, which had chosen that moment to poke its nose out of his scarf and sniff curiously at Hetta.

"That was part of what I was coming to explain, before we got side-tracked into *completely irrelevant subjects*. It's a lowfae we rescued—that's why I arrived with Rake. It's a rather involved story." He began to tell it, leaving out the considerable quantities of nakedness. Hetta took his arm, and they walked slowly back along the lake as he spoke, concluding with: "Anyway, Rake has gone back to ThousandSpire to tell Cat what's happened. He thinks he can find the source in Faerie, though the more I think on it, the more I suspect he might have been overconfident in that."

"Rakken, overconfident. I'm shocked, of course," Hetta said so drily that Marius was forced to laugh. "Technically, he ought to have told *Wyn* about this first rather than Cat, since it involves the Mortal Realm, though I suppose I can't really fault him for his loyalties." She looked troubled. "Fae murdering people and dealing in magical plants—there's a problem we didn't need right in the middle of the talks."

"Should I ask how they're going?" He had only the vaguest idea of what the actual negotiations involved between Faerie and Mortal, except that they seemed to involve a lot of functions at the palace in Meridon and frequent meetings in Stariel. Rakken had mentioned subcommittees, which sounded ominous.

"They're... going. Obviously the fae courts want all the

advantage to *fae* and Queen Matilda wants all the advantage to *humans*, so everything turns into the worst game of tit-for-tat you can imagine. Wyn and I keep getting called in to mediate, or to explain mortal culture to fae and vice versa." She gave a deep sigh.

"Surely that's what trained diplomats are for, fae and human both, sorting out these sorts of details between them? Do you really need to be so involved in the minutiae? Especially when you're—" He bit off the end of the sentence at the look she gave him. "Well, you can't pretend you're *not*, Hetta, or that both of you aren't about to be busy with other matters!"

She gave a wry smile. "No, I expect you're right. It's all so lowering, waddling about like a duck and napping *constantly*. I am decidedly ready for these two to be out." She patted her stomach. "But it's also why it's hard to delegate. No one else has as much of a foot in both camps as we do."

"Is there anything I can do to help?" he asked, though he was about as far from a trained diplomat as could be. His specialty lay in making things *more* awkward between any two groups of people.

She shook her head, though less in rejection than in an attempt to shake herself into a better mood. "I'm sure we'll find a way through; we always do. Is Rake planning to return, do you know?"

"Yes, although he was extremely vague about when."

"He can be very aggravating," she agreed, a slight frown forming between her brows. "Are you sure—"

"How is the estate?" he asked quickly. "Didn't Jack say something about a new breed of sheep? Tell me more."

She huffed. "Subtle change of subject, brother mine. Fine, I'll let it drop, but just let me say that I want you to be happy, first, and you can tell me if you're not, you know."

He gave a monosyllabic grumble in response.

"What about the telepathy? Are you still getting the headaches?"

"It's manageable."

"*Marius.*"

"I can see you're already practising your offspring-chastising voice, but it won't work on me. I'm a grown man and older than you. I can handle my own business. I'd much rather hear about how things are going with you and the rest of the family. How are our siblings?"

Hetta opened her mouth, clearly having no intention of letting him escape interrogation so easily, and he was deeply grateful that his brother-in-law chose that moment to drop out of the sky. Literally.

Wyn landed on the path with a crunch of gravel, his wings shining blue and silver. Marius had known Wyn for a good decade or more, but for most of that, he'd been pretending to be human. It was still strange to see him in his fae form, winged and horned and with a sharper cast to his features. There was a strong family resemblance between him and Rakken, though they had different colouring. Wyn's brown skin was a touch lighter than Rakken's, his eyes brown rather than green, and his hair silver rather than ebony.

Wyn changed to the human form Marius was more familiar with a moment after landing, straightened his clothing, and beamed at him.

"Marius! To what do we owe the honour?"

"Wicked fae have attacked," Hetta told him blandly, a private joke from the way Wyn's lips curved.

"Oh dear," he said.

Hetta unlinked her arm from Marius's and went to her husband. Wyn bent to kiss her cheek in greeting. The two of them shared a soft moment, love shining in them so brightly that Marius had to look away, his heart squeezing painfully. How had the two of them ever managed to hide their romance?

He couldn't help remembering his own secret relationship with John. At the time, he'd thought it love, but he was nearly certain no one would have observed a similar softness in his and John's interactions, even in private.

"I shouldn't make light of it, though—one of Marius's colleagues in Knoxbridge has been murdered, probably by a fae," Hetta said.

Wyn's expression sobered instantly. He turned to Marius.

"Dr Martin Vane," Marius said, and began to tell his tale for the second time, again leaving out all the nudity, though Wyn at one point piped up to ask: "How did you follow the tracking spell to Vane's flat?"

"We flew," Marius said shortly, hurrying on to the next part. Wyn's expression became worryingly thoughtful.

Their path took them beneath the shadowy boughs of the Home Wood. Hetta absently summoned a mage-light to bob in the air above them.

"— but I don't mean to add to your burdens," Marius said when he'd finished telling them the whole. "I thought you ought to know, in case—well, it's bound to leak out in some form or other eventually. But Rake and I will get to the bottom of it, between us. Well, between us and the local police."

Wyn searched Marius's face, his deep russet-brown eyes holding the same concern that Hetta's had earlier. It made Marius want to protest that he wasn't some fragile creature in need of protecting. But all Wyn said was, "Will you dine with us while you wait for my brother's return?"

Marius thought about refusing, but now that he was here, he would like to see his younger siblings, and it *was* Saturday. He didn't need to rush back, even if he wasn't waiting for an aggravating fae prince.

"You could take the Gate back to Meridon tomorrow, catch the early train. Though you're welcome to stay longer," Hetta put in.

"Why do you have a helichaun draped about your neck?" Wyn asked suddenly, frowning at the lowfae, which had poked its head out of Marius's scarf again.

"Oh, is that what it's called? It was one of the lowfae imprisoned at Vane's flat."

Wyn was still frowning at it, and Marius got the impression he'd done something very fae when the helichaun gave a startled squawk and fluffed up its coat in outrage, its trio of ear tufts fanning out.

Wyn laughed, his brow clearing. "She seems to think she owes you."

"Well, she doesn't. Honestly, you're free to go," Marius told the creature, frowning at her. She merely burrowed back into his scarf.

They reached Stariel House. It was a building best described as having character rather than beauty. Old and immense, with three stone towers and a variety of architectural styles from its long history, it was full of draughty chambers and unexpectedly failing plumbing. Marius was bloody glad he hadn't been the one to inherit it.

He had only just removed his coat in the entrance hall when there came a high-pitched shriek from the top of the landing and an excited ten-year-old barrelled down the stairs.

"Marius!" his youngest sister Laurel cried, nearly knocking his briefcase flying in her enthusiasm to hug him.

"Careful, Laurel-lion!" he said, laughing at her enthusiasm as he placed it safely down and swept her up in his arms.

"Sorry! I didn't know you were coming home! When are you—" She made another bat-pitched sound as the helichaun poked its head out of his scarf. "A kitten! Where did it come from?"

Marius shot the helichaun a swift look—glamour. "She's a lowfae in disguise," he explained, replacing Laurel on her feet. "You must ask first before you touch her," he said, beckoning the creature out.

Laurel nodded furiously, eyes huge. "Can I touch you?" she asked the helichaun, holding out her hands. "I'll be ever so careful."

The helichaun warily consented to put out a dainty paw.

Laurel was thrilled. "She shakes hands!" She touched a fingertip gently to the helichaun's paw. "My name is Laurel. Does she have a name?"

"Thistlefel," Marius said, and then paused and eyed the creature suspiciously because he hadn't known that two seconds ago either.

Various other relatives arrived on the scene, no doubt drawn by Laurel's shrieking, and Marius was carried off to take tea and be asked kindly how he was getting on (Lady Phoebe, his stepmother), presented with a slightly misshapen woollen hat that she was sorry she'd lost a stitch somewhere but she'd been meaning to post it since the weather had turned (Grandmamma), and asked if they'd had the same thunderstorms this last week in Knoxbridge as they'd been having here (Jack, his cousin, coming in only briefly, covered in mud, and immediately banished to clean himself up by Lady Sybil, Marius's aunt).

It was good to see them, even if it had the curious effect of making him feel more alone than ever. He didn't belong at Stariel anymore, not really.

LATER THAT NIGHT, HE found himself unable to sleep even after the household had gone to bed. Giving up, he wrapped himself in an old dressing gown and pushed his feet into slippers. Thistlefel, who had curled up on the end of his bed and feigned deafness when he'd protested, cracked open an eye, debated following him, and then wriggled back into the duvet, warmth clearly winning out.

He left her there and walked down memory lane, the route he had always taken through the house over many years of insomnia. The atmosphere had changed since Hetta had come into her lordship. Hallways no longer felt strewn with crushed eggshells, with Father's ghost lurking around every door. He made his way up to the tallest tower, the nip of cold seeping through his coat as he stood and stared up at the twinkling night sky. Winter always came sooner to Stariel. The moon was just off full now, lighting enough of the landscape to form familiar shadows.

The last couple of days had been a whirlwind, full of grim facts and up-turnings he hadn't really had time to process. Vane, murdered so bloodily, a life cut short. Those poor dead lowfae they'd been too late to rescue, and his own culpability for that.

And Rakken, being his usual cryptic and confusing self, and that bothering Marius more than all the rest together, which said something about how skewed his priorities were. He wished he wasn't so affected by the man. It reminded him rather too much of the earliest days of his infatuation with John—and look how that had ended. He pushed his hands deeper into his dressing gown.

Wyn found him there, as he had so many times during the years they'd both lived here, two outsiders of different sorts. They'd both been prone to night-time excursions, and many times they'd sat up on the old tower, drinking whisky smuggled up from the cellars. In those days, Wyn had climbed the tower, since he'd been pretending to be human, but tonight, for the first time, he landed winged next to Marius.

"Am I intruding?" he asked. He had a bottle in one hand and a pair of tumblers in the other.

"Not with those offerings."

Wyn poured them both a measure and settled against the tower stones with a soft rustle of feathers. One of the things Marius both valued and disliked about Wyn was his ability to hold his silence. He had a way of outwaiting people until the force of it made them spill their secrets unprompted.

But it was Wyn who spoke first tonight, saying softly: "The law is going to be repealed. They will be introducing the bill into Parliament next month."

Marius took a sip of whisky. He knew which law Wyn meant: Unnatural Offences Against the Person. It was an old and controversial law, only rarely enforced, but the threat of it had hung over him his entire adult life, ever since he'd figured out that he wasn't going to grow out of 'schoolboy behaviour'.

Wyn had made repealing it a non-negotiable part of the

treaty talks between Faerie and Mortal. Wyn had warned him when the topic first arose and, upon seeing Marius's discomfit, added gently, "This is not solely about you, you know; it affects all of us. Unjust as it is to humans, this is a human law that cannot continue, if my people and yours are to mix with any kind of success." Wyn had smiled, then, a hint of mischief in it. "In all senses of the word 'mix'."

Us—tacit acknowledgement of something Marius had always known about his friend. Ironically, he'd once thought it their shared secret, but Wyn had turned out to be hiding a much bigger and more feathery one.

Marius leaned back against the tower. "It won't change things."

"Not overnight, no. But it's a start."

He was right. Marius had thought of himself as subtly wrong for the greater part of his life, but the fae were so far from seeing it as wrong that the concept of making any societal distinction about it had had to be explained to them. That might not yet have made any impact on Prydinian culture, but it had already made a difference to Marius.

He picked at the crumbling mortar between flagstones and abruptly admitted: "The headaches are getting worse. The exercises you gave me aren't doing much anymore. Rake said I flamed out yesterday, but the telepathy has come back again since."

The line of Wyn's mouth grew grim. "So far I have only a thin whisper of possibility that I have not yet managed to confirm. But I will keep looking until we find a teacher for you."

Marius felt terrible yet again that Wyn, who already had too many balls to juggle, was taking on this extra piece of work too. But what else was he to do?

Wyn frowned at his tumbler. "It *is* better here since Hetta had a talk with Stariel, though? Could you not—"

"I can't stay holed up here, Wyn," Marius said, anticipating his next words.

"But if it is getting worse... I do not know what my brother told you, but flameout is not a trivial matter."

Marius sighed. "It worried him too. But I have my work in Knoxbridge, and even if I didn't, the more I think about it, the less inclined I am to leave Rake to investigate this fae-plant murder unsupervised. You know what he's like. Even if he weren't, I feel... responsible. Vane was using a version of my own quizzing glass construction to find those lowfae."

Wyn's brow creased as he considered Marius. "Be careful. A mortal has already been murdered over this, and Rake has been wrong before. Bloodlock is serious business. These are deep waters."

Marius was tired of everyone he knew *worrying* about him when they would do far better to worry about themselves. "It's a bit much to tell *me* to be careful when I'm not the one with a history of accidental lightning storms or disappearing into Deeper Faerie for weeks."

Wyn allowed the point with a smile and began to get to his feet. "I need to check on Hetta."

"She really is all right, isn't she?"

"The midwife is not concerned, despite the... unusualness of the children's parentage. And I trust Stariel would know if something was amiss."

"You're still afraid something will go wrong."

Wyn let out a long breath. "I am trying hard not to be."

Marius squeezed his shoulder. "It's a bloody nerve-wracking thing, even without everything she's been through. But I'm sure Stariel won't let anything happen to her, as you say."

The faeland was more awake than it had ever been, and it loved its lord.

Wyn gave a wry smile. "As you say."

Marius stayed where he was after Wyn left, brooding in the cold night until he'd about frozen solid, thinking of change, plants, murder, and not at all of fae princes.

13

UNSOLICITED ADVICE

W HEN MARIUS WOKE the next morning, the helichaun was still in his room, perched on the end of his bed and watching him brightly. Her multi-lobed ears perked up, and so did the ruff of spikes around her neck. Spikes? He hadn't noticed those yesterday. They were the same silvery-grey as her pelt.

He shifted self-consciously under her beady gaze. Why hadn't she scampered off to join the rest of her brethren? "You really don't need to stick around, you know. Or do you want me to take you back to the Botanical Gardens in Knoxbridge?"

Her ear tufts flattened, which he took as an emphatic neg-ative. He got up and hesitated as he was about to pull off his night shirt. Her gaze remained fixed on him.

"You just go stare at the wall or something while I change, all right?"

He could've sworn the helichaun rolled her eyes, but she dutifully curled herself around so she wasn't facing him, at least. He got dressed and left his bedroom. Thistlefel followed him as he made his way down to the breakfast room, choosing to trot along at his heels.

He felt oddly flat. Rakken hadn't returned, and the prospect of returning to Knoxbridge alone felt a bit like the day after a holiday, a mundane comedown.

A man being murdered is not a holiday! It was a sign of Rakken's bad influence that he'd found himself almost enjoying their investigations. One shouldn't enjoy murder investigations. Even if the last couple of days had felt like waking up after a long winter, sap stirring to life.

Giving himself a shake, he arrived at the top of the main stairs, only to find Irokoi perched precariously on the banister with his wings draped behind him. Irokoi was Rakken's and Wyn's oldest brother—considerably older, Marius understood, even though Irokoi sometimes seemed as ingenuous as a child. Marius hadn't realised he was here rather than in the Spires.

He pulled up short, wondering if he could feign having forgotten something and return to his room and so avoid him. Childish—Irokoi wasn't an ogre. It was only that he was unsettling, his mind a castle full of fractured mirrors.

"Good morning," Marius said cautiously.

"Morning's greetings, Marius Valstar," Irokoi said sunnily. He had silver hair, black wings, and mismatched gold-and-blue eyes; the blue one was blind and marked by a scar down that side of his face.

The helichaun eyed Irokoi and gave a low growl. Irokoi started and swivelled, wings flaring as he regained his balance. She'd approached on his blind side, Marius realised. "And morning's greeting to your companion also! I didn't know helichauns could get that large."

"Er, I'll just be going down to breakfast then…" Marius made to continue.

"We are not unalike, you know." The playfulness had drained from Irokoi's tone. Now he sounded old, old and serious.

Marius stopped, sighed deeply, and turned back. "All right, having lain in wait here to ambush me, have at it with the unasked-for and probably unhelpful advice."

Irokoi laughed. "One must find one's fun somehow. But we *are* alike, so you may find my advice more useful than not. We see the world in ways that others don't."

Marius grimaced. Irokoi could generously be described as 'extremely eccentric'. "That's reaching, surely. Hearing people's thoughts and seeing the future, or whatever it is you do, isn't the same thing."

Irokoi gave him a sober look that sent a chill down his spine. "When one is buffeted between the half-formed shapes of what-ifs and what-thens in the sea of possibles, one must find a central tenet of self-certainty on which to stand. What are you, without artifice or vanity, when you are stripped back to your bones? Not what you hope or feel you ought to be; not what others label you. Not the lies you tell yourself so you can sleep at night. Who are you, in the unflinching truth of now? What is it about you that cannot be mistaken for something other, that is not open to doubt?"

"So what's your answer, then?" Marius said, feeling rather ruffled. He hadn't had any coffee yet.

Irokoi shrugged. "You must find your own."

"Yes, *very* helpful," he grumbled, and stalked off down the stairs. Thistlefel hurried to catch up. Once in the breakfast room, she sat looking mournfully up at the sausages until he relented and gave her one. "Look—you can't just... attach yourself to my side," he told her, because he was getting a strong feeling that she intended to do exactly that. "I'm going back to Knoxbridge after breakfast, and I'm not allowed pets at my college. You're much better off staying here."

She was not a pet, and no one would see her unless she wanted them to anyway, he was informed in a way that wasn't quite words. He blinked.

"Oh!" His sister Alexandra came into the room and paused mid-step at the sight of the little fae. Alexandra was just sixteen. "Oh, isn't she adorable! Does she have a name?"

"Thistlefel." Thistlefel continued eating her sausage in neat bites. "And have a care, you. Alex has the Sight and can see you perfectly well. Other people might be able to as well." He thought of his quizzing glass lying on Vane's workbench and abruptly lost his appetite.

Thistlefel ignored his words but allowed Alex to bribe her into jumping up into her lap with more breakfast foods.

"I haven't seen one like her before," Alexandra said, stroking Thistlefel's fur. "I've been trying to sketch all the wyldfae on the estate, but I keep finding new ones, and some are hard to get a good look at. Did you know there really is a nessan in the lake?"

Marius nearly spat out his tea, half-choked, and had to take a few moments to recover himself. The nessan was a lake monster that featured heavily in local children's tales.

Alex grinned impishly at his reaction. "Don't worry; I don't think he's dangerous, and Hetta said she told him he mustn't eat anyone, just in case. He let me pat his nose once."

Thistlefel let out a trill, looking pointedly at the next bit of sausage on Alex's plate. Alex obediently forked it and held it out to her. Thistlefel gobbled it down and lay on her back, paws folded over her engorged stomach. Alexandra should pet her, she suggested.

"You could stay here with my sisters," Marius pointed out.

"Think of all the sausages to be had."

Thistlefel just huffed. Thistlefel had taken *his* blood offering. Sausages were not comparable.

"That wasn't a blood offering. You bit me. You don't owe me anything," he tried telling her. Thistlefel once again ignored him. What was it about fairies and their determination not to listen to him?

Grandmamma made one of her erratic appearances at breakfast, and Marius obediently made up a plate for her. She thanked him and then paused, mid-sip of her tea, as Thistlefel peered over the edge of the table and made another chirping sound. Grandmamma put her cup down.

"I do not think that animals at table are appropriate, Alexandra," she said. "Not even fae ones, as I assume that one is."

"Yes, Grandmamma," Alex said in a meek tone, setting Thistlefel back on the ground.

"And you, dear boy." Grandmamma turned her dark eyes on Marius. "You're not eating enough. What's got you so long faced?"

Marius hurried to assure her there was nothing wrong with him. "But I do need to take my leave—I must get back in time to catch the early train." He rose. There was no sign of Rakken, but Marius had no inclination to await his pleasure.

"All this to-ing and fro-ing cannot be good for a person," Grandmamma said, shaking her head. "In my day, we didn't even have trains, and now here you all are jumping about like fleas with these Gates of yours. Make sure you don't wear yourself out, my boy. And take that hat I made you; it'll keep your ears warm, and the nights are getting cold."

"I will," Marius promised, leaning down to kiss her cheek.

Alexandra bounced out of her chair and demanded her own

farewell hug. He obliged and told her he'd expect an update on her bestiary when he was next up.

Thistlefel followed him back upstairs as he went to fetch his things, feigning deafness once again when he repeated that she was under no obligation to accompany him. When he paused to snap closed his case, she scrambled up his clothing and draped herself around his neck like a fur scarf. She felt heavier than she had yesterday, more than a couple of sausages ought to account for. Some magical effect from being freed, or the influence of Stariel, maybe?

The advantage of a permanent Gate over a portal was that it didn't require magic to activate, which meant Marius was quite capable of stomping back to the Dower House to return to Meridon alone. He did so, the chill darkness of the early morning bringing him to full wakefulness. A few ducks quacked on the lake shore, objecting to his passing.

Just what was he planning to do alone, back in Knoxbridge? He'd assured Hetta and Wyn that he and Rakken would figure out the affair, but that had been with the assumption of Rakken's presence. Despite Rakken's many, *many* aggravating qualities, he exuded such an aura of competence that it had made Marius feel as if he too could handle such things as untangling a fae murder mystery, just to pick a hypothetical example.

Still, he didn't *need* Rakken, he told himself. He would be perfectly fine alone.

14

WHO CARES ABOUT FAE PRINCES ANYWAY?

I T WAS SHOCKING, really, how the universe ground on with barely a stutter after a man had been murdered, Marius thought two days later. Oh, there had been official regret expressed and talk of some sort of memorial—plus a firm decree from the higher-ups not to talk to the reporters—but otherwise the everyday business of the department rolled onwards, barring some hastily adjusted timetables. Thankfully, the reporters hadn't connected his name to Vane's murder yet. Undoubtedly there would be a stir once it came out, since 'Valstar' was becoming synonymous with 'fairy business'.

He finished putting a set of slides back into their box and looked around the now-emptied lab, which had held first-years until about five minutes ago. He'd been assisting the professor in theory but in reality solely supervising the lot of them. Thistlefel gave an inquiring chirp from the windowsill. No one had seen her, she pointed out. She'd told him so.

"That's because you spent the class sleeping out of sight." Still, he extended an arm, and she clambered up to perch on his shoulders. Carrying her over to a set of scales, he put her down. She climbed onto them, patiently suffering through his need to quantify things. He wrote down the numbers in his notebook.

"Do you know if you're supposed to be getting bigger so quickly? I won't be able to carry you around for much longer if this keeps up."

Thistlefel was supremely unconcerned as she climbed back up. If she had fierce, fast legs, so much the better for the chasing and biting.

"You are not to bite anyone," he told her as they left the lab, only to run into a pair of gossiping undergrads just around the corner.

"—receiving black-market goods. Reckon someone offed Vane so he could sell the loot himself?" Marius heard one man ask another. The Knoxbridge City Watch was almost as watertight as the botany department. "Who knows what fairy plants might be worth…" the student trailed off suggestively. They both froze as Marius came into sight. He raised his eyebrows at them, and they hurriedly found somewhere else to be.

He rubbed the bridge of his nose. Fairy plants indeed. The rumours had spread through the department like wildfire. He wondered whether the police had found Vane's flat in Meridon yet, and whether he ought to tell them about it if they hadn't. But then that would entail explaining why Rakken had destroyed the plants there and deciding whether he ought to tell them about Bakir as well.

Damn Rakken. Had he found the supplier in Faerie? Maybe that was why he remained absent. Maybe he'd already discovered who had murdered Vane. Marius wished he'd hurry up and return. Marius had no gift for approaching strangers or untangling rumours, and his presence at the scene of the murder had made everyone reluctant to broach the subject with him. Rakken could have been of some bloody use for once.

Still, he had to try. With this in mind, he overruled Thistlefel's protests and left her to hide under his desk in the office he shared with five other post-grads while he went to see Professor Greenbriars for his weekly supervisory meeting. He couldn't help feeling some trepidation as he approached Greenbriars' office. He hadn't seen Jenny since his return. Was she avoiding him? Had she known about Vane's partnership with Bakir? Did Greenbriars know about any of it?

If Vane's office had been impersonal, Professor Greenbriars' might qualify as its own life-form. Papers, curios, and specimens were stacked messily on every spare surface, including the extra chair. Greenbriars had been with the department for going on forty years, and by the time he retired, his office would be considered an archaeological dig site.

"Ah, yes, Marius. How are you getting on?" Greenbriars said, looking up from his work. He waved vaguely at the chair across from him. "Sorry about that," he said, as he did every week. Marius dutifully redistributed the papers so he could sit down, as he also did every week.

"Er… it's been a challenging few days, sir," he said. "Obviously I don't have access to the greenhouse at the moment. I'm not sure how much damage there is." That officer had planned to ask Greenbriars to check the plants in there—had he done so?

Greenbriars gave him a look of soft reproach that most unfortunately answered that line of thought in the affirmative. "The police said you'd been talking with Vane about a research project."

He'd already been dreading this conversation; introducing murder hadn't improved it. Greenbriars had sponsored his return to the university and stood by him despite all the controversy surrounding his family name. Admittedly, Marius wasn't sure how much of his support stemmed from a lack of interest in anything that didn't photosynthesise.

"We discussed some of the things Vane was working on," he admitted.

Greenbriars frowned. "How does his work relate to yours?"

"I thought there might be a mechanism in common, growth in response to stimulus," he lied. It wasn't as if he could switch to Vane's supervision now. How did one shift the conversation where one wanted it to go? Rakken made it look so easy. "I didn't know he already had access to fae specimens. Did you?"

Greenbriars gave an uncomfortable shrug. "He implied he might have something of the sort when we spoke about the latest funding round. I didn't inquire further." *Impertinent puppy. How dare he speak to me like that?*

Marius got a brief impression of Vane saying mockingly, *"I must thank you for your help. The board wouldn't have been half so interested in my proposal if you hadn't bored them into a stupor beforehand."*

He shook his head, trying to rid himself of the unwanted images. Suddenly, he remembered that note he and Rakken had found in Vane's office. Had Greenbriars known of his daughter's affair? Could *he* have written the note? Before he could stop himself, he asked, "You weren't there that night, were you? Er, at the department, I mean. I thought Jenny might have been with you before she saw the light on in my greenhouse."

Greenbriars frowned at him. "No, I was at home. I've told Jenny she oughtn't to be out so late. I don't mind saying it's been keeping me awake, thinking of what might have happened if she'd met Vane's killer that night! I've told the Head we must have more security on campus. A bad business all round."

Instinctually, Marius reached out and heard Greenbriars

think, *Better for Jenny that he's dead, though. Poor girl. But she'll come round,* he comforted himself. Greenbriars hadn't wanted to believe that glimpse he'd caught of her with Vane, but it seemed she *had* lost her heart to the damn womaniser. Sneaking out to meet with him! Thank goodness no one else seemed to have seen them together, and Marius was too well-bred to mention it, if he *had* wondered what Jenny had been doing meeting Vane in his greenhouse so late. Now if only Jenny would take an interest in that direction…

Marius pinched himself, hard, appalled by what he'd just done and feeling a headache germinating. *Deliberately* trying to read a man's mind? What was he thinking? Just because Greenbriars and Vane had been professional rivals didn't mean Greenbriars had anything to do with Vane's death. And even if he *had* been somehow involved, Marius shouldn't have been trying to read his mind because… Wait. What were the ethics of this when it involved murder?

He wished, sharply, that Rakken were here. Rakken would undoubtedly tell him he was being too nice in his principles, but at least Rakken understood what it was like to *have* problematic mind-magic. He remembered Rakken's expression after he'd compelled Bakir.

He surreptitiously rubbed at his head to try to stop the pounding. "What's going to happen to the fae plants, if they're recovered? Shouldn't we—"

But Greenbriars shook his head. "The department will decide if and when the matter arises, but I think the question of magic and botany is best left alone for now. At present it is much too political. Especially for you." His eyes were kind, a tacit acknowledgement of Marius's personal connections. "I know you've been… distracted, and this business with Vane has certainly not helped, but you need to focus, Marius. There will be time enough for"—he searched for a phrase—"more *whimsical* research tangents later in your career. But that is not how one achieves a doctorate. I see great potential in you— almost, you remind me much of myself as a younger man, if it does not offend you for me to say so," Greenbriars said gruffly, and Marius squirmed with self-consciousness and guilt. "So, putting unsavoury subjects aside and returning to the subject of *your* research…"

Marius then had to scramble to cover his complete lack of progress. When he eventually extracted himself, it was with the knowledge that he'd left his supervisor full of that worst of emotions: disappointment.

"LOOKS LIKE IT'S JUST you and me," he told Thistlefel several days later, when he finally got access to his greenhouse again. "At least plants are easier to talk to than people. Maybe *they'll* be able to tell us something useful." His awkward attempts at poking about the department for information had so far drawn only blanks.

It was a relief to be back in here, even if the state of it reminded him all over again of the horror of that night. Thankfully someone had mopped up the blood and cleared away the worst of the broken glass, so the mess was of decomposing plants rather than flesh. They'd taken away the fallen rake. Marius couldn't help staring down at the patch of scrubbed tiles where Vane's body had lain.

He shivered and went to find a broom. As he began to clear

up, he separated out any plant bits that looked unfamiliar and placed them in a growing pile on the workbench. It was slow going—wilting leaves and stems had a tendency to all look alike until he carefully unfolded them. Thistlefel noticed what he was doing after a few minutes and began to nose through the wreckage as well, her long plumed tail wagging furiously whenever she found something. He assessed the damage to his own specimens as he went. Some had been damaged by cold, despite boarding up the windows. Others had been snapped off at the base; too late to take cuttings of those. The snapdragons were mostly alive but squashed and muddled up. Accurately recording the seeds was going to be tricky. Or, well, impossible.

When the worst of it was cleared away, he sat down at the workbench to more closely examine the handful of unfamiliar greenery. The fragments he'd gathered came from at least three different plants, he decided, none of which resembled the ones Rakken had destroyed on the roof in Meridon, though it was hard to be certain. It would've been significantly easier to judge if a certain fae prince hadn't destroyed that evidence in a fit of temper. Or if the ones in front of him weren't so damaged.

He sighed and began to sketch the fragments he'd found before they degraded further. He'd press them afterwards. Unlike his sister Alex, he wasn't a gifted artist, but he'd always enjoyed botanical drawing. The process could be almost hypnotic, and his work was competent enough. If Rakken ever showed up, perhaps he'd be able to identify them.

If he ever showed up.

Thistlefel spent the time nosing into every corner, scrambling up on the raised containers so she could look inside each one. She'd gotten even bigger in the last few days and was now about the size of a large cat. Marius was charting her growth, and the rate of change was a bit worrying. Was this normal for helichauns? He'd tried searching the library for reference material, but folkloric literature was in high demand.

His cousin Caro came into the greenhouse, wrapped up warmly against the chill, red curls escaping her own Grandmamma-hat. "Marius!" *I've caught you, finally. Have you been avoiding me? Are you allowed to be in here?* "I dropped by the department after my shift, and a rather shy young man kindly told me I'd find you here. I suppose the police are done with this place, then?"

Marius winced at the combination of thoughts and words.

"Em?" Caro was still smiling, but it had gone a bit tight around the edges.

What had she asked? The police. "Er, yes. They said I could have it back." He gestured at the broken windows. "Maintenance are supposed to be sending someone to fix those, though the gods know when they'll get round to it. Could be years," he said philosophically.

Caro looked warily about, and it didn't take telepathy to know what was on her mind. Marius couldn't help his own gaze being drawn again to the patch of tiles.

Caro followed his gaze and shuddered. "Is that where…? No, don't tell me. It must have been awful."

She was thinking of the morning after Vane died, when Marius had been practically swaying on his feet. *He looked so sick, then, and he doesn't look a whole lot better now, with those shadows under his eyes. Poor Marius. I ought to have made the effort to come round sooner, but I've been so busy lately with Jane away and Dr Mortimer wanting me to pick up extra shifts.*

Marius tried to rein in his telepathy, with mixed success. Irokoi's harsh advice didn't seem to be making any difference.

Not that he'd figured out how to apply it.

"I heard his fiancée has just arrived back in the country for the funeral from abroad," Caro was saying. "It's horrible, isn't it? Even if it wasn't a love match."

Marius floundered for a moment, re-finding his place in the conversation. "Oh. *Vane's* fiancée. What makes you say that?"

Caro shrugged. "Well, your man was known to be... not exactly the picture of devoted fidelity, you know. His fiancée, a Miss Claridge, comes from money, and word is Vane's father is on the verge of selling off the ancestral home. It's not a kind thought but also rather an obvious one—and it's what people are saying." She looked again at the tiles. "It must make things rather awkward for Miss Claridge. Oh, what am I saying—a man is dead. Gossip seems so trivial set against that."

"Yes," he agreed softly. He thought of Jenny Greenbriars. Maybe Vane really had loved her, if his arrangement with his fiancée was driven by financial need. He still doubted it, somehow.

Thistlefel came and shoved her nose into Caro's shin. Caro started and then began to stroke her ears. "When did you get a dog? And where on earth do you keep him? I thought the colleges weren't keen on pets."

Marius couldn't tell half the time when Thistlefel was using glamour or not; he'd gotten better at seeing through it. He squinted down at the lowfae. "Her. This is Thistlefel. She's a lowfae. I—well, Rake and I—found a collection of trapped lowfae at Vane's place in town."

It was a relief to tell someone else about the whole sorry business. He'd missed having someone to talk plainly to about it all, and Caro understood the intricacies of the university's politics better than he did. She hadn't known Vane, but she knew the impact his murder had had on the academic grapevine.

"So when is Prince Rakken to descend back upon us in all his magnificence?" she asked after absorbing the whole of it.

Marius shrugged. "He didn't say."

"Typical," Caro said. She searched his face again. "Sorry. You're friends with him, aren't you? This is where you reassure me I did the right thing, leaving him to take care of you the other morning."

"I—you did the right thing," he said. "I suppose we are friends. Or at least, at truce."

"And you're all right?"

He shrugged, wondering what it was about him that made people constantly ask him this. Did he *look* like there was something wrong with him?

There IS something wrong with you.

Yes, but the telepathy is technically invisible.

He moved his hands restlessly on the bench, picking up his pencil and fiddling with it. "Er, actually there's something I need to tell you." He'd read Caro's mind too many times now, and his powers seemed to be getting worse rather than better. The incident with Greenbriars had worried him deeply. "Something I ought to have told you sooner. I beg your pardon for that—I suppose I just didn't want you to second-guess yourself around me."

Caro blinked up at him, then put a hand on his arm. "It's fine, Em." She looked serious. "And, you know—"

"I can read minds," he blurted out before he could lose courage.

"—it's not all that uncommon..." Caro trailed off.

"What?"

"What?"

He stared at her. "Your what first."

"You can read minds?!"

He put a hand over his face. "Gods, you *did* invite me to that party for a reason."

"What?"

"With the"—he flailed a hand about—"unconventional people."

Caro gave a choke of amusement. He looked up, and whatever she saw in his face made her sober. "A bit," she admitted. "I saw you talking to Thomas Bakir. He's lovely, isn't he?"

Marius shook his head, not denying Bakir's loveliness but this entire conversation. A small part of him spluttered indignantly. This was supposed to be his innermost secret, and yet apparently he might as well have posted flyers announcing it on every pasteboard in Knoxbridge. It bothered him less than it would have a year ago, but still! One ought to be allowed to pick one's moments and not have people treat it as old news!

"Sorry," Caro said into his silence. "I've overstepped, haven't I? You just—you get so wound up and you've been holed up like a hermit so much lately. I thought it might help to have someone to talk to. And I did mean it when I said it's not that uncommon. Um. You said you can read minds?!"

Marius launched himself at the subject change. "Yes. Well, not all the time. It was after that fae attack last year. Wyn thinks it may have triggered a latent ability. I thought it might go away, but it seems to be getting worse."

Caro, to her credit, swallowed but didn't flee screaming. "Are you reading my mind now?"

Marius shook his head. "Not right now. It happens erratically. Sorry. I don't mean to do it, but sometimes it just happens. Mainly I hear surface thoughts, especially if they're emotional. I heard you worrying about me when you came in."

"Oh." Caro digested this and made a face. "I'm not going to lie. It's… a lot, and I don't much like it. One can think the most terrible things safe in the privacy of one's own mind; it's rather awful imagining someone overhearing that. And of course now I can't help but think of the most shocking things." Her cheeks flushed.

"I'm still not hearing anything right now," he reassured her hastily. "But I shouldn't judge you even if I did. It's as you say—people can't help what comes to mind, and I shouldn't be invading their privacy in any case. I can't blame people for their thoughts." He sighed. "I wish I could figure out how to turn it off permanently."

Thistlefel made an odd yip of a sound, and both of them turned towards the door to the potting shed.

"Am I interrupting?" Rakken stood there. He was in his human form and in human attire besides, very much a proper gentleman but for the length of his hair, which was tied at the nape of his neck. Smiling, he gave a slight bow of his head to Caro, all his company manners switched on.

It was as if colour had rushed back into the world. Warmth spread through Marius's body, and his first, unfiltered thought was how glad he was to see him. He took a sharp breath, appalled by the strength of his reaction. *And that is exactly why you need to take care.*

"Where have you been?" he demanded. Rakken could waltz in all conciliatory smiles if he liked, but Marius hadn't forgotten the high-handed manner in which he'd left, or his tardiness in returning.

Rakken raised an eyebrow. "In ThousandSpire, for the main, though also briefly in Meridon for a meeting before I came here, with a detour to your Gardens to return the dead."

That brought Marius up short. "Oh." He swallowed. "Did you find who supplied Vane with the plants while you were in the Spires?"

Rakken came into the greenhouse. "Miss Caroline Valstar. You don't look at all surprised by these topics of conversation."

Caro eyed him warily. "That's because I'm not. Marius told me about Vane's experiments. Did you mean him to keep it secret from me? I don't see why you should get to decide that. Or do you imagine I'm going to go to the papers about it?"

Rakken made a show of displaying his open palms. "I was merely establishing to what degree I need explain myself."

"Oh." Caro's bristles went down. "Well, in that case, please do answer Marius's questions."

Rakken leaned back against the workbench. His expression remained open and pleasant, and it made Marius irrationally irritated. "I regret that I have not found whoever supplied Vane. I suspect I must go to the Goblin Market for that information, but the market is unfortunately not for some days yet. It is held only on the full moon."

"That's a real thing?" Marius asked, surprised. "I thought the Goblin Market was—"

"—a fairy tale?" Rakken finished for him, looking amused. "I suppose technically it is, but it is also real, and where one goes for this sort of trade."

"And it's only open at full moon?" Marius frowned. "It was full moon the night Vane was murdered."

"Yes," Rakken agreed. "As I said, it is where one goes for this sort of trade. If I were batch-growing bloodlock and trying to avoid notice by growing it outside Faerie, that is when I would move it." He smiled. "That was a hypothetical example, Marius Valstar; I am not growing bloodlock, before you ask." Despite his attempts at lightness, he seemed subdued. Even… tired.

"Was that all that kept you so long in ThousandSpire?" Marius asked.

"That and court politics." Rakken shrugged. "I admit I am glad to bring my focus back to this matter instead."

Marius studied him. Rakken generally *liked* politics, odd creature that he was. "They must have been bad, if you'd rather hang out with lowly mortals."

"I should not call your cousin any such thing," Rakken said, aiming another of his brilliant smiles at Caro.

Caro chuckled appreciatively whilst Marius spluttered.

Rakken straightened. "Now, lowly mortal, tell me what you have been doing in my absence."

Marius waved at where his sketchbook lay. "I found a few remnants that our plant thief left behind. Do you know them?"

Marius carefully laid out the fragments, and Rakken frowned down at them. Eventually, he shook his head. "I would need to check these against my own reference texts; I do not recognise them on sight."

"Could you use them to trace the rest of the plants?"

Rakken hovered his palm over the scraps and closed his eyes. After a moment, he let his arm fall and shook his head again. "These are in too poor a condition, and any remaining sympathy has been ruined by blood, death, and time."

That reminded Marius. "What about the…" He trailed off, glancing at Caro. He hadn't told her about the blackmail note they'd found in Vane's office. Murder was one thing, but revealing an affair between Vane and Jenny felt wrong. Not that Caro was likely to be shocked, but he found himself flushing at the thought of revealing the crude double entendre of the note to her.

Caro saw his flush and reached some horribly incorrect conclusions. Standing, she announced, "I'm becoming too much,
aren't I? Very well. I do have other things to do, you know. I
shall take myself away, but you're to tell me if there's anything
more I can do to help."

"I will," Marius said, clasping her hands in thanks. She went
up on her toes to press a brief kiss to his cheek. Her grey eyes—
Valstar eyes—searched his, and he thought she was going to say
something maudlin and sentimental, but in the end she just
pressed her lips together and took her leave.

Rakken watched her go, a bit of wickedness lurking around
his mouth. "I didn't know you had such levels of subterfuge in
you. Are you protecting her ears or Miss Jennifer Greenbriars'
reputation?"

"Both," Marius admitted. "It's not a proper subject to discuss
in mixed company."

Rakken looked blank.

"You know, with women."

Rakken shook his head in bemusement. "Whenever I think
I have grasped your mortal cultural oddities, I find there
are yet more eddies of peculiarity left to fly. I thought your
culture favoured sexual congress between men and women
over others? But how are they supposed to have such without
talking about it?"

Marius rubbed the bridge of his nose, mainly to cope with
Rakken saying 'sexual congress'. "They're supposed to wait
until after they're married."

Rakken's eyes danced. "That has not been my experience."

Marius choked. "I do *not* want to hear about that. Also, you
understand mortal culture perfectly well. Stop winding me up
by pretending you don't."

A RAKE OF HIS OWN

"But I am right. Also, it is so much fun winding you up," Rakken complained. He ran a hand idly along the workbench, his eyes going distant for a moment. "A quality this week has been sorely lacking in. But come," he said before Marius could dig any deeper at that remark. "Let us see if I can trace anything at all from the note. It cannot be here—the leylines remain too disturbed. I have a notion."

This notion, as it turned out, was to commandeer an empty lab in the botany department. Rakken didn't even have to compel anyone to do it; he dazzled the lab assistant with smiling entreaty, and the assistant fell over himself to lend the space to Rakken 'for a few minutes'.

Marius eyed him sourly when they were alone. "What are we doing here, then?"

Rakken fished out the blackmail note he'd taken from Vane's office. "Tracking spells rely on sympathy, the connection between two things, but this note will only have a weak sympathy with whoever composed it. It is not hand-written, it is more than a week old, and there was no personal essence involved in making it. We must hope that whoever wrote it did so in a heightened emotional state. That will increase the connection, but even then, the trace is likely to be weak. A traditional tracking spell would draw me directly to whoever wrote it, but in this case the magic required to cast it would overpower any sympathy present. It would also destroy the note. I am therefore going to use a weaker, more generalised, proximity-based spell."

"You're going to see if it registers a connection with anyone currently in the building?" Marius guessed.

Rakken gave him a measuring look. "Yes. You would have made a good sorcerer, if you were fae."

Marius was too startled to say anything more as Rakken began to push benches and stools about, clearing a bigger space in the centre of the lab. Startled—and flattered, in a strange way, though part of that strangeness was that he hadn't really thought about the fact that Rakken had studied magic. Human mages might need to be trained, but fae magic seemed so innate.

He thought about it as he helped Rakken rearrange the room. It was only logical, wasn't it? He already knew that Rakken was a sorcerer in a way that Wyn was not, even though they both had magic. Of course Rakken couldn't have sprung into the world fully formed, even if it was hard to imagine him as anything other than the self-assured man now defacing the better part of the lab floor with a stick of chalk liberated from the blackboard.

How does he get me involved in this sort of nonsense? he wondered, bemused. Rakken hadn't even been back a whole hour yet.

Apparently satisfied with his spell lines, Rakken folded himself into the centre of the design. Marius perched on a lab stool pushed up against the wall to watch. Rakken closed his eyes and began to murmur softly to himself, and after a brief internal struggle, Marius gave in to the temptation to stare at him shamelessly.

Rakken looked so out of place and yet simultaneously the realest thing in the room, as if the world had oriented itself on him as its true north. He gestured as he wove his magic, the graceful motions alternately tightening and loosening the fabric across his shoulders, and Marius found it hard not to imagine the muscles beneath, flexing. As Rakken's magic rose, his features grew sharper, his skin and hair more vibrant. The sharp-sweet tang of tangerines expanded alongside the feel of rain on leaves, as if Marius stood beneath the boughs of trees in a storm.

One by one, the intricate chalk lines lit up. Rakken held the spell for several minutes. Nothing more seemed to happen, and the touch-smell of Rakken's signature eased. He opened his eyes, which glowed a brighter emerald for a moment, but Marius read the negative there before he spoke. "Whoever sent this is not nearby." Some of his earlier tiredness seeped through into his posture.

"Not Professor Greenbriars, then," Marius said, glad to have it confirmed. He'd wondered, after catching Greenbriars' thoughts the other day, if perhaps the professor had wanted to frighten Vane off. Though he couldn't imagine him cutting out letters from newspapers.

"No," Rakken said, putting the note back in his pocket. He looked pensively at his spellwork and made a gesture. Wind whipped across the floor, blowing chalk dust into the air and making Rakken's hair flare out. The wind swept the chalk into a neat white pile in the corner. Rakken rose to his feet and, to Marius's mild surprise, began to put the room back to rights.

He hurried to help. Their shoes clicked on the hard floor, the thump and scratch of furniture shifting.

"What was it like, growing up in Faerie?" he asked as he put down a stool.

"What was it like, growing up a mortal?" Rakken returned evenly.

He supposed he'd deserved that, but he gave the question a proper answer anyway. "Something of a mixed bag. I didn't get on with my father." Understatement of the century.

Rakken gave a dark laugh. "Nor did I, if it comes to it."

An even greater understatement, since Marius knew Rakken

had plotted to overthrow his father before King Aeros's death.

Rakken slid him a curious glance. "What of your mother? Lady Phoebe did not birth you."

"No, Father married her when I was ten. Phoebe was just seventeen." A young seventeen, too, in hindsight. She and Marius could have resented each other; him for being the reminder of a previous marriage; her as his mother's replacement. Instead, Phoebe had become one of the things that had gotten him through those terrible teenage years before he'd escaped the estate.

"My mother died when Hetta was born," he said.

"Do you remember her?"

Marius picked at a blemish in the bench's varnish. "A little. I was only four. I remember things like sitting on the back lawn making daisy chains, and her reading to me." Even after all these years, it made his chest ache. "What about your mother?" Wyn had been close-lipped about her. He knew only that she'd been missing for some time but was still alive.

"My mother wilfully abandoned us to our father's cruelty, and I do not forgive it." And then, as if the words had slipped out unguarded: "Wyn was always his favourite, and that remains the case even now."

"*His* favourite?" Marius asked, not sure if he'd heard that right.

Rakken nodded with a wave of his hand, as if the pronoun were only so much trivia. Perhaps in Faerie, it was.

"Oh. Like the High King?"

Rakken gave a bark of laughter, his dark mood breaking. "Very much so."

"Perhaps he just didn't think you needed him as much," Marius said. "Wyn's the youngest, isn't he? And you've got a twin." On impulse, he reached out and put his hand over

Rakken's where he had rested it against a bench.

Rakken froze for a moment, surprise flashing in his expression. Then he pulled away, his mask firmly in place as he moved back across the room to fetch the last stack of stools.

Marius studied his profile and added: "Or, alternatively, you've every right to be angry. Father always favoured Jack over me, it wasn't fair, and I resented the hell out of it."

Rakken paused, his back still turned. "Do you resent Jack still?"

Marius took a sharp breath, that Rakken had seen that ugly truth beneath his words. "I used to, but not anymore. Jack never asked for Father to favour him over me. Of course, it helps that Father's dead now and Jack didn't inherit either," he added wryly. "And you?"

Rakken turned, raising an eyebrow. "Do I resent your cousin Jack?"

Marius gave him a flat look. "Don't be disingenuous."

Rakken sighed, the tension in him unravelling all at once. "I try not to," he admitted.

15

EVEN MORE TERRIBLE FAE TURN UP

LATER THAT NIGHT, when he holed up for a marking session in his room at the college, Marius found himself still unsettled by the earlier interaction with Rakken. The conversation had been worryingly lacking in their usual antagonism, and he didn't know what to make of that.

Thistlefel settled herself by the desk lamp and watched his pen hand with bright interest. A paw flashed out to tap the nib, sending a line wobbling halfway across the page. Bollocks. No doubt the student would assume he'd been marking drunk.

He gave the lowfae a meaningful look. "No. This is my work, and you're not a dumb animal. I know you can understand me."

Thistlefel waggled her hindquarters in that way cats had when they were lining up to pounce.

He let out a breath of exasperation. "Look, leave my marking alone, and I'll drag a string or something about for you to chase after I'm done."

Thistlefel considered this offer and found it acceptable. He returned to his marking, only briefly interrupted when Thistlefel leapt up and walked across his papers, ignoring his protest, and settled down in his lap. He looked down at her suspiciously. Her expression remained innocent.

"Fine, then," he grumbled. He only realised he was petting her absentmindedly some minutes later, when he became aware of the sound. It was more birdlike than a usual cat's purr, a sort of warbling. All her spikes lay smoothly against her back, vibrating. He smiled and went back to marking.

He was deep in untangling a multi-clause, paragraph-length carcass of a sentence sprinkled with a frankly criminal number of commas when some small sound made him look up. Thistlefel jumped out of his lap with a growl, ear tufts and spikes both standing on end. He stood in the same moment, driven by an instinct of danger he didn't understand.

The door slammed open. An unfamiliar fae woman with an imperious expression stood in the frame. She was a stormdancer like Rakken, tall and curvaceous, with olive-toned skin, dark hair, and grey wings and horns.

"You are Marius Valstar?" she demanded.

"Yes? What—" The flash of contempt in her eyes sent him stumbling backwards. It saved his life. The knife aimed at his head instead whooshed past the space he'd so recently occupied and stuck in the wall, shuddering with the impact.

The fae woman who'd thrown it hissed her displeasure.

Marius made a garbled sound that indicated *his* displeasure, but she had already closed the distance between them, another knife in hand. He scrambled back, arms raised to grapple with her, but she was so quick.

Pain, a sudden shock of it, surreal and confusing, and his

head became a starburst of agony.

This is he? Truly? Thin and slow with mortal clumsiness. Pathetic. She ought to have sent someone else for this. But she'd wanted to know, wanted to see what had caught the prince's attention. A disappointment; she was even more furious now than she'd been before. How dare Rake think he could humiliate her without consequences? She'd scratch out his eyes for reducing her—*her*, whose name rightfully inspired worship and terror in equal measure—to this wretchedness. Oh, she would send such a message. She would make this one—

The pain rose to a peak, and something shattered. Marius was barely aware of his back hitting the wall, knocking the breath out of him. Cold air rushed in, curtains billowing, and for a moment he didn't understand what had happened or why the fae woman had disappeared mid-attack. Was he dead?

Sense returned. He wasn't dead. The windows had shattered; Emyranthus had gone out through them. No, not gone—been *thrown* through them. How? He hadn't done it. Had he? Could you throw people with telepathy?

How did he know her name?

His head throbbed like a bruise. He could feel Emyranthus in his mind, the tart taste of her magic and anger alongside the disorienting awareness of how she'd seen him: an obstacle, a pointed message, not a person.

He pushed unsteadily off the wall and sucked in a breath of pain as he jostled his shoulder. He was bleeding. She'd stabbed him. Whilst marking essays, which was deeply unfair because he only had one more left to do. He stared stupidly down at the pile of papers flung askew.

A cold nose bumped against his hand. Thistlefel. He started. Never mind the damn essays. He stumbled towards the windows. His ears rang with white noise, making it impossible to hear anything.

He could see, though, as Emyranthus rose like a vengeful spirit, grey wings sweeping her up into the sky. Blood ran from her nose, and her long dark hair spread out like a halo behind her. Her eyes fixed on him, and Marius knew that she was finally seeing *him* and not a human proxy for the man she was truly angry at.

"Emyranthus!" he called out. "There's—it's not what you think! There's nothing between us." Though even if there had been, was that really an excuse for attempting to murder him? Just what sort of people did Rakken take as lovers, if this was how they reacted to being wronged?

They stared at each other, and he had an odd double-vision effect of seeing himself from the outside. Gods, he looked dire, with his face drained of colour and blood blossoming bright against his white shirt. He couldn't seem to move, stuck in the frozen horror of the moment.

Emyranthus sneered. The winds rose around her, and she launched herself through the broken window. But then the winds changed, no longer obeying her but bowing to another, stronger, hand. She gave an outraged cry, swiftly cut off. The scent of storms and citrus rolled over Marius. Oh, thank Mighty Pyrania and all the little gods.

He could move his feet again, though his heart hammered in his chest, and he felt like a disconnected set of ligaments and bones, only loosely strung together. He stumbled backwards as the two fae crashed into his room.

Rakken stood between him and Emyranthus, sweeping out his wings until his feathers brushed each wall, making his shoulders seem impossibly broad. Little sparks of lightning shivered down his wings and crackled between his feathers, spooling down his arms to arc around his clenched fists. The temperature of the room dropped to ice.

Marius was torn between relief and an overwhelming sense of irritation, because this seemed very much a problem of Rakken's causing; he *ought* to bloody be the one to deal with it. And despite that, he felt a prick of concern for Rakken, because Emyranthus had a weapon and didn't seem too shy about using it.

Emyranthus got to her feet with feline grace. She looked rather wind-blown. Glass glittered in her dark hair between her grey horns. The blood trickling from her nose had smeared over her face.

"What are you doing here, Emyranthus Gracehame?" Rakken growled.

Emyranthus waved her knife in Marius's direction. "Don't be dense, Rake. I'm trying to maim your pet mortal, obviously." She gave an angry laugh. "You didn't think I'd really stand for such an insult? You didn't mention he was a telepath. Is that the true reason for your interest here?"

She threw the knife. Marius moved, too slowly, but the wind snapped out and threw it off course. The knife bounced off the wall and clattered across the carpet, where Thistlefel pounced on it with a growl, but Emyranthus had already folded her wings and leapt from the window.

Air rushed back into his lungs. His head felt about to split open, and he slumped, the wall the only thing keeping him upright. Rakken prowled to the window to satisfy himself that the stabby fae woman—his ex-lover?—had taken herself off.

Marius's fingers felt slippery, and he looked down at his left hand. There was smeared blood between his fingers. He was leaving bloody handprints on the wallpaper.

Just like that, the pain hit him. Fuck. Ow. He'd been *stabbed*. The whole thing was so unreal. He was not the sort of person who got himself into situations where 'stabbed' was a possible outcome. Just how bad was it? It *looked* bad, blood soaking through his shirt-sleeve, but even a scratch would look serious through the white fabric. He tried to undo his cuff, but his hands shook too badly. Something odd was happening with the elektric lights, making stray shimmery shapes appear in his vision, like bacteria swimming across a microscope. He blinked rapidly, trying to clear them.

Rakken was abruptly in his space, providing a welcome bit of relief from the light's glare. His eyes blazed with fierce anger.

No, he realised with a shock. Fear. That's what the emotion was. Rakken was afraid in ways he rarely felt. Mortals were so blasted *fragile*. What if he'd arrived a few moments later? Did Marius have any idea how vulnerable he was?

"I'm not defenceless," he protested. He hadn't used his telepathic powers on purpose, but he *had* thrown Emyranthus out a window. Somehow. That was both a thrilling and sobering thought.

But Rakken wasn't listening, something feverish in his expression. "You're injured." He'd become intensely fae in the grip of strong emotion, the planes of his face knife-sharp, skin a deeper, more vibrant brown. His fingers were at Marius's cuffs, undoing buttons with quick grace, and Marius was too surprised to resist as Rakken stripped the shirt off him. The wound on his arm was long and shallow, not life-threatening, but Marius swallowed, feeling light-headed all of a sudden. The high-pitched ringing in his ears went up a tone.

Hands framing his face, Rakken's eyes boring into him from

only an inch away. Marius gasped, feeling himself bleeding into chaos.

Marius's own face reflected back at him. Storms. That's what those soulful grey eyes inevitably brought to mind, deceptively clear one moment and turbulent the next. Tonight they were wide and lost as a foggy sky, the expression in them almost pleading.

"Marius Valstar," he said, holding the mortal's face in his hands, but no comprehension came into his gaze. Marius was breathing too fast, lips parted softly. Under other circumstances, Rakken might have appreciated the picture he made; as it was, he debated how best to shock him back to his senses. He made an idle circle on Marius's jawline with his thumb, feeling the intriguing hint of stubble. Marius's breathing hitched in a satisfying way. Promising, but his expression remained too blank.

Storms, but he was tired of resisting this pull. Perhaps he ought to change tack, since distance and will had failed to excise desire? Rid himself of this unwanted fixation through satiation instead?

Of course, the aggravating mortal chose this moment to slide down the wall into unconsciousness.

"Oh, Marius," he said, catching him. He was all bones and sinew, whatever he'd protested earlier. *The mind taking too much from the body*, Rakken thought grimly. The tension in Marius's face hadn't eased even in unconsciousness. Rakken bared his teeth at the distressingly soft urges that filled him and tightened his grip.

Someone pounded on the door, demanding to know if everything was all right in there.

Rakken began to weave glamour as he hefted the mortal into

his arms. Now, where would be safe while he dealt with things?

The helichaun emerged from beneath the desk and gave an indignant meep, a half-hearted challenge to his authority.

"No," Rakken told her. "My claim pre-dates yours."

16

MILD KIDNAPPING, FOR HIS OWN GOOD

ARIUS WOKE DISORIENTED and flailed his way to sitting. He found himself on a long low-backed sofa in front of a fireplace, not just in an unfamiliar room but in a *world* he didn't recognise, judging from the blurry but nonetheless startling view he glimpsed through the floor-to-ceiling windows.

The view was of a fairy-tale city made of a thousand—or, well, he supposed *ten* thousand—rock towers. That had to be where he was, didn't it? Even if he didn't remember how he'd gotten here. What looked like bridges were strung between the towers, sparkling in the sunlight. Wonder and curiosity stirred. He'd never been in Faerie before. Where were his spectacles? He wanted to see properly!

A subtle scraping sound had him twisting around and forgetting the view as he spotted the woman. She was seated on a round covered chair without arms or back, sharpening a short, narrow blade in practised motions. Catsmere—Queen Catsmere—was a tall woman with cropped dark hair and almost the same colouring as her twin. Her feathers were slightly more golden, and the green shading of their tips didn't extend quite as far up as Rakken's. While both twins gave an impression of physical athleticism, where Rakken would lounge in an—ironically—feline way, Catsmere always gave an impression of stillness, of being poised before the strike.

He couldn't tell at all what she was thinking; his head had that same blissful clear-water feeling it had had the day after Vane's murder. Had he flamed out again, or was it just that Catsmere had damn tight shields?

"Er. Hello," he said. He realised he was wearing only his undershirt and trousers and hunched in on himself self-consciously. *Fae don't care about modest dress, remember?* But it was hard to shake the unease of being half-dressed in front of a lady. Not that Catsmere was exactly a lady.

Catsmere looked up, too-green eyes slamming his heart into overdrive with the ancient presence they contained. It was the same look that Hetta got on occasion, he realised with a start. At least with Hetta, he *knew* the ancient presence in question, since Stariel shared a bit of his own soul. Here, there was nothing lurking at the back of his mind but confusion.

"Good afternoon, Marius Valstar," she said, that hint of power outside herself draining from her eyes. "Your spectacles are on the table." She tilted her chin at the coffee table, which was made of a single slice of an enormous geode, polished to reveal its inside. She went back to sharpening her blade. It felt just a tad threatening.

He scrabbled for his spectacles, and something sharing his sofa made a sound of protest. Looking down, he found Thistlefel curled up at his feet. She was now roughly the size of a beagle.

"Is it normal for lowfae to get bigger at this rate?"

Thistlefel bunted her head affectionately at his knees and

jumped down onto the rug. Catsmere chuckled. "No."

"Do you know why this one is?"

"I do not. I admit I expected you to ask different questions when you woke, more along the lines of 'where am I and how did I get here?'."

He swung his legs off the sofa, balling the blanket up and putting it at the other end. "Well, I'm in ThousandSpire, aren't I, and Rakken must have brought me, since I can't see how else I could have gotten here."

Catsmere's mouth curved. "Yes. These are my brother's quarters."

This was Rakken's? His curiosity increased. The room was large and circular with a high, soaring ceiling holding a vast sky-light far above. One half of the room's curve was taken up with the immense windows—goodness knows how they'd gotten a glazier to make panes that large and seamless. Probably there was magic involved. The other wall was lined with bookshelves, with a closed door set between them and a staircase leading up to the half-level above. The furniture was eclectic but aesthetically pleasing, in muted shades of golds and greens. Chosen to complement Rakken's feathers, he realised with a touch of amusement. Vanity, thy name is Rakken.

"Why did Rake bring me here?" He didn't remember anything after Emyranthus had attacked. He touched the bandaged wound around his arm and winced.

Catsmere put down her blade and sighed. "Because he trusts me to keep you safe, and apparently you are in need of safe-keeping."

"How long was I out for?"

"Most of a day."

Just like last time. That probably wasn't good, was it?

"That fae woman who attacked me. She…" He stopped, unsure whether to broach Rakken's personal affairs with his twin.

"Yes. Emyranthus. One of my brother's lovers," Catsmere said without embarrassment. "Did you get any sense of where she might have fled, if you saw into her mind?"

Marius frowned, wading through the blurred impressions he remembered, but eventually had to shake his head. "No. Er, why was she trying to kill me?" Had Emyranthus been the fae who killed Vane? Was this who Rakken had been referring to, worrying about mistaken identity?

"You had better ask my twin that than me." Catsmere folded her legs up into her chair, sitting cross-legged as she weighed him up.

He fought the urge to fidget under her gaze. He wasn't sure if his telepathy was still gone or if Catsmere just had particularly good shields, but he wasn't picking up anything not obviously originating from his own mind. Or perhaps it was her connection to ThousandSpire—Hetta was quiet like that too, within Stariel's bounds.

"Do you understand what my brother has done, bringing you here, Marius?"

Something bad, based on her solemn demeanour. "I didn't *ask* him to bring me here, and I can hop straight back to Stariel if someone will make me a portal or bring me to a Gate. I don't want to cause trouble."

"A mortal involved with fae is dead, someone is supplying highly dangerous plants from Faerie to Mortal, and a greater fae of my court just attacked a mortal. We are mid-negotiations on the conduct of greater fae in your realm. Politics," she summarised. "This is not simply about Rakken finding a convenient reason to kidnap you. Bringing you here for sanctuary makes this more than a family matter. It brings ThousandSpire's honour into seeing it righted."

"Oh. Wait—a family matter?" he asked.

"You are connected to my brother." She paused for a meaningful beat, and he felt his cheeks heat. "He is married to your sister, after all."

He choked. Catsmere's expression was pure innocence.

"You have too many brothers," he complained.

A brief, sharp smile before her expression sobered. Her gaze swept him from top to toe. "Do you have any strengths to your name, or are you only a collection of weaknesses, Marius Valstar?"

"What?" It came out strangled.

She continued to hold his gaze blandly, as if she hadn't just insulted him. "You are no warrior, and you cannot control whatever peculiar magic you possess. I have seen you show no great guile, cunning, or charm. You fear excessively what others think of you and are apt to freeze in a moment of crisis. On this basis, you have nothing useful to contribute other than whatever fleeting attraction you hold for my brother. Can you explain why it is necessary that you involve yourself in this matter at all?"

"I—" It was horrible, the way she listed off all his deepest insecurities so matter-of-factly, without malice. It would've been easier to cope with malice. "It's... Dr Vane was my colleague, murdered in my greenhouse. And I'm not—just because I'm not a warrior or a diplomat or a sorcerer doesn't make me useless! Those aren't the only things of value in the world, good gods. In this instance, I know plants, and I knew Vane." It seemed a pretty pitiful offering. He swallowed. "Was it Emyranthus who killed him?"

"I don't know. That is what Rake is currently trying to discover." Her countenance remained unblinking. "He is not widely known for constancy in his entanglements, and I think that is what you seek, isn't it?"

"I— No." Marius shook his head out of pure reflex, even though he knew that sort of thing didn't matter in Faerie.

"What *are* your intentions here, then, Marius Valstar?"

"I'm not—none of your business!"

She moved so fast, unnaturally fast, and he hadn't time to process her intent before the blade left her hand. It hit the sofa and stuck, quivering, in the leather between his parted legs. He looked down at the handle and swallowed hard, feeling a bit light-headed at how close it was to the unmentionables.

"Are you threatening me?" he asked incredulously. "I'm in your kingdom, in the heart of your power; you don't need to throw knives to make a point!"

"I did not *need* to, no." Her gaze lifted over his shoulder, and she smiled and threw another knife. It bounced off something behind him and skittered across the rug.

He turned to see Rakken standing in the door, one hand raised in a warding gesture Marius had seen him make before. He looked from Marius to his twin with narrowed eyes, although he seemed much less surprised to be greeted by a thrown knife than Marius expected. Maybe that was a perfectly normal greeting in Faerie. Terrible thought.

Catsmere rose and went to her twin, bending fluidly as she passed Marius to pull the knife in the sofa free. Marius reflexively got to his feet, wincing as it made the pain flare in his arm.

Rakken frowned briefly at him. "Have you been threatening him?" he asked his sister.

"Only a little bit for his own good." Catsmere embraced

Rakken, and when she stepped back, a silent conversation passed between the two of them. They always tried to keep their disagreements hidden from outsiders, but Marius could read some of the charged currents there, if not the specifics. They were both angry, though not entirely at each other, he thought. Rakken was worried about something and… ashamed, maybe? Not an emotion he'd known Rakken possessed.

"I have kept your wounded dove safe," Catsmere said after a beat, putting a hand on her twin's shoulder. "Emyranthus?"

Rakken shook his head. "I have not located her hiding place, but I have planted enough seeds that I will hear of it sooner rather than later."

"Do you want me to kill her?" Catsmere said, a careful offer.

Rakken's gaze fleetingly touched Marius's where he stood in horrified curiosity. "*I* will do it, if it is necessary."

"Will it be?" Catsmere asked.

Rakken spoke so easily, as if they were discussing the weather. He didn't look at Marius again. "If Emyr was responsible for the mortal's death, it will be more difficult to avoid, but that is not yet certain. Has the mortal queen raised it with you yet?"

"No. I go there now." Catsmere waved at Marius. "Go and fuss over your mortal and get it out of your system. We'll speak later, when you're less hopelessly distracted."

Rakken muttered something in stormtongue that made Catsmere grin as she sauntered over to the windows and let herself out onto the balcony. The balcony had only a low lip around it, which wouldn't prevent anyone from falling off, and Marius realised why when Catsmere unfurled her wings and walked straight off it without hesitation, winging up and away.

17

THE SEDUCTIVE POWERS OF WATER LILIES

"How is your head, Marius Valstar?" Rakken still stood by the internal door.

Marius shrugged. "Fine. I flamed out again, I think."

"And your arm?"

"I haven't looked under the bandages, but I assume I'm not going to die from it. Hurts like blazes though. Now what is—"

"Drink that; it ought to help with the pain," Rakken said, pointing to the sideboard, where a vial of something rested.

"Are you sure fae medicine is compatible with humans?" Marius asked, picking it up, wincing as the movement jostled his stab wound. Various bruises were also making their presence known.

"In this case, yes. I checked—this has been used on mortals before. I would not poison you by *accident*."

He couldn't help a grin at Rakken's emphasis, but he uncapped the vial without further debate. It tasted cool and faintly of mint, and the sensation of coolness spread quickly to his arm, bringing with it relief. Magic. He let out a long breath, glad for it.

"You." Rakken clicked his fingers to summon Thistlefel, who trotted over in a way that managed to convey that she was merely *choosing* to wander in Rakken's direction. "You may leave us for the moment. All the levels on this tower are mine." She huffed but went out the door he held open, leaving Marius alone with Rakken. His stomach gave an odd flip.

Rakken closed the door firmly behind him and made a gesture. A subtle spark between his fingers, and the walls and windows of the room flared in response, a brief glow that made Marius blink.

"Wards," Rakken explained without prompting.

Emyranthus had shattered the windows back at the college, Marius remembered. Or rather, he had inadvertently made her do so. "My room. Gods, what must the Dean think."

Rakken sighed. "Your college is persuaded that the damage was not your fault."

"Oh. Persuaded how?" he asked suspiciously.

Rakken walked closer. "I do not know why you have such trouble believing I can charm others without the use of magic, but rest assured, so it was. Though I cannot say they were precisely happy about the affair."

Marius swallowed, the silence between them feeling more awkward than it ever had. Rakken's manner was... different, in a way Marius couldn't pinpoint. Softer? Except Rakken didn't look at all soft. He watched Marius with an intensity that made him want to look away except that that felt like conceding something he didn't wish to concede.

A dozen half-formed questions and accusations crowded in

his throat. What in the hells was going on, and just what did Rakken mean by any of it, especially this talk of killing? Why had Catsmere just done a good impression of an old-fashioned guardian trying to intimidate her ward's suitor?

"Rake—" he began, at the same time as Rakken said: "I am sorry."

They each paused, and he waved for Rakken to continue.

Rakken grimaced. "I am sorry that Emyr targeted you, that it was because of me, and that I erred in concluding that you were not in danger from her."

Marius stared at him.

Rakken picked his way across the room as if he were approaching a horse he was afraid of startling. He stopped at the chair Cat had recently vacated and waved at the sofa. "Sit."

Marius remained standing. Rakken settled into an armchair with a sardonic expression. The armchair had an oddly low back; designed for stormdancers, Marius realised as Rakken arranged his wings.

"Emyranthus. The woman who attacked me," he said abruptly. "She was your"—he fished about for a word—"ex-paramour."

"A past lover, yes."

"She's who you meant when you said you had enemies, isn't she?"

"Yes."

"Did she kill Vane by mistake?"

"I do not know."

Marius was getting bloody tired of these less-than-informative answers. He touched the bandage on his arm. "Well, thank you for coming to my rescue, I suppose. Even if your deranged ex-lover was the reason I needed rescuing in the first place. And just why was she trying to kill me anyway?"

Rakken matched his fingertips together and inspected his hands. "Spite, perhaps. I offended her with my waning desire, so she targeted that for which my desire has waxed." He looked up and met Marius's eyes.

Marius felt like he needed at least three feet of solid brick between him and the heat of that gaze. Maybe more. Maybe several city blocks. He wanted to protest that one couldn't just *say* things like that and then *look* at people as if they hadn't already mutually agreed that nothing was going to happen between them.

Instead, he looked away and swallowed. "Things ended badly between you, I take it?"

"There was nothing to end," Rakken said sharply. "If you are imagining either of us kept to some quaint notion of fidelity, you can rid yourself of it. I have never taken an exclusive lover, and neither has Emyranthus. We have each swived our way through a great portion of Faerie, together and separately, and wished the other well in the doing."

"So why did you end it, then?"

Rakken huffed. "I have told you; there was nothing to end. I was simply uninterested in an assignation when our paths most recently crossed. She didn't accept my refusal, and I do not tolerate such behaviour in a lover, casual or otherwise." His voice had gone hard, his eyes flaring in a way that was more than metaphorical. "When I made this clear to her, she took it… badly."

"You don't say." Marius's heart was hammering. "How long were you together?"

"We were never together, not in the sense you mean. There were no promises, no expectations between us."

"How long?"

Rakken sighed. "We do not count time as you do in Mortal. Especially before the Iron Law was rescinded."

Marius looked at him. "How long, Rake?"

Rakken rolled his eyes. "A few decades, probably."

"*What?*"

Rakken bared his teeth. "We fucked now and then on a casual, non-exclusive, mutually pleasurable basis. That's all it was."

"For *decades*. And you just ended it like that. Gods, no wonder she was so hurt." That had been the emotion he'd seen, beneath Emyranthus's rage, a distilled bitterness and pain he empathised with all too well. She'd loved Rakken, whatever he had to say about the matter, and unrequited love was the absolute worst. Marius still had nightmares sometimes about the expression on John's face when Marius had declared himself, the pitying scorn.

Wait, how had he found himself on the side of the woman who'd tried to kill him?

"She wanted to punish you," he said, the disorienting swirl of her borrowed memories swimming up.

"She has no claim on me regardless, but she should not have brought you into this," Rakken said stiffly, and Marius knew he would rather be speaking of practically anything else. It was almost worth getting stabbed to see him made this awkward. Almost.

"And now you're going to kill her, if that's what that nice little chat with Cat was about?" What sort of person could do that?

Rakken sighed again and crossed his long legs. "I will try to avoid it if I can, but Emyr has made it difficult by involving the Mortal Realm. That directly flouts her queen's instructions, and Cat cannot be seen to tolerate it, not if she is to keep the court's respect. If I can resolve this as a personal matter between myself and Emyr, I can keep it from involving the queen's justice, but if Emyr has killed a mortal unconnected to me, Cat cannot appear influenced by my connection to her."

"You're her twin."

"And Cat cannot afford to be seen as half a ruler, with me as the true power behind the throne. Our previous cultivated image of complementary strengths—me as diplomat, her as warrior—is to our detriment now."

Marius was a little surprised Rakken had admitted his and Cat's front had always been deliberate. No wonder Rakken's emotions regarding his twin were so uneven. His relationship with Cat was central to his identity, and this would be a cataclysmic shift in that. It occurred to Marius that this conversation was the most personal information Rakken had ever willingly revealed. Or unwillingly, rather; he was pretty sure Rakken was only being this explicit because he felt he owed him for Emyr's attack.

"It would have been easier if ThousandSpire had chosen you rather than her," Marius said. He knew that was what Rakken had hoped for, and he could see how it would have fitted with the image they'd presented to the world, Rakken charming and manipulative with Cat as his strongman. Strongwoman.

"Easier in some ways, perhaps. But better? No. It was no accident that ThousandSpire chose her over me. She chose it first, after all."

No hint of hurt in Rakken's tone or expression, but Marius wasn't fooled. He thought of Stariel and his own failure to be chosen. Not that he'd wanted it, unlike Rakken, but it wasn't exactly an ego boost to know that you weren't your faeland's favourite person.

He walked closer to the window on the heels of that thought. A faeland that wasn't Stariel. A fae *city*. Sunset had painted the view in jewel tones; he was pretty sure there were jewels inset in the towers as well. Despite everything, a soft wonder filled him.

His stomach gave an audible growl.

"You should eat, after the power you expended on Emyranthus," Rakken said abruptly. "I will have food brought."

"No—I mean, yes, fine, good idea—but can we go out?" He waved at the towers in the distance. "Assuming they have places to eat in ThousandSpire? It seems a shame to be standing in a fae city and not to see any of it. It's not dangerous, is it?" he added when Rakken stared at him as if he'd said something outlandish.

"The city does indeed contain food," Rakken said after a pause. "The city of *Aerest*. ThousandSpire comprises much more than one city. And you will be safe enough with me. It would in fact be advantageous for us to be seen together here. It will emphasise that you are under my protection and might draw out Emyr." He strode to the balcony, opened the doors, and held out a hand. "Come."

Marius followed him reluctantly. "Isn't there another way to get around?"

Rakken smiled. "This tower is more than three hundred wings high."

"Oh, all right, but I'm beginning to think you're coming up with these situations on purpose," he grumbled.

"Oh?" Rakken put a hand on his heart with a wounded expression. His eyes gleamed.

Marius snorted, but his amusement ebbed into something else as he put his hands behind Rakken's neck. Rakken's smile grew wicked, but before he could protest, they had dropped off the balcony. He let out a stream of profanities and felt Rakken chuckle.

Once the initial shock had worn off, it was less alarming than last time. Mostly because he trusted Rakken not to drop him. Not that he'd exactly expected Rakken to drop him on previous occasions, but repeated exposure had increased his confidence. It wasn't pure wingpower keeping them airborne, he knew—the wing-span ratio wasn't sufficient for the weight. Rakken's magic wove around them, fresh rain and citrus, but there was less wind whipping at them than Marius had expected; Rakken was doing something with the air currents.

It was… exhilarating whilst remaining mildly terrifying. Intimate, since he could feel Rakken's muscles flex with the exertion, pressed up against his chest as he was. Fascinating, flying through a fae city and knowing he was probably the only human here.

"Welcome to Aerest," Rakken said.

Marius's breath caught, looking down at the city. Everything was so different. As they flew, Rakken murmured the names for the different parts of the city. The towering rock formations— the ten thousand spires—varied hugely. Some were heavily modified, hollowed out to contain homes and shops and elaborate hanging gardens, whilst others remained bare rock. Strange birds took flight as they passed, bowing to the presence of a larger predator. Rakken flew them past sky bridges, where a mixture of winged and unwinged fae looked up to watch. Most of them were stormdancers like Rakken, but there were other kinds of fae too, a wild variety of horns, wings, fur, and various nonhuman appendages.

"It must be a hard city for those who can't fly?" Marius asked.

"There are sky barges that dock at many of the towers in

addition to the bridges."

"And we couldn't have used one of those methods?"

"Oh, but it would have been so much less fun!" Rakken said with such a showy bit of aerial manoeuvring for emphasis that Marius couldn't help laughing. Rakken joined in. It was, Marius thought with a start, the first time he'd ever heard Rakken sound happy.

"What is that?" he asked, glimpsing a dark churning mass of clouds in the distance, lit with flashes of lightning.

"The Maelstrom," Rakken said.

Marius shivered; he'd heard Wyn talk about the nightmare storm.

"You are safe, Marius Valstar. It will not come into the city." He turned, and the view of the maelstrom disappeared behind another spire.

With a stomach-flipping turn, Rakken flared out his wings and landed neatly on a rooftop plaza. It was tiled in pale blue and white, and a shallow pool filled with large water lilies dominated the centre of the space. Around the edges were various stalls, most of which seemed to sell food, judging from the smells.

Marius slid out of Rakken's grip, feeling abruptly self-conscious as everyone in the outdoor market turned to look at them before recovering themselves and turning back to their business. In the human world, he would have said the sight of a flying man dropping out of the sky carrying another (horrifically under-dressed) justified extreme surprise, but it didn't seem so out of the ordinary here. There were many others setting down and taking off, and he wasn't even the only one being carried. His improper attire wasn't even noteworthy amongst the outlandish and in some cases barely-there clothing styles. But he didn't think it was his imagination that the crowd was paying them particular attention.

"You're a prince," he realised abruptly. And these were Rakken's people. *Of course* they were paying their prince particular attention.

"Well spotted."

"Do people always watch you when you're about?"

"They would be fools not to notice me, but in this case, they are watching you, starling. You are the first mortal many of them have ever seen. It helps that you are accompanying *me*, of course."

"Oh."

Rakken held out a hand again, as if casual public hand-holding were a thing that one did. Looking about, Marius supposed perhaps it was. The Spires' fashions were so different to home, and the range of body types and forms so varied that gender wasn't all that obvious in many cases, but there was what looked very much like a woman with feathery tufted ears sitting practically in the lap of another in a loveseat under the gently swaying trees. As Marius watched, they shared a kiss that made his cheeks burn. He looked quickly away, feeling unmoored.

He took Rakken's hand. His heart hammered. What were they doing? What did Rakken mean by this increase in flirtatiousness? Was he increasing in flirtatiousness or was Marius imagining it?

Rakken led him to one of the stalls. A wide variety of unfamiliar foods were piled on different trays along its frontage.

The vendor was a slim, elegant… person, with turquoise scales running down their throat and eyes of an unnatural amber shade.

"Rake," the vendor said with a warm smile. Their eyes flicked curiously to Marius.

"Salamank," Rakken said with equal warmth. This was Rakken on his home ground, Marius realised suddenly—a place Marius had never seen him. Maybe that was the reason for the change in Rakken's manner since Marius had woken.

"The usual?"

Rakken tilted his head at Marius. "Some of everything, I think."

Salamank gave it to him with a smile. "Making sure he keeps up his energy? You'll need it," they said to Marius, which made him want to sink through the rock of the tower and die.

Rakken chuckled and completed the transaction. Knowing shot through Marius, sharp and unwanted, and embarrassed him nearly as much as Salamank's words had.

"That was another former lover, wasn't it?" he asked quietly when they were a little distance away.

Rakken shrugged as if this was uninteresting information. "Yes. Not all of my previous lovers take up knives against me."

"Did you bring me here specifically to make that point?"

Rakken seemed surprised. "I brought you here because the food is good, and I thought you would appreciate the water lilies."

Marius's suspicion must've shown on his face.

Rakken's lips curved. "No need for jealousy. Salamank and I have not shared sheets for many years."

"I'm not jealous," he said quickly. *He is not widely known for his constancy.* "Why are you being…" He broke off and gestured inarticulately. "Oh, never mind."

Rakken continued to smile in an aggravating way. The setting sun reflected in his feathers, hair, and horns, picking up the metallic highlights.

The back of Marius's neck itched with the weight of all the

curious glances the fae were giving him—he could tell it was him, now that Rakken had pointed it out, though they clearly knew who Rakken was too. A few murmured "your highness" in absent greeting as they passed, which Rakken acknowledged with aloof nods.

Marius, in turn, tried not to stare too much. *I am the strange thing here* was such an odd thing to get his head around, amidst all this.

They sat down on a wooden bench in one of the many nooks surrounding the water lily pond. Rakken was being far less careful with his personal space than usual, and their legs pressed against each other. Marius shuffled sideways, flustered.

"So, the fae plants," he said hurriedly, trying to focus on things that weren't sitting sensually next to him. "Could Emyranthus have taken the missing plants from the greenhouse?"

"Perhaps. She would take exception to fae plants in mortal hands, certainly, and might have felt moved to destroy them."

Marius thought about it as they ate. The food was good but unfamiliar, sorted into many smaller papery containers within the larger vessel. There were dumplings with different kinds of meat, a spicy mixture that contained nuts, and oddly textured bread.

"I don't think Emyranthus killed Vane," he said eventually.

Rakken slid him a look. "Is that true knowledge or speculation?"

"Speculation. But I got a glimpse into her mind, and it didn't feel like it was her *second* attempt to murder me. I got the impression that Mortal was a new experience for her. She did ask my name first, though," he admitted.

"Which could mean she wanted to be certain she'd identified you correctly after a mistake the first time," Rakken pointed out. His brows knit together. "But your judgement is usually sound, so I will assume you are right and it was not she who killed Vane."

Marius blinked at him. Rakken thought his judgement was *usually sound*? He'd said it absently, as if it went without saying.

To cover his confusion, Marius fixed his focus back on his food and did not look up again until Rakken said softly: "Watch." He nodded towards the pond. One of his wings furled out, brushing Marius's back.

The sunset colours of the city had deepened. As the pond fell into shadow, the giant water lilies began to bloom. Great soft-pink petals unfurled, revealing blue stamens and releasing a heavy perfume into the evening air. Tiny glowing lights began to gather above the lilies as what Marius assumed were magical pollinators were drawn to the scent. The effect was to gild the flowers with light and set the whole pool glittering with the reflections.

Marius let out a soft breath of wonder. "In the Kebulyn jungles, giant water lilies trap beetles overnight to pollinate them. There's a specimen in one of the greenhouses back home. Do these work the same way, do you know?"

Rakken's laugh was low. "I do not know, and now I will not be able to stop wondering until I do. Oh, Marius Valstar."

Marius turned to find that Rakken's wing had curled around the two of them, creating a sort of privacy screen so that it felt like the entire world was only them, facing the glittering pond. Rakken was very close, the heat in his eyes stripping Marius bare. He felt as if he were falling.

Come on, even you're not this much of an idiot, his inner logician pointed out. *You recognise this scenario, even if it's been a while. An intimate meal with just the two of you? Deliberately*

romantic choice of scenery? This is a date, Marius, and you're an
idiot if you fall for it.

John never gave me water lilies, a quiet voice said.

"Are you trying to seduce me?" he asked, aiming for lightly
amused, but his voice came out hoarse instead.

Rakken smiled, slow and dangerously attractive. "Yes. Is
it working?"

"No," he said. *Yes,* he thought traitorously. And then, to his
mortification, "*Why?*"

"Because you are worth seducing."

The words slid right under his determined armour, a needle
of pleasure-pain. He took a shuddering breath, his throat suddenly tight.

Rakken leaned closer until his breath warmed Marius's lips.
He met Marius's eyes, raised one eyebrow, and closed the gap
with excruciating slowness, so that Marius had plenty of time
to move away.

He didn't, gods help him.

The first contact still startled him, a shot of heat and adrenaline. Did he want this? Was this all right here, in public? But
then, this was Faerie, and those two women had... And they
were hidden within Rakken's wings, after all, even if someone
could probably guess what they might be doing.

Rakken slid a hand around his waist, pulling them together
more firmly, and Marius gave in, burying his hands in Rakken's
hair. His pulse thundered in his ears, and he thought rather
wildly that he could taste storms.

When Rakken pulled back, Marius stared at him, panting,
aroused to the point of discomfort. He felt dizzy, as if they
were still mid-air. His hands were caught in Rakken's hair, the
dark strands soft against his fingers.

There was a moment when Rakken looked similarly dazed. He searched Marius's face with wide eyes, as if seeing something he hadn't anticipated, but the expression was gone in a heartbeat, quickly folded under a practised, self-satisfied smile.

If I kiss him again, will that shake off the mask? he wondered.

Again? Hadn't Marius decided—several times now—that there ought to be no kissing whatsoever between them?

"We—what happened to agreeing it would only complicate matters?" he managed to croak.

"I have changed my mind, since complications have found us regardless. Why not enjoy our mutual interest while it lasts? Where is the harm in casual pleasure, if both parties wish to seek it? It doesn't have to mean anything. I have begun to think it is *more* complicated to ignore it, and perhaps it will burn out quicker this way. Or are you pretending you do not want me? Why do you fear your own lust so greatly?"

"I don't fear it!" He stood.

"Don't you?"

"No!" He ran a hand through his hair, agitated. He'd bent both himself and reality out of shape before to keep the world rose-tinted when he looked at a man. He couldn't do it again.

But this wasn't that, was it?

He tried to sort through the logic, the various parts of himself caught equally between NO and YES. Rakken was the walking personification of everything Marius had sworn to avoid, and yet, what he was proposing... there was no pretence to it. Casual. Uncomplicated. Something that could end at any moment. Something that *would* end.

Maybe it *was* a good idea to get this foolishness out of his system, to prove to himself that he could enjoy things without getting painfully attached. Maybe then he could stop fearing it.

It wasn't as if Rakken was proposing anything that led to *love*, Marius thought with an internal cringe, and that was what he truly feared, more than anything else.

As if Rakken could sense how unsettled his thoughts were, he dropped the subject. "Come—let us search my library for any relevant texts about the plants you salvaged, while we are here." He stood and held out his hand.

Marius took it.

18

RAKKEN ABANDONS SUBTLETY

THEY WENT BACK to the tower. Rakken made no more mention of his indecent proposal, but Marius could hardly think of anything else, even when presented with the quite magnificent distraction of stacks and stacks of fascinating books. Especially when Rakken stood in the middle of the shelves and began weaving sorcery whilst explaining his cataloguing system. This, Marius felt, was playing dirty.

Rakken's hands moved in graceful shapes as he murmured to himself: "Plants, as a starting point." Spine after spine began to glow with a soft green light. There must have been hundreds, perhaps thousands, of books lit up amongst the shelves. Rakken grimaced. "The web of this spell will only recall what I have put into it, alas, and botany is no speciality of mine, so works are only tagged at the broadest subject level. Let us cross-reference against magical texts." Another gesture, and most of the glowing volumes changed from green to gold. "And specifically, dark magic." This time a much smaller portion changed colour, shifting to glowing bronze.

"Did you choose the colour scheme for your cataloguing magic to match your décor?" Marius asked with a laugh.

"Of course," Rakken said primly. "What is the point of being a dread sorcerer if one cannot indulge aesthetic whims?" He fanned out his wings so that the light of the glowing volumes reflected in his feathers, highlighting all their different shades.

Marius laughed again but sobered as he took in the still-overwhelming number of books highlighted. "This is going to take some time."

Rakken hummed agreement. "Perhaps something more straightforward. Encyclopaedias." He made another gesture. This time only three volumes changed colour, turning a deeper shade of green.

Marius retrieved the closest, which was on a low shelf amongst several other glowing results from Rakken's wider searches. The encyclopaedia was a large, leather-bound book about two feet tall and several inches thick, and the weight of it made him search out the nearest flat surface and set it down there with a thump. Opening it revealed page after page of gorgeous botanical illustrations, each with a brief note, not so dissimilar to its human equivalents except that the species were largely unfamiliar. His heart skipped, a wild thrill of discovery rising in him.

"Oh, you are bad for my ego," Rakken said, making Marius's head snap up. "You never look at *me* with that much ardour."

"Sprout leaves and roots," Marius advised, determined to focus, and went back to examining the pages, eventually retreating to a leather sofa with his find. Nothing jumped out at him, but he didn't trust his memory in any case. He'd have to retrieve his sketches to compare with.

Some time later, he put the book down, even the thrill of

new plants unable to keep his mind from what Rakken had suggested earlier. Rakken was perched next to a high table, working through his own stack. He looked absorbed in the task, a slight frown between his brows as he read. How could he be so *nonchalant* about all this?

"You disapprove of my experiments," Marius said suddenly. "We argue like cats in a bag. And you're—"

"I am what?" Rakken asked, his voice gone soft and dangerous.

Untrustworthy. Too bloody tempting by half.

"The sort of person who has murderous ex-lovers!" he said.

"I have far more *non*-murderous ones. What is your phrase? Emyr is an outlier and should be disregarded for statistical purposes."

Marius gave a startled laugh, amazed Rakken had been *actually listening* to enough of his rambles to pick up that bit of jargon. "What happens if it goes wrong, after?"

"How? I am proposing mutual pleasure for as long as that lasts, not to wed you."

"…is that possible, in Faerie?" he asked faintly.

Rakken blinked. "What? Oh, your mortal customs. Yes, of course it's possible, though as fae royalty I would need the High King's permission, and I will *not* ask him for anything." His expression went dark for a moment.

"You can talk about 'casual pleasure' all you like, but it's not as if we're going to be able to avoid each other afterwards if this turns sour. Your brother is married to my sister. We're supposed to be solving a murder investigation together." Was he actually considering this?

Rakken gave him a dry look. "However shall we cope with a degree of antagonism between us? If only we had some way to expend such energy."

Marius burst out laughing despite himself, and before he'd recovered, Rakken had moved so fast that Marius couldn't process anything except that the world had become suddenly and shockingly intimate.

What? How? Rakken was basically in his lap. Or, well, over his lap. Rakken had positioned himself so that his knees were on the outside of Marius's, trapping his legs. His hands gripped Marius's shoulders, wings draped to either side. Marius became aware in a single, elektric moment of the heat of Rakken's thighs pressed against his, of Rakken's face near enough that his breath warmed his lips. Of the scent of him, warm and— damn it all—*alluring*. Rakken's eyes gleamed.

"You are entirely easy to shock," Rakken said with satisfaction. He released Marius's shoulders and shifted his weight back, partially flaring his wings and holding himself poised like a heron about to strike. He took the book from Marius's unresisting fingers and set it aside. One eyebrow rose in a silent question.

"What are you—" He had to swallow, his throat was so dry. "What are you doing?"

"Seducing you with increasingly less subtlety. Do tell me to stop, if you're not enjoying it." And with that, Rakken set one hand under his chin, leaned forwards, and kissed him.

Rakken kissed with firm arrogance, as if having kissed Marius before had conferred some sort of ownership. *I know the shape of you now*, the kiss seemed to say. *I know how you like your pleasure.* And gods, he did.

Marius couldn't help responding, couldn't help the way his body arched or the way his hands reached out blindly and found Rakken's waist. Pulling the hard muscle of him closer, he scrabbled at the fabric between them. Rakken pressed him back into the couch, deepening the kiss without letting go, his tongue sliding against Marius's, hot and wicked.

Some disoriented part of him remained frozen, but his body knew what it wanted. Sensation, enough to drown in, enough to leave no space for thought or doubt or aching loneliness. He could regret this at leisure later.

He hissed at the single grind of Rakken's hips that was all it took to bring matters to the point of uncomfortable tightness. His hands moved down Rakken's back to dig into the curve of his arse, which—of sodding course—was inhumanly firm.

Rakken pulled back and smirked. He could hardly be unaware of Marius's state, given his position. Black nearly overpowered the green of his irises, and he was breathing faster than usual.

"Are you interested in particular parts of my anatomy, starling?" Rakken said, voice dark as thirty-year malt. He caught Marius's wrists and rolled his pelvis, leaving him in no doubt as to his own condition. He leaned forward until his breath tickled in Marius's ear. "My cock, for instance?"

The word, said in a tone of pure sin and combined with Rakken's accompanying movement, startled a sound out of Marius that was half-snort, half-groan. "You're insufferable, you know that?"

"Am I now?" He licked Marius's earlobe, repeating the motion. Marius strained upwards, desperate for more contact. Rakken held him in place, the weight of him utterly ungiving but for that faint, teasing friction as he nibbled his way down Marius's jawbone.

Sweet Mother Eostre, this was madness, but he thought he might die if it stopped. *Rubbish! People do not die of sexual frustration!*

"Marius Rufus Valstar." Rakken's breath curled against the skin he'd just licked.

"None of that. It's just Marius, or you can get off," he said firmly. Or tried to say firmly—it came out embarrassingly breathy.

"Oh, I intend to get us both off." Rakken grinned and added, "...Marius." The way Rakken said his name, setting it down like a dare, with eyes half-lidded, sent quivers running through Marius, and with that a frisson of anxiety.

He didn't want another experience like John. He knew how quickly desire could lead to infatuation, how that could twist everything out of true, including yourself, until you warped yourself into unhappiness. He couldn't do that again.

But Rakken was nothing like John. John had always held out the promise of more, a bauble forever just out of reach. Rakken had been clear he wasn't offering more than the purely physical. Casual pleasure, he'd said. And judging from his truly appalling attitude towards his past lovers, an attraction that might burn out arbitrarily at any moment.

Marius gripped that thought like a lifeline. It made this thing between them safe.

Rakken released his wrists then, nimble fingers moving to his shirtfront. "While you argue with yourself, shall I get on with things?"

"You utter—" Marius began to protest, his words muffled by the removal of his undershirt. So exposed, he squirmed, a touch self-conscious. Rakken was such an unnatural specimen, after all.

"Indeed," Rakken agreed and kissed him again, hands moving to his bared skin.

Marius lost the ability to string words together for a bit. At least he wasn't the only one.

Storms above, how can a mortal threaten my self-control so? I will purge this from my system, if I have to fuck this one so thoroughly he wears my scent for days.

It took several seconds to process Rakken's thoughts, and when Marius had done so, he gasped the first thing that came to mind: "Is that a euphemism or a literal possibility?"

Rakken swayed back. His mouth was painted a brighter red than usual, almost obscene. He gave Marius a narrow-eyed look.

"Flameout over, I suppose."

A trace of a frown appeared between Rakken's brows, smoothing out after a moment. Marius had the sense of walls rising; Rakken had bolstered his own mental shields. "Probably not literal." He traced one hand over Marius's chest, the other wandering lower. "But I am certainly game to try. Do you want me to?"

Marius swallowed, mouth suddenly dry. His voice emerged as a bare whisper. "Yes."

Rakken's lips curved. "You need not sound like you're agreeing to your death warrant."

"Well, perhaps you'd better stop mucking about and show me some reason for enthusiasm." The words were out before he could stop them. He didn't quite know what to make of himself and this sudden boldness.

"Yes," Rakken agreed, eyes smouldering. "Perhaps I should." His hands trailed lower, unfastening, and Marius exhaled at the sudden relief from constriction—and then sucked in a breath as Rake's fingers moved lightly over him.

"Feeling more enthusiastic?" Rakken growled.

Before Marius could object that Rakken was still fully clothed, he slid down off the couch and settled between his legs. Marius stiffened in surprise. Rakken couldn't be—but he was, smirking at Marius's expression before taking him in his mouth.

Marius fisted his hands, fighting not to embarrass himself then and there. It had been a long time since any touch save his own, after all, and he hadn't thought—well, there were fellows who did this sort of thing and fellows who didn't, and Marius had assumed princes fell firmly in the latter category.

Clearly this specific prince very much did because—oh, gods. This was torture, from someone highly skilled in the art. Heat enveloped him. Desperate to touch, he sank his hands into Rakken's hair and then hesitated as he found Rakken's horns. Rakken murmured softly in the back of his throat, tipping his head forwards in encouragement. When Marius wrapped his fingers around the bronzed ridges, Rakken did something impossible with his tongue, and Marius struggled to remember some bloody manners and not thrust mindlessly.

Rakken wasn't helping matters, hand and mouth working in concert. Pleasure coiled, tighter and tighter.

"Rake, I can't—I'm going to—" Marius gasped a warning.

Rakken did not stop.

For a single, glorious moment, the world went quiet. There was no thought, only a long, drawn-out note of pure sensation. He hung weightless in a void.

And then thought rushed back in, in pulses of pleasure.

Maelstrom take me, I will not—

"Fuck," Rakken cursed. He pulled away from Marius and sagged sideways against the sofa. His head fell back. His mouth was wet, lips parted, his hair pulled partially loose. His eyes were half closed, and he looked… utterly undone. Sated.

"Fucking telepaths," Rakken complained to the ceiling.

Oh. *Oh.* Marius laughed. "Yes. That *is* what you wanted to do, remember?"

"I am not a callow youth. I had no intention of"—Rakken waved irritably—"finishing yet." He released a harsh breath, expression caught in slack awe. "Untouched. Storms above. That was not a side effect of telepathic projection I had anticipated."

"Should I apologise, then?" Marius asked, a bit archly.

Rakken chuckled, one hand curling possessively around the back of Marius's calf. He shot Marius a look of pure wickedness. "No, since I suppose I have only my own efforts to blame. I'm glad you so enjoyed them." *If they'd used you when I was learning mental shields, it would have been a much more enjoyable process. Although possibly less effective.*

Telepathic projection. That should probably worry Marius, but right now all he felt was happily limp. He reached out and brushed a tentative hand over Rakken's hair. Rakken gave an encouraging hum, so Marius pulled the rest of his hair free, running his fingers through the soft waves, too warm a hue to be true black. Deepest ebony threaded with glints of gold, giving the whole a rich sable lustre, a dark contrast to the bronze of his horns.

"Even your hair is ridiculous," he mused. "Unless—is gold a fae sign of age like grey is for humans?"

Rakken turned and glared. "No, it most certainly is not."

"You don't have to sound so appalled. I have grey hairs, after all." He ran a hand through his own locks self-consciously. Why was he talking about hair? Maybe it just seemed a safe subject, so much less awkward than saying, "So you just unexpectedly sucked me off, and I'm not quite sure what to do next."

The first pricklings of self-consciousness began to germinate, but before they could send down roots, Rakken got up and smoothly dropped back down onto the couch beside him, matter-of-factly crowding into his space. The edge of his wing brushed against Marius's bare thigh, the feathers softer than he'd expected.

"And yet you accuse me of vanity." Rakken sounded amused. He traced an idle line down Marius's shoulder.

"*Some* of us aren't quasi-immortal fae with unfair genetic advantages. How old are you, anyway?"

Rakken shrugged. "I cannot give you an exact answer; I do not know myself. You know time passes differently here."

"You have to be less than three hundred years old, since I know you weren't around when the Iron Law came into place," Marius reasoned.

"I am much less than three hundred years old," Rakken promised.

"There's a lot of ages that are less than three hundred. Two hundred and ninety-nine, in fact."

"Less than two hundred years old, then, impertinent fledgling," Rakken said.

The address reminded him of something Rakken had called him earlier. "Why 'starling', before?"

Rakken's eyes danced, and Marius wasn't sure if it was telepathy or sudden inspiration that made the meaning click.

"A diminutive of Valstar," he grumbled. "Little Valstar."

"Valstarling seemed too much of a mouthful," Rakken agreed and began to kiss him with slow, thorough exactness. Languor shifted to something tighter, more urgent, and Marius fumbled at Rakken's clothing, determined to get his hands on him properly this time.

Flashes of Rakken's thoughts came through, on much the

same theme, and Rakken was as clumsy as Marius had ever seen him in his impatience. The things he wanted to do to this mortal, to make him shudder, to see some measure of his own desperation reflected back. They kissed hungrily, mouths clashing.

"How in blazes does this come off?" Marius exclaimed, tugging futilely at Rakken's shirt.

Rakken's response was a low rumble of amusement as he directed him to the hidden buttons behind his neck. It took far too long to extract him from the infernal garment, but it was worth it to run hands over bare skin, up to the glory of all that excessive shoulder muscle. From there, Marius couldn't help brushing curiously over the small feathers where wings met skin.

Rakken arched into the touch with a sound of almost catlike pleasure. Marius did it again, rewarded by another sensual murmur. He brought his hands down to tug at Rakken's belt, which at least seemed to unfasten in a relatively normal way, feeling like Rakken was wearing altogether too much clothing. Rakken gave a soft laugh and rose, taking the task of shedding his remaining clothing in his own hands.

He made a show of it, unselfconscious and deliberate, holding Marius's gaze like a dare as he unbuttoned himself. Marius couldn't have made himself look away for anything.

Of course he was glorious, damn him, intimidatingly large and slightly curved, jutting out from his body in obscene invitation. Rakken proffered a hand and pulled him up, bringing them flush together from chest to groin. Marius's mind stuttered into incoherence as Rakken caught his mouth once more, hands moving down between them. The slide of his tongue echoing what his hands were doing made Marius scrabble at his shoulders for balance, knees gone weak.

"Can I," he murmured in Marius's ear, "interest you in buggery?"

Marius choked. "You really have given up on subtlety, haven't you?" And yet it did things to him, the way Rakken said such shameless things in that smooth, confident voice.

"Mmmm, yes. There are few things I don't like, and I'll tell you if you somehow manage to find them. Otherwise, I want to take you and be taken in every possible configuration, in the extremely immediate future, just to bring us to absolute clarity on the subject. What do *you* want?" His gaze was a challenge, pinning Marius.

Every possible configuration. Marius's cheeks flamed, but his desire rose even higher along with something like... relief. Rakken's gaze blazed up and down Marius's body, and he knew with a bone-deep intuition that there was nothing he could say, no desire he could express, that would make Rakken think less of him.

"Yes," he said, throat thick. "Gods. Yes. All of that."

Rakken's wings snapped out, and Marius clung to him for a few dizzying wingbeats before he landed them clumsily on the half-floor above.

"On the bed," Rakken growled. His eyes were glowing slightly. "Now."

"Anything else, your bloody highness?"

"Oh, plenty."

Marius snorted but stumbled backwards and onto the bed, heart thundering so that his whole body seemed to pulse with arousal. He reached down and took himself in hand, enjoying the flare in Rakken's eyes as he followed his movements.

Rakken stalked closer. He was so powerfully erotic that Marius almost couldn't bear to look at him. He felt pinned by his intensity, overly aware of the loudness of his own breaths, yearning for touch as if he might burst out of his skin waiting for it.

"Oh, I do like you like this, awaiting my arrival." But Rakken hesitated at the edge of the bed, attention flicking to the bandage around his bicep. "Your arm—"

"Sod my arm. It's still numbed anyway. And I want this." Whatever had been in that vial was still doing its job.

Rakken weighed him with an oddly serious light in his gaze. For a moment, Marius thought he was about to change his mind, walk away as he'd done so cruelly once before.

"I want it, Rake," he repeated and pulled him roughly down. Rakken chuckled and didn't resist.

They tangled together. Rakken's mouth was everywhere, nipping and sucking in turns, finding places Marius hadn't even known could be so sensitive, kissing his wrists, the hollow at his throat, his nipples. He was so caught up in sensation that he barely registered the signature scent of storms and citrus, only the jerk of slightly cool oil against overheated skin and Rakken's hands, moving lower. He tensed at that first intrusion, but Rakken's fingers were patient and oil-slick, his mouth a distracting counterpoint, and the tension slowly drained out of him, replaced with a growing ache of need.

His hips began to buck. "Please."

"So impatient," Rakken murmured, continuing that maddening rhythm with his hand, finding the exact place that made him shudder. "Do you want my cock, then?"

"No, I thought you were—proposing—a round of—sodding—tennis!" he panted, squirming.

Rakken chuckled and moved to cover Marius's body with his own. His breath tickled in his ear. "Oh, since you ask so sweetly, then."

A thrill of anticipation went through him, and he tensed, even knowing it would make matters worse. It had been a while, and this had been the rare exception rather than the usual way of things between him and John. There were... conventions about who and how one did this, which was mad if you thought about it, when the entire act was illegal, although possibly not for much longer, and—oh.

"Breathe."

Marius did, a gulp of air. Rakken soothed a hand along his spine and murmured low in his throat, holding still. Marius caught the edge of his thoughts, rough and possessive though he moved with excruciating control.

Marius's breaths came in small, rapid gasps as he adjusted, briefly dancing the edge between pain and pleasure until it firmly settled into the latter. Rakken was inside him, and the shocking intimacy of that tangled his thoughts into incoherency.

"Marius Rufus Valstar," Rakken growled. He shifted slightly, and Marius's finger's spasmed in the sheets.

"Gods, Rake. *Rake*."

Rakken began to thrust in a tortuous rolling motion. Each oiled slide of flesh jerked pleasure through him, maddening in its slowness. He couldn't form words; he made an inarticulate noise instead. More, he needed more. He grabbed at Rakken, not physically but mentally. *More.*

Sensation abruptly doubled back on itself, taking and being taken in the same moment. Rakken gave a harsh, guttural cry. The rhythm between them grew hard and frantic, and Marius lost his bracing, flattening against the bed as Rakken's nails dug into his hips. The twinned pleasure spiked through him so intensely he cried out, pressed into the mattress. When Rakken bit him hard on the neck, they came unravelled together.

Both of them were panting and clutching for the other, desperate to touch skin to skin. He wanted to curl his body around this mortal with a craving so intense it frightened him, but he'd examine that thought later. Later, when he had his wings wrapped about them both. *Mine*, he thought, sudden and savage, nipping at the mortal's neck again. The sight of his earlier mark filled him with primitive satisfaction.

Marius came back to himself to find he was trapped in a cage of Rakken's limbs with his back pressed against Rake's chest, silky feathers draped over them. Rakken had one arm around Marius's waist and had hooked a leg over his. The air was thick with the smell of sex, though there was less mess than expected, thanks to a casual bit of magic on Rakken's part.

"There are certain fringe benefits to bedding sorcerers," Rakken agreed.

Marius's head was ringing like a struck bell, and little flashes of emotion not his own seeped through. Thank the gods it was primarily satisfaction, because he didn't know what he'd say if Rakken was radiating disappointment instead. Still… what did he do now? What did you say when you'd just had the most intensely erotic experience of your life with a man—fae—you trusted about as far as you could throw him?

"Thank you, your highness, would be appropriate," Rakken murmured, nuzzling at his neck. Marius stiffened, and Rakken paused. "Interesting. You're projecting again. You really ought to work on your shields."

As if Rakken's shields were any better! Marius wasn't the one wanting to stretch his wings out possessively! He didn't have wings.

"True. You do test my control." Stormwinds, that was

irritating to admit, even if this had been a thoroughly enjoyable testing.

Marius panicked, unable to separate where he began and Rakken ended. He struggled to escape and knew Rakken considered not releasing him for a second before drawing back his limbs with a sigh. Marius shouldn't like knowing that Rakken could overpower him if he wanted. He didn't like that. What was he thinking?

He scrambled up and felt Rakken's echo of displeasure, much like a cat being ejected from a sunspot. Was he still projecting?

"You are," Rakken confirmed, propping himself up onto an elbow. He winced as Marius's alarm beat at him. Marius was right—he should look to his own shields first. He frowned as he realised they had frayed to the point of insubstance. Careless. He wasn't a fledgling to be so easily overwhelmed, but then nothing about this little mortal had ever been easy, had it?

"I'm not little," Marius snapped.

No, he wasn't where it counted, was he? Marius choked and stumbled, disoriented at the image. Gods.

"Get out of my head, Rake." Flattering though the thought had been, he had to find his way back to mental solitude or he would go mad. What if he was still projecting? He didn't know how to stop if he was. What if Rakken heard all his most embarrassing thoughts? He mustn't think them, but now it was impossible not to, a flurry of shameful images: dark fantasies; the hurtful things John had said before he'd left; Lord Valstar standing over him and telling him he'd beat the nancy out of him.

Suddenly Rakken was in front of him, his hands on Marius's shoulders. His green eyes filled Marius's whole field of vision.

"Shield," Rakken commanded, and the word had magic in

it, the force of his willpower bearing down on Marius like an arrow. Compulsion, from the fae whose compulsive abilities were the most powerful in all of Faerie, bending Marius as if he were green willow.

And then something in Marius bent back with shocking speed, like a green branch released from pressure. It snapped out between them, shoving Rakken away with such force that he went tumbling over the edge of the bed with a muffled oath and a thump as he hit the ground. Exactly like Emyranthus had.

Marius was alone in his head again, which would have been wonderful if it hadn't hurt so much.

He swayed, and Rakken's hands steadied him. How had he gotten back across the room again so fast? Rakken's eyes blazed emerald a handspan away, heat emanating from him. Blood trickled from one nostril. Was that Marius's fault? They were both still naked, and it was somehow more intimate now that he couldn't hear what Rakken was thinking.

"I am sorry, Marius. I should have thought to try that earlier."

Rakken's apology unbalanced Marius nearly as badly as his ringing head.

"You're apologising?" he blurted out. "Wait, you're apologising for not compelling me sooner?"

"It did not work, so technically I did not compel you despite my attempting to do so."

Marius sucked in a sharp breath. "That's dancing a hell of a technicality. Did you know it would have that effect?"

Rakken shrugged. "I thought it worth trying." He winced and rubbed at the nape of his neck. "I also thought I'd brought my own shields up fast enough to avoid any side effect, but clearly I am out of practice. Or you are growing in power. I warned you that was a possible side effect of flaming out."

"I didn't exactly choose to do it either time. Or now." Little warning lights were sparking at the edges of his vision. It struck him that of all his fantasies of the two of them naked—and truthfully there had been rather a lot—none had included feeling ill and using Rakken to steady himself as his legs threatened to give out.

Rakken frowned and then, without ceremony, bent and scooped him up as if he were a child and not a grown man. Marius squawked indignantly. Rakken dumped him on the mattress and crawled in after him, and Marius found himself once again caged in a nest of warm limbs and feathers as Rakken began to knead his shoulders. To Marius's combined irritation and relief, it actually helped with his pounding temples.

"I don't—what—you can't just—" he grumbled, but it came out drowsy.

"Go to sleep, starling," Rakken said. "The world will be just as complicated in the morning."

19

HINTS OF TRAGIC BACKSTORY

A FAE WITH HAIR striped like a golden tiger smiled, and Marius woke with a start, mind blurry with unfamiliar images and heart thudding with the need to escape. The image faded as he realised it wasn't his, but the emotion stayed, leaving his gut churning.

Rakken didn't wake from his nightmare. He lay curled like a twitching spider on the other side of the massive bed, the rich brown of his skin drained of vibrancy by the moonlight. His long hair was a nest of coiling tentacles, ink against the white sheets. He shifted, the lines of his face strained.

"No," Rakken muttered. He sounded wrong; he sounded afraid. He jerked his head, hands fisting at the sheets. "No."

"Rake," Marius said, putting a tentative hand on Rakken's chest.

The next few moments were both disorienting and alarming. Rakken reacted with sudden violence, on top of him, the movement rough and driving the air from Marius's lungs. Something cold and sharp touched Marius's neck. "Rake!" Marius croaked, panicked.

Awareness snapped into those green eyes, horror following
on its heels. Rakken flung the blade he'd summoned across the
room, where it clattered somewhere out of sight. He stared
down at Marius, pinned under him, his expression as rattled
as Marius felt. "I could have killed you. Storms, I could have killed you."
Rakken's voice shook.

He'd slept, somehow—and Maelstrom knew how that had
happened. How could he have slept, with someone else in the
same room, in the same bed? He hadn't even considered that
might be a risk. He'd intended to let Marius fall asleep and then
withdraw. What if he'd come to his senses a mere half-second
later? Mortals were so fragile, and if he'd harmed this one—

"I'm fine. Well, slightly squashed, but otherwise fine,"
Marius said.

Rakken put a hand to Marius's neck, fingers lightly brushing
the line where the knife had pressed. He gave a deep, shuddering breath and rolled off him—off the bed too. He was gone
straight out of the room—naked as the bloody day—before
Marius had quite registered what was going on.

Marius sat up and stared fuzzily about the empty bedroom,
his heart pounding with ebbing adrenaline. He put a hand to
his neck. It came away clean; Rakken hadn't broken the skin.
What had he been dreaming of that had left him so rattled?
The way Rakken had mumbled in his sleep, how frightened he'd sounded—that wasn't like Rakken at all. Concern
rubbed at him.

Marius put on his spectacles and borrowed one of the silk
robes hanging on a hook by the door, blue embroidered with
peach snapdragons. Some people might be happy to wander
about nude, but he wasn't one of them.

Downstairs, the living area was dark and empty. Had Rakken left the tower? But then Marius spotted the open door to the balcony, saw the figure standing in shadow, looking out over the dark city.

Rakken didn't turn as he padded over. The balcony made him anxious, since it had no railing and dropped away to sheer, terrifying verticality, but the night was still. Eyeing the edge of the balcony, he kept Rakken between him and the drop. He hesitated a moment as he drew closer, then slung an arm around Rakken's waist. Rakken gave a soft sigh and raised his wing to better accommodate him, which was equivalent to a public announcement that he wanted the comfort.

They stood for a while. Rakken radiated heat through the thin silk of Marius's robe. Even in darkness, the differences between Aerest and Meridon were apparent. For one thing, the sky was far clearer and full of swirling, unfamiliar constellations, interrupted by the dark shapes of the many towers. Even the lights were subtly different to those at home. Less harsh, Marius thought—a city lit entirely with magic.

"So, do you try to kill people in your sleep often?" he asked Rakken.

Rakken let out a soft breath, almost a laugh. "No. But I do not usually sleep in the presence of others; it may have triggered something in my subconscious." Had his subconscious decided that Marius Valstar was no threat? Was that why he'd inadvertently slept?

"Thanks for that," Marius couldn't help grumbling. On the one hand, of course he didn't want Rakken to see him as an enemy. On the other, he was man enough not to want to be seen as weak. "Also, you're not shielding."

"I could equally claim that neither are you." But there was

that sense of pressure easing that meant Rakken had bolstered his mental walls. "I am sorry. I did not mean to endanger you, but it does not lessen the fact that I did." He made an aggravated sound. "I detest the number of apologies I am making these days."

"Maybe you should take the knives out of your pocket dimension at night. There's a finite number of them in there, isn't there?" Marius wasn't sure what point he was arguing. He didn't want to repeat tonight's awakening either, but he'd, well, he'd liked it up until then, sharing a bed. And insult aside, he liked that Rakken had let himself be vulnerable enough to sleep.

Rakken's eyes were full of shadows. "Knives are not my only weapon."

"What a reassuring thing to say," Marius said drily. "But also, that being the case, I don't actually think you were trying to kill me. You hesitated." Unpleasant as the thought was, he didn't think he could have stopped Rakken otherwise, not with how fast fae could move.

Rakken's mouth formed a hard line, but he didn't pull away. If anything, his fingers spread on Marius's waist, warm through the thin fabric of the robe, the tiniest of invitations to draw closer. There was an odd hesitancy to him as he searched Marius's expression, as if he were waiting for something. As if he wanted something he could not voice.

On instinct, Marius lifted a hand and traced down Rakken's cheek. Rakken leaned into the touch like a cat, turning his face against Marius's palm and pressing his lips to his fingertips. This time Marius recognised the question in his eyes, and he answered it by hugging him.

There was a moment where Rakken was all rigid angles before his tension dropped away. He buried his nose in Marius's neck and inhaled, feathers rustling as he brought his wings in more tightly. Marius wondered how often he let himself accept comfort from anyone.

"You are coddling me like a frightened child, when it is I who must have frightened you," Rakken murmured, his lips warm against Marius's skin, a contrast to the cool of the night.

He shivered. "You definitely *alarmed* me," he admitted.

Rakken pulled back, shadows in his eyes as he searched Marius's face. Marius didn't know what he was looking for, or if he found it. "It will not happen again. Sleep was not part of this arrangement in any case."

Right. Neither was this intimate scene of comfort between them now, Marius supposed. Still, he wasn't so inhuman as to leave Rakken to it.

"Do you want to talk about whatever gave you nightmares?" he asked.

"No. Talk of something else. Tell me about John Tidwell."

Marius jerked. "What?"

"John Tidwell," Rakken repeated. "He was one of your past lovers, was he not? Indulge me, since I have bared an inordinate amount of my own love life in the past day."

Try *only* past lover. Which Marius had no intention of revealing.

"Um. Yes. He was. He was… good looking. Charming. I loved him. More fool me, as it turned out." Why had he said that? But it was a relief to say it. So few people knew of his relationship with John, and none of them had really understood why Marius hadn't gotten over it sooner. But, foolish or not, he had loved John, and he hadn't been able to switch the emotion off simply and cleanly, despite everything.

The truth of that past tense felt odd but good, a hard

foundation of strength. It had taken an agonisingly long time to feel it, the freedom from love's toxic bindings. He looked out over this strange fae city, hushed in the darkness, and felt the relief of the knowledge. He didn't love John anymore.

"Why did you fall in love with him?" Rakken sounded genuinely curious.

No one else had ever asked Marius that.

Marius had puzzled over the same question, as love had withered into despair and regret, then bloomed again as anger, then finally—finally—begun to fade. He didn't like any of the answers he'd come up with. *Because he was handsome and charming and paid attention to me, and I was so lonely.* Because Marius was stupid and naïve in ways he was determined never to be again.

"I don't know," he said.

Rakken canted his head. "Do you fall in love frequently?"

"I'm not going to fall in love with you, if that's what you're worried about," he snapped, irritated. "'It's just sex'," he said, quoting Rakken's own words back at him.

"If you can use the word 'just' to describe it, I need to try harder," Rakken murmured, in a tone that sent a shiver of arousal through Marius.

"Come back to bed, then," Marius said.

He did, but afterwards, as Marius lay in loose-limbed drowsiness, he left, and Marius fell asleep alone. He told himself it didn't bother him.

20

THE AWKWARD MORNING AFTER

MARIUS WOKE SORE and thirsty. *The wages of sin*, he supposed, stretching and expecting to encounter—but there was nothing. He opened his eyes. The other side of the bed was empty. When he touched the rumpled sheets, they were cool. Then he remembered that Rakken hadn't slept, afterwards. Or at least, he hadn't slept here.

Which was… fine, obviously. This wasn't a romance.

The warm dregs of sleep fell away, and he sat up, feeling self-conscious and wary. He was alone in Rakken's vast bedroom, in a pool of light from the skylight. Clouds moved across the glass, far above. How late had he slept? Probably not that late, since the skylight's lack of curtains allowed the light to stream down undiluted.

Did Rakken never wish to have a lie-in? Oh gods, he was one of nature's early riser types, wasn't he? Marius added this offence to the list of Rakken's other vices. Unless Rakken possessed a second, darker bedroom that he used for actual sleeping. *Also possible*, he allowed, remembering Rakken's night terror. The episode felt like a dream in daylight, that glimpse between Rakken's impenetrable armour. Strangely intimate.

Unsettled by the direction of his thoughts, he got out of the bed and purloined a dressing gown again. Now just what was the etiquette in this situation? He spotted a stack of towels, clean clothes, and bandages left meaningfully out. They were topped with another vial of the pain-easing potion from yesterday. Marius eyed it, wondering if this represented consideration or a hint that Rakken wished to limit further interaction. Perhaps last night had been 'sufficient' for him, enough to snuff out his half of the desire that simmered between them.

Maybe it's sufficient for me also, Marius thought hopefully. Maybe now he knew what all that burning tension led to, he'd—

Oh, who was he trying to fool? That had been the best sex of his life; he was hardly going to turn down the opportunity for more if it arose. Though he'd feign nonchalance if he had to. He couldn't imagine anything worse than Rakken treating the entire thing as an average Tuesday.

He padded through to the bathroom. It was even more impressive in daylight, with a sunken pool filled with slow-moving heated water. The benefits of royalty, he thought, watching the current. An image of the sunset reflecting in the water lily pond came to him, and his heart gave an odd squeeze.

No, he told his heart sternly as he washed. None of that. *Just because he can be personable when he chooses and hints at possessing a tragic backstory in the dark of night doesn't magically make him anything but a bad idea. Remember how insufferable he can be? Remember how casually he cast off Emyranthus, a lover of several decades? Remember how miserable you made yourself pining after John? Hmmm?*

Drying himself off made the wound on his arm ache, and he unstopped the vial of potion Rakken had left and swallowed it down before sorting through the clothes. They were not as outlandish as some of the fashions he'd seen in Aerest yesterday, but they were decidedly not Prydinian in style. The trousers were gathered at the ankles and a bit snugger than he'd prefer, and the borrowed shirt had a strange neckline and was made of a silky dove-grey fabric with tiny leaves embroidered in the design. It had sleeves adorned with a thousand buttons along the inside of each forearm. Marius grew tired of doing them up before he'd gotten halfway down the first one, gave up, and rolled the sleeves up to his elbows instead.

He inspected the result doubtfully in the mirror afterwards, noting absently that he needed to shave. His fingertips ghosted over the bruise on his neck where Rakken had bitten him. He flushed. Oh well. He could borrow a scarf too before he went out.

He was half-prepared to find himself alone in the tower, so it was a slight shock to find Rakken in the main lounge as he came downstairs. Rakken was sprawled reading on the low-backed sofa with his wings spread. Thistlefel had returned and sat just inside the glass balcony doors, watching the flying denizens of the city pass.

"Er, good morning," Marius said.

Rakken didn't look up but made a faint sound of acknowledgement and waved at a covered tray and teapot on the coffee table. Not exactly the greeting one hoped for from a lover the morning after. Though what greeting should one hope for? There hadn't been that many morning afters with John. Often they'd parted late the night before rather than take the risk.

The times they had awoken together, Marius mostly remembered feeling pathetically desperate to please, trying to ensure John didn't regret staying.

He didn't feel at all desperate to please now, but he did feel... off balance. Thistlefel turned from the view and gave a soft chirp of acknowledgement before trotting over to Marius and pushing her head against his leg. Had she gotten larger in just the last day? He bent to pet her ear tufts whilst surreptitiously watching Rakken.

Last night didn't seem to have made Rakken any softer or more approachable. If anything, he was giving off a strong do-not-approach aura, turning the page he was reading as if it were far more interesting than Marius's arrival. Too pointed a setup to be accidental, though.

Fine, Marius thought with exasperation. *Cue taken. Boundary lines firmly re-drawn after you unintentionally showed a single moment of vulnerability last night. Gods forbid.*

"Find anything useful?" he asked and went over to make himself tea.

Rakken turned another page. "I'm trying to discover why that helichaun"—he waved in Thistlefel's direction without looking up—"has altered so. This text is from before the Iron Law, and there is some reference to the effects of fae magic on mortals, but only an enticing hint of the reverse. Severenn always does favour portence over clarity in her writings."

"*You're* complaining about someone else being vague?"

"I do not..." Rakken looked up, and Marius had the satisfaction of seeing him utterly lose his train of thought. His eyes widened as he took in Marius's damp hair and borrowed outfit, lingering on his bare forearms and the snugly fitted trousers in a way that could only be described as hungry.

Guess it's not out of his system, then, Marius thought with satisfaction. He grinned, unable to resist saying: "That look was very good for my ego, Rakken Tempestren."

Rakken gave a choked laugh and shifted his long legs from the sofa, making space. "Come and have it stroked further then, distracting mortal," he suggested.

Marius calmly added milk to his tea and indicated Thistlefel with the cup. "Is she changing because she consumed my blood? Because I'm telepathic?"

There was a hint of a smile playing about Rakken's mouth. "If you come here, I will show you the relevant passage and you may take what you can from it."

Marius put the cup down and went and sat primly on the other end of the sofa. "Well? Show me this book," he prompted.

Rakken's hint of smile blossomed into open delight. The full effect of that hit Marius in the chest and knocked the breath out of him. When was the last time he'd seen Rakken smile without an edge of caution or deceit? Had he ever? It left him feeling rather dazed and made him helpless to resist when Rakken pulled him into his lap and began to kiss him in a slow, leisurely manner.

Marius was so thoroughly addled by the time Rakken released him that he gasped, "Book!" incoherently.

"*Not* the ejaculation one hopes for, but very well." Rakken reached matter-of-factly past him to pick up the book he'd set down.

Marius took a few blinks to process what Rakken had said and then gave a soft groan. "The more dirty puns you make, the more I wonder how anyone can take your 'Fear me, I'm a Terrible Fae Prince' persona seriously."

Rakken only smirked as he began to read aloud: "'I have

heard reports that the Mortal Realm may influence certain types of lowfae, but I have not been able to substantiate any of these claims. There is good evidence that some lowfae are more tolerant of iron, such as house-brownies, but this may be merely due to their low baseline magic.'" Rakken put the book down. "Severenn then goes on to espouse her theories on iron and magic, but there is no other mention I can find of other effects on lowfae, and nothing at all on helichauns specifically." He shifted, the motion rustling his feathers against the back of the sofa.

Marius put a hand on Rakken's wing, and Rakken's eyes heated.

"I wasn't imagining that last night, then. You do like your wings being touched."

"Yes. More so in the inner wing." Rakken watched intently as Marius walked his fingers up the curve of his wing and shivered as he got closer to his shoulders. "You have my full encouragement to continue this voyage of discovery." His voice had roughened.

At that moment, the wards flared with a soft chiming sound, and Rakken swore, his attention snapping towards his balcony. A winged figure landed in a flash of blue and silver.

Marius stared through the glass in horror, but it must have had some magic to it, because Wyn showed no sign of having seen them even though Marius was looking directly at him. Marius shot to his feet, almost tripping in his haste to untangle himself from Rakken.

Rakken sighed deeply and snapped his fingers. "Oh, very well. Go and welcome my interfering little brother."

The wards flared, and Wyn pushed open the balcony door. He looked worried, and he let out an audible sound of relief when he saw Marius.

"Marius! Are you all right?" Wyn crossed the distance between them in rapid strides and went to clasp his shoulder. But before he completed the motion, he reared back. His startled gaze met Marius's, as if he hadn't fully taken in his appearance or borrowed clothing until that moment.

He knows. He couldn't know. There was no logical way Wyn could know. But Marius flushed anyway, recalling Rakken's drawled promise to drive his scent into Marius's skin.

He heard Wyn's thought then, clear as crystal: *I'm going to strangle Rake. Can't he keep his storms-tossed hands to himself?*

It wasn't Rakken's hands Wyn should be worried about, Marius thought, followed by a desperate hope that he wasn't projecting right now. He avoided Wyn's gaze and scrabbled for some control over his telepathy, trying to will the heat in his cheeks to cool. Gods. Damn. It. He could do what he liked. What did it matter what Wyn did or didn't think?

"Marius?"

Right. He'd gotten distracted and had now forgotten what the actual question had been. Wyn seemed to realise this, for he repeated himself gently: "Are you all right? We got word from Caroline that there was an attack at your college last night and that you'd disappeared. Cat sent word you'd been injured and were in ThousandSpire. This morning." Wyn shot his brother a pointed look, and Marius caught in it the echo of twenty-four hours' concern, of Caroline catching a glimpse of broken windows, and Hetta desperately prodding Stariel for a clue to her brother's wellbeing.

"Sorry," Marius said. "I didn't think."

"There was no need for you to fret, little Hollow," Rakken said to his brother. "I had things in hand." He got up with studied insouciance, wandered over to Marius, and draped an arm around his waist. Marius startled at the touch and flushed even hotter, not helped by the *Truly?* he felt coming off Wyn in waves.

"Tea?" Marius said helplessly, moving away from them both in a horrible tangle of awkwardness.

"Ah, yes, thank you," Wyn said with less than his usual composure, looking between Marius and Rakken. Marius could count on one hand the number of times he'd seen Wyn embarrassed, but there were faint stripes of colour on his cheekbones now. "I'm... glad you're all right. What exactly happened? With the attack yesterday," he added hastily. *Storms know I don't want to know about between then and now.*

Marius winced at the stray thought.

"Your shields are fraying, Hollow," Rakken murmured.

A sense of something easing, and Wyn sent Marius an apologetic look. "My apologies; Stariel has made me careless." He frowned, searching his face. "Is it getting worse?"

Marius shrugged. "I don't know." Yes. It was, and he didn't want to think about what that might mean if the trend continued.

Wyn accepted the cup of tea Marius offered and sat warily in one of Rakken's armchairs. "The attack yesterday?" he prompted.

Marius shot a quick glance at Rakken, who had re-draped himself along the sofa as if he hadn't a care in the world. "Rake's, er, former lover turned up at my college and stabbed me—a woman named Emyranthus. Rake arrived and frightened her off before she could finish me off." Marius touched the wound on his arm, feeling the bandage through the shirt.

Wyn blinked at his brother. "The sorceress?"

The fact that Wyn knew Emyranthus was a strange reminder of Wyn's personal history. Marius was so used to thinking of him as falling firmly on the human, Stariel side of things—but he had grown up in ThousandSpire, after all, even if he'd spent the last decade or so in the human world.

Rakken gave a careless shrug. "The very same."

"And she was trying to kill Marius because…?" Wyn asked.

"Spires business, little brother." There was a warning note in Rakken's voice.

Wyn stiffened. "Not if it involves fae attacking humans— and my family. Word has already reached Queen Matilda of a fae altercation, and it is only a matter of time before the story breaks publicly. They will want explanations—and reassurance."

Marius wasn't sure whether to be touched at being so easily claimed as family or annoyed at yet again being seen as a burden in need of shielding.

"I will deal with Emyr, and I will deal with the mortal fallout, should it become necessary. Perhaps you forget that I am already on the relevant subcommittee in Meridon; I am perfectly capable of providing an official explanation to them myself." Rakken was still sprawled like a lazy cat, but his edges had sharpened, and there was a hint of storms in the air. Marius knew it was Rakken's magic even though all the Tempestren siblings had that storm edge to their signatures. And he knew, moreover, that it was deliberate. Rakken had far too much control to let it spill over accidentally.

"So you don't know where Emyranthus is now, then?" Wyn's voice hardened. "Did she kill Vane?"

"If she did, she will face the justice of the Spires. You are not required here, Hollow."

"That's not how this works, Rake, and you know it. What

if she attacks a mortal again? Is that why you've brought Marius here?"

Rakken and Wyn glared at each other, at an impasse. Marius had a hysterical urge to laugh. He was intelligent enough to know this wasn't about him, even if he felt a bit like a bone between two dogs; Rakken was Wyn's older brother by some margin, and Wyn was still fighting to be taken seriously as a grown man—fae—in Rakken's eyes. Fae were hierarchical, and Wyn's new role as both Consort to a faelord and the High King's designated ambassador to Mortal arguably gave him a greater position than Rakken within that.

He had a sense that Wyn, too, was reminding himself of these facts at this moment.

Both brothers' heads snapped towards the balcony. It was Catsmere, landing with quick precision. She stretched out her wings for a moment before folding them behind her. Coming through the doors, she took in the situation in a single glance. "Hallowyn."

Wyn had risen at her entrance, and they clasped hands in greeting, genuine warmth in the interaction. "Thank you for sending word, though I would have appreciated it sooner."

Catsmere gave him a cool look. "Don't blame me. I tried to frighten Marius off back to Mortal yesterday. I doubt you would have been more effective."

"What?" Marius spluttered, feeling dim. "That's what that was?"

She inspected Marius from head to toe without a change in expression and then looked blandly at her twin. "Mouse?"

"I was explaining to our dear little brother that his interference is neither needed nor wanted."

"And I was explaining that this isn't only Spires business,

since it involves mortals," Wyn said tersely.

"If by mortals, we mean only Marius Valstar, then this is a matter between members of my court, and I will deal justice to Emyranthus accordingly."

"Cat," Rakken said, a warning. Wyn looked equally displeased.

"Could we stop talking about me as if I'm not standing right here, please?" Marius said. "Also, it seems like the main thing is to discover whether Emyranthus killed Vane or not. If it was her, you can argue about what to do about it once you know for sure. If she didn't, then as the person she did actually attack, I should get a say in this, not your bloody fae or mortal politics."

Wyn searched his face and nodded. "You are right. How likely am I to persuade you to come to Stariel until Emyranthus is found?"

"Not very. It's the middle of term, and the university won't grant me leave. I'm already on thin ice there as it is."

Wyn frowned. "Thin ice is better than dead, Marius. I cannot be in Knoxbridge full time."

It was a mark of Wyn's concern that he'd even considered it, given Hetta's current condition and his other responsibilities. Marius touched the wound on his arm. Rakken had been his bodyguard once before, and he found himself waiting for Rakken to raise the subject again.

But it was Catsmere who spoke, matter-of-factly. "Rakken will act as his bodyguard and get to the bottom of this mortal mystery while he is doing so."

"Oh, will I?" Rakken asked. "I am hardly free of duties either. What of the negotiations with the mortal court?"

"Take him with you as needed."

"Very well," Rakken said after a moment. "I suppose it is my fault he is in danger, after all. A debt I should repay." He met

Marius's eyes, and Marius had no idea what he was thinking.

Is that how you think of me? It was on Marius's tongue to say, but he wasn't fool enough to refuse the offer of protection. He didn't fancy meeting Emyranthus alone again. "Fine," Marius said. It came out as a bite of a word.

There was an awkward lull that he told himself he was imagining.

Wyn cleared his throat. "I had another reason to find you, Marius. I had word of a telepath who might be able to teach you."

Marius looked up, hope beating in his throat.

"In Galial—" Wyn began, but Rakken cut him off.

"Your information is out of date," Rakken said. "I have already spoken to them. They cannot help."

Both Wyn and Marius stared at Rakken. Catsmere, however, did not look as if this were news to her.

Marius took a sharp breath, intuition hitting in a sudden rush. "That's where you were, when you stumbled out of that portal na—near me."

Rakken smiled, but it faded as he spoke. "Yes. I found the telepath in question, but they were not in control of their powers. They were mad, or close to it, though they hid it well at first." *Which I wish I'd realised before I dropped my shielding as part of the bargain I negotiated.* It would have saved him a ringing head and a precarious exit that had involved a humiliating tumble into the darksink full of blade-ghasts that had guarded the telepath's lair.

"That's what had you so addled when you arrived!" Marius accused. "When were you planning to tell me this?" Darksinks were places of dark magic in Faerie.

Rakken shrugged. "What purpose would it have served?

As I have just said, that telepath was not a useful source of information."

"Don't try to tell me that's why you kept it secret—you just didn't want to admit someone had bested you!" He narrowed his eyes. "Or that you were trying to do something nice, for once."

Rakken didn't react to this entirely true accusation. "Hardly. An uncontrolled telepath connected to my allies profits me nothing, and my brother has offered considerable reward for finding a teacher. It was logical to search my own sources for answers. But since it seems increasingly unlikely we will discover a telepathic teacher for you, I think the best option is for you to teach yourself, using my compulsion as a tool in that."

Marius frowned. "How?"

"Your powers react instinctively to compulsion. Triggering them in such a manner could be a starting point for you to develop a better awareness of them, and from there, control."

"Every time that happens, I flame out and end up unconscious shortly afterwards," Marius pointed out. He didn't like this at all, though he wasn't sure how much of that was anger at Rakken for being so opaque. Again. Couldn't he have just told Marius why he'd been in Knoxbridge? Why did everything with him have to be so bloody difficult?

"A question of calibration, I suspect. I used too strong a compulsion last time."

Wyn frowned, and a hint of his magic lit the air. "You compelled him?"

Rakken gave Wyn a sardonic look. "Yes, under quite enjoyable circumstances for us both."

Wyn winced, but Marius's attention went to Catsmere, who had gone even stiller than her usual watchfulness for a moment.

"Mouse…" she said, sounding worried.

Rakken shook his head. "Nothing like that, Cat."

"Nothing like what?" Wyn asked sharply.

But it was clear that Rakken had worn through his patience. He rose in a rustle of feathers, every inch the imperious prince. "I do not owe you an account of my personal affairs, brother. We are done here."

"*You* are done," Marius said evenly. "I want to talk to Wyn. Alone."

It was satisfying to have three pairs of eyes look at him in surprise.

Catsmere was first to rise. "Let us fly, then, Mouse. If you are to be in Mortal for an extended period, there are things we must discuss before you go."

Rakken gave an exasperated huff but acceded to the request. The twins left, matching wings glittering as they dropped over the balcony.

Wyn remained seated. He canted his head, fixing Marius with a quizzical look.

Marius squirmed a bit.

"Are you going to tell Hetta?" he burst out.

Wyn blinked. "Tell her what, exactly?"

Marius grumbled. "Oh, don't be so bloody disingenuous; I know you know. Tell her about"—he waved at the windows, where it was just possible to see the small specks of flying figures in the distance—"him."

Wyn didn't say anything, and Marius found himself hurrying to justify himself. "It's just, she'll worry, and want to *talk* about it, gods forbid, and—it's nothing. Nothing serious. Just a, a bit of fun." He winced even as he used the phrase, the awkwardness of spelling out anything at all.

Wyn searched his face. "Ah." It was said so neutrally that Marius couldn't tell what judgement it contained, positive or negative.

"So there's no point bringing it up with her, right?"

Wyn sighed. "Hetta is not as easily shocked as you seem to think, but if you do not want me to tell her, I won't. But she has eyes." There was a long pause. "Have you learnt anything more about the circumstances surrounding Vane's murder?"

Marius clutched at the new subject gratefully. "There were some plant fragments left at the scene that we're still trying to identify. Rake didn't have any luck with tracking them back to their source. We've been looking through his library, but I really need to fetch the sketches I made for comparison. I suppose we're waiting for full moon, otherwise, and this Goblin Market, to find whoever sold the plants to Vane."

Wyn frowned. "The Goblin Market," he repeated slowly. "Not the safest of places for mortals. Or fae. Be careful, my friend." There was a penetrating look in his brown eyes that said he wasn't talking merely about the market.

21

ANTAGONISTIC ACQUAINTANCES
TO LOVERS

MARIUS STOOD IN his room back at the college, amidst strewn books and glass shards glittering in the carpet. It had rained the night of the attack, and consequently everything near the broken window was rather damp. Why did this keep happening to him, his places of sanctuary violated? At least the essays he'd been marking seemed intact, if disordered. Next to him, Rakken said nothing.

The college Keeper, Mrs Wright, spoke anxiously beside them, largely addressing her remarks to Rakken. Whatever Rakken had said to the Dean had left the college's domestic staff in awe of him, but there was a thread of unease below that, with Mrs Wright silently wondering if there would be any *more* fae attacks and if the staff were in danger. Aloud, Mrs Wright was promising that the glazier would be round on Tuesday; they'd get the windows boarded up smartly, but a bed could be made up for Mr Valstar temporarily somewhere. Marius heard her only distantly. The wound on his arm gave a twinge.

A hand pressed on his shoulder and made him start. Rakken

squeezed and then let his hand drop. "No need," Rakken said to Mrs Wright. "I will accommodate Mr Valstar until the repairs are done."

"As you say, Your Highness."

Marius flushed, even though there was nothing outwardly improper in Rakken's offer, and he *was* grateful for an escape from the college for a few days, while the initial furore died down. He'd been aware of whispers following him on his way in, stray bits of forceful thoughts and speculation rubbing against him.

He covered his awkwardness by starting to gather his things, including the sketch book that contained the drawings of the plant fragments. Perhaps if he brought them to Rakken's library, he'd have more success identifying them. This inevitably made him think of other things that had already occurred in Rakken's library, and he flushed again.

Gods, how did one *do* this, act naturally around a lover? What even *was* acting naturally around Rakken, who had to be the cause of more unnatural behaviour than any living creature? Why must Marius feel the awkwardness like an itch under his skin? No one would know anything simply by *looking* at the two of them. No one would bat an eyelid. He had perfectly above-board reasons for being in Rakken's company, given their family's connection. People would assume they were friends.

Were they friends?

It was *fine*. Everything, in fact, was fine. Extremely fine.

"Thanks for, er, accommodating me," Marius said after they left the college.

"As you pointed out, it is my fault Emyranthus attacked you and thus damaged your current abode."

Right. Debts, which must be paid in fae culture.

"I brought the sketches I made of the fae plants. Might have more luck trawling through your library with them. Er. Are we going back there? How is this going to work, exactly? I have a meeting later this afternoon with my supervisor. And you have… committee meetings at the palace? When exactly?" They hadn't discussed anything properly, and it felt easier to focus on logistics rather than more fraught subjects. They could not attend the Goblin Market until full moon, but Rakken was hopeful that he might hear word of Emyranthus before then.

"For much of this coming week. I will need to reassure your politicians I have things in hand here," Rakken said. They talked of their respective schedules, which somehow managed to make Marius feel even further off-balance, too close as it was to domesticity.

That feeling only increased as Rakken showed him into the flat he'd taken on Pennyroyal Lane, not far from the gardens. Being Rakken, the place was fit for a prince. There were even multiple bedrooms, for form's sake.

And for when he gets bored of you, Marius couldn't help thinking, and then told his brain to shush as he dumped his things there. That was what he wanted anyway—for this to end neatly and cleanly and without emotional investment from either party. Why let that spoil the present enjoyment to be had?

He turned around slowly in the centre of the living room, taking it in. Outside, it began to rain, falling at first in dainty patters but steadily thickening until the view blurred into light and shadow. There was a chessboard set up by the windows, between two armchairs. It was a custom table, inlaid with the squares of the board, and the pieces were carved of heavy stone. Of course Rakken would find accommodations with that sort of nicety included.

For a moment Marius stood back in Stariel's drawing room on a winter's night, with the storm outside and the firelight glinting off the chess pieces. A bittersweet memory; the games had been well enough, but those years at Stariel before his father's death…

He gave himself a shake. "Do you play?" he asked.

"Of course. Do you?"

"Yes," he said. "I'm no grand master, but I can account for myself. Wyn and I used to play a lot. He's better than I am, though I didn't always lose."

"Cat and I taught him and Torquil to play," Rakken said, sounding almost wistful. "I had forgotten."

Marius had an odd moment of realising that Wyn was, despite everything, Rakken's little brother. A little brother whose life he hadn't been part of for the decade when Wyn had lived at Stariel.

"Where is Torquil now?" Marius had only met the brother who came between Wyn and the twins once.

"EdgeSmoke. Another court. He defected there some years ago rather than continue under our father's rule. Cat has been trying to persuade him to return his allegiance to ThousandSpire." Rakken stared out at the pouring rain. "Seven children of the great King Aeros Tempestren, and none of them now at ThousandSpire but Cat and me. What does that say about us?"

"That you have an even more complicated family than the Valstars." He hesitated. "Or perhaps that you respect each other's freedom. Hetta didn't come home for half a decade while I was stuck there, but now she's inherited, *I* don't live at Stariel anymore, and that's a good thing."

"This is a terrible attempt at comfort," Rakken said, still

watching the rain. "I assume you were attempting comfort?"

"Fine, just keep staring at the rain and brooding, then, Prince Melodramatic."

Rakken's lips curved. "No, I think I am done now." He turned away from the window.

Marius told himself it would be immature to throw a chess piece at him. Instead, he moved away from the table and began to unpack the sketches he'd made. He was strangely *aware* of Rakken in a way he couldn't quite ignore. Would Rakken want to try the experimental telepathy lessons he'd suggested now? Marius wasn't looking forward to it, remembering how much his head had ached last time.

Rakken sighed. "What is wrong, Marius Valstar?"

"What makes you think anything is wrong?"

"You protested about my claiming possession of you far less than I expected, earlier, and you are being suspiciously quiet now."

That startled him. "Claiming *possession* of me? Offering me temporary house-room because your terrible ex-lover destroyed my room is hardly—" Rakken smiled, and Marius broke off, muttering, "—and you're winding me up on purpose."

"Well done."

Marius rolled his eyes. "It's just… this doesn't feel especially casual." He gestured around at the flat and his own stack of things.

Rakken shrugged. "Why should it not be? Your room being damaged was a convenient excuse to relocate you in any case; I cannot ward your nights from a distance. It shall also be easier not to have to go so far to fetch you, since I must take you with me when I traipse back and forth." His grin grew a bit wicked. "There are also other benefits."

Marius put the papers down, feeling both reassured and strangely annoyed. "Of course."

But Rakken had gone abruptly and oddly sober, all the wickedness drained from his expression. He looked, if anything, alarmed. "I do not accept sex as payment or out of obligation. If you—"

"I know that! Honestly, of all things." Marius shook his head in disbelief. "Also, I don't feel particularly obliged to you right now."

The moment of oddness faded, replaced with a flaring ember of interest. "You don't, do you?" Rakken said archly, prowling closer.

We ought to have started shagging sooner, Marius reflected. *It would have shortened a lot of arguments.*

22

VOYEURISTIC SPELL CASTING

"—AND THEN, OF course, Papa started waxing lyrical about Archetypes of the Unconscious," Caroline said, putting her fork down. Her father was a professor of psychology. "Gods help us if he really does try to set up a study on fae psychology."

"Gods help us if he tries to start with Rakken," Marius said, and Caro laughed.

The two of them were having lunch at a small riverside inn, Marmalade Punts, in the sheltered courtyard that directly overlooked the water. It had been some days since Emyranthus's attack. He and Rakken had been shuttling back and forth between their various commitments in Knoxbridge and Meridon all week until he'd begun to feel like a sycamore seed in the wind. Sometimes they took the train; sometimes they flew. Portals within the Mortal Realm were currently limited to emergencies only, in a gesture meant to reassure everybody that greater fae would not be popping up from under every rock without warning. The fact that there had been two violent portal-related incidents in Knoxbridge—Vane's murder and Emyranthus's attack on Marius—was reportedly causing Rakken some difficulties with said reassurance.

Autumn sunshine had warmed the courtyard enough to make dining outdoors almost pleasant, and he'd removed his greatcoat and folded it over the spare seat beside them. Thistlefel lay curled up snoozing in a pool of sunshine, but she looked up hopefully at the scrape of cutlery. Caro laughed and flicked her a bit of leftover crust, which Thistlefel caught and wolfed down in a single smooth movement. He'd so far found few foods that she would turn her nose up at.

The Marmalade was an old favourite of Caro's, but he suspected that wasn't the only reason she'd suggested it today. It was a quieter establishment, away from the main thoroughfares. Just now there was only one other occupied table in the courtyard, an elderly couple. In other words, there were few minds here to overwhelm him, and few people who might see through his 'dog's' glamour. He was grateful for the consideration and annoyed at having to be.

"She's growing at quite a rate, isn't she?" Caro observed, watching Thistlefel. "Do you know how big she'll end up?"

"No, and neither does Rake," he said. "This isn't standard behaviour for helichauns, apparently. I've been taking measurements and plotting her growth curve, and it does *seem* to be slowing." He played with the edge of his napkin.

Caro gave him a measuring sort of look. "And where is your royal bodyguard today?"

"Talking to the police, I think." He sighed. Rakken had quickly had both the local police force and the entire botany department sorted along a spectrum between eating-out-of-his-hand and in-worried-awe-of-him. There had been no sign of Emyranthus so far, for all the 'feelers' both Rakken and Wyn had sent out and all the scrying Rakken had cast.

"It doesn't seem like very good bodyguarding, leaving you alone like this." There were questions in her grey eyes that made him itch with awkwardness, even though there was no way she could *know* anything, whatever she suspected. It was none of her business in any case. He was a grown man, and he could do what he liked. Or who he liked.

"He gave me a personal shield spell," he said, reaching a hand to his neck, where the amulet hung beneath his collar. "And he's still in Knoxbridge." He sighed again. "How do I keep ending up in situations where I *need* a bodyguard?" This was the second time he'd been lumped with Rakken for that reason, although last time there had been more arguing and fewer... other activities.

"And you really think this Emyranthus person killed Vane?"

"It could have been her, if she came to my greenhouse for me and, I don't know, happened to find Vane there instead. Maybe she realised what Vane was doing with the lowfae and decided to destroy the fae plants for good measure." Marius ticked off the thoughts on his fingers. He'd been worrying the same ones round and round as he went to classes, taught tutorials, replanted the seedlings that had been destroyed and made notes on the growth of those that hadn't, and tried not to look over his shoulder for Emyranthus every time his healing arm itched. "It could have been whichever fae was supplying Vane with the plants, who might or might not be the same person as the dryad who made the blade. Maybe they fell out over their agreement and he took the plants back."

"It could also have been a human, couldn't it? Vane might have had an assistant who killed him and took the fae plants for himself?" Caro grimaced.

"We found Vane's assistant, and it wasn't him." Marius had seen Thomas Bakir only once since the encounter at Vane's flat, awkwardly passing him in the quad. Bakir's eyes had widened at the sight of Thistlefel trotting at his heels, but he had said nothing.

"Are you sure?"

"Yes. Rake compelled him."

Caro looked troubled. "Well, what about someone else, for reasons we haven't thought of yet? What would motivate someone to kill?"

"Love," Marius said, thinking of Emyranthus.

"Money. Power," Caro said. "If we list off the usual suspects."

"Revenge," said a deep, familiar voice that sent a shiver through him. They turned to find Rakken had silently approached while they'd been talking. He was in his mortal form, wingless, probably for the ease of sneaking up on them through the furniture maze of the courtyard. Familiarity, rather than lessening the effect of him, had only made things worse, because now Marius knew exactly what all that coiled masculine potential felt like. Every part of him rushed to maximum wakefulness.

Everything and nothing had changed between them. Rakken remained frequently aggravating, although he'd been right about having an alternative to strangling each other giving them something else to do with their energy. Sometimes, when they were alone in the evenings after long days, when Marius was grumbling about hidebound academics or Rakken was attempting to explain some bit of fae magic, it felt almost as if they were friends.

Other times, Marius felt as far away from understanding

the man as ever. Beneath it all ran an undertow of tension, the knowledge that no matter what, he had to hold himself a little detached.

Rakken took a seat at the table.

"You think someone killed Dr Vane from a desire for vengeance?" Caro asked.

Rakken shrugged. "Possibly. I thought we were merely listing motivations for murder more generally."

Marius thought of the blackmail note they'd found in Vane's desk. They still didn't know who had sent it; Rakken had tried his proximity-based tracking spell again several times now in various locations around the university without success.

Caro was saying something else, but he found himself caught in the green of Rakken's eyes. Abruptly, he was seeing *himself*, bespectacled with wind-ruffled hair, in his grey herringbone suit. The image was overlain with a memory, skin bared and sweat-slick, eyes closed and head thrown back.

How have I not yet sated this desire? Though perhaps it is for the best that my interest remains so close to hand. It would take time Rake currently did not have to seek diversion elsewhere, and it seemed likely he must be here until at least full moon and the Goblin Market, with Emyr proving so elusive. This arrangement was convenient.

Marius reared back, nearly tipping over his chair and managing to knock a teaspoon flying. Rakken caught it before it could clatter on the cobblestones and placed it back on the table.

"Sorry," he mumbled, since both his cousin and Rakken were now staring at him. He couldn't read Rakken's expression except that there was a sudden sense of smooth darkness to him. He'd bolstered his mental shields.

Marius shuffled his chair straight and tried to cover his

reaction by taking a sip of his drink. Gods. Why in Simulsen's name had his telepathy kicked in with such terrible timing? It had lain relatively quiescent since the last flameout, and he'd begun to hope that perhaps he wouldn't need to try Rakken's threatened experimental teaching methods after all. Not that Rakken had brought it up since ThousandSpire.

It was easier to focus on that than on what he'd heard Rakken thinking. His cheeks burned. Of course there was no reason why Rakken shouldn't take other lovers if he wanted. None at all. Even if he found it convenient right now not to do so, which infuriated Marius so much that he wanted to immediately seek out Bakir and anyone else Bakir knew and— No. He didn't want that either. What was *wrong* with him? He was *getting* what he wanted.

Rakken was still frowning at him, but he made a flourishing gesture with his left hand and pulled the dryad blade out of thin air. "I have been talking with your mortal authorities."

"Shouldn't that be kept as evidence?" Caro said.

Rakken ignored this. "I attended the—what is the word for the ritual butchering of a person?"

"Autopsy," he said, wincing. He thought about objecting that this was yet another subject not to be spoken of in mixed company or at the very least not over lunch, looked at Caro (who he had once seen matter-of-factly extract a bullet from a bleeding wound), and kept quiet.

"Ah, yes. I attended the autopsy. The interesting thing is that Vane wasn't killed by this blade, according to the pathologist's opinion. He was stabbed after he died. The death-wound was a blow to the head with a blunt instrument. The iron head of a nearby garden tool was used to do the deed—a rake. The object, not myself, I feel a need to emphasise here." Rakken flipped the dryad blade idly. *Was Emyr making a rather unsubtle point with that choice of implement?*

Marius remembered seeing a short, heavy rake, fallen on its side, spattered with blood. He shuddered.

"Why would someone want to stab him after he was dead?" Caro asked.

"An excellent question to which I do not yet know the answer." Rakken flipped the blade again.

"Why do you have that? I thought you said any resonance in the knife would be ruined by the violence?" Marius said.

"I thought I might identify the maker by less magical means than a spell. If the dryad who made it is at the Goblin Market, they will recognise it, and we will discover if they were Vane's contact in Faerie or if they had passed the blade to another." He pocketed it. "I did not think your mortal authorities could achieve anything more with it."

"Did you *ask* them if you could take it?" asked Caro, who by this time had some familiarity with how Rakken operated.

Rakken grinned, sudden and dazzling, and even phlegmatic Caro smiled back before she could help herself.

"Rake," Marius objected.

"You are both so ready to believe me committing crimes," Rakken complained in a wounded tone. "But I did not take this without your police's knowledge." The grin was back. "Although it would be more accurate to say that I informed them I was taking it rather than asking. I thought I might also try an experimental spell and see if I can cleanse the weapon of negative influence. The original site of contamination will be best."

"My greenhouse?"

"Yes, when you are done here. You do not have classes this

afternoon, do you? But do not let me hurry your lunch; I am content to sit quietly and be admired by you both while you finish," he said magnanimously.

Marius choked. Caro giggled.

"Generous of you, but I'm sure Marius will be sufficient," Caro said, beginning to hunt for her bag. "We were finishing up in any case."

"Have I ever told you that you are my *least* favourite cousin, Caro?"

"Oh, that's all right. It's good to have some point of distinction amongst the masses. I haven't even thought about it beyond my top five or so favourites, so I've no idea where you sit in *my* ranking of cousins," Caro said, her eyes twinkling.

Rakken chuckled. Marius glowered at both of them.

"You said you thought you could help with my telepathy," Marius said reluctantly as they walked back towards the gardens. Thistlefel trotted at their heels.

A flicker of expression, there and gone too quick to read. "I did."

"We've both been putting it off, and I hoped it might just go away by itself, but it's clearly not going to. I think we ought to test your theory and see if it helps."

Rakken went quiet for a beat. They passed the rounded dome of the Blucrag Camera, and Marius shook his head at the paperboy on the steps, who'd perked up hopefully. He didn't want to see whether Vane was still making the headlines.

Eventually, Rakken spoke. "Very well. After this."

Marius let out the breath he'd been holding. "All right."

Knoxbridge's streets were busy at this time of day. Normally he'd have to weave through bicycles, rowdy undergrads, and townsfolk, but with Rakken, there was no need. The crowds simply parted as naturally as a school of fish. Every time he was in danger of forgetting just what Rakken was capable of, something like this would happen to remind him. It was simultaneously worrying and, currently, convenient.

"What makes it an experimental spell? The one you want to try on the knife?" he asked as they reached his greenhouse.

"It means it has not yet been confirmed in the Codex as a spell that can be reproduced successfully," Rakken said, turning thoughtfully to survey the interior of the greenhouse. Marius's gaze automatically went to the patch of tiles where Vane had died, even though all evidence had long since been scrubbed away.

Rakken continued, drawing forth a tattered volume with a snap of his fingers. "I am not sure whether Severenn herself ever performed this one or if it was purely theoretical. I found it while trying to discover if she had written anything more regarding influences on lowfae. Unfortunately, I cannot find that she wrote anything more on the subject. However, she did have an interesting theory about how 'mortal influences' more generally might be stripped away by cleansing rituals. I need to search my library further."

"I want to search your library for more plant references when we're next back there," Marius said absently. He hadn't had any luck identifying the fragments from the books they'd brought with them. He flushed, realising how presumptuous he'd sounded. "Are we going back to ThousandSpire again?"

"On Saturday, unless you had some other engagement?"

Marius shook his head, feeling odd.

Rakken began to draw spell lines with chalk, which Marius supposed was at least easy to clean up afterwards. He pretended to measure seedlings but in reality couldn't help watching Rakken work. There was an air of suppressed excitement about him that he recognised; the thrill of following a theory through and seeing how far it went.

Satisfied with his work, Rakken arranged his braid over his shoulder and settled himself in the centre of the design, hands lying palm-up on his knees, one of them holding the knife. But the spell lines did not light up as Marius was used to, and a frown slowly formed between Rakken's brows.

"Nothing?"

"The spell isn't catching. Perhaps if I alter some of the parameters." But after several more attempts, it was clear that the experiment wasn't going to be successful any time soon. Rakken spun the blade and sighed. "It was such an elegant piece of magical theory."

"That's the nature of theories," Marius said. "Do you come across new spells a lot?" he asked, fascinated by this further glimpse into fae sorcery despite his current ambivalence towards said sorcerer.

"It is quite common to encounter variations on existing themes. Almost every sorcerer likes to make a few modifications to personalise their work. But I have lived long enough that I rarely encounter spells that are wholly unfamiliar to me. However, there is also a great deal of magical theory that no one has tested in practice."

"Why not?"

"Any number of reasons, from a lack of raw power to a fear of unforeseen consequences, but most often because there is a great deal of mundane work involved in developing a spell from the broad strokes of an elegant theory to a functional working, and time is limited in supply."

"Is that what you would do, if you weren't a prince? Test experimental spells?" Because it didn't take a genius to recognise that Rakken shared the same intellectual curiosity as the academics Marius worked with, even if it ran in an unusual direction. He had a suspicion most fae did not line their fantastical towers with books.

"I have never thought about what I would do if I weren't a prince," Rakken admitted. He pondered his answer as he stood and began to stretch, eventually deciding: "No, I do not think I would. I enjoy testing those spells that most interest me, but I was not made to sit for long in solitary splendour."

"You need people to admire your enormous ego."

A wicked gleam in his eyes. "Admire something enormous, in any case."

Marius groaned even as his pulse quickened.

Rakken took a step towards him.

Marius instinctively gripped the workbench behind him. "You can't... someone might see."

Let them see!

Marius's temper rose, burning out the desire that had been stirring. "All very well for you to say that! This isn't Faerie!"

Rakken frowned. "I did not say anything. But no one will see." It wasn't an idle reassurance; Rakken's magic lit the air, glamouring them.

Marius eased his grip and gave a sharp jerk of his head. "That's the second time today I've caught the edge of your thoughts. You said you'd help me try to control it, afterwards. It's afterwards."

Rakken's feathers twitched, his body tensing. "Very well." He withdrew to the far end of the greenhouse and held up a hand to stop Marius from coming any closer when he would have followed. "No. It is best if we do not risk touching, for this."

Obediently, Marius sank down on the nearest bench and looked expectantly at Rakken. "How do you want to do this, then?"

Rakken folded and refolded his wings, a rare sign of restlessness. "If you were greater fae, we would be practising the art of both giving and resisting compulsion. It is usual to start with very little compulsive strength and trivial commands, learning to give and resist compulsion in turn."

"I think I know what you mean. That's what Wyn did with my sister Alexandra—used tea flavours she disliked and told her to drink them."

Rakken's eyebrows went up.

"You can't exactly disapprove of him teaching humans, considering what we're doing right now."

"Farewell, moral high ground," Rakken said mournfully.

"I'm immune to compulsion already, though, so you're not trying to teach me to resist compulsion. You think my mental shields are related to my telepathy?"

"Yes, although I am not sure precisely how except that on several occasions you have reacted to the use of strong compulsion with psychic projection, instinctively rather than consciously activated. My proposal is very rough-edged: forcibly activate your telepathy and hope that with repetition, you will learn to recognise the trigger and from that first step, control when it triggers. My concern is that this may require the opposite approach to that one would usually take when teaching a fledgling."

Marius worked that one out. He didn't love the phrase 'forcibly activate'. "You think you'll need to compel me strongly rather than weakly for this to work?"

Rakken nodded. "At least at first. If this experiment is a success and you can become more sensitised to being triggered, I should need to use less over time to achieve the same effect. And in theory, once you can recognise that activation, you can learn how to take control over it."

"That's why you've been delaying." Marius didn't blame him, thinking of how Emyranthus had gone through that window—and how addled Rakken had been after his own encounter with the out-of-control telepath that he'd tried to keep secret. He grimaced. "Is there any way to make this safer for you?"

Rakken stared at him for long moments, blinking, and then gave a bark of laughter. "I am not worried about *my* safety. You caught me unawares before, but I should be able to shield against the psychic backlash if I am expecting it."

"Should I be worried about *my* safety, then?"

Rakken was as serious as Marius had ever seen him, holding himself taut as a bowstring. "I will keep you safe." The oath thrummed into existence.

It wasn't the most reassuring exchange they'd ever had. There was something here, some undercurrent of tension he couldn't pinpoint the reason for. "How do we start?"

Rakken swallowed, his feathers flexing restlessly again. He settled himself as far away as the space would permit and laced his hands together. The air changed, became edged with storms and citrus. Rakken's eyes were fathomless, emerald pools of too intense a colour to be real. Stray strands of his hair seemed to curl in the air like the fronds of an anemone, and the bones of his face lay sharp beneath the skin. Power beat against

Marius's eardrums.

"Marius Valstar," Rakken said, his voice primal in a way that went directly to Marius's hindbrain. "Pick up the book beside you."

Something in him uncoiled, striking out like a viper. Rakken let out an *oof* of breath and scrabbled for balance, his back hitting the wall of the potting shed with a thump. A wash of images and emotions rolled over Marius: dappled jungle, a fae with golden tiger-stripes in his hair, and a sharp cut of fear.

He shook his head, trying to clear it, and found Rakken watching him with that same fear clear in his eyes.

"I'd rather not," Marius said mildly, his head aching. "Or— am I supposed to do the things you tell me, or will this work better if I don't? *Did* it work, do you think?"

Rakken put his head in his hands and laughed and laughed. It sounded slightly hysterical.

"Rake? Are you all right?" He crossed the distance between them. When he put a hand on Rakken's shoulder, he found that he was trembling.

Rakken steadied at the touch, pulling himself back together so that by the time he looked up, that fractured vulnerability had all but disappeared. "I am fine," he said, which meant he'd come within touching distance of the opposite sentiment. "How is your head?"

"Hurts like hell," Marius admitted. "I wonder if we're going about this wrong, though. Wouldn't it make more sense to start with weak compulsion and figure out what degree of it triggers the psychic backlash from the bottom up rather than the top down, as it were?"

Rakken blinked at him and then made a sound of disgust and put his head back in his hands. Marius found it weirdly endearing but couldn't resist the temptation to tease. Turnabout and all that. "I want to hear you say, 'I think you're right, Marius; let's try it your way rather than needlessly approaching this from the point of maximum pain for us both'," he said merrily.

Rakken lifted his head again, this time to glare. "*Fine.* Fine. I do think you're right."

What was it that had so unsettled Rakken? It was something about using compulsion but not *just* about using compulsion. Rakken compelled people all the time, even if he was more judicious about it than he liked to pretend. He'd piled far stronger compulsion onto Bakir than he'd used just now and hadn't verged on hysterical relief afterwards.

"What were you afraid of?" he asked.

Rakken looked at his hands. "We are lovers," he said finally.

Marius stared at him, bewildered, before the pieces slipped into place. Just when he despaired of Rakken's amorality, he would display some finely tuned principle like this, something it hadn't even occurred to Marius could *be* a principle.

"You were worried you'd influence me. Though I'm not sure how you thought you'd get from me picking up a book to making me want to get into bed with you—even I'm not *that* much of a bibliophile. But you can't compel me, Rake. Even if you wanted to," he said firmly, because Rakken was looking at him as if he needed the reassurance. He didn't understand why Rakken should hold so much fear on this subject, but it was clear that he did.

"That much is now apparent," Rakken said, getting up. "Let us try again, then."

23

INCONVENIENT JEALOUSY

O N THE DAY of full moon, Marius found himself hiding in an alcove in the palace library in Meridon, waiting for Rakken to be done with today's political engagement. Well, *hiding* might have been overstating things. The palace library was a long room with a trio of alcoves along its length, and Marius had retreated into the one furthest from the entrance in order to get away from the sharp gaze of the librarian.

Mr Featherstonehaugh did not mind Marius, who maintained a proper library hush and handled books with the appropriate respect (the minimum bar for moral decency). However, these qualities were outweighed by Marius bringing his strange 'dog' with him (a book-destroyer in waiting if ever Mr Featherstonehaugh had seen one). Gods knew what Rakken had said to wrangle Marius access to the library, because Mr Featherstonehaugh clearly did not feel he could cast them out on their heels.

Thistlefel jumped up next to him on the sofa, which was elegantly upholstered in butter yellow. Marius sighed and put the book he was reading down.

"You know you're not allowed on the furniture here," Marius told the lowfae. "You'll give the poor librarian apoplexy."

Thistlefel meaningfully pointed her nose along Marius's legs, which were stretched out on the sofa. Marius guiltily shifted position and put his feet back on the floor, but Thistlefel only settled down where she was. Her body retained the sleek length of a polecat, but the ruff of spikes had grown into a mane. She was now too large for him to pick up, though her growth rate was slowing, as if she was closing in on its endpoint.

Marius glanced back through the alcove's arched entrance towards the main part of the library, but there was no sign of Mr Featherstonehaugh prowling. The library had elektric lights, set so that they illuminated the painted ceilings portraying various woodland scenes. Marius found his gaze drawn to a deer whose disapproving expression bore an uncomfortable resemblance to the librarian's.

He checked the time: seven o'clock. He'd been here a little over two hours already. Rakken had been confident he'd be done with this meeting in plenty of time before moonrise, but it itched at Marius. Outside the mullion windows, the palace gardens had fallen into darkness punctuated by a single glowing lamp.

He picked up his book again, talking to Thistlefel in a low voice. "This book has a section about how the life stages of some lowfae are affected by catalysts. You wouldn't happen to know anything about that, would you? Blood is listed as a known catalyst, and you did eat some of mine."

Thistlefel only snuffled her way further into the sofa. She did not find books very interesting.

Marius set the book aside and picked up his journal to make a note of the passage. He had enough speculation and observations now to write a whole paper. Several whole papers, if he included what he'd found out about fae plants so far. He carefully did not turn to the section of his notebook that was supposed to contain the latest iteration of his research proposal for Greenbriars.

He shut his notebook. Though fascinating, this wasn't shedding any more light on their murder problem. He'd managed to identify some of the plant fragments found in the greenhouse with help from Rakken's library and was currently trying to figure out *why* Vane had wanted them. As far as Marius could work out, they were common species in Faerie with minimal magical properties. Had Vane known that? In which case, why had he wanted them? Unlike the black-market stuff Vane had been growing at his apartment, there seemed no real reason to meet at midnight to deal in such things. Or had whoever had stolen the plants simply been careful not to leave any trace of the more interesting specimens?

His temples began to ache, and he rubbed at his head before fishing his spectacles out of his pocket and replacing them. Getting up, he stretched out his limbs, ignoring Thistlefel's grumble of protest.

Thank the gods it was full moon tonight. He was beginning to chafe not just at the waiting but at the fact that this routine with Rakken had begun to feel almost mundane, as if they might continue in this manner indefinitely. Which they weren't going to. If they found the plant seller, and they turned out to be Vane's murderer, this whole business would be wrapped up. Or nearly so. There had still been no word of Emyranthus.

A.J. LANCASTER

He turned at the sound of approaching conversation. Two women in evening gowns appeared alongside Rakken, framed by the arch of the alcove entrance. Mr Featherstonehaugh hovered some distance behind them. Rakken was at his most ambassadorial, draped in black-and-green finery, though in his mortal form. Marius's heart gave an erratic beat despite himself. Gods, he was so unreasonably magnificent. It wasn't fair.

"Ah, Marius," Rakken said, as if it were somehow a surprise to see him exactly where he'd left him.

Marius frowned. *What are you up to, Rake?* But Rakken's walls were high and smooth—he'd been getting harder and harder to read telepathically the more time they spent together. His eyes were bright, movements energised, extremely pleased with himself, but he was often so after one of these functions. He liked manipulating people.

Just as he was manipulating Marius now, somehow. It would no doubt become apparent why shortly. Marius got to his feet and bowed acknowledgements, casting a sideways glance at Rakken. Why had he brought people here from the evening's function? Rakken pretended not to notice his silent inquiry.

The two women looked Marius over in return, politely but ultimately without much interest. The glamorous younger woman had the classic milky peaches-and-cream complexion of a Southerner and was wondering if Prince Rakken might be amenable to a tête-a-tête in a less crowded location and if she could conveniently lose her companion in the process of getting there. Her companion was just as suspicious of fae men as human ones, maybe more. *Doesn't anyone else think it odd that this prince paid Emma so much attention tonight?* Well, she had no intention of being shaken off; let this too-shiny prince just try it.

Marius winced.

"Mr Marius Valstar," Rakken introduced him, and there was a kind of 'aha' moment on the women's faces as they recognised his last name. The younger woman's gaze sharpened for a moment, but then he heard her dismissal as clear as a bell, *another dull scholar.*

"This is Miss Claridge and her companion, Mrs du Plessis. Miss Claridge was lately engaged to your colleague, Dr Vane. Marius worked with Dr Vane in the botany department at the university."

Understanding and anger flickered to life. This was Vane's fiancée, and Rakken wanted him to use his abilities on her; that's why he'd brought them here. Marius didn't know whether Rakken was counting on the fact that his control was so non-existent that he'd accidentally overhear something or if he wanted him to read this poor woman's mind on purpose. How dare he in either case?

"My condolences," Marius said, trying to keep the anger out of his voice. Miss Claridge didn't deserve it. "Dr Vane will be much missed in the department."

Miss Claridge shrugged. "Thank you." *Honestly, if I have to keep playing the dutifully mourning widow, I will scream. How long is this going to go on for? It was just like Martin to get himself murdered before I could break things off.*

"Oh," Marius said. "That... must have been awkward."

Miss Claridge gave him an odd look. Damn. She hadn't said anything, had she? Rakken saved the moment, turning things nimbly in another direction. Miss Claridge smiled up at him and laid a pale hand on his sleeve. Mrs du Plessis cleared her throat, and Miss Claridge removed her hand with a laugh, making the movement look natural.

Marius's own hands flexed into fists that he had to force to un-clench. Miss Claridge and Rakken leaned towards each other as if they were old friends sharing a joke. By the time Marius had given himself a stern mental talking to and returned to the conversation, Rakken had somehow turned the topic to love-notes and the art of constructing them.

Marius couldn't think of a subject he wanted to hear Rakken discuss with someone else *less*, but then he heard Miss Claridge think, in response to Rakken's arch question about whether she had a favoured style for her suitors to adopt when writing such notes to her, *I wish I hadn't sent that dratted threat to Martin, though I suppose he must have burnt it. I only wanted to punish him for taking up with that other woman and thinking he could keep it from me!*

So *that* was why Rakken had raised the subject. It didn't make him feel much better about it. He waited for Rakken to brush the pair off, but when he showed no signs of doing so after several minutes, Marius broke.

"We need to get on," he said, aware he was committing a social sin. He put a hand on Rakken's shoulder. "It's late—I have to be getting back."

"Must you go too, Your Highness?" Miss Claridge cooed. She did not at all mind if the prince's awkward companion took himself away. At least Mrs du Plessis looked at him with approval.

"Alas, I take my leave of you," Rakken said, managing to sound regretful.

Marius packed up his books with stiff-necked irritation and didn't say a word to Rakken as they left the palace.

Rakken dropped his casual manner as soon as they were clear of the building. The long drive that led to the palace was free of crowds at this time of day, though brightly lit by lamps to either side. Rakken strode right down the centre of it as if he owned the space.

There was none of his earlier lightheartedness in his voice when he spoke. Instead, he sounded darkly satisfied. "Miss Claridge is an ambassador's daughter. That is how Vane made contact with Faerie—he attended a function at the palace with Miss Claridge. There were fae from several courts in attendance."

This was enough to briefly distract Marius from his brooding. "Including Emyranthus?"

Rakken shook his head. "No, but I did not expect her to be involved in Vane's experiments. I can acquire a list of those who attended. One of them is either his supplier or introduced him to the fae who became such."

"Right." It was good news and explained why Rakken had showered so much attention on Vane's fiancée. He knew Rakken hadn't really been interested in her. But. *But.* It had put him in a temper anyway, a kind of prickling jealousy he hated.

I have no right to jealousy, he told himself. He kicked at a loose bit of gravel, sending it clattering over the cobblestones. "You shouldn't have brought her to me hoping I would read her mind. That's why you did it, isn't it?"

"Of course."

Marius did not kick the next bit of gravel at Rakken, which he thought showed strength of character. "It's wrong."

"Why? Neither of us did her any harm."

The guard at the end of the long drive eyed them with interest as they turned onto the footpath. Marius lowered his voice. "People ought to be allowed to keep their secrets."

"Even when they relate to murder? Do your own mortal authorities not ask questions and demand private information when they seek to solve a crime?"

"That's different. There's a process, rules about how they can go about it, to stop them abusing their power." He groped for the right words.

"Are you planning to abuse yours?"

"No, but who would stop me if I was?"

"Me," Rakken said with so much hardness in his voice that Marius's stride faltered. Rakken did not pause, and he hurried to catch up. When they were once more side-by-side, Rakken added: "Perhaps you do not recognise fae conventions as holding the same validity as mortal ones, but it does not mean we do not have them. An uncontrolled telepath is dangerous; I did not offer to try to teach you out of sheer altruism."

Marius shoved his hands into his pockets, scowling. "You still should have at least *asked* me if I wanted to be party to this first. You know I can't control it. I'm not another pawn in your game. It's my telepathy, and at the very least I ought to get to decide when I use it."

"I will be the villain of this piece then, if you insist; I am content with the judgement I made. However, I think you have more control over your abilities than you wish to acknowledge. Would it be so terrible to admit you trust yourself to use them?" Rakken said.

"Yes, I've so much control that I willingly give myself head-aches on a daily basis!"

"I did not say you had *complete* control yet. If you like, we have time for another practice session, before the Market."

Marius ground his teeth together. They walked in silence for several blocks, other pedestrians diverting around them without hesitation, although a corgi on a leash did resist its owner's efforts to pull it away for a few moments, growling at

Rakken. Thistlefel hissed at it in response. Animals were harder to fool with glamour than people, Rakken had told him.

Eventually, Marius said, without looking at Rakken: "Miss Claridge wrote that note we thought was blackmail. She knew about Jenny Greenbriars and was about to break the engagement. She's sorry Vane died but mostly because it's forced her to pretend to a public mourning she feels is false. She can hardly disavow Vane now he's been murdered—it wouldn't reflect well on her."

"Ah. I thought Miss Claridge's feelings for her ex-fiancée seemed more complicated than simple grief; I was hoping you might have some insight as to why. One loose end tied up." Rakken sounded a bit smug, although he at least didn't point out how convenient it was that Marius had heard this fact from Miss Claridge.

Was he right that Marius had more control over his telepathy than he thought? Surely that couldn't be the case? "Do we still need to attend this Goblin Market then, if you can get a list of the fae who Vane might have met through the palace?"

"The Goblin Market opens only once every moon. I would rather go and search the black-market trade there for a lead than gamble everything on this new information and risk losing the opportunity for a month." Rakken paused. "You need not accompany me. You would be safe from Emyranthus at FallingStar."

"It's a market, not a battlefield," Marius pointed out. He steeled himself to argue. He didn't trust Rakken to look out for human interests, left unsupervised. Rakken had had no qualms about destroying the evidence at Vane's apartment because he thought it best.

Rakken sighed. "You would be a useful addition, but if you

come, you must follow my lead, and you must be careful."

Marius had been so prepared to argue that it took him a moment to rearrange his train of thought around the fact that Rakken wasn't flatly against the idea. "I'm not stupid; I know fae play by different rules. I'm not planning on doing anything reckless."

Rakken's lips curved. "You never do."

They reached Malvern Place.

"Open the door for me, will you?" Rakken said, the thread of compulsion subtle enough that Marius almost did as he asked simply because it was a reasonable enough request.

Instead, he huffed and folded his arms. "Open it yourself."

Rakken grinned. Now that he was confident he couldn't compel Marius, he seemed to enjoy issuing random orders despite Marius obeying none of them (or more probably *because* of that fact; Rakken had a strong streak of contrarian in him).

They went inside. The familiar smell of dust and mildew assaulted Marius's nose. Rakken did not walk straight through to the back door but instead turned right into the drawing room. Aged furniture made misshapen icebergs under the dust cloths.

Rakken shook out his wings. "Come and preen my feathers," he suggested. He used only a thread of compulsion this time, and Marius's telepathy quivered but didn't trigger.

Marius rolled his eyes. "Let's just get back. I'm not in the mood for experimenting tonight." He was angry, and hurt, both for reasons he didn't care to examine too closely. Accidentally projecting them was the last thing he wanted, which sometimes still happened during their sessions. He likewise didn't want to catch a memory of Rakken seducing Miss Claridge.

"We do not need to go anywhere—we can reach the Goblin Market from here when the moon rises. You are the one who was angry at your own lack of control, earlier," Rakken pointed out. "How else are you proposing to improve?"

"Why was Vane's ex-fiancée there tonight anyway? I thought you said it was a committee meeting, but she was dressed for a ball. And surely she's not part of the committee." Why was he bringing her up again? He knew Rakken had been flirting with her for purely tactical reasons. Even if he'd clearly been enjoying himself. Marius couldn't get it out of his mind, that brief, unsubtle way Miss Claridge had caressed Rakken's sleeve.

"There was a social function after the meeting, and Miss Claridge came to join her father there, who is an ambassador. I suspect he thought it would improve negotiations." A touch of a smile in his voice.

Marius didn't smile. "She was sizing you up as a matrimonial possibility, you know. Hetta has given everybody ideas."

"I know," Rakken said. "But I am a prince, and Miss Claridge is far from a princess, even if fae were as casual about marriage as mortals."

That made him snort. "Yes, call us casual whilst you screw around with half the kingdom."

"I am doing no such thing, at present. I am touched by your faith in my prowess, but even I have only so much time and energy." He undid his cuffs.

Marius hated that *at present* and hated even more the spark of jealousy burning in his breast. He was being stupid about this, about Rakken, and he hated that too. Everything was terrible.

He shook his head. "It doesn't matter."

Rakken took a step forward. "Are you jealous at the thought that I might indulge elsewhere, starling?"

"No." Marius refused to look at him.

The compulsion this time held the weight of an anvil, wordless and powerful, pushing with the relentless power of the tide.

"Come," Rakken said, deep and sonorous. "And take these." He held out his cufflinks.

Marius sucked in a sharp breath, struggling to catch hold of the rebellious *thing* that rose up inside him. He was generally able to stop his psyche from lashing out physically now, but Rakken hadn't used this much compulsion since that first night in the Spires. It was like snatching at bees, keeping his internal *something* from instinctively swarming out to attack. He gasped a warning for Rakken to shield.

Rakken, the bloody moronic contrarian, bared his teeth and lowered his shields to nothing at all. The full force of his thoughts hit Marius. Not compulsion but deliberate provocation, for Rakken was focusing on suggestive imagery with single-minded intensity. The taste of sweat. Muscles, straining. Salt. Heat. Feathers brushing against overheated skin.

"Stop it," Marius hissed. He was only holding back the great coiled spring of energy inside him by the barest thread. If it unleashed and hit Rakken unshielded, it would knock him senseless. He'd seen Rakken telepathy-addled once already; he didn't want to see it again. Why was Rakken taking such a foolish risk? Especially when they were supposed to be attending the market in not so many hours now.

The explicitness of his mental images only increased. "Make me."

Aroused, angry, and wondering how bad it would be if he actually did strangle Rakken, Marius crossed the distance and shoved at his shoulders. Rakken laughed and went with the motion, though as Marius pressed him back against the wall, his laughter rumbled away into an interested murmur in the back of his throat.

Without breaking eye contact, Rakken spread his wings with slow leisure, the feathers scraping against the wood panelling behind him. "Physical force is cheating, starling. Or are your thoughts running in other directions?" He looked down to where Marius's fingers were curled tightly into the fabric of his shirt.

Rakken's voice ought to be some sort of controlled substance, available only in small doses under the cover of darkness. The suggestive way his head fell back against the wall, exposing the clean line of his throat, the way he licked his lips, it was all too much, even setting aside the flurry of mental imagery that came alongside it.

Marius kissed him. It lowered the intensity of the psychic assault mainly because it derailed Rakken's focus. However, Rakken remained unshielded, and so his thoughts bled into Marius's, kissing and being kissed simultaneously, pleasures so muddled together that he couldn't separate out one from the other.

He pulled back, breathing hard, leaning his weight on Rakken. "I can't—no one else, Rake. Not while we're doing this."

Rakken arched a brow. "I thought this didn't mean anything between us? Or are you in danger of falling in love with me?"

Marius flinched. "No! No, I am not," he repeated. "I just don't want to share."

Rakken's eyes were dark. Anger or arousal, Marius couldn't tell. "Are you issuing me an ultimatum?" he asked softly.

Marius realised with a sharp thrill of shock: *This might be it.* The moment this madness ended. The moment he pushed too far and found the edge of what Rakken was prepared to give.

Part of him wanted it. He could still recover now, but the longer this went on, the less certain he was that his heart wouldn't go and do something stupid and make it impossible to go back to how it was before. It hadn't been happiness, exactly, before, but he'd been safe.

This wasn't safe.

He felt eerily calm as he responded. "Yes. You can sleep with all of Meridon if you like, but not if you want to come back to my bed. Not while this thing lasts. Unless you're ready to be done with it now?"

A dart of painful apprehension shot through him. But he couldn't regret pushing, even though it hurt. It was such a relief to know that he *could* push, that he hadn't already lost himself like he had with John, who had muddled him up so badly that he'd been unable to draw a single line in the sand.

Rakken pulled himself taut, his eyes narrowing. Marius braced himself for the refusal.

"The reverse would also apply," Rakken said abruptly.

"What?" Marius gaped at him.

"That you would not take other lovers."

Marius wrinkled his nose but managed to bite back the words: *as if that's likely.*

Rakken canted his head, softening a fraction. "Do you truly not know your own desirability?"

If Rakken believed he was fighting off offers with a stick, Marius wasn't going to disabuse him of the notion. "All right, no other lovers while this lasts, then, for either of us. Do you agree?"

Rakken looked at him through heavy-lidded eyes for an endless moment. Marius's heart pounded, but he couldn't look away, couldn't move.

Rakken brought his hands to his waist. "While this thing lasts, then, I am yours alone." A slow, wicked smile, the brush of feathers spreading further. "So take me."

24

TO THE GOBLIN MARKET

THEY WAITED FOR moonrise in the back garden of Malvern Place. In the city, only the brightest stars would normally be visible, but tonight grey clouds obscured even those. Marius couldn't see the moon at all.

He remembered how the moonlight had glittered on broken glass the night of Vane's murder. A whole month ago, now. A whole month since he and Rakken had been thrust together. It felt both longer and shorter.

"Will this work even if it stays overcast?" he asked, looking doubtfully up to the dark sky.

"The moon is there, clouds or no. Can you not feel it?" Rakken shot him a swift, searching glance, as if this genuinely surprised him.

"No, humans can't feel the phases of the moon."

"You are not entirely human."

"One fae ancestor a thousand years ago is as near to human as makes no difference. So no, I can't feel the moon. What does it feel like?"

Rakken threw his head back, his eyes glowing subtly in that way that meant he was calling up his leysight. "The tide," he said after some consideration.

He gave himself a shake and withdrew a feather from his pocket. It caught the light of the street lamp spilling over the garden wall. Emerald filaments glinted, shading towards bronze at the nib. He held out the feather towards Marius.

He didn't take it. "If this is a token of your undying affection..."

Rakken rolled his eyes. "It's to keep your mortal hide safe. We are going to unclaimed lands, which makes you the same. The feather is to signal you fall under my protection."

Marius worked that one out. "Hang on, what do you mean by an unclaimed mortal? Fae don't... abduct humans, do they?" An alarming number of fairy tales from his childhood were springing to mind. He ought to have questioned Rakken more strongly on this point earlier.

Rakken shrugged. "Historically, perhaps. It hasn't been common practice since the Iron Law, for obvious reasons, and even before that, abduction was always less popular than luring mortals away of their own free will."

"And since the Iron Law was rescinded?"

"I only kidnapped you to Faerie the once, and for your own good besides. Ungrateful to complain of it," Rakken said drily. "But, yes, it is something that will likely end up in the final agreement between this realm and mine. No abducting unwilling mortals: a tedious but necessary trade for the greater good. But for mortals already within Faerie..." He flourished the feather at Marius.

Marius hesitated. A feather felt personal, like a lock of hair. On the other hand, he didn't wish to be abducted. "Oh, all right." He reached for it, but Rakken kept hold of his end.

He grinned. "You must wear it somewhere it can be seen. Braided into one's hair is traditional."

Marius let the feather go and stood back. "My hair isn't long enough." He was not wearing a feather in his hair like a child playing dress-up. Especially not Rakken's feather.

"Untrue." Rakken stepped close. The heat of him thickened the air between them with the faint citrus-and-storms of his magic and the more personal scent that was just *him*. It froze Marius stupid for a heartbeat, which was long enough for Rakken to raise his hands in neat, rapid movements.

Something silky tickled his ear, and he put up a hand to tug it free. "I'm not—" he began, but Rakken caught his wrist and stopped him. His fingers were warm, wrapped around his pulse.

"Wear it," Rakken said, expression serious. His eyes shone more brilliantly than ever, lit with magic. "I'm not only trying to provoke you; it truly is for your protection."

"Oh, all right. Can we go now that you've tied a bloody feather to me?"

"A bloody feather would carry an entirely different meaning." A laugh in Rakken's voice.

Marius went to run a hand through his hair out of habit and stopped himself. "I feel ridiculous."

"You do not look ridiculous." There was a different light in Rakken's eyes now.

Marius swallowed. "If you keep looking at me like that, we're going to miss this market."

Rakken sighed. "The sacrifices one must make." He knelt fluidly. "Now, do not distract me with your own ogling. I know how much you like to watch me."

"You and your bloody ego."

"I can only speak truth, starling."

Marius crossed his arms and huffed, making Rakken chuckle. He was right, damn him; Marius did like to watch him. There was something so *vital* about Rakken when he performed magic. Besides, Marius wouldn't be a scientist if he wasn't interested in how things worked.

I'm not sure ogling counts as science, his irrepressible inner critic pointed out.

Rakken rested a hand on the worn stones of the path, where dandelions had pushed their way into the cracks. Marius had always had a soft spot for dandelions. His mother used to hold them out and tell him to make a wish before he blew the seeds free on their downy tufts. But there was no real magic in dandelions, as far as he knew. Or was there? he wondered, as Rakken pulled up a stalk and withdrew several items from his pouch.

"Dandelions?"

Rakken shook his head, not a deliberate evasion but a signal that he was concentrating. Marius stayed quiet as Rakken pulled out an old gold coin of unfamiliar currency and a knife, but he couldn't help making a sound of protest as Rakken sliced the back of his own forearm. Rakken, in contrast, remained perfectly expressionless as he held the coin where it could catch the blood, counting silently—one, two, three drops—before placing it on the flagstones.

Marius tried to work out the methodology. So much of fae magic had to do with sympathy, making connections to things that were alike. That got him as far as the coin—the Goblin Market presumably involving money—but blood seemed excessive. Blood was powerful. Intimate. Dangerous. Rakken disliked shedding it, even under as controlled a circumstance as this.

That last thought had held too much of Rakken for comfort, and Marius carefully checked, but it wasn't telepathy, he didn't think. *Maybe I'm just getting too familiar with how he thinks.* Worrying thought.

Rakken murmured something too low to hear and looked up. The clouds parted, and the full moon shone down upon them. Had he parted the clouds with magic, or was that a superb bit of timing and showmanship?

Rakken blew on the dandelion, and the seeds took flight. They sparkled in the moonlight, leaving a trail of silver in their wake. The trail expanded, until a ribbon of silver extended beyond where Rakken stood into the shadows of the back garden.

He held out a hand. "Come."

"Is this a portal?"

"Of a sort. It's a way of a more flexible sort, opened by ritual rather than resonance."

"Full moon and dandelions?"

"Their inclusion isn't essential: a handful of dust or leaves would have worked as well to open the moon path."

"Something capable of travelling," Marius guessed.

Rakken shot him a sharp look. "You pick up the principles of fae magic impressively quickly for someone who does not practice it." He flourished his hand again. "Come. The way will not remain open long."

Marius turned to Thistlefel, who had been watching the proceedings from the back door of the house. Her eyes brightened, her trio of ear tufts flicking out. "You stay here," he told her.

She hissed.

"Marius is right, helichaun."

Thistlefel grumbled but settled herself into the rough shape of a loaf of bread, paws tucked underneath. She would wait for them to return.

Rakken's attention lingered on the feather attached behind Marius's ear. "The market is not a place I would tread lightly. You will be careful and do as I say."

"Within reason," Marius murmured, taking his hand.

Rakken gave a sharp grin at that and pulled him forward.

The world went strange. It wasn't like stepping through a portal. Instead, it was as if they'd entered a dark tunnel, the world narrowing to only the silver path beneath their feet. There was no sound but for them, their breathing, their footsteps, but somehow Marius had the sense that just out of sight, hidden in the shadows, was an ancient wood, a sense of slumbering hush. He thought of the turn of seasons, and blood sacrifices on stone altars, and the damp, rich loam of the forest.

"What happens if we step off the path?" he whispered.

"I would be extremely inconvenienced trying to find you again, and we would not reach the Goblin Market this moon."

Well, at least the answer wasn't 'instant death'. He tightened his grip on Rakken's hand, the warmth in contrast to the eerie chill they walked through.

The world opened out again, and they emerged at the edge of a field as if they had stepped out of a shadow. They stood beneath a trio of trees that were not oaks but looked a lot like them at first glance. Bare branches reached towards a sky full of strange constellations, dark against the bright silver of a truly enormous full moon.

Before them stood a simple wooden gate, of the ordinary rather than magical-portal sort. A large, free-standing sign was staked into the ground next to it. It read:

Beyond the gate, the market spread across the field and out of sight, tents and stalls lit up in many colours—by magic — and figures moving. Even at a distance, the noise of the crowd was audible, as were the strains of music. A wild, merry reel played, the beat the sort that made your feet itch to move.

"What happens if you're still inside when the gates close at sunrise?" Marius asked after reading the sign.

"Immediate ejection from the market," Rakken said. Marius realised they were still holding hands and released his grip.

Rakken frowned at him. "Shield as much as you can and stay close to me. Do not bargain with anyone. If we are separated, meet me at the Wayside Inn. It is nearest this entrance; we will pass it on our way, and I will point it out."

"I'll be good, I promise," Marius said drily.

Rakken's mouth curved in a brief smile, but his sober mood didn't lift. He straightened, flexing his wings, and when they crossed the market's threshold, Marius felt very much that it was a fae prince beside him.

The market was overwhelming even to his normal senses, and Marius pulled the woolly-feeling reins on his telepathy even tighter. Fae of all kinds strode and flew and slithered between stalls or hawked their wares. The people at the marketplace in ThousandSpire had been homogenous by comparison.

Rakken wasn't referring to any map, and the paths between stalls were laid out in confusing, non-linear patterns, so that Marius quickly lost all sense of which direction he was facing. Not that he'd exactly known which direction they'd been facing to start anyway—how did one figure out such things in Faerie?

He tried hard not to stare, but he couldn't help being aware of the curious glances thrown their way. He couldn't blame them; even among other fae, Rakken was striking. He looked like something out of a tale, dressed in black and striding under the moonlight with his hair gleaming. A creature of blood and sacrifice and ancient gods.

Ancient gods? Marius made a fervent vow to himself to never let that thought out. It would make Rakken even more insufferable.

Stall owners and hawkers called out to them both, or rather, mainly to Marius, as Rakken ignored them with a smooth arrogance Marius secretly envied. The wares on display were truly astonishing in their variety. One shadowy cave of a stall seemed to be filled entirely with pulsing, bioluminescent fungi (Rakken had to drag him away). Another held scarves that moved of their own will, slithering about the wooden roof poles like snakes. They passed stalls selling enchanted cloaks, glittering weapons, clothing of wondrous variety, and glass bottles in fantastical shades.

"Is that a dragon?" Marius screeched to a halt in front of a stall selling a glittering collection of jewelled clockwork artefacts. A tiny reptilian head rose from behind an ornate pocket watch to stare back at him.

"A minor construct," Rakken said dismissively.

"Minor? This is the work of a skilled artificer!" The vendor hurried over to them.

"What does it do?" Marius asked, fascinated. The dragon was smaller than his palm and made of metal, he realised on closer inspection, though it appeared quite life-like. It reminded him a little of a technomantic construct, except that there was no sign of gears or elektrical circuits.

"Keeps tea at the perfect temperature." The stall holder pressed an indentation on the tiny dragon's head, whereupon it curled into a tight spiral and flattened out, becoming a thick disk of interlocking joints. The jewel of its eye gleamed. The stall holder placed a dainty teacup full of liquid on the disc, which after a few moments began to steam. The stall holder removed the cup and tapped the disc, whereby it uncurled itself and became a dragon again.

"The warming spell will wear off sooner rather than later, I suspect," Rakken said over Marius's shoulder. "Come."

"How much for it?" Marius asked. His little sister Laurel would love this. The vendor eyed him up and down, deciding how much to inflate her price. *A mortal, here?* Marius heard the thought, the touch of surprise, and then the, *ah, but he's claimed*, as the vendor noticed the feather tickling Marius's ear. Marius winced.

"Well, something like this, you understand, has a rare value that—"

"Here," Rakken said with a sigh, placing a stack of coins on the vendor's table. "Give my companion the teacup dragon."

The vendor opened her mouth as if to attempt to haggle,

met Rakken's gaze, and closed it again.

The tiny dragon perched in Marius's breast pocket as they walked, blinking interestedly at the crowds as if it were real.

"Thanks," Marius said, feeling odd about the fact that Rakken had sort of bought him a gift, even if the act had seemed largely driven by impatience. "You didn't have to do that. Sorry for getting distracted."

Rakken shrugged off the thanks. "Your lowfae isn't going to be pleased that you've adopted another small nuisance." But he sounded amused rather than annoyed.

The crowds grew thicker the deeper they got into the market, as did the noise. Marius spun, trying to find the source of the wild rhythm that seemed to be drawing ever closer.

"The midnight dance," Rakken murmured. "It winds its way through the market. Best avoided, I think."

But the dance seemed determined to follow them. Between one moment and the next, they were swept up in the parade of musicians and dancers, fae with multiple limbs gyrating and flexing in impossible ways. Marius's mouth fell open for about the thousandth time, and by the time he realised what was happening, the path had become too narrow to retreat.

Rakken was fortunately easy to spot, there not being many tall and darkly handsome feathered princes about. He had gotten caught up on the other side of the procession, wings flared slightly in annoyance. He met Marius's eyes as Marius was borne helplessly away, but he didn't look worried—merely put out, which was reassuring. Marius gestured back in the direction of the teacup dragon stall, since that was the direction the dance was bearing him and he remembered the path being somewhat wider there. Rakken nodded.

It was like being caught in a river of bodies, carried away

and deafened by music. His temples began to throb, and by the time he'd forced his way to the edges, a truly terrific headache was spiking. It was a relief to step free in the wider path, and he rubbed at his head, breathing deeply for a second. He ran a hand through his hair, settling himself.

He stopped. Ran his hand through his hair again, slowly this time.

Rakken's feather was missing.

It must have come loose in the dance, Marius told himself. No need to panic. Rakken couldn't be that far away, and in any case, Marius wasn't helpless.

He turned and found himself face to face with the stallholder who'd sold him the teacup dragon. She was holding a pipe. Marius opened his mouth to speak, but before he could, she lifted her pipe and blew. Small motes of golden dust puffed out, like mushroom spores, and then—

—the world went dark.

25

IS IT EVEN A GOBLIN MARKET IF NO ONE GETS ABDUCTED?

MARIUS WAS SICK of waking up in strange places with an aching head. Upon this occasion, he found himself lying on a dirt floor in a warehouse, surrounded by towers of crates. His limbs felt stiff and cold.

Blearily, he tried to work out how he'd gotten here. The golden dust the fae had blown at him must have been some kind of drug, or perhaps a spell? What about the rules of the Goblin Market? How did sending someone to sleep not count as violence? Trust fae to make that sort of ridiculously technical argument.

He sat up, his muscles protesting, and—

—discovered the shackles. He stared at them in disbelief: thick metal cuffs on his wrists and ankles with a length of chain between them. The chain on his wrists went to a heavy ring embedded in the floor. What in Almighty Pyrania's name?

He got to his feet, rolling his shoulders to loosen them. The chains clanked as he pulled against the anchor in the floor, which didn't budge even when he leaned his whole body weight against it.

He stood panting, filled with a sort of bemused outrage. He had been, quite clearly, kidnapped and taken… where? Was he still inside the Goblin Market?

Between the stacks of crates, he could see cages, he realised with a shock. The cages contained creatures. Lowfae? He stared at them, appalled by the thought, and the memory of Vane's flat. A crocodile-like creature with pink fur paced circles. Birds with jewel-like feathers clustered forlornly inside a delicately wrought birdcage. Through a narrow gap he could just make out something small and dust-coloured sleeping in an oversized cage. The creatures were all eerily silent, even though the crocodile-fae's mouth stretched open periodically as if it were roaring.

Marius might not be in a cage, but he was inside a circle, he realised with a sharp jolt. A metal one, inlaid in the floor. He knew enough of fae magic to feel deeply uneasy about that.

A figure was making its way through the warehouse, holding a clipboard and stopping at intervals to inspect the wares.

"Hey!" Marius shouted at him. "I say!"

Or—tried to shout. No sound emerged. His hands went to his throat, felt the cool metal of some sort of collar. A spell?

The figure continued as if he hadn't heard Marius at all. The figure was fae, of course, with pointed ears and spiralling ram's horns emerging from his short, gleaming locks. Tall and broad, he put Marius in mind of a bull even before glimpsing the cloven hooves beneath the long golden robe. The fae wore a long gold chain about his thick neck, from which hung a medallion in the shape of an auctioneer's hammer. Oh, bloody hell. That couldn't mean what he very much feared it meant, could it?

The fae stopped at the pile of crates nearest Marius and lifted the lids, revealing brilliant magenta flowers. Bloodlock. A thrill went through him.

"You do know those are highly illegal, don't you? Who are you and why have you brought me here?" Again, nothing came out.

The fae didn't react. He put the lid back on the crates containing the bloodlock and called to an assistant to come and fetch the next lot. Continuing on to inspect the next section, he passed near Marius's circle and paused, grinning. He had large flat teeth. "Oh good, you're awake. Live'uns always go better than sleeping."

"Let me out immediately!"

The grin widened. "You're under a sound shield, you know, so no use yelling at me; I can't hear you."

Marius reached up to where Rakken's feather had hung, realising only now that the hair there was slightly shorter than it ought to have been—the feather had been cut off. "You took my feather—how does not that count as theft?" Why were the only rules of the market turning out to be completely useless?

The fae got his meaning, even without being able to hear him. "Oh, I don't have your token. I imagine it's been kicked into the Dance and is leading your companion a merry chase by now."

Not stolen—lost. *Deliberately* lost. Only fae would make that sort of distinction.

Marius almost said, *Do you know who I am?* But he managed to snap the words off in time. If the fae didn't know, Marius didn't want to get his family tangled up in this. Instead, he gestured angrily, making his shackles clank.

The fae's eyes flicked up and down Marius's body in a chillingly clinical assessment. "A pretty price you'd fetch, I should think, even without the psychic abilities I'm told you have."

Marius stared at him, appalled by literally every word of that. This was outrageous! They weren't really going to auction him off, were they? How did they even know he was a telepath? Why would they care what he looked like? Wait. They wouldn't be auctioning him off for... that, surely? No.

On the brighter side, at least he'd found the black-market plants. Did this... auctioneer know anything about the ones that Vane had had?

Marius decided ethical qualms on the subject of telepathy did not apply to people who had put him in chains and were apparently planning to *sell him*. He glared at the auctioneer and imagined himself reaching across the distance between them.

And met—something. A shield, less familiar than Rakken's, but giving off the same sort of blank sensation.

The auctioneer laughed. "I can feel you scrabbling, but I'm no weak-minded lesser fae. That's a valuable gift you have there, pretty mind-reader, though I'd avoid using it on whoever buys you if you want to please them."

He wandered off. Marius watched him go, thoughts in turmoil.

Other fae came, shifting goods in and out of the warehouse through a door at the far end. Taking them to the auction block? Surely this had to mean they were still in the market? The other fae deferred to the bullish auctioneer, who spared Marius no further attention. Marius tried to read their minds and partially succeeded this time, catching odd flashes, though nothing useful. His headache worsened.

One of the assistants came to wheel away the bloodlock. She was a gangly fae woman—he assumed—with blue-tinged skin, a long neck, and legs that came to delicate cloven hooves.

"Where did they come from?" Marius asked and thought

as loudly towards her as he could, hoping he was projecting. For a moment, he thought it had worked, for the fae looked up at him, blinking in surprise. Marius got a fleeting impression of something—an unfamiliar landscape—and a... name? *Stoneholm.*

But then the fae shook her head and carted the plants away, and Marius was left to wonder if it had been only his imagination.

When the bullish auctioneer returned, he carried a long golden wand. Marius was determined to do violence if the man came into arm's reach; getting forcibly ejected from the market seemed like a fantastic option right now. But he didn't get the chance, for the auctioneer waved his wand, and gravity abruptly upended. Marius flailed, floating helplessly in the air, unable to do anything at all as the auctioneer undid the chain linking him to the floor and began to tow him in the direction the other wares had been taken.

Marius swore, soundlessly, thrashing without gaining purchase in the air. Now would be a wonderful time for his aggressive telepathic projection to kick in, but the threatening vertigo made it impossible to focus.

He had thought things couldn't get any worse, but being towed like a flailing balloon into a vast dark tent full of people was definitely worse. The auctioneer directed his wand and set Marius down on a plinth, attaching the chain to the anchor there. Marius couldn't help tugging at it just in case. It didn't budge.

His face on fire, he glared out at the crowd. He might as well have been under a damn spotlight, since the plinth was well-lit whilst the rest of the tent had been left in dimly lit shadows. There were a lot of hoods and cloaks being put to good use, making the figures into shapeless blobs.

I suppose if you're going to attend a black-market auction, you don't necessarily want to announce that fact.

The auctioneer addressed the crowd. "Our next lot is a rare prize indeed: a human telepath."

There was a murmur of interest from the crowd. Marius's hands balled into fists. He tried again to project telepathically as he shouted the words: "I am not for sale!" but it didn't seem to do anything. He tried again to lash out, but he couldn't find the trigger that activated that instinctive response. He'd never yet managed it without Rakken's compulsion, and he'd never tried to use it to psychically attack someone on purpose before.

His fingers curled into fists as the bidding began. It was even more humiliating than Marius had expected. Voices emerged from darkened hoods, calling out strange bids, egged on by the auctioneer in a horrible caricature of a stock agent at a farmer's market. The bidders didn't bid coin. They bid in currencies that under other circumstances Marius might have found fascinating, but right now each one hit like a blow.

"A casket of lightning!"

"The breath of a dying unicorn!"

This was outrageous. It couldn't really be happening, could it? Fear began to rise beneath the anger; what would happen when the bidding *stopped*? He tugged at the chain and tried to project again. His only reward was a worsening pounding in his temples.

The bidders dropped out one by one until there were only two left, each bidding equally ridiculous things against the other. Marius squinted into the darkness, trying to figure out who was attempting to purchase him. The two figures were both cloaked, but he caught a flash of something from one that might have been a furred tail, and his heart sank. A DuskRose fae? Oh, gods. On the one hand, they'd probably return him to Stariel and his family. On the other, they would use him as leverage against Hetta to gain political capital, wouldn't they? His stomach twisted. He hadn't thought about the fact that he might be used against his family.

He turned his attention to the other cloaked figure, who had upped their latest bid to something called sorcerer's tears, to general gasps. They had wings, he realised, only partially disguised by the shadows and the bulk of their cloak. His heart lifted, but then, no. This figure's wings were grey rather than bronze-and-green.

Oh no.

Emyranthus had grey wings.

Sorcerer's tears proved hard to top, for there was a long pause. The auctioneer lifted his gavel suggestively, to urge the potential-DuskRose fae to up their bid.

Rakken came like a storm.

A dark, churning aura of charge flickered over his wings and burned in his eyes, which were not their usual green but the blue-white of lightning. Thunder hummed in the air, and power flared up each of his horns, lighting them with the same brilliance. He *glowed*, pulsing with power.

The ranks of cloaked figures leaned away as he strode through without giving them the smallest piece of his attention. He was magnificent and inhuman, and relief flooded Marius so strongly it made his legs shake. Rakken—terrible, insufferable prince—would get him out of this. He knew it not because he suspected Rakken of sentiment, but because he knew how strongly Rakken felt his duty towards lesser creatures. Gods, he hated that he currently fell into that category.

The auctioneer held up a hand. "Are you here to bid?"

"This human is mine and stolen from me. I claim him." Rakken gave the auctioneer a look so threatening it made Marius take a step back, but the auctioneer remained unmoved.

"The market's rules have not been breached."

"If you do not give him over to me, I will make you regret it. I am Prince Rakken Tempestren, dread sorcerer of the Spires and the most powerful compulsionist in all of Faerie bar the High King. I killed DuskRose's golden prince. Do you wish to make an enemy of me?"

The auctioneer remained unmoved. "And I am Mammona, older than your court, invulnerable to the harms you offer. You are hardly the first princeling to think they can threaten the Midnight Exchange. If you want the mortal so badly, then bargain for him. Bidding stands at three vials of sorcerer's tears."

"Ten thousand derenti," Rakken said without hesitation.

"That is not the sort of coin we bargain in, and you know it, youngling."

Rakken's eyes met Marius's.

"No," Marius said, soundlessly.

Rakken turned away, his face hard as he looked back to the auctioneer.

"Very well, then. Make me your enemy." He gave an ironic flourish at himself, flaring his wings slightly. His smile was dagger-sharp, promising violence. "Sunrise to sundown. Anak's rules. Next full moon."

Marius could only understand the value of what he was offering by the reaction of everyone else in the room. The silence spilled out, absolute, and even the auctioneer seemed frozen with surprise, though he was the first to shake it off.

"Any other bids?" he asked. No one spoke. The auctioneer

went to raise his hammer.

"No!" Marius shouted, though of course no sound emerged. He held Rakken's gaze. "Rake, compel me!"

Rakken's mouth tightened, and for a moment Marius thought he wouldn't do it, wouldn't think Marius capable of this. Why would he, when Marius had gotten himself into this? No one ever thought of him as anything but an endearing burden, at best.

But then he felt Rakken's will fall over the assembled crowd, stopping the auctioneer mid-motion, holding them all in thrall. Terrifying. Irresistible as gravity.

"Come here," he told Marius, and Marius clung to that anvil of force with all his might, feeling his defences trigger and feeding all his panic, humiliation, and anger directly into a wave that burst out of him with the force of an explosion.

The auctioneer staggered, falling off the podium with a clatter of hooves. Marius had only time to feel darkly smug about that before the world spun. There was a wrenching sensation, nausea rising in his stomach, and then he was falling forward onto soft ground.

He sat up, coughing, feeling as if he'd been thumped all over. His head rang. Beside him, Rakken lay groaning. They were in the long grass in an empty field. In the distance, Marius could hear the lights and sounds of the Goblin Market, muted. The air smelled of crushed grass and damp earth. Above them stood the sign.

No violence. No compulsion, Marius read with satisfaction.

Rakken sat up too. His features were sharp with strong emotion, almost gaunt. He reached to the collar around Marius's neck and muttered something harsh. The collar snapped open.

Rakken removed it and threw it hard to the side without looking, his eyes flashing. "That was a damnable risk, Marius Valstar. If it hadn't worked, I would not have been able to rescue you."

Before Marius could voice his apology-slash-defence, Rakken had toppled him, pressed him into the grass, and begun kissing the living daylights out of him. His mouth moved feverishly, his hands scrabbling at his body as if he were trying to eliminate every space between them and make certain of every inch of him.

Rakken had been afraid, Marius realised when they pulled apart, his wide green eyes only inches away. That's what his Terrible Dread Prince mask had been hiding.

"Oh, gods." His own bubble of denial popped, and he started to shake, the full horror of the last few hours, of what had nearly happened, hitting him all at once. Rakken held him as he buried his face in his neck, feeling pathetic but unable to let go. They lay in the grass for a while without speaking. Rakken was so warm and solid, and the weight and smell of him went straight to Marius's hindbrain and said: safe.

"Are you hurt?" Rakken asked eventually.

"No, I'm fine," Marius said. He took a gulp of air and made himself stop clinging to Rakken like an invasive species of climber. Sitting up, he asked: "What are Anak's rules? You... tried to sell yourself, somehow, didn't you?"

Rakken shrugged. "Yes. My service for a single day. Anak's rules are a set of conditions for such cases: No permanent injury done to me; I will do no harm to my kin. Otherwise, I do as I am told and accept whatever humiliation is given."

"This happens often enough that there's a named set of conditions for it?" Marius said, followed by, "Oh, gods, why? Why would you do that?" He found himself shaking Rakken's shoulders, anger, guilt, fear, relief a churning nausea. "What the fuck were you planning to do if I hadn't—gods!" He shook Rakken's shoulders again, making his feathers rustle in the long grass.

"The alternative was telling my brother I'd left you to the mercies of the Midnight Exchange." Rakken seemed amused by Marius's outburst. "There is no debt between us for that; I said I would protect you here."

"It's your debt I'm worried about! What... what do you mean by service?" *Sex*, Marius thought before he could stop himself.

"I would have been thankful for something that trivial," Rakken said, and Marius realised he'd inadvertently projected the last bit.

Rakken began untangling himself from Marius's grip and stood up, his feathers fluffed in a way that meant he was ruffled in the emotional as well as literal sense. "That is hardly my most valuable attribute, though I suppose I ought to be flattered that you rate my prowess so highly. I was much more concerned someone might avail themselves of my powers, and that this trap was too neat not to be planned. Do you think it a small thing, to be the most powerful compulsionist in Faerie next to the High King himself?"

Marius had offended him. He wasn't sure whether to laugh or cry at that. "Hells, Rake, of course I know you're worth more than that. It was just the most horrifying thing I could think of, and I was furious that you might have had to—that I got myself into this situation at all. How is the Midnight Exchange allowed to carry on like that, selling people? There were lowfae in cages there too."

"Faerie holds just as many horrors as your own realm, and no laws govern the market but for those signposted," Rakken said.

"I did not give you one of my feathers for no reason."

Marius rested his hands on his knees, not ready to stand and face the world quite yet. There was mud on his trousers, along with pale lines of broken seedheads. He recognised some of the species from Rakken's botanical texts. "Someone cut the feather off deliberately, and the auctioneer knew I was a telepath. I saw—I think one of the people there had a cat's tail. Could it have been DuskRose behind this? And there was another bidder with grey wings, who I thought might have been Emyranthus."

Rakken's mouth thinned. "I would rather she was behind this than DuskRose. But that is for later." He tipped his head back to examine the sky, where the moon was now barely above the horizon. "I have not found the plant seller who dealt with Vane, and the market will not let us back in this night. We have both broken its rules."

Marius blew out a breath. "I saw bloodlock in the auction house. It was the lot sold before me. I tried to read the seller's mind. I got a name, a location, I think—Stoneholm. Does it mean anything to you?"

Rakken's frown deepened. "No. But it is more than we had."

Marius didn't find this much consolation. He'd told himself he'd be doing something worthwhile in accompanying Rakken to the market, but instead he'd only made things worse.

THEY FOLLOWED THE SILVER path back to Malvern Place. The sky had lightened with a hint of pre-dawn, but the streetlights were still burning. It was very cold. The city around them lay quiet with only the occasional sound of a vehicle in the distance breaking the stillness. Their breaths fogged in the air.

Marius pulled his coat closer and tried to remember what day of the week it was and what time the first train left Meridon for Knoxbridge. His brain felt muddled with more than just fatigue. With some effort, he worked out it was probably Saturday. That meant he could safely fall into bed—once he reached a bed—and not have to worry about getting up for anything. Or, wait, had he said he'd help out Peter Kendrick with his *Nepenthes* in the greenhouses? No, that was tomorrow. Today was the lecture from a guest speaker he was supposed to be attending, but that wasn't until this evening.

Thistlefel burst out from beneath a rose bush and began a thorough inspection of his boots and lower trouser legs, as if determined to read everything about where they'd been from that. Maybe she could. Marius watched her sniff his ankles, his thoughts moving sluggishly.

His hands found a metal disc in his pocket. He pulled it out and stared at it blankly, having almost forgotten about the teacup dragon that Rakken had… given him, sort of. Thistlefel looked up and yipped, but he shook his head and put it back in his pocket. He didn't have the energy for introductions.

Rakken brushed his palms together as if ridding them of the last of the magic he'd cast. He too seemed tired, or perhaps just lost to reflection. Perhaps he was cursing Marius for having mucked the whole thing up, he thought with detachment. The whole night felt like a dream. A *bad* dream.

He cleared his throat. "I don't think the trains will be running for a while yet. I'm minded to traipse back to Stariel and avail myself of my bed there rather than wait. You?" Not since that first night had they slept in the same bed. Probably he ought to be in favour of not risking a knife in his throat, but in truth he disliked waking up alone. It made things feel so much more transactional.

Because they are, idiot, he scolded himself.

Rakken frowned at Thistlefel. "Koi may know of Stoneholm. His knowledge of Faerie surpasses mine." He didn't sound thrilled at the prospect of talking to his oldest brother.

"I can ask him," Marius said. "Least I can do, really."

"You do not owe me, Marius Valstar," Rakken said formally.

"I have a rather vivid and recent memory of standing on an auction block that says otherwise."

"As I have already explained—"

Marius shook his head. "That doesn't change it. I'm not fae; this isn't some formal oath-debt you can absolve or tot up. And don't try to brush this aside as some matter of political expediency or family obligation." He straightened his shoulders. "You could have left me there, and you didn't. You offered yourself up to save me, and I'm damned grateful, all right, even if I hate that you needed to." Awkwardness scratched at him, but he wasn't so much a coward as to leave it unsaid.

Rakken's eyes narrowed. "The auctioneer was a fool to accept so low a price for you. If they had known your full worth, nothing I had to offer would have sufficed. Come." He turned and strode to the Gate, activating it with brisk efficiency.

Marius gaped after him. That was... perhaps the nicest thing anyone had ever said to him, or at least the nicest thing he'd ever believed. Many people—his stepmother, Wyn, Hetta—were willing to gush reassurances at him whenever they thought he needed bolstering, but he'd always held their words at arm's length. They were nice people, and they loved him; they would say what they thought he needed to hear.

Rakken was not nice, and he did not coddle people. Marius turned his words over and over in his mind. He knew that Rakken had likely meant that Marius's mortal connections were highly valuable to dodgy fae, but Marius was still unreasonably flattered by the *way* he'd said it, as if it might not be just that.

"I was not planning to hold the Gate open all day."

With a start, Marius followed him through to the Dower House, his mind awhirl.

Rakken was not inviting comment as they walked through the dark corridors, but Marius couldn't leave it. "Thank you," he said eventually. "For saying that."

Rakken made an impatient sound. "I said it because it was true." His tone was curt.

They emerged onto the front lawn, where the pale light of the stars glittered on the lake. Marius frowned at a deeper patch of shadow near what he knew was an ornamental garden bench. There was something odd about it, but just as he thought this, the shadow moved, transforming from an ominous blob into a winged fae as Irokoi rose from where he'd been sitting.

Irokoi's black wings merged into the shadows, his silver hair a pale contrast where it spilled over them. He came urgently towards Rakken. "You are not injured? No one stabbed you?"

Rakken narrowed his eyes. "No, Koi, I am not."

"Are you sold to the DuskRose queen?"

"I am not that either."

Irokoi turned to Marius, eyes wide and fearful. "He is not?"

Marius shook his head, reflecting that he ought to have known that Irokoi would find a way to make the night even stranger. "No. He tried to martyr himself, but I—we—got out before the auctioneer took him up on it. Neither of us is hurt. What did you see?"

Irokoi sagged with relief, his wings brushing the lawns. "Nothing real. A bad dream. Only a dream! Oh, I am glad, brother." He laughed and embraced Rakken, heedless of Rakken's bristling objection.

Rakken extricated himself. "Gratifying, brother, but I am not distracted. You saw this? Why didn't you warn me? And what more do you know of it—was there a plot, or was this mere opportunism?"

"I see a lot of things that never happen, broken bits that make no sense until after they have already come to pass. Should I tell you nonsense?"

"You could at least try."

Irokoi stiffened. "And how would you feel, how would you act, hearing of the deaths of those who you love? Deaths that never happened—or perhaps have not yet? Of sins no one has committed against you but still may? Lives we did not live, unless we do? That I might have kissed this one instead of you?" Irokoi waved at Marius.

Rakken took a half step forward, as if he would put himself between them, and then stopped, looking annoyed with himself. His wings fanned out a few inches before he got them under control.

Irokoi arched an eyebrow. "Oh, do not fluff up at me, Mossfeathers; I was being rhetorical. I have no designs on your lover. No offence intended—I am sure you are a very good kisser," he said earnestly to Marius past Rakken's shoulder.

"Er... thanks?" Marius said in a rather strangled tone. *What the hells was that about, Rake?* What the hells was any of this about, tonight? But then, he supposed he knew already that

Rakken could be possessive. A terrible part of him quite liked it.

"You were waiting here tonight, expecting bad news," Rakken said, scowling at his brother. "Do not try to change the subject or use your disingenuous act with me, Koi. If you are plotting something…"

Irokoi opened his eyes wide. "Act?" But his expression sobered, his wings shifting, and the lines of his face made him look suddenly older. "I dreamed it only tonight. I do not—I do not usually see things so clearly unless they are very likely or very imminent, but there was no time to do anything but wait in either case. So, I… waited."

Waited alone in the dark, to see what had become of his little brother, seeking reassurance after a nightmare. Marius softened.

Rakken did not soften, still frowning suspiciously. Irokoi radiated sincerity, but then, he always did.

Rakken sighed, giving up on making sense of his brother. "Well, since you are here, what do you know of Stoneholm?"

Irokoi frowned and then shook his head. "I do not know the name. Is it a place or a person?"

Rakken turned inquiringly to Marius.

"I'm not sure," Marius said. "It could be either, I suppose."

"I do know where to find an excellent map of Faerie," Irokoi mused. "I will go and find it for you and see if your Stoneholm is on it, though it will take me a little while." He gave Rakken's elbow an encouraging pat.

Rakken looked coolly at Irokoi's hand until he removed it. "I don't suppose your precognition has given you anything useful to share regarding this matter?"

Irokoi grinned. "You suppose correctly."

Rakken sighed. His wings drew against his spine as he looked down at his brother. "You are welcome in the Spires, you know."

"Am I?"

"Cat would like you there."

A smile pulled at Irokoi's lips. "And you?"

"I can tolerate your presence."

Irokoi laughed and patted Rakken's arm again. "Flattering, Mossfeathers. One day, maybe, but for now I am happy enough to shamelessly take advantage of Lord Valstar's hospitality. There are going to be *babies* soon, too! There are no niephlings in ThousandSpire, yet."

"I bid you good night, then, Koi," Rakken said, and turned and pulled Marius into his arms.

Marius made a token grumbled protest, but not much, because he was tired enough to appreciate not having to walk the rest of the way up to the house. Also, Rakken was gloriously warm, and Marius's hands and feet were starting to freeze. He shamelessly turned his face into Rakken's neck and let himself breathe him in for the few minutes the flight took them.

When they landed at Stariel House, Marius trudged inside and climbed tiredly up the stairs. The servants weren't up yet, and the quiet magnified their footsteps. Rakken followed him, saying nothing. Fatigue made Marius's movements clumsy as he opened the door to his room, and he managed to bang his shin on the frame.

"Damn," he swore, limping into the room.

Rakken didn't move from the threshold, watching Marius in an oddly intent way.

Marius began shrugging out of his jacket. "I'm planning to collapse, just in case you thought I had the energy for anything else."

"No," Rakken agreed. A flicker of uncertainty in him. "Even so, I would like to remain for a little while, if you will permit it."

"Yes, of course you can come in for a cuddle, Prince Melodramatic. Gods know I could use the comfort tonight, though I warn you my feet are icicles, so enter at your own risk."

Rakken chuckled and came in, closing the door with a soft click. Marius ducked his head, feeling awkward and fumbling at his cuffs to disguise it. Gods knew why he should feel awkward—it wasn't like Rakken hadn't seen every inch of him many times before. And yet it felt like something important had shifted between them. Marius was too tired to figure it out.

Rakken hummed in the back of his throat and began to help, fingers soft and graceful as he unbuttoned Marius's shirt. It made something tighten in Marius's chest, and he found it difficult to meet Rakken's eyes as he returned the favour.

They got into bed.

"I was concerned, tonight, when you disappeared," Rakken murmured. He was in mortal form; he wouldn't fit winged in Marius's bed. He wrapped his arms around Marius and pulled him close so that the warm heat of his body pressed against Marius's spine.

Marius wasn't quite sure what to say. Any reasonable person would've been worried about their companion disappearing in a dodgy fairy market—and yet Rakken admitting as much felt like a confession on par with a governmental declaration.

"Me too," Marius said eventually. He wriggled until Rakken relaxed enough to allow Marius to roll to face him. Rakken's expression was uncharacteristically soft, a question in his eyes.

Marius kissed him, and Rakken responded like warm water, pliant but undemanding. He raised an eyebrow as Marius's hands trailed down his body.

"Maybe I have a little energy left," Marius admitted. "If you do?"

Rakken chuckled, but his response was unequivocal.

It was softer and slower than usual, drowsiness and desire in equal measure, mouths and fingers and small gasps as they rutted against each other, the dreamlike languidness of release blurring easily into dreams in truth. Marius's last thought as he succumbed was that perhaps Rakken actually could be quite nice, on occasion.

HE WOKE LATER THAT day to the sound of brisk knocking. Rakken was already awake—and in the bed with him, Marius realised with a jolt of surprise. When Marius untangled himself and stumbled out of the bed, he made a disgruntled sound and propped himself up on one elbow to watch through slitted eyes as Marius found his dressing gown.

"I suppose this is some sort of payback," Rakken muttered, but Marius didn't work out what he meant by that until after he'd opened the door a fraction and seen who it was knocking.

"Good morning—or rather, good afternoon, sleepyhead," Hetta said.

"I was up all night," Marius said and then realised how that sounded. He flushed and spluttered: "No—I meant, I got back just before dawn. I've been sleeping!" It occurred to him rather belatedly that the lord of Stariel would certainly know about the presence of a greater fae on her faeland and the fact that said greater fae hadn't left yet. And was in Marius's bedroom.

Hetta grimaced, holding up her hands as if to stop him. "It's fine, Marius. I came to tell you Caro called from Knoxbridge.

There's been another murder. Go and get dressed." She grimaced again, already turning away. "And bring His Royal Highness with you."

He shut the door and turned back to Rakken, cheeks hot. Half of him was stuck on Hetta's words. Another murder? Who? How? The other half was more trivially occupied with wanting to die of embarrassment.

Rakken had already risen, un-self-conscious as always as he dressed. Marius found it impossible to look away, and Rakken paused in braiding his hair. His mouth ticked up. "Much as it pains me to say it, this is perhaps not the time to do nought but stare admiringly at me."

"You slept here," Marius said unthinkingly. "You never do that."

"No," Rakken said.

"You didn't sleep?"

Rakken considered his appearance in Marius's mirror and flicked an invisible bit of lint off his collar. "I didn't think you would enjoy being attacked in your sleep again."

"You said that doesn't happen often—and you didn't hurt me so much as give me a fright, last time. I'm prepared to take the risk."

Rakken said coolly: "Then you are a fool."

Marius hunched at that, his temper snapping. "Yes, clearly. I'll see you downstairs."

Why did he keep trying, anyway? Clearly *nothing* had shifted between them, for all his sentimental musings last night.

26

WAIT. ANOTHER MURDER?

THE SUN HUNG low in the sky when they made it back to Knoxbridge, and the mood between them remained strange and tense. Maybe it was knowing what lay ahead and that they'd failed to prevent another death. It didn't feel like it, though; it felt personal, something gone awry between the two of them. *Blurred lines*, Marius thought. Their casual arrangement had never felt less casual than last night. *Just make sure to keep yourself on the right side of that line*, he reminded himself. Rakken clearly was.

The second murder had also occurred in a greenhouse, though at least not Marius's this time. It felt wrong to be grateful for that; a man was still dead. Where he'd died didn't change it.

They went straight from the station to the gardens, which had already been closed to the public. A crowd of reporters and rubbernecking undergrads clustered at the public entrance.

The murmur of rumours being exchanged rose and fell in volume as reporters caught sight of people through the iron railings and called out questions, which were generally ignored.

Caro hadn't known who'd been killed—just that someone had been in one of the greenhouses. Marius's stomach twisted with wondering: who? When? Was it related to Vane's murder? How could it not be? If he hadn't bungled up their visit to the Goblin Market last night and they'd managed to find Vane's supplier, could they have prevented it?

The crowd parted for Rakken, though they didn't notice themselves doing it even as they shuffled to make way. Marius caught a flurry of images and emotions as they went through, their excitement leaving a bad taste in his mouth. He was grateful for the glamour; if the reporters realised who he and Rakken were, it would be open slaughter.

The relative quiet of the gardens was a relief. Even from some distance away, it was clear which greenhouse was the scene of the crime from the knot of police officers and university staff hovering about aside. Jungle House was one of the architectural jewels of the university, rising to a height of sixty feet at the apex of its curved roof. It housed a huge number of tropical plants from around the world and had a viewing gallery around its perimeter that was open to the public on weekends. Obviously not open on this one.

He recognised the diminutive Miss Dauntry, the police 'sniffer'. She was arguing with one of the officers. Said officer threw up his hands and walked off. Miss Dauntry was still frowning after him when he and Rakken drew close.

"Ah, Emily. I regret the circumstances in which we meet again. What is the situation here?" Rakken asked. When had he gotten on first-name terms with her?

She turned towards them. "Good; you're here. None of my sort of magic was used, but I told them you'd need to check for your sort." Her lips tightened. "Is there some way for me to detect it? I'm not much use as a magic consultant if I can't tell whether fae magic has been used, and this is becoming too much of a trend for my liking."

"Fae magic often has a signature unique to the person who cast it. Usually it manifests as smell, but it sometimes makes you think of strange textures or other senses as well," Marius offered.

Miss Dauntry's eyes brightened, and Marius caught the edge of a thought along the lines of, *oh, thank goodness; this one talks.* She wanted to know everything she could about fae magic, but Prince Rakken kept slipping past her questions. "How do you tell it from real smells?" she asked.

"You can ask my colleague more about it later," Rakken said hastily. "It will be best if I see the scene sooner rather than later. The magic fades."

Miss Dauntry looked like she was considering dragging Marius off to the nearest pub to interrogate him but decided that murder took priority. She escorted them through the police, who accepted Rakken without a blink. Marius, however, was given significant side-eye.

The greenhouse's humid air hit like a wall. An enormous monstera wound about one of the internal supports, but large sections of it had been ripped off so that huge, perforated leaves covered the central path through the greenhouse. The whole greenhouse looked as if a windstorm had run the length of it, leaving snapped trunks and broken vines in its wake. Gods. Some of these specimens were extremely rare. Would they be salvageable?

But what they found at the far end of the greenhouse drove all thoughts of plants out of his head. The second murder scene looked a lot like the first. Distressingly so. A dark-haired man in a tweed jacket lay in a pool of blood amidst a mess of plants and glass.

Marius's throat squeezed, recognising the man. Peter Kendrick, who he'd been meant to be helping with his *Nepenthes* tonight. His chest felt hollow, a bleak despair rushing to fill it with almost physical pain. Peter was another of Greenbriars' post-grads. Marius had liked him.

He turned away, unable to look at Peter's death-pale face staring silently up at the steel-and-glass of the dome.

"Can you sense anything?" he asked Rakken.

Rakken's eyes slipped out of focus as he leaned on his leysight. "Something fae was here," he said slowly. "I do not recognise it, and there is too much blood and death swamping the signature for much nuance. Not Emyr, unless she was deliberately laying a false trace."

"How does that work?"

"It is difficult to set a false signature; much easier to simply mask and leave none. But Emyr has skill enough for it. In such cases, mimicking someone else's signature is easier than fabricating one, so it could be that this signature belongs to someone Emyr knows. But I do not recognise it. More than that; there is a strangeness to it deeper than a lack of recognition. Perhaps it *is* a fabricated signature, to feel so." He frowned and moved his fingers as if he were trying to separate threads.

"Is the trace the same as last time?"

"Yes and no. The same signature, but it's stronger this time." Rakken turned to the officers examining the scene and gestured at poor Peter. "Was he killed in the same way as Vane?"

Marius stared down at Peter's body, hearing their answer only distantly. From the conversation, he gathered that, yes, Peter had been murdered in the same manner as Vane: killed by a blow to the head and then stabbed, although no weapons had been found this time.

He couldn't bear it anymore. Turning away, he left Rakken to it and walked back towards the main entrance. Almost automatically, he began to catalogue as he went, trying to work out what had been most damaged underneath all the mess. It was better than thinking about Peter.

His gaze fell on the colourful central stem of a bromeliad, snapped clean off—and caught on the plant next to it. His heart stuttered. It couldn't be, could it? But he'd spent hours poring over drawings of plants in books from Rakken's library. Not sure what to think, he left the tiled path and pushed aside leaves and trailing roots, only distantly hearing someone start to object. He crouched down.

The plants were a bit worse for wear, camouflaged beneath the shaggy detritus of a banana palm. The ones that hadn't been bumped about by last night's murderer all had their leaves oriented to best receive light, and some of the stems had begun to grow sideways as well, which meant they'd been here for a while.

"I've found the missing fae plants," he said, softly, and then stood to repeat himself more loudly.

The greenhouse went quiet. He met Rakken's eyes across the distance, read a reflection of his own puzzlement there. How had the plants gotten here? Had Peter known? Was this why he'd been killed? But then, why hadn't the killer taken them?

There came a sound of raised voices outside: Professor Greenbriars, demanding to know what was going on inside *his* greenhouse. Rakken's expression changed, turning thoughtful. Marius knew what he was thinking: Greenbriars had been Peter Kendrick's supervisor, and that made it two of Greenbriars' students affected. Greenbriars had been Vane's professional rival—and Vane had been having a secret affair with his daughter. Greenbriars could have moved plants in here easily. That was means and motive both.

Marius jerked his head—he'd deal with it. Greenbriars was *his* supervisor; he knew the man, and he wasn't capable of murder. Except... did he really know that? Greenbriars had hated Vane, after all.

No, it had to be coincidence.

Rakken nodded and turned back to speak further with the police.

Outside, Greenbriars started when he saw Marius and then sagged with relief.

"Marius! Oh, thank the gods; I heard a student was killed." *I feared you'd gotten mixed up in something you shouldn't, with those relatives of yours.*

The thought made Marius's tension abruptly ease. Gods, had he really thought for a moment that his supervisor might be a murderer? He wasn't thinking straight.

He led Greenbriars a little way away from the greenhouse, out of earshot of the police.

"It's Peter Kendrick, sir. He's dead—murdered. I'm sorry."

Greenbriars scowled. "They won't let me in. Why did they let you in?"

"Ah, Prince Rakken is liaising with the police. He, er, brought me with him."

Greenbriars' eyes went wide. "A fairy killed Peter too? The same one mixed up with Vane? What did Peter have to do with that?"

"We don't know yet. Maybe. There was fae magic used at the scene again."

Greenbriars looked shellshocked. "Peter was a very promising young man. I was talking to him only yesterday. He was so enthusiastic about the latest field trials. Gods, what a terrible thing." He sank down onto the nearby garden bench. His normally florid complexion had drained of colour, making his skin look papery and thin.

Marius sat down next to him, the impact of Peter's death hitting him like a sudden weight in his stomach. With Jungle House behind them, the view was disconcertingly peaceful, as if a man hadn't been murdered so nearby. The wind rustled a row of silver birches lining the walkway. A single yellow leaf broke free and floated lazily down.

Greenbriars leaned forward, staring at his hands. "Have Peter's parents been told?"

"I don't know."

Greenbriars gave himself a shake. "I must find out from his dean. He was from the Isle of Lowe, you know. His father's the temple priest there. There'll be an inquest, I suppose; I'm sure his parents will want to come up for it." He began to get up but stiffened before he'd fully risen.

Marius turned. Rakken had emerged from the greenhouse. He was in his mortal form and dressed in Prydinian fashion besides, but there remained something subtly other about him. Greenbriars watched him approach as if he expected Rakken to turn feral at any moment.

He's not dangerous, Marius had an impulse to say, and yet that wasn't true. '*You shouldn't suspect him*' probably wouldn't go down well either, given the department was currently swimming in rumours about fae plants, fae magic, and fae murderers.

"He's a good man," Marius said instead, and then wondered whether that was true either. And what did it say about Marius, that he was drawn to him regardless? "He'll find out who killed Peter." That, at least, he was sure of. Rakken did not give up.

Rakken strode towards them with a deceptive lack of concern and stopped, looking calmly down at Greenbriars. "Did you kill Peter Kendrick?" he asked without preamble, the thread of compulsion humming in his deep voice.

Greenbriars started. "What? Of course not!"

"Did you know Vane's fae plants had been moved to this greenhouse?"

"No!" Greenbriars said, looking even more bewildered. "They're here?"

"Yes." Rakken turned towards Marius. "I have told the mortal authorities that you would help me identify them, but that it would be better done away from the scene of the murder."

Greenbriars swung accusingly to Marius. "You, identifying fae plants? How?"

Marius couldn't quite meet his eyes. "I've been doing a lot of reading, in the light of Vane's murder, and I, er—"

"Reading fairy tales?" Greenbriars said. "I'm not sure magic and plants ought to mix."

"They do already, though, even if we only consider human magic! What about the technomantic advances in greenhouse technology? The experiments Wiesner did with plants growing under different spectra using illusionary magic?"

Greenbriars was no less taken aback than Marius by his own outburst. He shifted uneasily, some colour returning to his cheeks. When he spoke, there was a gruffness to his voice.

"I take your point, but none of that research involved plants themselves being considered magical. And none of it involved murder. Vane's interests have already brought enough bad press upon the department." He scowled. "If they get wind of this…"

"There's no reason they should. And it might help us learn who murdered Peter and Dr Vane."

"I suppose you must, then, but do not let yourself get too much distracted with this, Marius." Greenbriars rose, shaking his head.

Marius got to his feet as well.

"Not our murderer, then," Rakken murmured as Greenbriars walked away.

Marius watched him go, feeling oddly heavy. "No."

"Why do you let them have so much power over you?"

Marius spun back to face him. "What? Who?"

"These academics at your university. They ought to be courting *your* favour, not the reverse."

Marius gave a hollow laugh. "That's unfortunately not how it works. We do as we're told, and one day, if we've been very good boys for many years, we might get to set our own research goals."

"But you are not just anyone, Marius Valstar. You are a prince of FallingStar, which has just become the most influential faeland in two realms. If you leave your mortal institute to pursue your own research, they will be the lesser for it, not you. You hold the high ground. Use that. Make them see what they have to lose: not only your brilliance but access to resources they cannot find a route to without you. Threaten them, if you must."

Marius rocked back on his heels. "Queen Matilda would have something to say if I started styling myself prince. That's not how mortal titles work," he said, to give himself time to think. *Threaten* the university? It was typical of Rakken to suggest it, but was he wrong that Marius had leverage? Rakken was not usually wrong about that sort of thing. But did Marius want to have to lean on his family connections for advancement? It felt off.

He said instead: "You think I'm brilliant?"

Rakken shrugged. "It was a statement of fact." *Though my judgement has never been more flawed than of late, when it comes to you.*

Marius winced.

There was an awkward pause before Rakken gestured back towards Jungle House. "What puzzles me most," he said, "is that Peter Kendrick was killed in the same manner as Martin Vane. The fact that stab wounds were made after the blow to the head originally suggested an unplanned, panicked attempt at misdirection. But an exact repetition of that method by definition cannot have been unplanned."

"There was no dryad blade left behind this time," Marius pointed out.

"No." Rakken's frown deepened.

Unbidden, the image rose of Rakken stalking into the auction house like a dark god. *I killed the golden prince*, he'd announced to the crowd last night. Greenbriars might not be a killer, but Rakken was. Marius had mostly managed to push that knowledge to the back of his mind, but it felt different today, after seeing yet another person lying in a pool of their own blood.

He swallowed. "Rake, how many people have you killed?"

Rakken froze, and for a long time Marius thought he wasn't going to answer. The wind had picked up, rattling dried leaves in the gutters. When Rakken spoke, his tone was carefully inflectionless.

"Four. Three on the battlefield; one in cold blood."

It didn't take a wild leap to work out who the one in cold blood was. "Prince Orenn. DuskRose's prince."

"Yes."

"Why did you kill him?" He'd asked Rakken this once before and received no answer, knew Rakken didn't want to discuss it. But Marius couldn't leave it alone. Not now.

Rakken drew a breath through his teeth. "Are you hoping I can give you some extenuating circumstance or noble reason that will allow you to salve your conscience about what you allow into your bed? That perhaps it was an accident, or in self-defence, or for some greater good? An honourable duel? I can tell you now I murdered Orenn in cold blood. I gave him no chance to defend himself before I slit his throat."

Marius flinched. Rakken was right; he did want there to be some extenuating circumstance. He couldn't believe that Rakken was just... a murderer, for the sake of it. Couldn't believe the man he'd caught glimpses of—who mourned dead lowfae and wryly insulted students' essays and patched up wounds—could be truly bad.

He swallowed. "I'd still like to understand," he said. "Please. Tell me."

The silence stretched even longer this time. Then a shiver ran through Rakken, and he closed his eyes. "Get out, Thistlefel."

The lowfae had been sitting next to the bench, but at this she hissed. Rakken opened his eyes and narrowed them at her, and she got grumbling to her feet and padded towards the greenhouse, looking back over her shoulder the entire time. Marius had better come back for her when she was done. She wasn't a pet to be dismissed for inconvenience.

Rakken ignored her complaint. He began to walk away from Jungle House, towards the arboretum. He wanted privacy for this conversation.

"You're starting to worry me," Marius said, following.

"You should have been worried long since." There was a sharpness to him, a bristling hostility lying just beneath the surface. He stopped under the boughs of a majestic copper beech and cast a spell, murmuring under his breath. A faint golden shimmer expanded around them, falling softly in a circle around the tree's dripline, shielding them from eavesdroppers.

"Well?" Marius asked, folding his arms. It was cooler in the shadows beneath the branches.

"There are two answers to why I killed Orenn, and neither of them reflect well on me."

Marius waited.

Rakken gazed up into the boughs. "The first thing you should know about Orenn is that he was much, much older than Cat and me; even older than Irokoi. Power generally grows with age, in Faerie. He was Queen Tayarenn's only child, the shining crown prince of DuskRose. No one of DuskRose had anything but praise for him."

"What was he like?"

Rakken shrugged. "We in ThousandSpire despised him on principle, of course, but to DuskRose he was a warrior-mage to rival the heroes of legend. They called him the golden prince for the armour he wore to battle, and the tiger prince for his prowess. DuskRose boasted of his beauty and his brilliance and prophesied that he alone would be enough to turn the tide of influence in DuskRose's favour—at that point the long enmity between our courts had not yet flared into outright battle. It remained in the arena of political games, occasional assassination attempts," Rakken said dismissively, as if this was a normal sort of thing to dismiss. "The shadowcats claimed ThousandSpire had spread its blood too thinly in its royals; DuskRose had not made the same mistake. Silently, we feared they were right."

"He sounds insufferable," Marius said frankly. "I notice you don't say anything about him being good."

Rakken hesitated but admitted, "Though the wyldfae of DuskRose would not speak ill of him, they could not always hide the fear in their eyes."

"And that's why you killed him?"

Rakken shook his head. "I told you it was not some noble impulse. Cat and I… you do not know what my father's court was like, in the years after our mother left. We were the middle children, not young enough to be afforded the protection of childhood, too powerful to be discounted in my father's games. That the two of us were able to defeat DuskRose's prince, the shining star of a powerful enemy court, bought us respect from those who might otherwise have been a danger to us."

"It kept you safe. Cat safe," Marius said. The motivation to protect one's loved ones was something he could empathise with, if not the actions that had resulted. *Really? You're really going to accept premeditated murder as acceptable on those grounds?*

"Killing Orenn brought us *power*," Rakken corrected. His fingers flexed into fists. "I am ambitious; I wanted that. I admit I didn't foresee that my actions would rekindle outright war, nor draw Hallowyn into the mess in the end. I regret that, but I will not deny I enjoyed the influence his death bought us."

"And that's why you did it? To further your own ambitions?"

"I certainly considered it as one of the benefits of the act."

Marius swallowed, thinking hard. Even if all that Rakken had said was true—which, technically, it had to be, though he knew how skilled fae were at stretching truth until it turned a complete circle—he'd also done his best to present matters in the least favourable light. Almost as if he wanted Marius to recoil. Part of him *did* recoil, hearing Rakken speak of killing someone for no reason but cool ambition.

Two answers, Rakken had said. Marius blew out a long breath. "What's the second answer, then?"

Rakken shrugged, all loose-limbed carelessness. "Why not simply accept the first? You will not find the second any more to your liking. There is no truth here that will absolve me; I own my dark deeds in their entirety."

"Yes, yes, you're doing a great job at convincing me of your inner terribleness. You might as well tell me the rest while you're at it."

Rakken began to pace, restless as a caged panther. Leaves crunched underfoot. After several strides, he gave a soft laugh. The sound made all the hair on Marius's neck stand on end, for there wasn't a bit of amusement in it. Whatever he was thinking, Marius wasn't picking up on it; Rakken's shields were hard, obsidian, giving nothing away.

He waited. Eventually Rakken stopped by the trunk and began to speak, each sentence coming with a pause in between, as if he were having to think about them too carefully. He didn't look at Marius, instead picking at the tree's bark.

"I have always had what Cat calls a dangerous degree of curiosity. Portal magic, especially, has always fascinated me. What makes any two places resonate? Does all of Faerie connect to somewhere? How many unclaimed lands are there? One should not portal without knowing the destination, but as a youth, I had a bad habit of ignoring that wisdom, stepping through portals without always knowing where they might lead. Sometimes, Cat would come with me. Other times, I preferred my own company. Occasionally I would run into trouble, but I was young and arrogant in my own power."

"Unlike now," Marius couldn't help interjecting.

Rakken gave him a brief smirk. "Oh, you should have known me as a youth—the poor decisions we could have made between us. But my arrogance was reinforced by the fact that I survived these encounters. Narrowly, on occasion, I must admit, but always with my skin intact."

"And then one day you didn't?" Marius guessed.

Again, Rakken laughed in that disturbing, unamused way. "Oh no, he left me very much intact. He wanted me to live with the knowledge of my own stupidity and how he had bested me forevermore between us."

Marius's insides turned to ice. "Orenn?"

Rakken gave a tight nod. "We met in unclaimed lands. I realised later that I had blindly portalled into the wild lands bordering DuskRose's territory, where Orenn liked to hunt for more challenging sport than that offered by the tamer woods of his mother's faeland. He was alone that day, and he was thrilled to have a stormprince fall right into his lap. I was so much younger; his power eclipsed mine completely. He quickly overcame me."

There was so much bitterness in Rakken's voice, and only the fact that he stood there, alive and whole while Orenn lay dead, made Marius able to keep breathing.

"It wasn't your fault. You couldn't have known."

Rakken gave a sharp jerk of his head. "I knew the risks of blind portals and chose to take them anyway. It was my own gamble that I lost." A spark of his usual self-satisfaction returned for a moment. "Not that it has stopped me gambling in such a way since." His gaze turned pensive. "I thought Orenn would kill me, or take me prisoner, the better to crow his triumph over ThousandSpire, but I had reckoned without his sadism." Rakken's fingers twitched restlessly, and he muttered a low curse. "Storms, I have never had to *tell* someone this before."

"You didn't tell Cat?"

Rakken shook his head. "She found me. I didn't need to explain what had happened. Only—who."

"It's all right, you don't need to tell me any details if you'd rather not," Marius said. "I can imagine well enough. He hurt you." It made him furious and sick to think of it. The nightmares; this was at the root of them.

Rakken made a frustrated hissing sound. "No. He didn't hurt me, actually. Orenn's compulsion was very good. Almost as good as mine has grown. Ironic, that. I enjoyed it, all of it; he made sure of that. I think he knew I would hate that most. And then he set me free as if I were a grounded nestling, as if I posed no possible threat to him. That humiliation was almost worse."

Marius couldn't speak, horror a lump in his throat.

"He had had me in his power and set me free: a debt I owed if I did not wish him to reveal to the world how his will had overpowered mine. He meant to hold it as leverage against me, and I think he liked the idea that I would have to live with the uncertainty that he might change his mind at any time." He bared his teeth. "But he had underestimated me. Even then, I was no trifling sorcerer, and he'd been carelessly arrogant to leave me with his essence. I used it to bind him to secrecy, and

I take some satisfaction from knowing he must have hated that, in return, once he realised what I'd done."

Rakken's eyes had gone faraway. "It took a long time for Cat and me to be sure enough of success to enact our assassination. Many years. It was quick, and cold-blooded, and my knife in his throat. He knew it was me that killed him when the light went out of his eyes."

"*Good*," Marius said emphatically.

"You think so? His death triggered a war. Many died, my own people among them. My brother forsworn and fled to the human realm, my father's court weakened, all on the altar of my need for revenge."

"I'm—well, I'm not glad for the war, but I'm not sorry he's dead."

Rakken bared his teeth, only now looking directly at him. "Don't you dare *pity* me. I am not so feeble; this happened long, long ago now, and I regret only that I let it—let *him*—influence any of my decisions. But it is done, and it does not pain me anymore."

"Of course I don't pity you! Gods, what an utter bastard Orenn was." Marius hadn't known he had it in him to wish a man dead, but he was glad—*glad*—that Orenn was. A directionless anger twisted in him alongside a terrible admiration. Rakken was so strong, a dark fortress of a man, and yet he should never have had to make himself so. His heart ached.

He needed to touch him like he needed air. It felt a bit like approaching an elektrical storm, Rakken was so bristling with defensiveness, but Marius paid it no mind. He put his arms around him, half expecting Rakken to throw him off, but instead he stood stiffly, neither welcoming nor rejecting the embrace. He growled. "Do not fool yourself into thinking this exonerates me, that I was but some hapless victim."

A terrible swell of fondness washed through him. He was so predictably prickly, so determined that no one would see his weaknesses. Marius hugged him tighter. "Thank you for telling me."

Rakken twisted, claiming his mouth with enough fierceness to bruise. When Marius hesitated, he growled, "No. Don't you dare be gentle with me, starling," and pushed him up against the trunk, bringing their bodies flush. He kissed Marius without mercy, grinding their hips together. It was tongues and teeth and wet, slick heat, moving feverishly.

Marius could only pant when Rakken pulled back to glare a challenge at him, as if he expected… what? For Marius not to want him anymore? He almost laughed except he felt that would give rather the opposite impression to what he intended.

"Of course I still want you," he said.

"Do you?" Rakken's eyes glittered in the dappled shadows, lit with their own inner fire.

"Yes." He put a hand on Rakken's waist. *Always*, lay on the tip of his tongue, and he hastily clarified: "I've always desired you, and this certainly doesn't change that."

Rakken smiled, a display of teeth rather than joy. For a moment, there was something wild in him, something dark with jagged edges, but it smoothed away as his personal shields rose, forming an obsidian wall between them. His voice was light. "Convenient, then, that my own desire has not yet run its course."

He kissed him, but it felt strangely perfunctory, as if he held Marius at a distance even when they were pressed chest-to-chest. Marius pulled him closer, trying to breach that invisible barrier. Rakken's words had unsettled him, and it unsettled him even more to realise how little he relished the reminder of the ticking clock counting down between them.

But Rakken withdrew from the embrace. "They ought to have moved the plants by now."

27

BOTANY NERDS UNITE

THEY COLLECTED A grumpy Thistlefel, who was unimpressed with people keeping things from her, and went to find the potting shed where the fae plants had been shifted to. Marius pulled up short. A police officer was standing guard outside, and Jenny Greenbriars was arguing with him. He and Jenny hadn't spoken since that day in Vane's office.

He'd always thought of Jenny as a bit mousy in both appearance and personality. Her recent lashing out at him he'd chalked up as an uncharacteristic one-off, but perhaps he ought to revise that assessment, because Jenny wasn't having any of the police officer's attempts to snub her.

Her eyes flashed as she argued, "*I'm* the person most familiar with Dr Vane's research—I've helped him catalogue new specimens before, and I make all my father's drawings for his articles."

"Sorry, miss; I've been told to keep everybody out."

The police officer spotted Marius before Jenny did and threw him a pleading look to deal with this unnatural bluestocking of a woman.

"Jenny," Marius said softly.

Jenny Greenbriars whirled to face him. She coloured, but her chin came up, and she glared daggers. "You!"

"I'm here to identify the plants," Marius told the officer, and Jenny made an angry sound.

"Miss Greenbriars will assist me," he found himself saying; Jenny's mouth closed with a snap. The officer looked between the two of them and then at Rakken. To Marius's relief, Rakken followed his lead and nodded.

They went in. The plants were arranged on a wooden work-table in the shed. Empty terracotta pots had been pushed to the side and stacked roughly to make space.

As soon as the door shut, Jenny bristled at him. "What are you doing here?" Her gaze flickered to Rakken. "You and your pet fairy. Did you kill Peter? And Martin?"

"What?! No, of course not! I was going to ask if you did, actually," Marius admitted.

"Me?"

"Because you clearly took Vane's plants and hid them in Jungle House," Marius said, surprising himself nearly as much as Jenny. Rakken made a quiet *ah*. "That night—you took the plants away before we arrived. You came back afterwards when you heard our voices, and you pretended you didn't already know Vane was dead. Did you kill Vane?" But surely Jenny wouldn't have? Her despair at Vane's death had seemed so *genuine*.

Jenny flinched. "No! No. I loved him." She hunched in on herself, voice cracking. "I loved him."

Marius felt Rakken's power flare and shot him a meaningful look. Rakken looked heavenwards, exasperated, but spread his hands in reluctant agreement that he would not compel the story out of her by force. The dark crackle of magic faded, and he withdrew to the far corner of the shed, leaving Marius to it.

Marius stepped closer to Jenny and pulled out a stool, perching on it so that he wouldn't loom over her. "But you were there that night, and you took the plants," he said gently.

Jenny gripped the edge of the bench so hard her knuckles were white. "I… I did take the plants. I can see now it was a stupid thing to do, but I wasn't thinking clearly. Father and the department and all those stupid arguments about funding and proper science—and why shouldn't fae plants be proper science?" Her eyes flared for a moment before her face fell. "And all I could think was that Martin had died for them, and I couldn't bear for them to be carted off—or, or incinerated or something for being dangerous or illegal. I knew they weren't properly legal, but you know how it is with foreign specimens…"

"Yes," Marius agreed. He did. "Why were you there that night?"

Jenny took a shuddering breath. "I'd been helping Martin for a while—he respected me, my expertise. He did!" she repeated, even though Marius hadn't made any sign of refuting her. "But he'd always kept me away from the actual exchanges. I don't believe he let anyone else in on those, not even his assistant."

"His assistant?"

"A grad student. Reading literature, if you can believe it," Jenny said with faint disdain for such idle pursuits. "I think they must have fallen out. But I know he couldn't have killed Martin because Amanda said she saw him out earlier that night, drinking, well before when I knew Martin was killed." She shuddered. "He was still… still warm when I found him."

Marius awkwardly patted her arm, feeling horrible.

Jenny took another gulp of breath, pushing the next words out in a rush: "I told my father I was meeting a girlfriend, but I'd really arranged to meet Vane after the exchange, to catalogue the new specimens. It was the first time he'd asked me if I would, and I thought it meant—" Her voice, which had been remarkably steady, broke off, and she gave a little hiccoughing sound, a sob catching in her throat. She'd thought it was a sign that Martin really did mean to break things off with his fiancée, that he loved her back with the same helpless intensity that she loved him.

Marius wished he did not know exactly how she felt. He thought of John and the tearing desperation of wanting whilst knowing deep down that his obsession wasn't reciprocated. It hardened something inside him. When things eventually ended between him and Rakken, he would not return to the place that John had sent him.

His gaze slid to the object of his thoughts, who had folded his arms and leaned back against the far corner of the shed. It was increasingly hard to imagine *after*, but he hoped that he and Rakken would manage to remain friends when it came. Were they friends now?

After a quavering moment, Jenny began to speak again. "I took the plants back, hid them where I knew I'd be able to check on them without anyone else knowing. I don't know what Peter was doing there last night, or if he knew about them. Maybe he saw me? I don't know. He was running his own project in Jungle House. He could have found the plants, I suppose."

"Did Martin Vane ever mention the name of his fae contact?" Rakken asked softly.

Jenny started, as if she'd forgotten he was there. She shook her head.

"Does the name Stoneholm mean anything to you?" Marius asked. Another negative.

A long silence fell.

Marius contemplated the plants set out on the workbench. He suspected they were going to need more reference texts from Rakken's library to identify them all, but he could make a start cataloguing now.

"What happens now?" Jenny asked.

He didn't know what justice was here, but he felt Jenny's need to *do* something. "You want to find Vane's murderer, don't you?" He waved at the line of plants. "Help me sort through these. Figuring out what they are might help us find them."

Jenny swallowed. "All right. How do you want to do this?"

"Systematically," Marius said. "And slowly." He looked to Rakken. "This is going to be dull for you."

Rakken's lips curved. "I shall cope."

There were fifty-two plants in total. Three matched the fragments Marius had already identified, and Rakken was able to identify another twelve on sight. None of the ones he knew had any especially worrying magical properties, he didn't think. "I am no expert, though," Rakken admitted.

Marius made a note of the names and prioritised cataloguing the rest.

He and Jenny divided the remainder between them and began to work, noting identifiable features and making quick sketches. Rakken wasn't a trained botanist, and Marius didn't trust him to make the observations—except for the magic. He asked Rakken to examine each plant using his leysight.

Rakken obediently did so, lifting each one to sniff it. Jenny watched this process with a peculiar expression but didn't question it.

Rakken looked thoughtful after he had finished. "I can tell these are all of Faerie, but I do not have any additional insight to offer beyond that."

"Is it just because they've recently been in Faerie and absorbed some of the ley energies there, or would you know them as fae plants regardless?" Marius asked.

Rakken looked amused. "Ley energies?"

Marius made an encompassing gesture. "You know, what all the books talk about, and you with your leysight. The way you see magic. And Severenn's talk of catalysts and environmental cues. I assumed the magic in different places must feel different somehow, like a signature."

Rakken's eyes flared in a way that made Marius fidget. It was a look he recognised well at this point because it meant Rakken was contemplating kissing him. He shifted a bit further away, just in case Rakken had forgotten Jenny's presence. Jenny had paused in her note-making, listening to their discussion about fae magic with quiet intensity.

"Yes," Rakken said after a beat. "Magic does feel different in different locations; it leaves an imprint on living things. That is why you taste of FallingStar, and I of the Spires." He frowned at the plants. "I am not sure if these would lose all taste of Faerie if they were grown long enough in the Mortal Realm. Something you might test."

"Could you trace these back to their point of origin, using the signature they absorbed?"

Rakken's gaze still held that molten heat. "I should not

be surprised at how quickly your mind works," he remarked. Rakken ran a finger over the nearest plant while Marius was figuring out what to do with the compliment. "But I do not know if I can trace these using that method. These plants may have passed through several locations on the way to Mortal, including portals, and they have spent at least a month here since. All of that would muddy any signature, even supposing the original location held sufficient magic to leave an impression in the first place. But it is worth trying." He picked up one of the plants that he had already identified—a nightshade species that he'd called black solaris—and retreated to the corner of the potting shed. Then he shook his head, looking up at the steel framing.

"Too much iron interference," Marius deduced.

Rakken nodded. "I will try outside." He hesitated.

"I'll be fine," Marius said. "I've still got your shield spell if Emyranthus turns up."

Rakken only made a humming sound in his throat before he left.

"You know a lot about fae magic," Jenny observed once they were alone.

"Rakken does. I've just picked up the odd bit here and there."

She cast him a sidelong glance, and his shoulders hunched up. "Is he…?"

"We're friends," he said shortly. "Just friends." They were that at least, weren't they? He certainly wasn't going to explain the benefits that friendship contained to Jenny of all people.

"Oh." She didn't say anything more (thank the gods), and they worked in silence for a bit, cataloguing specimens. After a while, she paused.

He looked up.

"Are there fae universities and researchers?" she asked, which made him laugh and then have to explain himself.

"I asked Rake the same thing not so long ago," he said. "But he says not."

"He's a scholar, though?"

"I suppose he is, a bit."

He could feel Jenny working her way up to her next question. "Did you find Martin's flat then, in Meridon?"

He thought of lying, but he'd been lied to too often himself to be comfortable doing it to someone else. Instead, he told her about the lowfae as diplomatically as he could.

"Thistlefel was one of them." He nodded at the helichaun, who was lying in a slant of sunlight. "I don't know exactly what Vane was planning to do with the lowfae he'd captured, but…"

"I'm not a child," Jenny said quietly. "I can guess. Martin had—you see it sometimes, that, that collecting mania. It's hardly uncommon amongst scientists."

"No," he said.

"You must think I'm a fool."

"No," he said again, more firmly. And then, without knowing quite why—"The last person I was… with… tried to black-mail my family and have my brother-in-law imprisoned for a crime he didn't commit."

"Oh." A long pause. "I'm sorry, for what I said before, in Martin's office. I shouldn't have said it. It's not my business."

Marius shook his head, not wanting to re-open that subject. "It's fine."

A hint of a smile. "And I'm sorry for thinking you might have murdered Martin."

"I'm, er, sorry as well. For thinking you might have."

The silence this time lay more comfortably between them.

Jenny picked up one of the smaller plants, a compact succulent the size of one hand. As he watched, she slipped it into her pocket.

"Um," he said. "What are you doing?"

Jenny whipped around, guilt blazing in her expression. And then, to his intense discomfort, she burst into tears.

He hated it when women cried; he never knew what to do. Awkwardly, he fished about for his handkerchief and offered it to her. Jenny took it with a gulp. After a few moments, she managed to swallow down her sobs.

"Sorry," she said between breathy gulps. "I'm being so… stupid… Martin's gone… and I don't have… anything of his."

"I don't think you're stupid at all," he said firmly.

She pulled the little grey-green succulent out of her pocket and looked at it curled in the palm of her hand. "I feel so stupid. Martin never trusted me, did he? I didn't know about the lowfae, or who he was trading with, or anything that mattered. He said I was different, but he didn't mean it at all. Just a stupid girl." Her lip began to wobble. "Half the time I'm glad he's dead, but then I think about never seeing him again and I just—I just can't bear it."

He patted her shoulder. "Keep it," he said. "You were Vane's unpaid co-researcher; these specimens are more yours than anyone else's. Assuming this one falls into the 'not highly illegal or dangerous' category of fae plants." He understood the desire for a lodestone amidst the chaos of grief.

Jenny gave a watery laugh but thankfully seemed to have stopped crying. She turned the succulent in her palm. "I doubt the police or the university will agree. They're probably planning to bury this lot in obscurity now their feathers are ruffled. You know how they are."

He did know. "Your father—"

Jenny shook her head. "I tried to talk to him about it, but he's worried about the impact on his reputation—and mine." She gave a bleak laugh. "I didn't tell him about Martin and me, but I think he guessed. Told me to look for surer prospects." She grimaced.

"Well, don't look at me," Marius said fervently.

Her grimace shifted into something worryingly thoughtful. "Why not?"

"Er…" he began, wondering if he should point out what Jenny *had already pointed out*, but Jenny shook her head.

"We wouldn't be the first marriage like that, and I wouldn't… interfere with you. You know my father would be thrilled. And you wouldn't expect me to—give up my career and be wifely and all that." Her mouth had gone hard. "My mother was one of the first class of female students at Knoxbridge, did you know that? She would have gotten a first if they'd given degrees to women in those days. And now all she does is type up my father's notes for him."

Marius wished rather helplessly that he were anywhere else. "I'm, er… sorry. I can't." It seemed so deeply impolite to refuse someone's marriage proposal that he had to stifle the urge to reflexively agree. He flailed around for something to soften the blow. "But it doesn't mean I don't want to work with you."

He told Jenny about his research plans. Her eyes brightened with interest, but eventually she shook her head. "My father won't go for it, and nor will the department. Not after this." She ran a hand along the workbench. "They were going to give the Roseward Grant to Martin, you know. It *should* have gone to Martin. I don't care if it's disloyal to say it; the existence of fae plants is the most exciting botanical development this century, and they'll all just ignore it now for being too scandalous, and then in five years' time they'll change their minds and claim credit for his ideas themselves."

Marius grimaced. Greenbriars had just been awarded the grant.

Rakken returned then, carrying the plant that he'd taken.

"Well? Did it work? Your tracking magic?" Jenny demanded.

Rakken put the plant back on the workbench. "Magic is not a simple matter, Jennifer Greenbriars."

"So, no, it didn't work?"

Rakken addressed himself to Marius. "There is a resonance there, but it's faint. I can set up the parameters of a tracking spell using it, but I will need to be within Faerie to try it, and it will take some time. I am not sure of my chances of success."

Marius checked the log they'd been making. "We still have a lot to do here, to work through this lot."

Rakken shook his head. "Emyranthus remains at large, and too many mortal botanists have been murdered of late for my liking. I will wait."

They worked. Day bled into night. Marius switched on the single bulb in the potting shed, but it was not long before his eyes began to blur. They still had most of the specimens to catalogue when the guard knocked on the door and asked how late they were planning to stay there. He wanted to lock up.

Rakken glanced at Marius. He hadn't slept last night, Marius remembered abruptly. "We'll come back to do the rest tomorrow," he found himself saying. "Come on, Jenny; time to pack it up."

Rakken looked faintly surprised but did not disagree.

They bade Jenny good night and waited while the guard locked the shed. Rakken, having little faith in mortal security, cast his own magic after the guard had left. He did look tired, Marius thought, a faint tightness around his eyes. Rakken had cast a lot of magic between yesterday and today without taking any time to restore himself. Not that he'd admit it, though.

They returned to Rakken's flat. Marius kept opening his mouth to speak and then closing it, so that they walked in silence. While they had been working on detective-related activities, the strange tension between them earlier had all but disappeared, but now it returned in full force.

"Are you all right?" he asked quietly, as they turned down Pennyroyal Lane.

Rakken hesitated with his hand on the gate. He turned back. His expression was unreadable, but there was a thread of anger in his tone. "Do not treat me as a wounded dove, Marius Valstar."

"No, of course not. I just—you keep telling me that magic expends energy, and I know you haven't had a chance to rest since—"

Rakken cut him off. "I am perfectly capable. You are still safe from Emyranthus while you are with me."

"That's not why—I'm just *concerned*—"

"It is not your business to be concerned about me. You are not my keeper."

"I am your *friend!*" he snapped.

"Are you." Rakken said the words flatly as he opened the door. He stepped through without waiting for a response.

Marius followed him in, about ready to strangle the man. "Yes! *We* are friends, Rake! It's *normal* to worry about your friends! Stop making this into the end of days!"

Rakken had withdrawn to the windows on the far side of the room, his back turned. He picked up a knight from the chessboard. "I did not ask you for friendship, Marius Valstar."

He threw up his hands. "Fine! What are we, then?" His heart pounded.

Rakken's voice was calm, almost bored. "A convenient arrangement. Unless you have changed your mind about that?"

Beneath his anger, Marius had just sense enough to wonder if this was Rakken's way of asking for reassurance. He resisted the urge to throw something. "I meant what I said earlier; I do still want you."

Rakken put the chess piece down. When he looked up, there was a dark fire burning in his eyes. "Show me, then." His tone was pure sin. "I would like to be convinced."

Marius gave a startled bark of laughter, fond and exasperated in equal measure. "You are utterly shameless," he grumbled, even as heat shot straight through him, pooling in his groin.

Rakken arched his neck. "Yes. Don't pretend you don't like it."

Gods help him, he did. Just as he knew Rakken was deflecting, using sex as a distraction. The problem was that it was such a *good* distraction. Surrendering to the inevitable, he drew closer. Rakken's gaze turned molten.

But before they touched, there came a loud knocking.

He jerked, unsure if he was grateful for the interruption or cursing it. Taking a few deep breaths to calm down certain matters, he opened the door.

A boy of about fifteen had his hand raised to knock again. He wore a courier's uniform. "Is a Mr Marius Valstar staying here, sir? I've a telegram for him."

Marius frowned. "I'm Mr Valstar. Let's see it."

The boy nodded and handed it over. "Evening, then." He doffed his hat before turning and trotting back down the lane to his bicycle.

Marius closed the door, frowning down at the telegram and puzzling it out. It was from Hetta. After a moment he looked up, heart beating faster. "Hetta says they checked the lists of who used the Gates at Stariel. There was a greater dryad on them—a dryad by the name of Ithras Stoneholm."

28

FINALLY. SOME PROGRESS

NEARLY A WEEK later, Marius stepped through the final portal and enjoyed the stable ground under his feet. Rakken had finally tracked Ithras Stoneholm to an unclaimed land in Faerie, but unclaimed lands meant few Gates. Marius had lost count of how many temporary portals Rakken had made today, charting a course between resonances. The dizzying sensation of stepping through one had taken longer and longer to dissipate each time.

The portal saw them emerge onto a large flat boulder in the midst of dense jungle. There was no sign of habitation nearby. He frowned at the greenery, trying to identify species. A lot of climbers. Loud, unfamiliar birds called in the distance. He could feel beads of sweat already breaking out on the back of his neck.

Rakken looked down at the boulder with satisfaction.

"You intended to end up here, then?" Marius asked.

"Yes. We will need to fly the rest of the way."

Marius didn't object. This might be one of the last times they flew together, if the dryad was responsible for the murders.

Rakken would have no reason to linger in Knoxbridge once they solved the murders.

He'll still have to protect me until we find Emyranthus, he reassured himself. This wasn't the *last* time. Not yet. His chest tightened. He would be all right; he had gone into this with his eyes open. They would be... friends, and it would be fine. He would not be the broken-hearted wreck that John had left him. It would just be a change. An adjustment.

They flew. He was grateful for the cool wind of Rakken's wings. Below, the jungle stretched in an endless green canopy. He would have missed the building completely, but Rakken began to descend, seeing some cue Marius had missed.

They set down, and Marius could see why it had been so hard to spot. The building looked like part of the jungle, its walls made of the twisted growing trunks of trees. There were windows set in those strange walls, and through them he could see feylights burning. A fenced area extended behind the building, covered over with green netting supported by large poles.

He slid out of Rakken's arms, shoes sinking into the soft earth. Back at ground level, the full heat of the jungle was considerable, and he rather wanted to take off his coat and several more layers besides. Probably not the time for it right now.

They didn't speak. He knew Rakken was glamouring them into invisibility so as not to give warning of their approach. It would be easier to maintain the less he had to mask.

Rakken made an intricate gesture, testing for wards. Marius would never get tired of watching him do that, the way his hands shaped invisible currents with such graceful strength. *I'll miss watching him,* he thought, and then squashed the curl of unhelpful sentiment.

Something flared briefly along the building's walls, and

Rakken muttered a few words, long fingers weaving. It sparked and went out. Satisfied, he strode forward with the sleek grace of a hunting cat.

Marius put his hands in his pockets and followed, knowing his approach would more aptly be compared to 'awkward family dog'.

For some reason, he'd expected subtlety, but Rakken was anything but. He blew the front door off with a blast of controlled air and strode into the building in the happy knowledge that he was the most dangerous thing there.

Must be nice, Marius reflected as he blinked at the splintered door.

By the time he'd recovered from his surprise and stepped over the ruin of the door, Rakken had already gone through the main building and disappeared into the fenced area at the rear. Marius hurried after him, gaining only a brief impression of the interior—rows of shelves, benches glittering with glassware and some sort of distillation equipment, a kitchen, a box of syringes filled with bright pink liquid. The kitchen door opened out to the fenced nursery.

He stepped outside and saw that Rakken had found the building's occupant. They were sprinting the length of the nursery, past raised beds and clusters of young saplings, towards the gate (mundane rather than magical) in the far wall.

"Stop." Rakken didn't shout, but the word rang with power. The strange fae twitched, faltering mid-step, and nearly fell over before they recovered their balance. They stood, held in place against their will, and waited. Rakken stalked towards them like a panther approaching a mouse.

The dryad trembled, their deep brown eyes wide and terrified. They were tall—even taller than Rakken—and slender, with a flat, smooth face and the usual alien fae beauty. Their hair was pale gold and tightly curled around pointed ears, and their skin was pale green with darker markings, mottled almost like the bark of a tree. Their claws, the deep green of winter grass, retracted in and out of their fingers.

"Ithras Stoneholm, greater dryad of no court," Rakken said with deadly menace. The humidity in the air had become something thicker, the heavy weight of thunderstorms pressing down, and the other botanical scents were smothered under the weight of citrus.

Ithras Stoneholm shuddered.

There was bloodlock growing in one of the rows, Marius recognised suddenly. Immature specimens. He took a closer look at his surroundings. *All* the highly controlled plants that Vane had been growing at his flat were here, all seedlings. Had they been planted since Vane's death? The dryad had lost their supplier, after all.

Stoneholm began to speak, words rolling out of them even though Rakken hadn't asked anything at all, such was the power of his compulsion. "I was trading with the mortal. I supplied him with new specimens in exchange for growing certain plants and regularly harvesting them for me. I don't like to grow them here, but there are no rules for what one may grow in Mortal. He didn't know their use, only that they were valuable."

"What of the other plants you supplied to him?" Rakken asked. His voice was warm and dark, coated in a persuasiveness so intense that even Marius found himself taking a step towards him before he shook it off.

Stoneholm swayed under it but made a dismissive gesture. "Worthless. Common species. The mortal bargained for plants with magical properties, but almost everything is, with the right preparation."

"Do you have a list?" Marius asked.

Stoneholm looked at him with glazed eyes. "There's a manifest," they said slowly.

"Show us."

The dryad moved jerkily, reaching into their voluminous pockets and coming out with a notebook. Marius took it from them, hearing Stoneholm think *the human* with a faint note of apprehension as he did so. "What happened that night? Did you kill Vane?" he asked.

"No! He delivered his side of the bargain as agreed, though he had become suspicious of what they were for. I gave him the plants. I left."

"What about your dryad blade?" Rakken pulled it from nothing with a snap.

Stoneholm's eyes widened. "The mortal needed reminding of his place. He asked too many questions. I made it to frighten him and left it there so he would remember it."

"Who killed him?"

But Stoneholm only shook their head. "I don't know! Who knows or cares why mortals do things? Please! I have told you all I know."

"You are growing bloodlock, Ithras Stoneholm. You traded dangerous plants with a mortal."

The dryad did something odd then. They turned pleading eyes towards a section of the garden wall, where a layer of creepers covered the wooden slats and a young tree with palm-sized lobed leaves grew. "Please. I gave you what you asked for."

Magic blossomed, and Marius jerked away even before his conscious mind had realised the reason for his reaction.

A silvery whip snaked out of the clear sky and cracked against an invisible barrier. His shield amulet had activated, so that the whip struck a wavering sphere around him. More whips manifested from thin air all around him, each one hitting with considerable force. The amulet around his neck grew painfully hot.

Rakken's wings flared as he whirled, trying to find the source. Marius pointed towards the creepers along the wall, instinctively knowing where she was hiding even though he couldn't see her—his telepathy doing something useful for once.

Rakken sprang into action without hesitation. There was a confused clash of magic and feathers and then Emyranthus's glamour fell away. She and Rakken grappled, magic and feathers filling the air.

Stoneholm made a run for it. Marius shouted and lunged for them, but Stoneholm evaded him, knocking a stack of seedlings into his path. Marius stumbled. Stoneholm took the opportunity to put distance between them, sprinting into full motion with a speed that was truly astonishing. Marius hadn't a hope in the hells of catching up, but it was only as he reached the threshold back into the main house and saw that Stoneholm had already fled through it and out via the splintered front door on the other side that he realised he might not *want* to. What had he even been planning to do against a fae who was probably just as strong—if not stronger—than he was, and with who knew what magic besides?

He turned back, panting, to find Rakken had Emyranthus hard up against the fence, bound with her own silvery ropes. She still held a dagger in one hand, and her expression promised violence. There was a strong smell of ozone in the air.

Rakken was breathing hard as Marius padded warily over to

them. "Enough," he growled at her. "Enough, Emyr. It's over."

She bared her teeth at him. "Why should you get to decide when it is done? *I* am not done. Are you not having fun, Rake?"

"You will swear not to harm this one, Emyranthus Gracehame," Rakken said in a menacing tone.

She raised an eyebrow, summoning her dignity. "Or what? Will you sell yourself off to the highest bidder again?" Her smile grew sly, and Marius hadn't realised he'd taken a step forward until Rakken shot out a hand to stop him. "You must admit that was terribly amusing to watch."

She didn't know, Marius saw with sudden clarity. She didn't know Rakken at all. She thought this was another of their games.

"Or I will kill you." Rakken said it without hesitation. The bottom dropped out of Marius's stomach.

Emyranthus looked equally shocked. Her mouth fell open, her wings giving a startled flare. "Truly, Rake?" Her tone was soft, and she shaped the diminutive with uncomfortable familiarity. "Is that what it has come to, between us?"

Rakken's grip didn't yield, and Emyranthus gasped, as if the ropes had tightened. Marius didn't think he'd ever seen him so coldly furious. "Swear it, Emyr."

Her lips pursed, full and red. She looked past Rakken's bristling presence and met Marius's eyes. Her eyes were pale, he noticed, a wintry blue. He could feel her contempt, her disbelief that Rake would go to such trouble over a pathetic mortal. It brought all his insecurities to the surface, and he resisted the urge to touch the silvering threads in his black hair.

She looked back to Rakken. "Why this mortal?"

Rakken didn't answer. "You will not seek harm to Marius Valstar, directly or indirectly. Swear it, Emyr."

Emyranthus's lips peeled back in a grimace. "I will not seek
harm to Marius Valstar, directly or indirectly."

"Did you kill Vane?" Marius asked her.

Emyranthus's eyes burned with hate this time when she
looked at him.

"The mortal who was killed with fae magic near where you
attacked Marius last time," Rakken clarified.

"I know who Vane is," Emyranthus hissed. Her eyes widened.
"You think I would kill the wrong mortal by *mistake*? Better take
my knife then, Rake, if you believe me so careless." She gave
a laugh that made Marius flinch and dropped the blade in her
hand. It clattered on the gravel. "You utter piece of excrement."

Marius would have sympathised with her pain if she hadn't
tried so hard to kill him.

Rakken's feathers were all bristling, making him a birdy
kind of hedgehog. "Why were you working with Stoneholm
then? Explain it to me, Emyr, and I may be able to keep this
from becoming very political."

Emyr rolled her eyes. She had buried her anger and hurt
beneath a smooth, mocking mask, and for the first time, he
saw what must have attracted Rakken to her. They had that
in common, that hardened bravado, that way of twisting pain
into just another game.

"Save your veiled threats, Rake; I wasn't working with the
dryad. I merely bargained with them for the opportunity to
kill your pretty plaything." She shot Marius a vicious glance.
"Which you have now taken from me. A shame. I knew you
were hunting for them because your precious baby telepath
inadvertently shared the information with me. Not like you, to
be enthralled by weakness. Let me know when you tire of it. *I*
certainly have. You're being very dull with this possessive act of

yours. Unless you're proposing to entertain me, you can release me now. I have sworn your foolish oath."

Rakken narrowed his eyes at her, but Marius could see he wasn't sure what else to do now. "I was not threatening you," he said after a moment. "I was warning you. Our queen has agreed to treat your actions so far as a personal matter, but you walk a fine line—"

Emyr scoffed, a hint of anger flashing. "Do not lecture me on how to fly. I am no fledgling."

Rakken sighed, but the silvery ropes began to slither free. Emyranthus pushed away from the wall, fanning her wings in and out. She went to lay a hand on Rakken's arm, but he moved out of reach.

She rolled her eyes. "So serious, Rake." But there was sadness there.

Marius felt intensely awkward. "I'm sorry," he said.

Her eyebrows went up. "Then you are a fool." She moved then, aggression in her intent, but Rakken reacted so quickly that he'd already caught her wrist even as Marius registered the action.

"Emyr," Rakken said softly. He looked down at her with a faintly puzzled expression. "I did not take you for an oathbreaker."

"I am not," Emyr said with satisfaction.

Rakken inhaled sharply. Alarm rushed through Marius in a quick, electrifying sensation. Something was wrong. Rakken released Emyranthus, shaking his head as if a fly were trying to settle. Something made of glass fell to the ground and smashed: a syringe. Empty, but for a few bright pink droplets clinging to the interior.

Understanding came like the shuttering slides of a projector.

The syringe had been filled with bloodlock. Emyr had stabbed Rakken with the syringe. Therefore, Rakken was now full of bloodlock.

It makes us biddable, Rakken had told him, but he hadn't understood the full horror of what that meant until now when Rakken, quivering, looked up with an unsettling blankness in his expression.

"Come here," Emyranthus told him, holding out a hand, and there was compulsion in it.

Rakken took it without hesitation.

Emyranthus looked past him to Marius. "You are lucky I have already sworn an oath, mortal." She shrugged, as if that was all the attention she was prepared to waste on him, and began to walk back towards the building. Rakken followed at her heels.

"What are you doing?" Marius asked. "You really think he'll forgive you for this? For drugging him and compelling him on top of that? You think his sister will forgive you?"

Emyranthus said coolly: "This will not come to her majesty's attention. Rake appreciates people who challenge him. We are fae; we find strength attractive. It doesn't surprise me that you cannot understand, simple human that you are."

Marius shook his head. Emyranthus didn't know Rakken at all, he realised. Rakken had been right to classify their relationship as no such thing because no one who knew him would ever have made such a wildly incorrect assumption.

"This isn't a game, Emyranthus. He will *never* forgive you, not for this. And if you do this, he will have to kill you. That will hurt him—but it won't stop him. Don't you know that?" Because Marius knew Rakken, knew that he had a streak of ruthless practicality in him that would not flinch from doing whatever he had to do to keep his sister's power secure.

But Emyranthus ignored him and began to stride towards the building, Rakken following at her heels.

"Rake!"

Rakken frowned and looked back, but Emyranthus snapped her fingers, and Marius knew she had doubled down on the compulsion. Expression going slack, Rakken turned away from him.

Compulsion. It wasn't aimed at Marius, but he clung to the feel of it, using it to find that unpredictable trigger within, balling up his horror into a weapon.

"Stop!" He flung the word with, he hoped, telepathic projection, and saw Emyranthus flinch. Her wings flared out and she stumbled and fell onto a raised bed. She sat amongst crushed seedlings, shaking her head dazedly.

He ran to Rakken and grabbed his hand. "Don't let her touch you," he told Rakken.

Rakken smiled at him and said, in an eerily placid voice: "As you wish. I don't want her to touch me."

Marius's head was ringing, but he tugged Rakken further away, back down the row, past more seedlings and raised beds, towards the gate in the back fence. The gate was fastened with a wooden bar, which he had to let go of Rakken's hand to lift. Unlatching it, he pulled Rakken through and closed the gate behind them, heart racing. How long would it take Emyranthus to recover? Could he bar the gate from this side somehow? No, that wouldn't stop her.

The jungle rose before them. Marius swallowed. "We need to get out of here—is there a resonance point somewhere close? Can you find one and make a portal?"

"Yes," said Rakken. "You always make portals easier. I don't know why. I do like portals," he said with a happy sigh, beginning to draw sigils in the air. "Even if Cat says I ought to be more careful with them. I don't know why Aroset was given enhanced portal-making abilities. It ought to have been me, logically. Why did I get stronger compulsion? Aroset should have gotten that, if it were based on our prior magic use. Though I suppose it's better that she didn't."

Marius stared at him. Behind him, the gate slammed open with a blast of air.

"Hurry!"

The portal flared to life, and Marius didn't even look at where it led before he pulled an unresisting Rakken through.

29

THIS IS YOUR RAKE ON DRUGS

THEY WERE ON a riverbank in a gloomy forest made up of species he knew well. A rough deer track ran along its edge. He stared at it, feeling a tickling sense of familiarity, and it clicked into place: They were back in the Mortal Realm, near Stariel. This was the river Starshine, which flowed south from Starwater.

He didn't question their luck, grabbing Rakken's hand and drawing him forward, stumbling over roots but not stopping until they were over the border. Only after the silent land guardian's presence rose in his soul did he relax. If Emyranthus followed them here, she wouldn't be able to get at them now.

He paused to catch his breath, feeling shaky. He put his hand against an oak trunk to steady himself. "Right. We're safe. How are you doing?"

Rakken's eyes were less blank away from Emyranthus's compulsion, but he wore a dreamy smile that twisted Marius's insides with its wrongness. Rakken never looked that blithely happy. "I am glad to be with you," he said, as if this answered the question. He stepped closer and nuzzled at Marius's neck. "I like the way your magic smells. Like old books and cut grass. It makes me want to lick it." He did exactly that, tickling Marius's ear.

Marius disentangled himself, putting the tree between Rakken and himself. "You know Emyranthus dosed you with bloodlock, don't you?"

"Yes." Rakken didn't seem at all concerned. He followed Marius around the tree, reaching for him. "You are so beautiful. I want to kiss you."

Marius was both charmed and alarmed. "I don't think that's a good idea right now. Let go, Rake."

Rakken let go immediately, though he gave a small pout as he did so, like a child being denied a treat.

Marius considered him rather helplessly. "Do you know how long the bloodlock will last?"

Rakken shrugged, blithely unconcerned. "I've never been dosed before. I don't know why I was so worried about it; it feels lovely." He laughed, soft and joyful.

A fierce, protective urge rose in his chest. This was Rakken without any barriers at all, and combined with the fact that fae couldn't lie… This was dangerous. Rakken might say anything in this state, secrets he would later regret revealing. He knew Rakken would hate being so open, after this drug wore off.

"Do you have to tell the truth even though you're drugged?" He knew fae could lie if they were compelled to do so.

"Oh yes," Rakken said. "That's one of the reasons bloodlock is so tightly controlled. What would you like to know?"

Marius sucked in a breath. "You're not… worried by that?"

"No. You're wonderful. I want to tell you anything that

would please you. What would please you?"

Well, that was both terrifying and terrifyingly tempting. "Er, not just now, thanks."

His land-sense wasn't strong, but he reached out with it now, hoping to draw Stariel's—and thereby Hetta's—attention. It felt a little bit like trying to project telepathically, he realised with surprise.

"Hetta!" he shouted, because it was easier to try to project things if he said the words aloud. The opposite was also true; he was most likely to 'hear' thoughts that were on the tip of someone's tongue. He felt a bit silly, yelling into the gloomy forest. All the birds went quiet at the racket he was making.

"Hallowyn Tempestren!" He added Wyn's name to the mix a few times for good measure. Maybe Wyn would know how to counteract the bloodlock, or at least when it might wear off.

He prodded at his land-sense, trying to judge whether his summons had worked. But if anything, Stariel seemed even *less* present than usual.

"I don't think that worked," he told Rakken. "Let's walk to the house." Flying would be faster, but he didn't trust Rakken in this state. There was an unsettling languidness to his movements, as if he weren't paying enough attention and might catch himself on every stray branch if left to his own devices.

They walked, following the deer track along the river. After a while, Rakken began humming, an unfamiliar melody.

"What are you singing?" he asked.

"A travel song," Rakken said, and then began to sing in full lyrics.

Marius had heard him sing once before, at Hetta and Wyn's wedding. He had a good voice (what a surprise), smooth and resonant, and as he sang, he became something other, like a part

of the forest come alive. The words were poetic, brief snippets
of imagery, though Marius noticed how carefully the sentences
were constructed to avoid the possibility of falsehood.

Eventually, they reached the southern end of Starwater. The
great lake sparkled under the sky, the house a pale blob in
the distance. Even out from under the boughs of the forest,
everything felt oddly hushed. He reached out again with his
land-sense, unable to shake the feeling that something was
amiss. Rakken waited with no sign of impatience, wearing an
unnervingly placid expression.

Eventually, Marius gave up, shaking his head. He pointed
towards the path that would lead them to the lake's edge. "We'll
go that way. It eventually meets up with the driveway. Let's go."

Rakken obediently started into motion, sidling closer to
Marius as he did so. His fingers twined with Marius's.

Marius pulled his hand free. "Wait—"

Rakken, who had been reaching for him again, froze
instantly.

"What are you doing?" Marius asked, feeling great moss-
filled quagmires beneath his feet.

"I want to hold your hand," Rakken said simply.

"All right," Marius said, his chest tightening painfully.

Rakken gave a happy sigh and curled his hand around
Marius's. "Can I kiss you now too?"

"Not right now. Please don't ask in front of anyone else,"
Marius said, his heart pounding.

"I won't. Don't worry, starling," Rakken said, squeezing his
hand, and it made Marius want to cry. Rakken was trying to
reassure *him*.

He felt sick at what Emyranthus had tried to do. "*You* don't
worry; I'll look after you."

"I am not worried," Rakken said, smiling. "I'm with you, and it is a nice day. I'm perfectly happy. Are you?" He lifted his face towards the sun.

"Yes," Marius lied. It was a nice day, cold but clear. He couldn't appreciate it. His mind turned back to Emyranthus. "If neither Emyranthus nor the dryad killed Vane," he said, thinking aloud, "who else does that leave?"

"I don't like Emyr anymore," Rakken offered.

Marius decided further ruminations would have to wait until the bloodlock wore off.

It took them the better part of two hours to work their way around the lake, but Rakken was still in the grip of the drug when they reached the house. A nameless apprehension filled him, which he didn't think was just due to Rakken's state. There was something strange going on with Stariel.

He found three of his siblings on the front lawn, throwing skittles. Well, Alexandra was throwing skittles and trying to interest Laurel in them. Gregory was pacing, hatless, blond locks in disarray.

"Marius!" Little Laurel spotted them and launched herself across the lawn at him, heedless of dignity.

He felt a wide smile stretch his face and caught her up, letting out a breath on impact. "Little Laurel-lion," he said, swinging her in a circle.

He set her down on the grass, and she told him eagerly, "I'm going to be an aunt! I want it to be today, but Alex says it might not be until tomorrow even though Hetta has been having the babies all day already. Apparently, it takes longer, the first time," she explained. "Did you know that?"

Oh. That explained why Stariel was so distracted—and also why Hetta and Wyn hadn't responded to his summons.

Alexandra and Gregory had followed Laurel over at a more sedate pace.

"Everything's going, er, all right?" he asked them, trying to sound more relaxed than he felt. He didn't want to transfer his own anxieties to his siblings.

"I think so," Alexandra said, a spark of amusement in her expression. "Mama is with her—and so is Wyn. The midwife was a bit ruffled about it."

"And Hetta swore at both of them," Laurel said with great relish. "But then they kicked us out."

Gregory had flushed beet red during this recounting.

"So we're distracting ourselves," Alexandra summarised. She looked towards the house, a combination of worry and excitement in her big blue eyes. She always was a sensitive soul.

"Oh! My niephlings are coming!" Rakken exclaimed, as if he had only just realised what they were talking about. He tucked a casual arm into Marius's and beamed at Marius's siblings.

Gregory frowned and turned to Marius. "What's wrong with him?"

"Mossfeathers!" Irokoi landed near them in a rustle of black wings.

"You know, I've always thought you call me that because you're jealous my wings are finer than yours," Rakken told Irokoi amiably.

"They are not." Irokoi blinked and turned to Marius as well. "What's wrong with him?"

"He's been drugged," Marius said, eyeing Laurel and choosing his words carefully. "We had some trouble in Faerie. Do you know how long the effects of bloodlock last?"

Irokoi's eyes widened. "Oh. Well, that explains it then. Topical or ingested?"

"Injected."

"Probably not until tomorrow at the earliest," Irokoi said. "Depending on how concentrated the dose was."

IT WAS A STRANGE night. Rakken remained eerily docile but would answer any question put to him without hesitation. This caused a few moments of intense awkwardness until Marius was able to explain the broad strokes of the situation. After that, the others found Rakken's state amusing. It helped that it was far from the most peculiar thing to happen at Stariel in recent times, and that they were all distracted, waiting for news.

The other source of awkwardness was that Rakken was endlessly affectionate and kept trying for opportunities to touch him. If Marius told him to let go or step back, he obeyed, but it was rather like trying to put off a cat determined to be petted—or an overly enthusiastic octopus.

As the night wore into the early hours of the morning, Marius gave up and let Rakken curl against his shoulder on the sofa in Carnelion Hall. It wasn't necessary to stay up waiting—something he'd told Laurel firmly when she'd grown grumpy and overtired and he'd bundled her off to bed. There would be plenty of time to see the babies tomorrow after they were born, he told her. It wasn't as if there was anything for her to do but wait in the meantime. She would be better to get some sleep.

The same logic applied to himself, but he knew he wouldn't sleep and didn't try. It surprised him that his cousin Jack felt the same; he did not usually share in Marius's nameless anxieties.

But Marius caught a stray thought of lambing season, a flicker of all the things Jack had seen go wrong.

Gregory and Alexandra remained awake too, and they were past the age where he could send them to bed. So midnight found them all gathered in Carnelion Hall, waiting. Gregory brought out a card game, which passed the time, though they had to ban Rakken from playing because he kept telling everyone what his hand was and guessing aloud about what cards everyone else held.

Jack gave Rakken a disgusted look and rolled his eyes. "Whiskey?" he offered Marius, finding his way to the cabinet.

"Yes, please," Marius said so fervently that Jack gave a bark of laughter.

"Do I get one?" Rakken asked sleepily against Marius's shoulder.

"No. We're trying to get the sources of intoxication *out* of you, not put more in," Marius said firmly.

"I do so enjoy it when you get all protective of me. You can be so fierce defending others in ways you never are for yourself. No wonder I can't help but love you."

Marius flushed. "Stop talking, Rake," he managed to get out.

Alexandra giggled and made a sugary *aww* sound that made Marius wish he could disappear. "Who knew he could be so sweet?"

Marius wriggled out of Rakken's hold and stood, muttering, "No, stay there for the moment," when Rakken tried to follow him up. Rakken obediently sat down, though he looked up at Marius like a dog being abandoned.

Fuck. *Fuck.* His heart was hammering.

Thank the gods something shifted right at that moment, something in his land-sense sparking.

"Is that…?" Gregory asked.

"Yes," said Jack, grinning broadly. "New Valstars." He handed Marius his glass and they clunked them together.

It was only a few minutes later that little Laurel appeared on the threshold in her white nightgown. She looked half-defiant, half-nervous. "Are the babies here?" she whispered. "I felt something."

"Yes," said Alexandra, holding out her arms. Laurel took this as permission to trot over and climb into her lap.

Some time later, Lady Phoebe arrived with Wyn in tow. He stood up to greet them, and Rakken followed suit. His heart pounded, though it was mostly with relief; Wyn would not have left his wife if something had gone wrong, even if he did look a bit shellshocked.

Then Marius noticed each carried a wrapped bundle.

"Two healthy girls!" Lady Phoebe said happily.

"Hetta?" Marius asked urgently.

"She's sleeping now," Wyn said. He looked down at the bundle he held, and his expression melted around the edges. "She was amazing. I'm a father. Storms above. They're so *tiny!*" His voice throbbed.

Marius smiled. "Congratulations. They're beautiful."

His two nieces were actually squishy red blobs with faces a lot like wrinkled old men, but he knew better than to say so. He'd seen newborns before and knew they improved significantly. Though it hit him that these were the first fae—or at least part fae—babies he'd ever seen.

"Do they have wings?" Laurel asked.

Wyn gave a soft huff of laughter, but his eyes were bright. Marius knew what it meant to him. "Yes. Extremely small ones."

"Like a baby chicken's?"

"Laurel!" Phoebe said. "We've talked about making personal

remarks about people's appearances."

"But they're babies," Laurel pointed out. "They won't mind. Besides, it's lovely that they have wings, isn't it? I wish I had wings." She gave Wyn's feathers an envious glance.

Rakken padded over and stared down at the baby Phoebe was holding. His expression grew awed. "Fae and human both. They are perfect, brother," he murmured.

It was a measure of Wyn's exhaustion that he didn't notice anything odd about Rakken's demeanour. Wyn and Phoebe didn't stay long, taking the docilely sleeping twins back before they could wake.

After that climax, the party began to disperse, though everyone was smiling. Rakken followed Marius out, grinning from ear to ear.

"We are uncles," he told Marius, catching Marius's hand in his.

"We are," he agreed, something in his heart stuttering. He thought about shaking Rakken off, but there was no one about, and anyway, everyone would no doubt chalk it up to either Rakken's condition or their friendship if they saw.

Rakken's artless declaration from earlier crept back. Marius had been doing a great job of not thinking about it. He wanted to ask Rakken to repeat his words, but it felt wrong to do so under the circumstances.

He tried to leave Rakken in one of the guest bedrooms, but Rakken clung to him like a limpet. "Don't leave me alone. Please," he said, and something like panic sparked behind the placid calm of his green eyes.

Marius didn't need much persuasion. Rakken was so horribly vulnerable like this, and his heart twisted again, thinking of how Emyranthus had intended to take advantage of that.

He took Rakken back to his own room. As soon as the door

shut, Rakken kissed him, and drugged or no, his lips had lost none of their persuasiveness.

"No," Marius told him when things naturally escalated. "Not when you can't say no."

Rakken pouted. "I don't want to say no!"

"Even so," Marius said, and turned away. "Come on. Can you change to mortal form? You won't fit like this."

"You need a larger bed," Rakken said, but obliged before settling in beside him, a warm line against Marius's back.

HE WOKE SOME TIME later with his heart racing from adrenaline not his own, his mind full of tigers. It was instinct to reach out: *It's me; we're here, and safe.*

Rakken lay stiff as a board next to him.

"You're safe, Rake," Marius mumbled, not sure if he was speaking or projecting, he was so sleep-muddled.

Rakken let out the breath he'd been holding in a long, slow exhalation, and Marius felt the dangerous moment pass. "Thank you," he said, so softly it was barely audible. He sounded much more himself, as if the drugs had finally worked their way out of his system.

Marius nosed into Rakken's neck as sleep rolled back over him. "You're welcome."

But when he woke for the second time, he was alone.

30

EVERYONE GETS SENTIMENTAL

MARIUS STARED AT his conspicuously empty bed, unsure whether to be concerned. Had the blood-lock worn off? Perhaps Rakken had simply gotten up earlier and wandered off to entertain himself. He did sleep less than a human, after all.

Or (considerably more likely), Rakken had done exactly what he always did whenever someone chipped at his armour: retreat.

No wonder I can't help but love you.

The words were a relentless drumbeat as Marius dressed and went down to breakfast. He pulled them into pieces, looking for some other interpretation.

I love you.

Rakken had said he loved him.

Rakken couldn't lie.

Ergo, Rakken loved him. Terminally anxious, difficult, bur-densome Marius. Even though that made no sense whatsoever.

There was no one else in the breakfast room. He poured himself tea with suddenly shaking hands and sank down into the nearest chair. He hadn't—he'd never—how could someone like Rakken love him? And where did Rakken get off with making that sort of declaration when they'd agreed this thing between them was only about baser desires. Hadn't they? He gave a shaky laugh. So this was what irony felt like. He'd resisted Rakken's advances for so long, worried about getting his heart shredded. He'd never worried about *Rakken's* heart, since he seemed about as likely to fall in love as the average housecat. *He's the one who said this thing between us needn't entail emotional attachment!*

He fisted his hands in his hair and laughed again, more bitterly, because what he wanted above everything at this moment was to find Rakken and ask: "Are you sure?"

That's not very promising, if your first reaction is that it must all be a terrible mistake!

Also not promising was that there continued to be no sign of Rakken. Was he even still at Stariel or had he returned to the Spires? Marius supposed that since Emyranthus had sworn that oath, he no longer needed a bodyguard.

Did he love Rakken?

He hadn't let his mind so much as whisper the word, and it sent a cold thrill of dread through him now. Love had pulled him under last time, made him pathetic and vulnerable, and when he'd finally torn free of it, it had taken something from him, something deep. How could you love again, knowing what waited for you afterwards? Because Marius knew there would be an afterwards. Assuming that Rakken loved him now, *hypothetically*, how long could that last?

He is not known for constancy in his entanglements. Cat had said it, and Marius had no reason to disbelieve it. Even if it didn't seem to fit the man he'd come to know. Rakken wanted people to believe he was all surface and idle games, but beneath that mask lay a vein of deep seriousness. Rakken was not a casual man.

Which meant... what?

In the midst of his crisis, Jack came in. Marius took another sip of tea and tried to pull himself together.

"You're up early. How is His Royal Highness?" Jack asked, serving himself a couple of eggs.

Marius tensed. "I don't know. I haven't seen him. I think he might have left." It came out more plaintive than he wanted.

Jack shrugged and went back to piling his plate. Marius laid his palms carefully on the white tablecloth, trying to calm the thunder of his pulse. Alexandra might have interpreted Rakken's speech last night through the generous lens of friendship, but Marius didn't think Jack was similarly naïve.

Jack sat down and began to methodically work through his food. Unlike Marius, he was a naturally earlier riser. Quite likely he'd already been out on the estate.

Marius fiddled with the tablecloth, wondering if he could bolt.

"How's the detective work going, then?" Jack asked. As if he hadn't heard Rakken professing his love less than twelve hours prior. Or at least, didn't care.

Marius felt a sudden surge of affection for his cousin. "We, um, found the dryad who sold the plants to my colleague," he said, and proceeded to give Jack a loose overview of the facts as they stood. He pulled the notebook he'd taken from Stoneholm out of his coat pocket—he'd worn the same coat yesterday.

As he opened it, a slip of paper fell out. Marius frowned at it, recognising the handwriting after a moment.

I have gone to speak to my sister; there are things I must deal with. My apologies for last night. You should be safe from Emyranthus now.

—Rake

Marius stared at it.

"A clue?"

Marius shook his head. "No, it's—Rake left me a note. Apologising."

"I can see how that would be surprising," Jack said drily. "Not an apologetic sort. Though I've seen men do far worse in their cups than he did. At least he's a happy drunk."

"He wasn't drunk; he was drugged." Marius couldn't help defending Rakken. "And it wasn't his fault in any case. He didn't *ask* to be drugged."

Irokoi came in at that moment, followed by Grandmamma and Alexandra. Irokoi was in his fae form, dark horns rising from his silver hair.

Irokoi had a stack of books under one arm and beamed upon seeing Marius. "Oh good; you're still here. I thought you might have gone with Mossfeathers, but I can't blame you for not, since he was in such a mood."

"What do you mean?" And what did Rakken mean by apologising for last night? Did that mean he hadn't meant what he said? What did anything mean?

Irokoi's mismatched eyes were too knowing. "He does not like his wounds to be touched, or even seen, that one." His mouth twisted. "Not that any of us do, really. Anyway, these are for you." He deposited the books next to Marius's plate.

"From the High King's library?" Marius asked, struggling to focus. Exactly what *things* did Rakken need to deal with?

"Yes. They're everything I found about magical plants, if you still need them. There might be more I haven't found; there are a lot of books. I think I've convinced the lake guardian not to eat humans, but no one will volunteer to test whether it worked or not." Irokoi looked downcast for a moment, and then his eyes brightened. "Do you want to try?" He added, thoughtfully: "You can run quite quickly if you need to, can't you?"

Jack gave a snort of laughter behind him.

In other circumstances, Marius would have been tempted. An undersea magical library filled with ancient books from another culture? It sounded fascinating. He also didn't believe Irokoi's haplessness; he suspected Irokoi's approach to risk was conservative, and that if Irokoi thought he'd made it safe, it was.

But he wanted Rakken to be the one to show it to him. As soon as he realised what he was thinking, he shook it angrily away. He took a deep breath, smiling at Irokoi with effort. "I'll let you know if I think it's necessary. I'd rather not risk my neck and then find out the book I needed was already here. Thank you for these." He patted the stack.

After breakfast, he went up to see Hetta. She was awake although not yet dressed, wrapped in a cosy dressing-gown and eating honey-drenched crumpets. Phoebe was there too, holding a sleeping babe.

"How are you feeling?" Marius asked his sister. She looked tired but very happy.

"Sore." She grimaced. "I don't recommend childbirth."

"I'll do my best to avoid it," he said. "Congratulations. They're beautiful."

She laughed, but her face changed as she looked down at the babes, suffused with an awed softness. "I love them so much, it's ridiculous. I didn't think I could love anything this much." There was a sheen of tears in her eyes.

Marius felt she was allowed some hormonal excesses under

the circumstances, but he still spoke quickly to avoid her bursting into tears. "That can only be a good thing, since they seem like quite a lot of work."

"The midwife says today is the grace-day," Hetta admitted.

The door opened to admit Wyn, carrying a tea tray. Or rather, a coffee tray. Hetta's eyes lit up. For her husband or the coffee, it was hard to say.

"You do know you're not the butler anymore?" she said as Wyn padded over and deposited it. There were spare cups, which was absolutely typical of Wyn, although Marius now suspected he used his leysight to give him that sort of extra preparedness.

"Just keeping my hand in," Wyn said. He picked up one of the babes, which looked even tinier in his arms.

"Do you know what you're going to name them?" Marius asked.

Hetta glanced at Wyn. "We thought Edith, for one."

"Edith," he repeated. It was their mother's name.

"You don't mind?" she asked anxiously.

Marius shook his head. "No—I think it's a lovely idea. That's only one name though. What about the other?"

"Aeryn," Wyn said softly. A fae name.

"Welcome to the world, Edith and Aeryn," Marius told his nieces.

He left Wyn and Hetta to their happily dazed bubble of family life, his heart aching. He had wanted to ask Wyn his advice, but it didn't feel right to intrude at such a time.

Instead, he packed up Irokoi's books and the manifest from Stoneholm and went back to Knoxbridge. Alone.

31

SAUSAGES FOR JUSTICE

MARIUS PAINSTAKINGLY WORKED his way through Stoneholm's manifest over the next few days, matching descriptions to names and identifying each in turn. It was slow going, and he wasn't entirely sure why he was doing it except that he couldn't think of what else to do now.

Also, it was a distraction from Rakken's absence. He felt adrift. He'd moved back into his room at the college, his windows now repaired (Thistlefel viewed the transition with disfavour). Logically, things there should not remind him of Rakken, and yet somehow, they did. He'd buried the teacup dragon in the bottom of his trunk.

Maybe he *did* love Rakken. He wasn't sure. He missed him, at least. He'd grown used to having the sharp-tongued presence over his shoulder. The way that Rakken could follow his scatterbrained jumps in conversation. Missed his sheer *presence*, which tended to dominate any space attempting to contain him.

But after a week with no sign of the aggravating fairy, Marius's ambivalence shifted towards anger. How dare Rakken tell him he loved him and then just *run away*?

It was in this mood that he encountered Bakir in the common room. They had run into each other enough times now that it was no longer excruciating, but there remained a line of tension between them. Still, Marius wasn't going to be awkwarded out of his own common room, and he was sick of his own room. It was too wet to walk off his restlessness. Outside, the rain came in intermittent grumbles.

He gave Bakir a wary nod of acknowledgement and settled down to work at a desk by the window. There was no one else around. Even if there had been, the Emyranthus incident had created a kind of fraught bubble around him that meant his peers tended to keep their distance.

After nearly an hour had passed, Marius looked up in surprise. Bakir had crossed the space between them and now stood over him, shuffling awkwardly from foot to foot. "Valstar," he began.

Marius put his pen down. "What is it?"

Bakir swallowed. "I want to apologise—not to you. To your… fae friend." He nodded at Thistlefel, who had stretched herself out in front of the fireplace. Marius was surprised that Bakir had noticed her. For the most part, people didn't, and the few people who did assumed he'd smuggled a dog in. He lived in nervous anticipation of someone complaining to the Dean.

Thistlefel raised her head and chirped an acknowledgement.

"Go ahead then. She can understand you," Marius translated.

Bakir awkwardly squatted down so that he was at the same level. "I didn't know you weren't just animals, but I should have worked it out sooner. I'm sorry."

Thistlefel's plumed tail flicked side to side. She did not have much use for apologies, but she would accept a debt-payment from him. Marius passed this on.

Bakir blinked. "A what?"

"It's a fae thing," Marius explained. "Since you are acknowledging you wronged her, she will accept a payment of her choosing as redress."

Bakir looked alarmed. "What sort of payment?"

Thistlefel was very fond of sausages. She got up, and her ear tufts fanned out to their full extent, a trio of them on either side of her head.

"Really?" Bakir looked at Marius for guidance. "Sausages?"

Marius started stacking his books. "Don't look at me; it's her right to set it. Lowfae have their own priorities. I would have set it higher."

Bakir got slowly to his feet. "All right. Sausages it is, then. You up for a drink? I've given up on these proofs for the night anyway." He looked back to his own stack of papers with distaste.

Marius hesitated. But this wasn't up to him, was it, if Thistlefel wanted to forgive the fellow? He thought of Vane's modified quizzing glasses and his own culpability. Had Bakir been guilty of any worse naiveté than himself? "All right," he said eventually.

Bakir swallowed. "The... other fellow isn't going to be coming, is he?"

"No," he said shortly.

Bakir relaxed. Marius almost apologised for how Rakken had compelled him but stopped himself. He was no longer sure whether it had been right or wrong, but it was not his to apologise for.

After returning his things to his room and fetching his coat, they left the college. Under the eaves of the shop fronts, the drizzle wasn't too bad, and the pub was only a few minutes' walk. "No fairies are going to attack us, I hope?" Bakir said, shooting Marius a curious look.

Marius shook his head. "Not anymore." He could tell Bakir was bursting to ask more, but manners held him back. It struck him, suddenly, that he could tell Bakir the truth, or some of it. "That was a lovers' quarrel. She and Rake had a, um, brief fling that he ended."

"Ohhhh." Bakir drew the syllable out in understanding. Then he laughed. "That's rather reassuring, to know fairies are just as petty as us. I know a fellow whose beau set the bed on fire when she found him, ah, in flagrante delicto with another. Women," he said with a shake of his head. "Hormonal creatures. Best avoided."

Marius snorted. "Men being such upstanding examples of rationality."

Bakir cut him a sharp glance, too much knowing in his eyes. "Feathered fellow not coming back?"

Marius blew out a long breath. "I don't know."

Bakir clearly got the message that he didn't want to talk about it and changed the subject. They grumbled about supervisors and marking and speculated on when the ice on the lake would grow thick enough for the winter curling competition.

When they reached the pub, Bakir ordered an extra lot of sausages for Thistlefel. She gobbled them down in a truly astonishing time and declared them adequate. But, she added, there were a great many mortal inn-places that sold sausages. Also butchers. She would let him know when next she felt like eating some.

"You didn't think she meant just *one* lot of sausages, did you?" Marius said, laughing at Bakir's expression.

Bakir manfully accepted this news. The talk turned to other things, but Marius caught the thread of something under it, a kind of low-boiling anxiety. Marius's control remained imperfect, and every now and then he would catch a snatch of something thought rather than spoken. It was still a marked improvement, being able to sit in a pub without becoming rapidly overwhelmed by the roar of the masses.

Bakir put his drink down. The simmering sense of anxiety Marius was getting off him increased. "So, to confront the elephant in the room: the police still haven't found whoever killed Vane or that other poor bloke, have they?"

"No, they haven't," Marius said.

Bakir slid him a sideways look. "But they think it must have been the fae fellow who was selling Vane the plants, right?"

Marius was about to answer when he felt it, a frisson of awareness. He looked up and found Rakken standing next to their booth, glowering down at the two of them. Every inch of skin flushed as he fought down competing urges to do something between strangle, kiss him, and demand explanations. Instead, he carefully put down his glass and said calmly, "Good evening."

Rakken's eyes narrowed at Bakir, who had gone completely stiff. "You may leave us, Thomas Bakir."

Anger rose in a rush. "Hey! You don't get to just chuck people out! You're the one who's turned up uninvited—you can jolly well wait."

Some of Bakir's stiffness eased, but he held up his hands. "I am not getting in the middle of this." He got up. Briefly, it looked as if he might say something else, but in the end, he just shook his head and left.

Rakken slid into the space he'd vacated. Marius drank him in hungrily, despite being furious at his high-handedness.

"You promised," Rakken said, throwing him into confusion for a moment before he realised what he was talking about, and the even more startling realisation that followed.

"You're jealous," he spluttered. "Really? You turn up here after giving no clue as to when you plan to return and throw out someone who I was having an entirely platonic drink with, just so's you know. You have no right."

Rakken relaxed at the words 'entirely platonic', and Marius stared at him in disbelief. "Do you really not trust me?"

"Humans can lie," Rakken said. *And you fell in love with a miserable excuse for a mortal once before on no basis I can see.*

Marius stood up, furious. Despite spending most of the last week wishing Rakken were here, he now wished to put as much distance between the two of them as possible. He pushed his way out of the pub and onto the dark streets, ignoring the spiky presence following him.

32

OUTSTANDING DECISION—MAKING, EVERYONE

R AKKEN DIDN'T SAY anything as Marius wove his way through the cobbled streets. Marius didn't think too hard about where he was going. "Since you're intent on following me, I'm not still in danger, am I?"

Rakken shook his head. "Emyr will not break an oath; she likes her power too well."

"What will happen to her?" The rain drizzled down. They both ignored it.

"Cat wanted to cast her out of ThousandSpire and declare her anathema," Rakken said softly.

"Good." He was in agreement with Cat on this one. "What she meant to do—hells, what she *did* do."

Rakken gave him a sideways glance. "You told her I would not forgive her for it, and you were right. I took her wings. She will be a long time regrowing them."

Marius swallowed. That's what Rakken had been busy doing, then. "You remember that night? I wasn't sure if you would."

"Yes. I remember everything." Rakken grimaced, and then said grudgingly: "Thank you for saving me from Emyr. I suppose playing entertainment to an assortment of Valstars was a trivial enough price to pay for that."

"I think it rather improved their opinion of you. Alexandra called you sweet."

Rakken's lip curled in disgust.

They arrived outside Rakken's hired lodgings in Pennyroyal Lane. Of course. It was logical—they were going to fight, he could feel, and he didn't want to do it in public or at the college, where the walls were all too thin.

His body prickled with anticipation, his breath coming too quick. *Riiiight. Fighting. That's definitely what you're anticipating*, his inner logician drawled in a voice that sounded a lot like Rakken's.

Thistlefel, sounding deeply unimpressed, said that she was going to stay out here in the garden for a bit. Rakken's eyes were bright, but he didn't comment as he unlocked the door.

The minute they were inside, Marius practically leapt to the opposite side of the room. The words *I love you* sat in the air between them, unspoken and deafening, until Marius couldn't bear it.

"Did you mean what you said about—"

"Yes." Rakken hissed the word.

"Oh. How long have you…?"

Rakken gave a hollow laugh. "A while. I cannot pinpoint the precise moment of its inception."

"But you never said anything," he felt bound to argue. "I thought you disliked me!"

Rakken gave him a dry look. "I bargained my life for yours, Marius."

"Well, yes, but you would have done the same for anyone in that circumstance!"

"I would *not*."

"But you can't—"

Rakken stiffened. "Do not tell me what I can or can't feel, Marius Valstar. I meant what I said."

"But I thought—we agreed this wasn't... And you despise mortals."

"I did not plan this." Rakken sounded tired. "And I do not despise *all* mortals."

Marius's shoulders went up, but he could not help the single humiliating syllable that escaped: "Why?"

Rakken said, without hesitation: "I defy anyone to spend significant time with you and not love you."

It was, again, a statement that left Marius winded. He almost wished Rakken hadn't said it. He couldn't believe it, and yet he couldn't *not* believe it.

Rakken's eyes were a bit wild, his thoughts as loud as a clarion call. *What am I doing? Maelstrom take me, I'm a fool.* A wave of panic came with the thoughts, which snapped off as Rakken brought up his shields, hard and impenetrable as adamantine. His expression went smooth as well, revealing nothing.

They stared at each other. Marius's heartbeat thundered in his ears, but he felt detached from his own body, as if directing the strings of a puppet from a distance.

"Storms, you are bad for my ego." Rakken cursed, turned on his heel, and would have stalked out.

"No, don't go." Marius jerked back into motion and took several steps forward, hands stretched out to stop him.

Rakken looked haughtily down at him. Despite his retreat into maximum chilliness, beneath that surface lay a vein of vulnerability that could shatter if struck just so. "I do not want your pity."

"I don't pity you!" His throat felt dry. His heart thudded against his ribs. "It's just, I never thought you would… so I didn't… *You're* the one who said it didn't mean anything, between us, that it could never work, who kept trying to claim we weren't even friends! Of course I was trying not to get attached, when I know you'll only—" He cut off and changed tack. "I missed you when you were gone, and I don't want you to go now."

He was fully aware of how inadequate this sentiment was under the circumstances, but he couldn't make himself say the words that he knew Rakken desperately wanted to hear. Even the thought of it paralysed him.

"You missed me." Rakken's voice held an edge. "What do you want from me?" A crack in the ice, the heat of anger showing beneath.

"For you to not run off into the night before I've had the chance to, to *adjust*! Can we just… try? Please? Behave slightly more like grown adults?" It made something in him scramble, the thought that this might not be enough, that Rakken might stalk off and out of his life. Again. Even if he would probably do that anyway, once he fell out of love with Marius.

"Try." Rakken said the word as if it might bite him.

"Try seeing how we go if we stop pretending this thing between us doesn't mean anything. Try seeing if it could be… more." It was hard to get the words out. Something like terror seized him, crushing his ribs. "Or if you—"

Rakken's eyes flashed. He closed the distance in a rush, looming large. "If I *what?*" Marius's back hit the wall. "If I *what*, Marius Valstar? Stop loving you because your damned

John did?" He gave an angry laugh, and a wash of power ran over him, sending the threads of gold in his dark hair glittering, making his brown skin almost seem to glow. "Perhaps you are right. Bloodlock is a mind-altering substance; you are an extremely powerful telepath capable of projecting. Perhaps the combination…"

Marius went cold. "You think I might have influenced you? I wouldn't—I didn't—is that *possible?*"

Rakken took another step forward, so close now that their bodies nearly but not quite touched, his breath hot on Marius's lips. Every nerve stretched, straining to cross that distance between them.

"Shall we see if it wears off? Shall we stop now and see if that makes it wear off sooner?" Rakken's voice was low and sensual, and his lips were curled nearly into a snarl. He had that cruel light in his eyes that meant torment of the most pleasurable sort, and Marius's body responded even as his mind raced, worrying over Rakken's words. Was Rakken just lashing out, or did he truly think some unlucky combination of drugs and telepathy responsible for his earlier declaration? Marius couldn't imagine anything more awful than Rakken being forced to feel something against his will.

"Rake…" he said, fighting his body's arousal. "I don't want you to feel coerced into anything. You know I wouldn't want that."

Rakken didn't touch him, but shivering rivulets of his magic began to trail over Marius's skin beneath his clothes, ghost-caresses. Marius gave a small, helpless gasp. They worked their way up his legs, down his abdomen, nibbling and tugging.

"Do not dare use me as a shield, Marius Valstar. I know what *I* want. Tell me to stop because *you* do not want it, because *you* are afraid. Tell me you do not want *me*. Tell. Me. To. Stop."

The sensations sharpened, moving lower, and Marius launched himself at Rakken. They met in a clash of lips and teeth. Rakken growled and buried his hands in Marius's hair, and Marius scrabbled for Rakken's clothing, not sure how they had gotten here but past caring. Rakken hissed as Marius got a hand down his trousers and palmed his cock. They were both already hard.

Marius went to his knees.

Rakken took a harsh breath. He held it as Marius unfastened him, as if afraid the slightest movement would be the wrong one. But when Marius rubbed his cheek against the thick length, Rakken jerked and exhaled in a rush.

Marius looked up. Rakken's eyes glittered beneath heavy lids. Anger and longing and something he was too terrified to name pulsed between them like a heartbeat.

Without breaking eye contact, he leaned forward. Rakken swore, something not Prydinian, his fingers curling into Marius's hair. "Don't stop," he said hoarsely.

He didn't, relishing it. He was so angry and so aroused and gods, he'd missed him. Missed *this*, the earthy taste, the way all his senses heightened. Everything between them felt so knotted up, but this, *this* was simple.

Rakken's breathing grew ragged, and the ghost-caresses began again in earnest, feathering over him until he had to fight not to spill there and then. He took Rakken so deep that he nearly gagged, but it didn't stop him, only fuelling his efforts.

Rakken groaned, fisting his hands in his hair. "Storms. Marius. *Marius*. I want to feel you."

And then he was pushing Marius away so he could sink down onto the rug as well. He toppled Marius, following him over so that Marius fell somewhat gracelessly onto his back with Rakken on top of him.

Rakken's mouth was on his, his lithe body pressing against him. Lips and tongue messy in his fervour. When he sat back, the curve of his buttocks pressed against Marius's hardness. He began to strip Marius of his shirt. Marius groaned, hips arching, unable to quite get enough friction. Rakken knew it too, devilry in his eyes as he held him down. The light touch of Rakken's magic began to quiver again over his skin, sensitising every inch of him.

"Rake, please."

"Soon," Rakken promised, stroking a possessive hand down Marius's chest. He leaned forwards to press a kiss where his hand had touched, licking and teasing. Pleasure spiked through him, almost painful in intensity. When Rakken reached down to free him of his trousers, he almost sobbed in relief.

And then Rakken was back kneeling over him, thighs pressing on either side of him, positioning himself. He'd prepared himself already, and Marius had a vague moment of wondering if magic could be used for that purpose too, but then warm heat enveloped him, pushing out everything but want.

It was too much and not quite enough, but Marius wasn't in control, Rakken setting a rhythm that drove him wild. Gods, he was so beautiful, the long lines of him rippling as he moved, all muscular grace. Rakken's head fell back as he rode him, his own cock hardening further.

Marius strained upwards, coming unravelled stroke by stroke. He became a creature without words, mindless begging sounds falling from his lips. His eyes would have screwed shut but Rakken growled, "No. Keep looking at me," and caught and held him in the burning emerald of his gaze.

There was a beat of magic and Rakken's wings unfurled behind him, horns rising suddenly from his dark hair. Marius was drowning in the taste of his magic, as if the world had reduced to only the sound of rain falling on orange leaves, falling on Marius's own body with that same soft relentlessness. Rakken's wings half beat with every stroke, impaling himself even deeper, and the intensity of his magic sharpened. Still his gaze didn't leave Marius's, and something frightening rose in his chest, an emotion he didn't want to name.

You are mine, starling.

He closed his eyes and came with a cry, felt Rakken follow him mere moments later, collapsing on top of him, a warm, heavy weight. Feathers closed around them.

"I think I'm dead," Marius said when he was able to string words together again, still unable to open his eyes. "You've killed me. Bloody hells, Rake."

Rakken's chuckle rumbled against him. "I have no regrets. Do you?"

"Much as I like the weight of you, I'd also like to breathe again."

Rakken obligingly rearranged himself so that they lay face-to-face, though one wing still spread over Marius's body. There was something soft in his eyes for all his smug expression.

Marius swallowed. "Do you—do you really think that the bloodlock…"

Rakken's fingers went to Marius's lips, gently shushing him. "No, I do not think that. Do not provoke me again. I am considering agreeing to your terms."

Marius frowned. "My terms?"

"You said we should… try and see what happens. In either direction," he added grimly. *Storms above, is this what I am reduced to?* "I must remain here until this small matter of murder is resolved. I see no need to deny myself pleasure in the meantime, unless you do? Fair warning, if so; I will continue to attempt to seduce you into bed."

Marius ought to tell Rakken that they should end this thing between them right now. One or both of them was going to get hurt, and despite Rakken's declared feelings, Marius rather suspected it would be himself.

Even if it hadn't been some horrifying side-effect of the bloodlock, it didn't seem likely that whatever Rakken felt would last. And yet... for now, Rakken loved him. Thinking of it sent something inside him panicking even as warmth curled in his chest, but he didn't want to let it go. Not yet.

Well done for making sense in your own head, he thought helplessly.

33

A REVIEW OF THE CASE SO FAR

H E'D EXPECTED THINGS to feel different, somehow, now that he knew that Rakken (deep breath) loved him. However, only two things changed over the next few days. The first was that Rakken did not leave his bed to sleep, which Marius rather liked. The second, which Marius did *not* like, was that things between them felt constrained, as if they were each on their best behaviour for fear of hurting the other.

Not that Marius was thinking about the fact that Rakken loved him. He was in fact doing his best to avoid thinking about it, but it was impossible in the same way that not thinking of pink elephants immediately after someone said 'don't think of pink elephants' was impossible.

Rakken never raised the subject. Sometimes, though, Marius caught him watching him with soft eyes, and his heart would pound. He couldn't trust it. Why had Rakken gone and made things so complicated? Everything had been *fine*. Hadn't it? Why did he feel so *muddled*, logic as impossible to grasp as mist?

He tried his best to distract himself and focus instead on his research, official and otherwise. Maybe everything would sort itself out if he gave it time. Or Rakken would grow bored. It wasn't as if there weren't precedent. He remembered the night of Hetta's wedding, when Rakken had changed his mind with such cutting cruelty. Not that that had been about love, but it highlighted Rakken's personality, didn't it? But then he wanted to argue that it didn't, that Rakken wasn't like that at all.

So he catalogued plants and buried himself in the texts Irokoi had given him while Rakken attended more diplomatic events. At Greenbriars' urging, he finally submitted a lacklustre but mundane-focused draft proposal. Meanwhile, his notes on fae plants, lowfae, and alternative research filled an entire binder.

"I have found an answer to your faithful companion's transformation," Rakken said, late one night in the Pennyroyal flat. They sat in the window, having just finished a game of chess. Love or not, Rakken didn't hold back, though Marius was starting to win occasionally. Not tonight, though.

"Oh?" Marius stopped cradling his downed king and put it back on the board.

Rakken retrieved a slender book with a snap of his fingers and handed it to him. It was titled *On Mortal Influences*. "It's by Cerseekai, who made a study of lowfae five centuries ago. I was right that Severenn was referencing an earlier study. Cerseekai observed occasional but unpredictable changes in some lowfae when exposed to what she termed 'mortal influences'. I suspect her vagueness was because she herself was unclear on the exact set of circumstances required.

"She theorised that it was some combination of powerful symbolic triggers—blood, for instance—and intent. Most of the lowfae were changed for the worse, twisted in some way.

I wonder if they might have inspired some of the darker tales you mortals tell of us. The beasts that lurk at the forest's heart, the creature in the well… One might say Mortal has its own darksinks."

"Thistlefel isn't twisted!"

Thistlefel gave a bark of agreement from the hearthrug.

Rakken leaned back in his chair. "No, but she wasn't exposed to blood with ill intent. You intended to see her safe without any notion of obligation between you. She bit you in fear, and you sympathised rather than lashing out. That was a powerful and very mortal act. You are also a projection-capable telepath. I suspect your feelings on the matter of imprisoning lowfae were conveyed rather strongly."

"Why should she feel herself bound to me, then?"

Rakken slid him a look. "You gave her something of your essence, and you are one of the most loyal people I know. It does not astonish me that a creature you influenced should also display such a characteristic."

Marius still didn't know what to do with these, these *compliments* Rakken kept bestowing. He felt flustered and had a sort of reflexive impulse to push them away, as if he didn't, he'd shatter what remained of his thin defences and he couldn't— he couldn't. Perhaps he was not *capable* of love; perhaps his experience with John had left something in him permanently broken.

He ducked his head, unable to meet Rakken's eyes.

Rakken straightened chess pieces, the soft clink of them against the board the only sound for long moments. "Cat has asked me for a full briefing on the investigation's progress. How close are you to matching the plants against Stoneholm's manifest?"

Marius looked up, grateful for the change of subject and simultaneously ashamed of his own cowardice. "Close. Another few hours' work, I should think. Shall I come with you to report the results? I want to ask Irokoi if he knows anything more about the plants Stoneholm listed; he's the one who brought me the reference book that's been the most use. We could do that on the way."

Rakken frowned. "Perhaps we ought to take the opportunity to bring all of our interested parties together. I cannot help but feel there is something here we are missing."

Marius agreed that this sounded sensible enough, but he couldn't help giving him a suspicious look alongside it. Rakken had some other motivation, he knew, but he didn't press.

IN THE END, THEY asked Caro, Irokoi, and after some careful consideration, Jenny, to come with them to ThousandSpire. It was awkward to include Jenny, but Marius knew she wanted to find Vane's murderer more than anyone, and if they were pooling ideas, she had a unique perspective on the situation. And she *had* been a great help cataloguing the plants. Hetta and Wyn had been excused for reasons of sleep deprivation.

After the journey through the Gates, Caro and Jenny stood on the steps of the palace in ThousandSpire with wide-eyed fascination. Both of them were primly dressed in stout woollen gowns, Caro's red hair pulled tight under her hat. Jenny looked even younger than she was with her face slack with wonder. It made Marius remember his own first time visiting. Fortunately, both women were too dazzled to notice that the fae citizenry was viewing the party of humans with the same degree of amazement.

Marius pointed out Rakken's tower rising in the distance. "That's where we're meeting."

"How do we get up there?" Caro asked.

"Fly," he said.

Caro's eyebrows went up, and she turned to Rakken. "You must have non-aerial ways of transporting goods up there. I am sure such a method can accommodate people as well. That's assuming you've been so foolish as to not allow any accommodation for non-winged people in your architecture." She remained unimpressed when Rakken tried his customary spiel about his tower being so many wings high.

Rakken smiled, one of his genuine ones. "My tower has an ascension platform," he admitted.

Marius whirled on him. "You never told *me* that!"

Caro snorted. Rakken looked entirely unrepentant. Jenny said nothing, watching the interaction with her habitual reserve, though her eyes were huge.

"I will show you the foot-way," Irokoi offered. "City flying is tricky, and I would rather go a different way to these two anyway so we will not have to watch them fondle each other. We can take one of the aer-hoppers. They go over the ground, and I think you will enjoy seeing them."

Both Jenny and Caro looked startled. Marius flushed, but before he could come up with a clever retort, Irokoi had held out his arms to the two women, and the three of them had begun to walk down the steps. Thistlefel gave a huff and bounded after them.

Rakken meaningfully unfurled his wings.

"You *were* finding excuses to fly around with me in your arms!" Marius accused.

Rakken didn't look at all apologetic. "And you deliberately didn't try very hard to think of alternatives. One might think you wanted the excuse as well. Come," he said, holding out an imperious arm. "Let me *fondle* you."

Marius snorted, but amusement shifted to something else as he stepped closer. Rakken did not immediately launch them skywards, his gaze resting on Marius's. His expression was unreadable, but Marius's heart sped up anyway.

Then Rakken shook his head, as if at his own folly, and took off in a rush of wings and magic.

They reached the tower first. Rakken summoned refreshments, and Marius wandered over to rearrange the piles of books so that they didn't cover all the chairs. Rakken wanted to add more detailed botanical tags to them before they were re-shelved.

Queen Catsmere arrived just as Marius was trying to find a good spot to set down the last stack.

"Marius Valstar," she said, her expression unreadable.

He eyed her warily. "Are you going to throw knives at me again?"

"Are you going to break his heart?" She nodded at Rakken, who had just re-emerged back into the main level of the tower.

Marius spluttered.

"Cat," Rakken said, a warning.

Catsmere smiled. "Of course I'm not going to throw any more knives. It didn't put him off last time anyway." She patted Marius's lapel in a comforting sort of way. He couldn't help a small flinch. Her smile widened.

A soft chime sounded, and they all turned towards it. The

smooth inner wall near the stairwell shimmered and opened, revealing Irokoi, Caro, and Jenny standing in whatever the magical fae equivalent of a hydraulic lift was. No wonder Marius hadn't noticed it before; when the door slid closed it became once again invisible.

Caro wore the bemused expression that most people got after spending too much time in Irokoi's company. She shook it off at the sight of Catsmere and, to his surprise, dipped a brief curtsy. "Your Majesty."

Jenny followed suit after a beat, flushing. Irokoi blinked and then did the same, startling Caro into a laugh.

"Oh. Was mine so very bad, then?" Irokoi asked her.

She shook her head. "No, you did it very creditably. It's only that men bow, usually."

Irokoi turned to his sister, his expression comically chagrined. "I should not have tried for a mortal greeting." He put his hands together and bowed, transforming to fae form as he did so, so that his black wings swept out and added an extra flourish to the movement. Jenny's eyes went even rounder. "Well met, little cat. Already the Spires feel very different from our father's time. I like it."

"You are welcome to stay, Koi," Catsmere told him.

"Thank you. One day I will, but I am having too much fun with Valstars at the moment. They're very... energising." He slid a sly look at Rakken. "Aren't they, Mossfeathers?"

Rakken didn't rise to this obvious bait. "Shall we commence?" He gestured to the various seating options and himself chose a seat on the short-backed sofa, arranging his wings behind. "Marius?"

After a moment of internal wrestling, Marius joined him, though he kept a decorous distance between them. His shoulders straightened. He had nothing to hide here, did he? He could sit next to his lover if he wished.

But no one batted an eyelid, taking the wind out of his defiant sails. Rakken fanned out a wing so that if Marius leaned his head back, he would touch feathers. He looked a bit smug. This, Marius realised, had been the other part of his motivation for arranging this gathering; he'd wanted to stake a claim publicly. Marius's heart gave a painful thud.

Catsmere had once again chosen to sit like a perched falcon on the round backless seat. Jenny had the armchair, possibly because it was furthest away from the rest of them, while Irokoi and Caro sat at either end of a chaise longue. All four of them looked at him and Rakken expectantly.

Marius took a deep breath. "We asked you to come because we've spent too much time inside this case. The more heads the better, and all that. You all know the main details already. We thought for a long time that the murderer was either a dryad illegally trading rare plants or the sorcerer Emyranthus, but we learnt recently that neither of them was responsible. So, effectively, we find ourselves back at square one." He swallowed. "Laying things out from first principles, we have two mortal botanists killed a month apart, with signs of fae magic present at both murders—"

Rakken liked listening to Marius speak, the way he would make several abortive attempts while he marshalled his thoughts. How what had begun chaotically would gain steam and become powerfully articulate until his whole countenance lit up with passion.

Marius broke off, muddled by the thought that wasn't his own. He glared at Rakken.

Rakken took up the explanation without missing a beat.

"The first mortal, Dr Martin Vane, was trading in fae plants with the dryad Stoneholm. Stoneholm did not kill Vane; though the dryad was there that night, they had already left before Vane died. Vane was killed by a blow to the head and then stabbed with the dryad blade Stoneholm had left behind. The fae plants were later taken from the scene by Vane's lover. Who we have also confirmed did not kill Vane."

Marius didn't look at Jenny.

"The second mortal, Peter Kendrick, was in the greenhouse with the stolen plants when he was killed. He was killed in the same manner as Vane—a blow to the head followed by stabbing to his chest, although this time no weapon was left at the scene. Peter Kendrick was similar in appearance and age to Vane. I could not identify the signature of the fae magic I sensed at either murder, though it was stronger at the second scene than the first."

"Vane was also trapping lowfae," Marius added, with a glance at Thistlefel, who was busily sniffing her way around the room's perimeter. "He had some notion of selling them, we think. He had an associate who knew about the lowfae. He didn't kill Vane either."

Caro was frowning. "You seem very sure that all these people didn't kill Vane."

Rakken and Marius exchanged glances. "Some of them, I, er, confirmed. Some of them Rake compelled. We didn't do it *lightly*!" he felt bound to add, even though Caro's expression hadn't changed.

"What about your professor? Didn't you say he was competing with Vane for funding?" Caro asked. Her eyes bored meaningfully into Marius, her thought transmitting clearly: *and it was his daughter sleeping with Vane. He wouldn't have liked that if he found out about it.*

Jenny stiffened. "Are you accusing my father of murder?"

"What, then, was the cause of the magic Rake sensed?" Irokoi quickly intervened. "I am assuming this professor has none such?"

"No, he does not," Rakken said. "Also, I confirmed that he did not kill Peter Kendrick."

Jenny slowly began to unbristle.

"Some fae vigilante who found out what Vane was doing to lowfae and strenuously objected?" Caro hazarded. "And came back to finish off poor Mr Kendrick on principle, perhaps assuming he was involved too because he was near the stolen fae plants?"

Rakken drummed his fingers on his seat. "The second attack is what stops me. I could believe the explanation for the first murder to be an attack of rage. An unplanned blow to the head, and then a weak attempt at misdirection by using the dryad blade after the fact. But why was the same method used again on the second mortal? If we assume the first murder was unplanned, the second must have been deliberately staged to imitate it. Why?"

No one answered him. Thistlefel finished her inspection and trotted over to the sofa, where she jumped up and inserted herself between Rakken and Marius. Rakken's eyes narrowed. Thistlefel turned in a circle and rested her chin on Marius's knee.

He gave her ears an absent stroke. "None of the plants listed in Stoneholm's manifest have any terribly exciting properties that we could find. I brought the list with me—I'm hoping you two might know more." He nodded at Irokoi and Catsmere and got up to fetch the things he'd brought with him.

Thistlefel grumbled at being dislodged and turned speculative eyes on Rakken. Rakken raised an eyebrow at her.

"I don't suppose you have any ideas, helichaun?"

Thistlefel was quite willing to bite people if that would be helpful, but she could not see that it was yet.

Rakken chuckled. "Noted."

Thistlefel shrugged, got down, and went to demand further petting from Caro while Marius distributed the list to Irokoi and Catsmere.

He returned to the sofa while they each read through it, handing his sketchbook to Rakken. He'd written the names from the manifest under each drawing as he and Jenny had identified them. It had been rather like a children's game, matching tiles.

After a few minutes, Catsmere shook her head. "I only know some of these, but there is nothing here that gives me qualms. Nothing in the same category as the bloodlock or the other plants you found at Vane's apartment. Koi?"

Irokoi's lips moved as his finger ran down the list. "I have used some of these in spells before, but I agree with Catling. There is nothing here that wakens dread in me."

"We finished matching the manifest to the live specimens yesterday. Well—nearly. There's one missing: something called myrtleaf. Do either of you know it?" Marius asked Catsmere and Irokoi. They shook their heads. "I can read the description." He found the page in *Common Plants of the Upper Courts*, which was one of Irokoi's finds from the High King's library, and held up the illustration. "It ought to have a large, flax-like form with mottled grey-green variegation. But none of the plants we found look like that." Marius nodded at Jenny, who had been watching proceedings with quiet intensity, her small form almost swallowed in the large armchair. "We're not sure whether Stoneholm never delivered it or if it was taken before the plants were moved from the original scene. It could have been destroyed in the original attack. Or we could have wrongly identified something." Jenny made a small sound of disagreement; she didn't think they would have made that sort of mistake.

"What of this one? It is unlabelled." Rakken shifted closer, so that their thighs touched, and tapped a page from Marius's sketchbook. The unlabelled sketch was of the plant that Jenny had taken custody of: a small, dense succulent with mottled grey-green leaves. It looked nothing like the illustration in the book.

Marius wrinkled his nose. "It could be, I suppose. It's a wildly different phenotype to the one illustrated, but that could be a bad likeness. Or perhaps myrtleaf has a wide natural variation; that happens with mortal plants all the time." He offered the sketch to both Catsmere and Irokoi in turn, but neither recognised it.

Taking it back, he lined up the book with his sketch to compare the two more closely. They didn't have much in common except for the colour. He read the description again. There was a note about the plant's flowering habits: *flowers only when exposed to the light of the full moon.* Unhelpfully, no drawing was included of the flowers. He frowned. It *had* been full moon the night of Vane's murder; could the form change that substantially after flowering? He gave this theory to Rakken, who agreed it might be possible. Jenny had straightened at this talk, and he saw her fingers twitch, as if she were itching to take notes.

"It would hardly be the most dramatic change the Mortal Realm has inspired in something of fae origin," Rakken said with a wry glance at Thistlefel. "Another mortal influence, perhaps."

"Doesn't get us any further though." Marius closed both books with a snap. "None of the plants in Stoneholm's list seem to be worth killing for, and if they were, why hasn't anybody tried again since? They're still in police custody."

"The university's custody, you mean. Where they seem likely to remain," Caro pointed out thoughtfully.

"You think someone in the botany department killed Vane to get access to fae plants? And Peter was, what, part of it? Seems a stretch. How could they have controlled where they'd end up?" Marius objected.

Jenny was frowning between the two of them, but she didn't say anything.

"Where else would confiscated rare specimens go, under the circumstances?" Caro asked.

Rakken's eyes brightened, feathers rustling as his shoulders straightened. "There are others in the department who would covet Vane's position or his specimens. I did not compel truth from them, so I could have missed their guilt. Perhaps I ought to, this time."

Caro looked alarmed. "What about the flare of dark magic you sensed, though? You said it came from a fae," she added quickly.

Rakken's shoulders drooped back. "Yes. Unmistakably so. The same signature both times."

Marius sat bolt upright. "They were both killed at full moon, which is a time of power. The path to the Goblin Market opens then. Are there other places you can only get through from at full moon?"

Rakken made a thoughtful sound in the back of his throat.

"Moon paths are a strange and wild form of connection. I don't think anyone has mapped them, or even tried to. There are primal beings that could use such ways, who would certainly have killed Vane for his temerity if he had attracted their attention, but I cannot see why they would try to throw suspicion on another or why they should return a month later to kill an unconnected mortal in the same fashion. Still, the method of killing could be an obscure form of ritual. Koi, do you know anything of such moon rituals?"

Irokoi looked bleak. "You are asking me if I know anything about blood sacrifice? That is what you are talking about, killing mortals under full moon for the power of it. That is dark magic, brother."

Rakken didn't blink. "Yes."

Irokoi sighed, curling his wings around himself. "I do not know of anything matching the descriptions you have given. Except that in all blood sacrifice, the choice of victim is always significant."

"A primal creature with a taste for dark-haired mortal botanists," Rakken said with disgust. "Untidy."

"It's full moon again soon," Marius said slowly. "And I'm a dark-haired mortal botanist."

34

A STAKEOUT

THEY WAITED IN Marius's greenhouse for moonrise. He had resolved the issue of whether to stake out his greenhouse or the fae plants by moving the plants to his greenhouse. Rakken sat with him, his magic damped down as far as it would go and under a powerful glamour. It didn't affect Marius, but anyone else—hopefully including the murderer—would assume Marius was alone.

He'd expected Rakken to veto this plan to use himself as bait in its entirety, but Rakken had surprised him. Or perhaps it shouldn't have surprised him; Rakken had never treated him as incapable of holding his own. He'd never made Marius feel fragile in the way his family so often did despite their best intentions.

It was quiet in the gardens at this time of night. Marius worked his way around his plants, inspecting each in turn for health. The cuttings he'd taken were rooting.

Thistlefel lay silently under a bench, pretending to be just another regular garden lowfae even though she now weighed five stone and her head reached his mid-thigh when standing. He had tried to persuade her to stay home, and she'd been having none of it. She did not much care who had murdered Vane, except possibly to thank them, but Marius was hers to guard.

He paused to watch Rakken lay out a detection spell, admiring the line of him, the way he moved. What would happen if they did find the murderer tonight? Would Rakken leave straightaway, after? Did Marius want him to? They'd never agreed exactly how long this 'trying' would go on for, but surely Rakken was growing tired of his vacillating? On cue, his heart began to race, his mind wanting to shy from the thought.

He couldn't just keep not thinking of it. What *did* he feel towards the man? He knew that he liked him, gods help him, despite or perhaps even because of his spikiness. Watching Rakken move, he let himself admit that underneath Rakken's intense guardedness was a man he liked rather a lot.

He wasn't sure he'd ever *liked* John. Loved, yes, but John had never made him laugh like Rakken did. He'd never met John's eyes across a table and known what he was about to say, telepathy notwithstanding.

With John, love had been like a madness, making him wilfully blind to all the man's faults. He did not feel particularly blind to Rakken's faults. Manipulative, ruthless, sharp-tongued man. And yet those same qualities were also his strengths. Rakken would go to any length for those he cared for, regardless of social convention, personal cost, or any other difficulty. He had absolutely no shame, and Marius found that a very reassuring quality when he himself had it in excess. He saw Marius as his equal, and his arrogance demanded that Marius must see himself in that same light.

The corner of Rakken's mouth lifted. "I am trying to work."

"I haven't said anything!"

"I can feel the intensity of your gaze." He rocked back on his heels, met Marius's eyes and preened—there was no other word for it.

"I like watching you work," Marius admitted softly.

"I know. I like you watching me also," Rakken said and continued working with a slight smirk.

Are you going to break his heart? Cat had asked point-blank. He'd been too flustered at the time to wonder at it, but Cat didn't ask idle questions. Nor did she make idle threats. Why *had* she tried to frighten Marius off long before Rakken had confessed his feelings? He couldn't imagine Cat generally bothered to threaten her twin's lovers.

He frowned. Rakken was so good at misdirection, at instantly curling away from things that meant something to him. He pretended he didn't care at all when he in fact cared too deeply, but Marius thought he had the true measure of him now. He knew Rakken had two ways of dealing with things that threatened to expose his vulnerabilities: avoidance and lashing out.

"That night at Hetta and Wyn's wedding. You tried to make me hate you. And then you avoided me afterwards," Marius said, feeling his way towards a conclusion.

Rakken finished tying off his spell. "I shall know if anything fae comes within the radius I have set." He turned back, shadows carving his face into familiar angles as he studied Marius.

"Rake," Marius said, a soft remonstrance. For a moment he thought that Rakken wouldn't answer or would say (quite reasonably) that this wasn't the time for intensely emotional dissections. If Marius had avoided raising the subject between them since that fraught argument, Rakken had avoided it with similar studiousness.

"I did treat you badly that night, and other times," Rakken said abruptly. "I regret it, but I do not have a pat excuse to give you. I wanted you. I wanted you too much. It is dangerous to want things. I wanted you so much that it frightened me, and so I decided to make sure I would not have you. It seemed better than waiting for the reverse to happen." A wry smile. "Ironic, in hindsight, though I find I do not mind the waiting as much as I thought."

Two methods of dealing with vulnerability, and this was neither of them. Here he was, baring his throat against all his instincts. *Oh, Rake,* Marius thought, his heart squeezing as blinding realisation hit him. *You love so rarely, and still everyone you love eventually leaves you in some way.*

"What happens after this?" he burst out.

"After?" Rakken repeated slowly.

"After we figure out who killed Vane. What happens with you and me? With us?"

"I was not intending to give you up. Unless..." Rakken shook his head. "No. I was about to say unless you wish me to go, but I am not so noble. Until I am convinced there is no hope left for me, I shall plague you to the full extent of my abilities. I shall turn up in your lecture theatres to aggravate you and skulk seductively in greenhouses and flirt shamelessly at every opportunity. Consider this your fair warning. I do not care for things *lightly;* it is not in me to relinquish them without a fight, and storms, I will fight for you, Marius Valstar. I'm told I can be very persuasive." His eyes gleamed.

"Rake," Marius said softly. He could do this, though his chest felt full of thorns and his heart beat so hard it hurt. He *could* trust this man, couldn't he? Oh, gods. It felt like he was dying. "I want you to know—"

But Rakken put a hand over his mouth. "No. Not tonight, when we go to face a murderer."

Then he jerked as if struck, all his feathers fluffing up. Beneath the bench, Thistlefel growled.

"Company?" Marius asked, looking wildly around. The plants were much as they'd left them. All the elektric lights were on, making it impossible to see what was out there in the darkness.

"Human," Rakken said, his attention pulling outside the greenhouse. "Coming closer and—no. They are waiting a little distance away."

They exchanged glances. "I'll go see who it is," Marius said. "If it's someone innocent, I'll get rid of them, and if not, you can come along all invisible and guard my back. I don't fancy being stabbed if we're wrong about this and our murderer turns out to be completely mundane and not an eldritch horror after all."

Thistlefel got up and announced that she was coming as well, pressing briefly against his side. A mortal would do well to be wary of her. Marius dug his fingers into her mane, careful of the hidden spikes. "No biting innocent humans," he reminded her.

They left the greenhouse, and Marius tried to think why anyone would be out here so late. Amorous lovers? Over-eager students? Rakken led the way, moving quietly as a cat outside the narrow beam of Marius's torch. With his wings and horns, he made an interesting silhouette. He stopped near a bed of dwarf rhododendrons and nodded tightly.

Marius swept the torch back and forth and jerked as a human face stared back at him with wide eyes, pale in the harsh light. Thistlefel gave one of her odd chirps.

"Jenny," he said blankly, followed immediately by understanding. Of course she'd come. She'd given in far too easily when he'd said she must leave it to them and taken re-possession of her plant.

Jenny picked her way out of her hiding place with dignity. Her chin was up.

"You shouldn't be here!" Marius hissed. "This isn't a game, Jenny!"

"Do you think I don't know that? Martin and Peter are dead! If this isn't a game, I'm not some child to be sent off to bed. I have every right to be here, and more than you. You didn't even like Martin! I want to know who killed him. I want to look in their eyes and ask them why."

"Keep your voice down." He didn't know when the murderer might make an appearance—what if they had already seen them and took fright? "If you stay, you'll just be another person in danger, for no gain."

Jenny gave him a withering look. "I'll be in exactly the same amount of danger as you, maybe less. I brought my grandmother's pistol. Iron works on fae, doesn't it?" She withdrew an ornate piece from her pocket that looked about seven thousand years old.

Marius sucked in a breath through clenched teeth. "Put it away! My gods. Why does your grandmother even *have* a pistol?"

"She was terribly paranoid about highwaymen," Jenny said matter-of-factly. She slid the pistol back into her pocket. "Don't worry; I know how to shoot. But you weren't planning to end up murdered, were you? Your fairy prince is around here somewhere, isn't he?"

There was a dark edge to her tone, and he frowned, suspicion blooming horribly in his gut. But no; Vane and Peter had been stabbed, not shot. He glared at her. "Fine. If you won't go, come back to the greenhouse with me then and keep quiet. You may have already ruined things."

But before either of them could move, footsteps crunched on the gravel path coming from the gate. They turned.

It was Professor Greenbriars, and he was extremely agitated, almost jogging in his haste. He drew to an abrupt halt at the sight of them.

"Jenny! Oh, thank the gods, you're all right. What are you doing, sneaking out at this time of night? Lying to your mother! If it was to meet Marius—" He stopped himself, looking torn. "Well, you shouldn't! Either of you! No need to sneak about, anyway, and—"

"Jenny is *not* here to meet me!" he couldn't help objecting. "I was just telling her to go home!"

Jenny made a sound like an angry cat. "I am not going home! You had no right to follow me!"

"I am your father! I have every right! And after Vane, it's clear your mother and I cannot trust you to act with—" Greenbriars broke off, flushing. So he did know the extent of his daughter's affair and was determined to prevent it happening again. Marius wished himself anywhere else and the Greenbriars on the opposite side of the planet. He slid a look at Rakken, who looked as if he was considering compelling the lot of them— that or forcibly picking both Greenbriars up and dropping them over the fence.

"You understand *nothing!*" Jenny told her father fiercely.

But Greenbriars had collected himself. "Whatever is going on, neither of you should be out here so late. What if that tree fairy who killed Vane and Kendrick comes back? It's not safe."

"The dryad didn't kill Vane," Marius said, and then froze. He'd answered in response to an image that had risen off Greenbriars—an image of Stoneholm, waving a dryad blade at Vane. "How do you know about that?"

Greenbriars' mouth fell open, colour draining from his face. "Well, it stands to reason, doesn't it?" he said hurriedly. "Vane was dealing in fae plants, and it was full moon both times. That's a fairy-tale thing, isn't it? No doubt the fellow who gave Vane the plants came back to find them and killed poor Peter Kendrick for being close by. That's why I told the department they ought to be destroyed!"

Rakken hissed a warning a fraction of a moment before a deafening crash split the night. They turned towards it.

From Marius's greenhouse, something rose.

A vast green shadow moved within, illuminated for only a moment before all the lights went out. Glass shattered, and the iron framing of the domed roof wrenched free with a tortured screech.

A creature emerged from that monstrous egg, lit only by full moon and starlight. Marius's horrified gaze travelled over its vast tentacled form, trying to make sense of it. Was this the eldritch abomination they'd feared, come through a moon path from Faerie? Thistlefel began to rumble in a low, continuous growl, her fur standing on end, ear tufts flattened back against her skull.

With further crashes, the creature pulled its way free of the building. His experiments were definitely ruined, he thought vaguely. At least Greenbriars wouldn't be able to blame him for the delay, not after seeing the cause with his own eyes.

Probably not the time to be worrying about his thesis.

He couldn't make sense of the creature's shape. It didn't

seem to have a head, only tentacles. Grey-green tentacles that stretched out, some as thick as tree trunks, some thin vine-like whips that lashed furiously at the air. Others were sharp-edged, cutting the air like blades. Something about it seemed strangely familiar.

Not tentacles, Marius realised with a shock. Not vine-like. Vines. Leaves. He recognised the grey-green variegation pattern. "It's one of Vane's *plants*," he whispered. "The myrtleaf."

"Triggered by full moon and mortal blood," Rakken said grimly, following Marius's thoughts. Jenny gave a yelp of surprise; Rakken had dropped his glamour.

As if the creature had heard them, the mass of vines swung in their direction. They reached down through the ruins of the greenhouse, grasping bits of iron framing and broken wood, raising them like weapons, akin to a crab wielding bits of shells.

The plant *spoke*.

It spoke in a voice that Marius recognised.

"Vane! How dare you! I saw you with that creature! The department will never stand for this!" It was Greenbriars' voice, distorted and underlain with gnarled roots, the rustle of leaves, and the groan of ancient woodland.

"Of course they will."

They all froze. Marius knew that voice too, though he hadn't heard it in two months. Vane's voice. He sounded contemptuous.

The creature *did* have a face, Marius realised with roiling nausea. Two faces, in fact. Within the nest of vines were two gnarled carvings of men's faces, their mouths opening and closing woodenly. Almost the most distressing thing about it was that neither face changed in expression, though their mimicked voices thrummed with strong emotion.

They were crude reproductions of Greenbriars and Vane's faces, Marius realised as the thing exchanged lines of dialogue with itself and each mouth opened in turn. They argued furiously. The Greenbriar-voice sounded almost apoplectic with rage as it reprimanded Vane for his shamelessness; the Vane-voice remained coolly uncaring, telling the old man to show himself out.

The creature moved towards them as it spoke, pulling itself along on thick, creeping roots. Its progress was strangely controlled, as if it were advancing according to the same inner script as its dialogue.

"It's re-enacting the night Vane was murdered," Marius said, looking to Rakken for confirmation. His heart pounded. He couldn't look at Greenbriars. "Isn't it?"

"It would appear so. Echoing the conditions under which it was born. Shall we let it run to its conclusion? It will probably try to kill one of us in a few moments, as it did Peter Kendrick." Rakken's hands began to spin in circles, a glow gathering in his palms.

"What are—what are you talking about?!" Greenbriars's face was ashen. "This is some cursed fairy monster. Don't listen to it, Jenny; it's all lies! I didn't kill Vane!"

Jenny gave a sob.

"I know what you're doing with my daughter!" the plant thundered.

The real Greenbriars gave a moan. "Oh, gods."

It was horrible, and Marius wanted to know what it was going to say next.

It lumbered forward, a mocking laugh emanating from the Vane-face. "Caught up, have you? You always were a slow-top. Anyone else would have seen what was plainly under their nose months ago."

"You stay away from Jenny! You're no good for her!"

"I'll do as I please, but don't worry, old man; I've no desire to be your son-in-law. My intentions are purely dishonourable."

The Greenbriars-face gave a roar of rage, and the Vane-face cried out in pain and cut off abruptly.

By the plant's previous motions, Marius had been fooled into thinking it was a slow-moving thing, awkward with bulk. But now it moved so rapidly there was no time to react. Not that he was good at quick thinking under the best of circumstances, but now his body helpfully froze in terror. The world became a shadowy jungle, vines blocking out the sky.

A mass of writhing tentacles holding sharp bits of broken greenhouse slammed down and hit light as a barrier flared to life. Rakken snarled, charge streaming off him. That's what he'd been building before, but he hadn't expected the creature to move so fast either, hadn't been fully prepared.

"Stop!" Rakken commanded the creature, and the world bent with the force of the compulsion.

The creature continued to pummel down without pause.

"Wrong kind of mind," Rakken said grimly. His eyes were glowing, the smell of his magic thick as his wings fanned out, lit up with power. "If I can just find a way *in*. Stop, you storm-cursed creature! Run, the rest of you foolish mortals. I will deal with this, but I cannot hit it with lightning with you standing next to me."

The plant was moaning now using only Greenbriars' voice; Vane's had gone silent. "Oh god, what have I done? What have I done?"

Marius broke out of his paralysis. He didn't much like the idea of running and leaving Rakken alone with the creature, but he trusted Rakken's magic. He shoved Greenbriars, who was closest. Greenbriars's expression had gone slack. He seemed immobilised with shock.

Marius tugged at him. "Come on, sir! Jenny, run!"

Jenny's face was pale with terror, but she took her father's elbow and pulled as well. Thistlefel bunted into the man's legs, and Greenbriars jerked suddenly into motion. They all ran for the gate to the gardens as Rakken held up his shield.

But it quickly became apparent that the creature was fixated on Marius. No matter how many shields and strikes Rakken threw at it, it ignored him in favour of its preferred prey, and it was so fast that Marius had barely made it as far as the gate before it was on him again.

Rakken dove on top of him, taking Marius to the ground. Above their prone bodies, the shield flared to life only a hand-span above Rakken's horns. Vines crashed down around them, creating a sinister cocoon of darkness for a moment, lit only by the glow of Rakken's green eyes.

Marius's mind had gone curiously calm. "Peter looked like Vane. *I* look like Vane. That's why it's going for me—to complete its cycle."

"You do not look like anyone else," Rakken growled fiercely.

"It's a plant; they're not known for their keen eyesight," Marius pointed out, panting, Rakken's weight pressing him down. "How *is* it seeing?"

Rakken's whole body glowed with the effort of his magic as he pushed his shield out a little further, giving him space to get off Marius and turn towards the creature. Shadows grew under his eyes and carved his cheekbones in stark knives as power drew from his very flesh. The vines around them were thick now, the drum of them on Rakken's shield relentlessly loud. At least the Greenbriars had made it out. He heard Thistlefel give an angry yowl in the distance, and his heart clenched.

"Stop!" Rakken told the creature again, pushing a powerful wave of compulsion out. It had no effect, and his shield faltered for a fraction of a moment before he bolstered it. He hissed through his teeth in frustration. "I cannot get a grip on it. It *must* have a mind, but it's nothing I have ever seen before."

Marius reached out with his telepathy and found... something. The strangest mind he'd ever encountered: forest shadows and the tang of blood and anger. So much anger. The need to do violence was so strong that Marius choked. It *needed* the dark pulse of death, the stab and blood, needed it with a hunger that was beyond compulsion.

"I can hear it, sort of," he said. He had to practically shout to be heard over the ceaseless thunder of the vines striking the shield. Metal clanged; the murder-plant had not only brought along its trophies from the greenhouse but now seemed to have added the iron railings of the gate to them. Wonderful.

He grabbed one of Rakken's hands and projected what he was sensing from the plant, hoping like blazes it would work. "Can you get a grip on it?"

Rakken bared his teeth, nodding, no energy left to spare for words. He was panting with the effort of keeping his shield up. He growled, drawing more energy. "Stop!" he cried again, and this time Marius felt the ache of the compulsion in his bones.

The shield broke. They were both thrown as the plant convulsed. Marius tumbled into a rose bush and lay stunned for a moment. There was a sudden crash of impact as Thistlefel landed in front of the bush, positioning herself between him and the myrtleaf. But the world seemed to have gone quiet.

Painfully, he extracted himself from the bush and rose to

his feet. Thistlefel's fur was all on end and she had her teeth bared as she growled at the myrtleaf, feet planted firmly to brace for attack.

But the myrtleaf had retracted in on itself, shrinking as Marius watched. A brick clattered to the ground, then a railing, as it let go of its treasures one by one. Its vines became thinner, more leaf-like, curling inwards. The whole process took only seconds, until a grey-green succulent lay innocently under the moonlight. It was larger than it had been before the transformation, but still only the size of a man's head.

Thistlefel pounced on it and seemed disconcerted when it did nothing more than roll when her paws landed on it.

"It worked," Marius breathed. "It worked! Rake?"

He looked around. Rakken was much quicker on his feet than Marius; no doubt he would have managed not to fall into a rose bush.

But Rakken was lying on the ground, up against the half-destroyed fence. His wings were flopped open at a strange angle. Marius's throat went tight, a terrible premonition filling him. Time slowed as he closed the distance, unwrapped the wing, and stared down in horror. Rakken's eyes were closed.

An iron railing protruded from his chest.

35

EVEN MORE BAD THINGS HAPPEN

MARIUS DESPERATELY SCRAMBLED out of his coat and pressed it against the gaping wound. Was Rakken still breathing? He couldn't tell. He had to be breathing. He simply had to be. Marius didn't realise he was screaming silently until Jenny ran up with her hands over her ears.

"Is it gone? What's that noise? I can't seem to block it out! Oh, gods," she added, gaze falling on Rakken. "Is he...?"

He jerked his head towards the unprepossessing myrtleaf. "It's dormant. He's alive." Marius wouldn't let him be anything else. "Help me hold him. I need to get this out."

"I don't think that's a good idea. We ought to—ought to leave it in and call for a doctor."

"No. Iron affects fae magic." He'd seen Wyn made insensible until a bullet was removed. "If you won't help me, I'll do it alone."

Jenny held Rakken down with more pragmatism than he'd expected, and Marius braced himself and pulled. At first his fingers were slippery with blood, and he had to stop and wipe them. It was horrible, and he didn't think he'd ever forget the sucking sound it made or the feeling of metal sliding past bone.

Rakken remained unconscious throughout, which was both a blessing and a very bad sign. He ought to have been screaming. The iron railing came free with a nauseating suck, and Marius threw it roughly aside. The metal clanged as it hit the ground. Rakken was bleeding freely, soaking his shirt, soaking his feathers, turning bronze to rust.

He still couldn't tell if Rakken was breathing, and distantly, a bone-chilling fear began to seep in his edges. He refused to let it in. He'd seen Rakken heal from life-threatening injuries before; he *had* to be able to heal from this, even if the iron had gone right through his heart. Marius would *make* him. Thistlefel pressed against his side, attempting comfort.

"Wake up," he told him, reaching out with his telepathy. *Wake up.*

Jenny's frightened thoughts swept over him, her mind reeling with the night's revelations and now a man dying in front of her. She didn't see how Prince Rakken could be anything but dead after that, even if Marius didn't want to know it yet.

Empathy and shame jockeyed for position; she knew what it was to lose the man you loved to sudden, unspeakable violence, and now Marius was about to know it too, making her a tiny bit less alone. Oh gods, her father. Would they blame him for this death, too? Did she want them to? She hated him for what he'd done and hated that she still cared. She'd left him a shattered man, sitting numbly on a garden bench.

It went on, a chaotic churn of thoughts that Jenny was rather impressively holding in check enough to say aloud, "I'll go and find help," in a remarkably even tone.

From Rakken, Marius heard nothing.

Something inside him snapped, and he grit his teeth and called again. Always before he'd tried to keep the walls between himself and the rest of the world strong and sure. Now he reached out, heedless of the danger.

Emotion flew ahead of logic, desperation driving action before he had time to second guess himself. Rakken needed help, more help than could be had in Mortal. There were hundreds and hundreds of miles between Knoxbridge and Stariel; he could not project that far. He focused on the place in his chest where his land-sense rested whenever he stood within Stariel's bounds. He couldn't feel it outside the estate, but there had to be a connection there, however dormant. Just as there had been a resonance point once between Stariel's greenhouse and his one here, before the murders.

Blood, emotion, sympathy: the key elements of fae magic. His head throbbed, and a succession of fractured images threatened to break his concentration. His telepathy spooled out more violently than it had ever done before, spreading past the quiet darkness of the gardens to the nearby blocks of townhouses and streets, picking up minds as it went until he was nearly lost in the cacophony of hundreds, *thousands*, of minds. He held on to himself grimly—all this noise was *not him*; he had been distilled down to a single point, a single thought, a single desire:

Help. Come here. To the greenhouse.

"I can't go and get help if I stay here!" Jenny said, sounding frantic. "There's nothing I can do here for him."

"Not you."

He really, really hoped he hadn't just mentally summoned the entire town of Knoxbridge to his side.

For a long, long time, nothing happened. And then a portal flickered into being with the smell of earth after rain and the spice of cardamom. Marius took a shuddering breath of relief, his shell of distant terror cracking.

Wyn took in the scene, wings already half-flared in alarm. His gaze fell on Rakken, and he took a sharp, quick breath before he rushed forward. "What happened?" he asked Marius, kneeling next to his brother.

"One of the fae plants. It metamorphosed and attacked at the full moon. It threw an iron railing at him. We pulled it out, but…" He could barely speak, words coming in little chokes. He waved at the now-dormant plant again.

"You did right," Wyn told him. "But he needs the Spires. Help me lift him." Wyn hoisted Rakken up with unnerving fae strength. Rakken's wings dragged on the ground, sticky with blood.

Wyn turned back to the portal, and Marius rose jerkily. His gaze fell on the myrtleaf. "Wait."

He made a sudden dash for it and scooped it into his arms. It didn't react, remaining an odd, rootless succulent. He stumbled after Wyn through the portal, leaving an open-mouthed Jenny staring after him. "My brother-in-law," he said to her, vaguely, before the portal snapped out.

Then Wyn was winging his way into the night. He would go to the Stones, Marius knew, and use the Gate from thence to ThousandSpire.

Marius stood for disoriented minutes in the open doorway of Stariel's old greenhouse where Wyn's portal had opened, holding the terrible plant against his chest. At least here, Hetta could stop it if the myrtleaf went rogue again.

It was raining, a light drizzle, with the full moon only a

blurry smear of light behind the clouds. There was just enough light to make out the familiar shadows of Stariel House and its gardens.

His mind was realms away, wondering if Wyn had reached the Standing Stones yet, and if Cat was already with Rakken. Hetta could magically transport herself within Stariel's grounds, but it had taken her a while to learn the trick of it, and he wasn't sure whether Cat had yet learnt to do the same thing.

Cat wouldn't let her twin die, he was sure, and he knew the power of faelands. Why then, did his heartbeat refuse to slow, his roiling nausea refuse to calm? He could not remember ever feeling so afraid. An old half-memory stirred, of the day of his mother's death, and how he had *known* everything was wrong and would never be quite right again. How icy dread had curled in a tight band around his chest even before his father had bent down to take his small boy's hand and tell him, pale-faced, that he had some bad news and Marius needed to be brave.

He hadn't realised he remembered that. Fuck, why was he remembering that? That wasn't going to happen again.

Thistlefel whined and rubbed her head against his leg. He was safe now; he should put the darkfae down.

He put the myrtleaf down. Its grey-green leaves were pristine. Had it absorbed the blood he'd smeared on it? It otherwise hadn't changed; Rakken's compulsion held. That meant he had to still be alive, didn't it? Or had the plant merely come to the end of its grotesque play-acting naturally? It had lusted for death, he remembered with a shudder.

He wanted to burn it, to watch it crack and split. No. He'd let Rakken do it, blast the cursed thing with a lightning bolt.

If Rakken survived.

Thistlefel licked his hand, and he stuttered into motion, stumbling out to the pump outside the greenhouse. Mechanically, he began to wash his hands, the water shockingly cold. He stared at his fingers, pale spiders in the darkness. His head throbbed, in time to his own heartbeat, he thought. Had he flamed out again?

The world warped.

He stumbled again, no longer standing in the drizzling darkness but in a bedroom—Hetta's bedroom. It was too much to deal with, and he stared blankly at the curtains, mind moving sluggishly. Translocation. Right. His sister could do that, within the bounds of the estate, although she'd never done it to him before.

"Dash it," Hetta said behind him. "Sorry, Marius. I didn't mean to shift you like that. I was only thinking how desperately I wanted to know what was going on, and I must've been more tired than I thought—" She broke off as he turned to face her, her eyes going wide. He realised his clothing was stained with Rakken's blood.

Hetta was wrapped in a dressing gown and holding a bundled infant against one shoulder, deep circles under her eyes. Her short auburn hair was disarrayed. "Are you hurt?"

"It's all Rake's blood, bar a few scratches. The plant—the thing it transformed into. It put an iron railing through him before he made it stop."

A sharp intake of breath. Hetta knew what iron did to fae. His niece made a mewling sound, and Hetta began to jiggle rhythmically from one foot to the other. His niece went quiet.

"Where's the other one? Which one is that?" he couldn't help asking.

"This one's Edith, and Aeryn is asleep, thank Simulsen; I

just got her down again. You woke them both up with your shouting."

"Sorry," he said reflexively. "They heard me?"

Her nose wrinkled. "It might have been me being startled awake that they heard," she allowed. "I didn't know you could speak telepathically that far. Or even speak telepathically at all, really. You were attacked by a plant creature?"

"I didn't know if you'd hear me either, but I don't think it would have worked with anyone else. My lord," he added.

She grimaced. It was a very fae sort of thing, reaching out to one's lord to appeal magically for help. He supposed his land-sense was also a sort of fae magic, but it had been part of the Valstars' inheritance for so long that it didn't feel strange in the same way that this did.

His thoughts chased each other like rabbits. "Gwendelfear! Where is she?" Gwendelfear was a fae with the power to heal who had recently become attached to Stariel through a some-what convoluted chain of events. It would have been quicker to take Rakken to her. Why hadn't he thought of that sooner?

"Gwendelfear isn't here at the moment," Hetta said calmly. "I've introduced her to the concept of 'paid holidays', and I think she's gone to Alverness. It's unfortunate timing, though I don't know if she would have healed Rakken in any case—"

"You could have made her," Marius said, which shocked Hetta. It shocked Marius to realise he meant it, that he'd have asked it of her.

"Yes, I suppose I could have," she said after a pause. Her eyes searched his face and softened. "Rake was alive when Wyn opened the Gate to the Spires. He'll be all right, Marius. I fed you energy once from Stariel, you know—I assume ThousandSpire can do the same. And he's fae. Wyn told me once they could heal from things that would kill a mortal."

"If Rake were mortal, he'd already be dead."

He didn't know what his expression said except that Hetta shifted her baby to a one-armed hold so that she could reach out and grip his shoulder in an awkward half-hug. "Oh, Marius. Sit down; you look about to faint. Wyn will come back as soon as he can with news." She gently pushed him down into the nearest chair. There was a tea service set out on the nearby table.

"The servants are all in bed, but I think there's still some tea left in the pot. I asked them to make me up a tray; I'm doing a lot of late-night snacking at the moment." She pressed her hand to the teapot, and he knew she was using her pyromancy to heat it.

A thin wail began from the nearby cot, and Hetta grimaced. Marius held out his arms. "Hand me the non-crying one."

She laughed but did so. Marius had held babies before, but Edith was at that alarmingly floppy newborn stage, so it was with relief that he managed the transfer. Edith gave a small grunt but stayed asleep.

Hetta went to soothe Aeryn, and Marius just sat and breathed, wishing he were in ThousandSpire. "I brought the plant to you. It's in the greenhouse," he said, when Aeryn had subsided into mere grumbles. "We should probably destroy it. It's... imprinted on a murder, and for all we know will keep trying to re-enact it every full moon. It was Professor Greenbriars, my supervisor, who killed Vane. Gods, I left him there with Jenny—his daughter. She was in love with Vane; it's why Greenbriars killed him, I think; it sounded unplanned. I think he must have picked something up and struck him with it in anger—the rake—and then realised what he'd done. He'd seen Vane talking to Stoneholm moments before, brandishing a blade at him in a threatening manner. He must have decided the dryad would make a good scapegoat. Blood would have gone everywhere—onto the plants. That must have been part of it. What a mess. All my experiments destroyed too."

"I'm so sorry, Marius."

He was less sorry about the experiments than he'd expected. He didn't know what he thought about Greenbriars. The room was jarringly warm and domestic, the sweet, milky scent of baby in his arms. He kept flashing back to the sight of Rakken lying crumpled on the ground.

"Oh gods. I can't stop thinking about him. What if—" He couldn't speak it. He kept his head down, focusing on Edith's tufty reddish hair, her tiny eyelashes as she slept. Hetta said nothing, and it felt like a dam inside him cracking. "I thought if I just made sure to never fall in love with him, he could never break my heart."

Hetta made an involuntary sound.

He didn't look up. "I know. Your uncle is a moron," he told little Edith. "Sorry about that."

There was a scratching at the door and Marius looked up wildly, but it was only Thistlefel, demanding to be let in and highly unimpressed that Marius had disappeared from under her nose, even if it was to see his lord. She inspected Marius's nieces curiously before settling her weight firmly on Marius's feet. They would hold vigil together, she told him.

Time moved strangely. It felt like forever waiting in this warm room, and yet he could not remember afterwards a single word of what he and Hetta talked of. The world only came back into focus at the sound of wingbeats, followed by boots hitting the balcony.

Wyn let himself in, his hair damp and windswept. He met

Marius's eyes, and Marius's throat tightened at the expression in them. The world narrowed, his heartbeat pounding in his ears. He felt dizzy.

"He's alive, Marius, and with the healers. He will live."

Marius began to sob, helplessly, the relief so sharp it made his whole body jerk. It woke Edith, who let out a thin cry.

Wyn came and retrieved his offspring.

"I'm sorry," Marius said between gasps. He put his head in his hands. "I'm sorry."

36

TIME FOR SOME COMFORT

RAKKEN WOKE FROM a dream in which a red-hot skewer was being forced beneath his ribs. Reality was almost as unpleasant. The dull throb of the injury bored into his chest, the pain cresting and falling with each breath. At least he appeared to be alive, conscious, and back in the Spires, which augured well for his chances of recovery. There had been a moment when he'd feared—but his mind flinched from remembering the full horror of the iron entering his flesh. No.

Out of habit, he took stock without opening his eyes or letting his breathing change. Touch and smell told him he was in his own rooms, in his own bed. He stretched out with his leysight; the tower wards were active, which meant Cat. She was the only one who had the key other than himself.

He wasn't alone. A spark of a lowfae—that damned heli-chaun—and the ember-glow of a mortal, which he recognised: Marius. He opened his eyes at once, heart flipping over.

Marius was curled up in a bowl chair next to the bed, which he must have shifted from its usual location. He was reading, though Rakken could not make out the book's title from this angle. As Rakken watched, Marius turned a page, a tiny crease forming briefly between his brows, his thoughts flitting across his expression as if he had spoken aloud. Whatever the author had said, Marius had his own opinions on it. But then, he always did.

Marius shifted in his seat, idly flicking a hair behind his ear. He was so characteristically artless, nestling into place with the graceful awkwardness of an adolescent deer. Rakken drank in the sight of him, wondering how long he had been sitting so. It gave him great satisfaction to think that Marius had been watching over his sickbed, even as he hoped someone had had practicality enough to drag him away and ensure he was getting enough sleep and sustenance.

He studied Marius's features, despairing at the depth of his obsession. Narrow shoulders, slim torso, bones too prominent; he needed to eat more reliably. He had rolled up his shirtsleeves, exposing the lean muscle of his forearms, the slightly paler skin where he was less tanned. His thick black hair was thoroughly rumpled as per usual, no doubt from its owner clutching handfuls of it in agitation. Rakken chose to believe that in this case the agitation was on his account.

He continued his helpless cataloguing. The silver streaks at the temples that Marius despaired of but Rakken thought only added to his attractiveness. The delicately rounded mortal ears. The long nose and fine bone structure of the skull. The beginnings of lines around the mouth and in the corners of the eyes. Every tiny imperfection made the longing in Rakken grow more intense. He knew that many of his past lovers had been objectively more beautiful, but something in this specific man was more potent than sensophorium.

Love is for fools and mortals. Rakken thought of the old adage. *And I am a fool.*

"Marius," he said softly.

The dark-haired mortal jerked out of his abstraction, dropping his book. It made a loud thud as it hit the rug, but Marius ignored it, his gaze snapping straight up to meet Rakken's. And there was the reason for Rakken's ensnarement, in the mind looking out through those deceptively clear grey eyes.

"You're awake!" Marius said, reaching out a hand as if the instinct had come before he could stop himself. "How are you feeling? I can call for a healer—Cat gave me this"—he waved at a summons disc on top of his pile of books.

"In a moment," Rakken said. He struggled his way to sitting, ignoring Marius's rather gratifying protests that he ought not to exert himself. The motion set his injury throbbing even harder and left him irritatingly breathless. "How long have I been asleep?" he asked when the room had stopped spinning.

"Three days!"

Rakken paused.

"Yes, exactly! Even you can't just shrug off being impaled through the heart. *Through the heart,* Rake. You came within an inch of dying, and I—" He swallowed, colour coming into his cheeks. "I want you to know that I—"

"Don't. I would rather you did not make emotionally charged deathbed declarations." His heart felt too tight in his chest.

"This is not your deathbed!" Marius said forcefully.

"No, it is not, but the circumstances are sufficiently close to make my sentiment stand." And that, he could not bear.

"Do you really think I'd say something I didn't mean only out of some vague sense of pity for you?"

Rakken arched his neck. "Not pity. Admiration for my heroics, surely."

Those clear grey eyes again, seeing through him even though

he knew his mental shields were in place.

"Do you expect your own feelings to change?" Marius asked, a gentle challenge. There was no escape.

"No." He felt as if he had bared his throat to a knife, the vulnerability cut so sharp. "I do not."

Marius's eyes softened. "You said once that you are not casual in this way; you must know I'm not either. But if it will reassure you, I'll hold my tongue until you've recovered, Prince Melodramatic."

He smiled, and Rakken wanted to simultaneously melt into a saccharine puddle and summon lightning enough to split the tower down to bare rock in disgust at his own sappiness.

"You may summon a healer, then. I might as well hear the full of it."

Marius hastily activated the summons. Putting it aside, he took one of Rakken's hands in his own. Rakken feared and hoped that he was about to lay aside his previous capitulation and say the thing that he wanted to hear more than anything in the world. He did not, but there was a strength of emotion in his eyes that carried its own meaning. "I'm glad you're back."

The healer arrived. Polyndel wasn't a stormdancer, his wings dark blue bat leather rather than feathered. Rakken had known him since his own boyhood, and Polyndel had not discernibly changed in appearance since then: smooth-faced with a grandfatherly manner. Polyndel did not seem surprised by Marius's presence, and Marius greeted him by name. Three days they had been in each other's company, Rakken mused. The high winds help him.

He wondered what the court knew of his injury, and what they made of a mortal at their prince's sickbed, and then decided that he did not care just now. Cat would have made it clear that Marius was off-limits, and Marius was not without his own sharp teeth.

Rakken would have to make sure that the story of Marius throwing Emyranthus out a window spread. The court did not need to know that Marius hadn't done it on purpose; open soft-heartedness was not a survival trait in Faerie.

Perhaps we will have to learn it, in this new world we find ourselves in, he could not help reflecting, thinking not only of Marius but of Hallowyn, who wielded his sentimentality like a weapon.

Marius offered to withdraw when Polyndel began to unwind the bandages on his torso, but Rakken bade him stay. "You need to know from Polyndel how best to coddle me, obviously," he said loftily. In truth, he did not want Marius to leave his side. Even he could not shake off the cold of so close a brush with death so quickly.

Polyndel's ears twitched, a sign of surprise to those who knew him. Rakken knew why; he had never previously allowed anyone other than Cat and the healers to see him while injured. Marius's presence here was aberration enough, but to expose a wound in his presence?

It will not make me any more or less vulnerable to this one, Rakken could have told Polyndel, but did not. No doubt the healer had already drawn his own conclusions, but Rakken had *some* pride left.

Rather less pride than I had, he thought ruefully as Polyndel poked and prodded. He tried not to wince too obviously.

"It's healing well," Polyndel eventually decided. "I will leave you some pain relief. You must treat yourself gently while this is recovering. No flying, for the moment. And no other strenuous activities either," he added, looking at Marius, who blushed furiously. "I'll expect you to enforce that one, since his highness is historically terrible at taking my advice."

"Er… yes," Marius managed to choke out.

Rakken couldn't help smirking at him.

Polyndel turned his attention back to Rakken, tucking the last of the fresh bandages into place. "And you—no lightning play, especially. The stormdancer native immunity to charge relies on the circuitry of the body being in full working order."

"Which I know perfectly well, seeing as I am a stormdancer and sorcerer both, and this is hardly the first time I have been injured," Rakken said acerbically.

"One would think that would make one remember it," Polyndel agreed. "And yet, I recall a boy—"

"That was *once*, and I was barely fledged at the time," Rakken protested.

"Lost all his hair, and his feathers stood on end for a month," Polyndel told Marius cheerfully. "The eyebrows in particular took ages to grow back."

He sighed. "Must you humiliate me in front of my lover, Polyndel?"

"It's a good incentive for you to remember yourself," Polyndel said, unruffled. "Consider how well he will like you bald when you find yourself tempted to try your magic before you should."

Marius gave a cough that sounded suspiciously like a laugh. Rakken attempted to glower at Polyndel, who ignored him as he always did and packed up his tools with serenity.

"I like Polyndel," Marius said after the healer had left.

"So do I," Rakken admitted. "Despite his lack of respect."

"I'd still want you if you were bald, you know," Marius told Rakken, a smile curving his lips. There was a softness in his eyes that he was not imagining.

Trying to cover how flustered the simple remark had made him, he smoothed his long hair and said lightly, "As you should. This is only the least part of my beauty."

"Yes," Marius agreed, clasping his hand and looking at him with steady grey eyes, cheeks flushed pink.

Maelstrom take him, how was he supposed to *cope* with this mortal when he said things like that and *looked* at him like that, with his whole heart in his expression? Rakken had thought unrequited love was terrible, but this was even more terrible. It felt far more dangerous than any amount of iron through the chest.

Ignoring Marius's protest, he pulled him onto the bed. It was worth the stab of pain to be able to wrap his arms around the thin man. He buried his face in his neck and breathed in his scent.

"The healer told you to take it easy literally less than two minutes ago!"

"Best that you stay here on the bed, then, to avoid me having to get up to retrieve you again."

Marius pretended to grumble, but he couldn't hide his smile as he arranged himself so that Rakken's head rested against his shoulder. He smelled of starch and old books, underlain with a warm masculine scent that was not exactly a magical signature but still unique to him.

A cheerful chirp made Rakken look up. Thistlefel scampered up the stairs to the bedroom.

"Of course you brought the dratted lowfae," Rakken said.

The dratted lowfae ignored this remark and leapt up onto the coverlet and settled herself.

"I used to inspire respect in lesser creatures, before I met you," he remarked to the ceiling. "I suppose this is what I can expect from now on, if it gets out that I was laid low by a plant, of all things. I take it I did dispose of the thing?"

"You definitely stopped it. It seems to have gone into some kind of hibernation, though I took it to Stariel for safekeeping. I thought you might like the honour of destroying it."

"Very much so," he said darkly.

"I feel sorry for it," Marius admitted. "It wasn't the plant's fault it had the bad luck to be splattered with mortal blood at a murder scene under the full moon. Maybe under different circumstances, it would have turned out more like Thistlefel."

Thistlefel made an indignant sound. She was not a plant.

Rakken agreed with her, though of course Marius felt sorry for the thing. "It did not have the mind of a lowfae."

They were silent for a moment, both remembering Rakken's final compulsion. He could hear Marius's heartbeat. Time drifted by, the pain medication slowly activating. He let the half-meditative state slip over him.

That was how Cat found them.

Marius stiffened and began to shift away but was prevented by Rakken absolutely refusing to move the arm he had slung across Marius's waist. "Cat has no illusions about my virtue, as you mortals would call it," Rakken murmured in his ear. "And I should get *some* benefit from being wounded. Coddle me."

An adorable blush spread over Marius's cheeks, but he stayed where he was. Rakken wondered if it was only his mortal prudishness that was ruffled or if he minded being openly linked to ThousandSpire's prince. If it was the latter, he ought not to have held bedside vigil for three days, Rakken thought with satisfaction. It was too late for that.

There was a line of tension in Cat's face that eased when she saw him awake. "Mouse." She frowned when she saw how he was positioned, propped up against Marius's shoulder. She arched an eyebrow—not for Marius on his bed, but that he'd felt the need to make such a statement to her.

Rakken remained unruffled. Cat might have suspected, but he wanted her to know his feelings were unequivocal.

A smile twitched at her lips. "I will throw your mortal out if you can't follow Polyndel's instructions."

"The sage Antorius held the belief that keeping an invalid content aided greatly in the healing process. Perhaps I shall send her book to Polyndel."

Cat was not convinced. There were signs of strain around her eyes, invisible to those who did not know her well.

He considered pointing out that this was but a small taste of how he had felt, the months when he'd feared her dead or worse, but said instead: "I will be well, Cat."

"I always feel like there is another conversation going on between you two beneath the one I can hear," Marius complained.

"In this case, Cat wishes us happiness and will promise to throw no further knives at you, won't she?"

Cat chuckled. "Very well." She came and sat next to him, hand pressing briefly against his wingbone in a gesture of comfort. "Has Marius told you the end of your little saga?"

"Not yet." He raised inquiring eyes to Marius's.

Marius made an unhappy sound. "Professor Greenbriars is under arrest for Vane's murder. He confessed. I feel like I ought to have worked it out sooner. He and Vane were always at odds. Very different philosophies and all that. They were competing for funding, not for the first time, but this time was different. Greenbriars is respected, a member of the old guard. But Vane is—was—"

"Hungry," Rakken summarised.

"Yes. And this time was different—Vane hinted he could gain access to rare fae plants to the funding committee. The department is sadly inclined to look the other way when it comes to provenance, provided their own hands are kept clean, but Greenbriars hates that sort of havey-cavey approach. He's always thought Vane's popularity was undeserved; he never respected him as a researcher. He liked to say that one should let the work stand on its own merits, and that reliability was more important than excitement. That the professional should always outweigh personal considerations."

"Vane represented not only the waning of his own power but the triumph of a philosophy he had spent his whole career fighting against."

"Yes. I was unwittingly part of it too. It annoyed him that external factors had interfered with my university career. He wanted to help me get back on the straight and narrow." Marius grimaced. "Certain things he said made me think he might suspect I wasn't... everything I ought to be."

"You are exactly what you ought to be," Rakken disagreed. Marius smiled, flushing a little. Past his shoulder, he could see that Cat was rolling her eyes at the pair of them. He grinned at her.

Marius sobered as he continued. "He saw Jenny with Vane, overheard their intention to meet again later that night. Greenbriars went instead, after telling his wife he would be working out in his own shed after dinner. He lives only a few minutes from the department; it would have been easy for him to sneak out. He didn't intend to kill Vane. I think he planned to warn him off, possibly threaten to expose him to the department—he knew Vane was already engaged."

"But Vane wasn't alone. Greenbriars saw him talking to the dryad who was supplying him with plants from Faerie in exchange for growing certain others in large quantity for him."

"The bloodlock," Cat murmured.

Rakken could not help a shiver, remembering. Even now, his memories of that night unsettled him, not merely for how recklessly he had shared secrets but how he had felt: so blissfully, falsely happy. He understood now why bloodlock was so addictive.

Marius rubbed his thumb over Rakken's skin. "You can stand right outside the greenhouse at night and not be seen from inside. Vane saw the dryad magic up the dryad blade and threaten Vane before leaving. Then Greenbriars confronted him.

"But it didn't go as he hoped. Instead of being penitent or afraid, Vane laughed at Greenbriars. He mocked him. He didn't care if Jenny was ruined; he had no intention of breaking things off with her—or of marrying her. It enraged Greenbriars. In anger, he picked up the nearest thing to hand—the rake—and struck him. He didn't mean to kill him, I don't think."

"One should not hit people on the head if one does not intend to kill them. Mortals are fragile."

"Well, yes, but a lot of people are hit on the head and don't die. It was bad luck," Marius argued. Of course he would feel sympathy for the murderer. He had been sympathetic to the damned murder-plant too.

"Bad luck did not stab Vane afterwards in an attempt to throw suspicion onto the dryad he had seen earlier in the evening. If one is driven to murder, one should own it," Rakken said.

"It would have ruined his career, everything he'd worked his entire life for. It would mean Vane winning from beyond the grave."

"And framing an innocent?"

Marius frowned. "I don't think he thought of Stoneholm as particularly innocent. He would have known they were engaging in black market dealing just as much as Vane, and remember he'd just seen Stoneholm threaten Vane with the knife in the first place. Perhaps he thought it unlikely they'd be found. I think mainly, though, that Greenbriars was thinking of his own family."

"His own family who have caused their own share of trouble," Rakken pointed out. "His daughter took the plants Vane had traded for from the scene."

"She couldn't have known one of them was going to turn into a monster and kill poor Peter Kendrick at the next full moon. She thought we were involved in the murder, since we turned up so promptly afterwards and you're fae. Of course she didn't trust us." Marius's gaze had turned inward. "She helped me get the iron railing out of you."

Rakken winced. "I am glad I do not remember that."

"Anyway, I think I've figured out what happened with the myrtleaf. I've been doing a lot of reading while you were unconscious. Stoneholm had no reason to suspect it was anything sinister. In Faerie, it is an innocuous plant with minor medicinal properties.

"I found a reference while you were unconscious to a creature called a wyrbark. I think that's what Greenbriars accidentally created the night of the murder. Vane's blood had sunk into the myrtleaf's flesh on the night of the murder, and it lay quiescent for a month until it was exposed to full moon again. It sought not just more blood but to replicate the original scene. It went for poor Peter, who bore a passing physical resemblance to Vane, and then returned to its inactive state. And then it went for me, since I also bear a passing physical resemblance to Vane," Marius added wryly.

"That plant had very little discernment," Rakken said and ignored Cat's low chuckle.

"Well, what do you expect from insane murder-plants?" Marius sighed. "I can't help but wonder how the plant might have transformed if exposed to a different set of circumstances—a kinder one."

"If it is power that triggers the transformation, it is hard to surpass murder at full moon."

"True, but there is Thistlefel as well." Marius had that faraway look he got when he was following his own internal line of logic. "The reference I found made me think that wyrbarks aren't any one specific species—just what you get if sensitive specimens are exposed to exactly the wrong circumstances. So what plants *are* sensitive to mortal influences? What makes them so? And how much influence do you need to apply?"

Rakken exchanged a meaningful glance with Cat. "Yes," she said drily. "You can see why the case has raised considerable interest in the mortal court. Some of their newspaper people have gotten hold of it."

"I am needed."

"You are," she said.

"Which is why you will be following Polyndel's recommendations to the letter," Marius put in.

Cat smirked at him. Rakken couldn't even pretend to be annoyed.

37

SAPPINESS ALL ROUND

S
OME WEEKS LATER, Marius lay with his head resting on Rake's chest. They were in the dilapidated upstairs of Malvern Place, having failed to make it any further before becoming distracted. Both of them, he thought lazily, had felt somewhat constrained by Polyndel's instructions and being in the Spires, where Cat had made it clear she wouldn't forgive either of them if they jeopardised Rakken's recovery. But Rakken had been given permission to use magic again, and his sister had sent him back to the Mortal Realm for the first time.

It was late afternoon. Dust motes sparked gold in the slanted light from the upper windows, the air currents as sleepily motionless as his own body, only the warm rise and fall of his breathing. He felt as if he were caught in the same golden light as the dust motes, every muscle loose and his thoughts for once blessedly quiet, just an empty house filled with bits of old furniture. He picked out the holes in the embroidered canopy above the solid four-poster. It created a small bit of gloom in the now-bright room, like a private tent.

He'd been too distracted earlier to ponder the shapes of the furniture beneath the heavy white dustsheets, but he traced them lazily now. Each thought came gently, like a stone pulled up from the water without leaving ripples. He was sure he could find something to worry about if he tried, but it was so nice to let this stillness wash over him. Even the press of his skin against Rake's was only a drowsy hum of niceness, absent the sharp need that had driven them earlier.

His fingers found the still-healing scar on Rake's chest. It was puckered under his touch, though the colour had faded from angry red to pale pink. Rake's hand was playing idly with his hair, the sensation curiously soothing.

"You could stay here," Rake said.

"I'm tempted to, for today at least."

"I meant beyond that. You do not like your college, and this is not so far from your university, even by mundane means."

This was true; only an hour's train journey. "The house is a wreck. I know Hetta would like to see the place refurbished, but I also know there's no money for it."

"I have sufficient mortal funds. Lease-rights are not an unknown concept to fae. I need a more permanent base to conduct my affairs in the mortal realm—why not here, where I can bed you much more conveniently than elsewhere?"

He rolled over and propped himself up on one elbow so he could look at him. "What are you thinking, Rake?"

Rake's expression was both more guarded and softer than usual. His long dark hair spilled over his shoulder, the wave of dishevelled curls dark against the white sheets. "There is a need for a more permanent ambassador here. My brother's heart lies in the north, not here. He will be glad to give at least some of that burden to me."

His heart beat too fast. "Wyn wouldn't do that. He knows your loyalties lie with the Spires."

"They do, but I think in this instance my loyalties and his are compatible, though no doubt I will have to make him certain promises to treat his precious mortals fairly." Rake sounded put-upon, but Marius knew it was a front. There was a coiled anticipation in him, the relish of a competitive man looking forward to the thrill of a tightly contested game. "My brother and Lord Valstar could continue to use the Gate, but they do not need this house. Or the greenhouse. And you could continue much of your work more effectively here, if you did not have to worry about security at your university."

It wasn't like Rake to over-explain himself, but here he was, arguing as if Marius had given him more objection than simple silence. "You'd do that for me?"

Rake moved then, a smooth show of strength, and Marius found himself abruptly on his back, pressed into the mattress by Rake's weight. Rake pinned Marius's arms above his head, a fierceness in his expression as he leaned forward, daring him to resist.

"There is very little I would not do for you, Marius Valstar." The words were at odds with the aggressiveness of his position. He held Marius pinned and squeezed his muscular thighs around him, as if he wanted to emphasise exactly how in control of the situation he was.

Did he really think he could distract him from the emotion implied in his words? Did he think Marius didn't *know* him now?

Okay, that actually was quite distracting. It wasn't fair that Rake had magic as well as hands, or that he was using the former to create phantom touches. No one could be expected to keep a straight line of thought under that kind of provocation. Oh gods. He arched against the sensation, helpless to do anything but submit to Rake's plans.

Well, not completely helpless. This wasn't fair, but then Rake wasn't playing fair either, so Marius slipped under his shields and projected, at full strength, everything he was feeling back at the damn fae.

A sharp breath, and Rake's grip loosened. Marius took the chance to break free and roll them over.

Rake blinked up at him, heat in his green eyes, his dark hair now spread out against the pillow. "What do you desire, then?"

"You."

Rake's lips curved. "You are welcome to have your way with me."

"No." He put a hand on his chest. "Well, yes. In a moment. But first I wanted to…"

The heat in Rake's gaze ebbed a little, his guard coming up as he waited.

Marius licked his lips, feeling strangely self-conscious. Rake was watching him intently.

"I love you," he said eventually. Hells, it sounded exactly as awkward and insincere as he'd feared. The entire point of waiting to say it had been to make it clear that it was true, because he knew Rake wouldn't trust anything less.

"Do you?"

Marius couldn't read his tone, or anything else. His entire aura had gone dark, his shields as tightly locked as possible.

"Yes!" He couldn't help giving Rake a shake. "I wanted to make sure you'd believe me when I said it."

Rake focused on him with blazing intensity. "Say it again."

"You only said it the once!"

"I also said it considerably sooner."

"Yes, well, I didn't want to lie to you."

"So you didn't love me before, then?"

"That isn't the thing to be focusing on here! I meant I wanted to be sure, and I am now. I love you, you great feathery sod. That is the point." This wasn't how he'd imagined this declaration going.

Rake swallowed. "Why?"

Marius stared down at him, but he appeared serious. "Are you fishing for compliments? No, you're not. You just don't think it's possible that anyone could choose you above anything else." Shock, before Rake's shields slammed down again.

Rake went to move—out from under him, off the bed, no doubt wanting to avoid this entire conversation. "No, don't. Stay. Please. You did say you'd do anything for me."

"Almost anything," Rake qualified, but he sighed and sat back down. "Which I see you're already taking advantage of. Mortals." He didn't quite manage his usual nonchalance; there was something fragile in him, glass under pressure.

Marius put a hand hesitantly in the small of his back, beneath his wings. A tremor went through him. "Do you think I would lie to you about this?" He'd never suspected this deep vein of insecurity; he'd thought he was the one providing all of that and more in their strange relationship. All at once he was angry. "Do you truly doubt me?"

"I... What do you feel for your John, now?"

Marius reared back. "You cannot possibly compare that to this."

Rake turned. His eyes were bright. "Can't I? You told me you loved him."

"Past tense." He stared at Rake in bewilderment. "Look, I'm trying very hard not to read your mind, but you're making it bloody tempting."

"Past tense," Rake said. "That is… How can you—how can you simply cease loving someone?" *And what if it happens again? How can I keep you, then?*

Oh. Rake had never loved anyone before? It daunted him, the magnitude of that admission. "John was…" He tried to answer it as it deserved. "I think there are different kinds of love. There is a kind of love that comes like madness, where it's almost more about the idea than the reality. Infatuation might be a better word for it. Intense but… fragile. It's all castles in the sky, and it can't last, not unless there's something beneath it. And with John, well, there wasn't. He wasn't the man I thought he was, the man I fell in love with the idea of."

"And me?"

"I'm not even sure I love the idea of you," Marius said honestly, startling a chuckle from Rake. "It seems like a bad idea, all around." An arrogant fae prince with ethically questionable magic and a tendency to see people as chess pieces? Who flaunted his sexuality in a way that Marius didn't think he'd ever feel comfortable with for himself? Who his closest family members had warned him away from?

"You're projecting," Rake said drily. "But thank you for listing my faults. Tell me, how is this supposed to persuade me of your affection, again?"

Marius didn't bother to bolster his shield, wrapping his arms around Rake from behind, pressing his head against his wings. "Gods, you're insufferable. I love you. Perhaps I shouldn't. But I know you. No—" he said fiercely when Rake would've spoken. "I *know* you. I know exactly what I love. You can't tell me I don't; I can read your bloody mind."

Rake had gone still in his arms, hardly breathing, but

Marius wasn't done: "You put up this, this mask against the world, pretending you don't care, that nothing matters, but you do. You're the smartest and most provoking man I know. I wish I had half an inch of your decisiveness, the way you face the world without apology. You make me braver, and you make me laugh. You always tell me the truth, even when you know I won't like it. It's mind-boggling that you think I could ever grow bored with you. I don't understand how you could love *me*, given your options. It's not like there's not a thousand other people who'd be happy to warm your bed."

"A thousand is perhaps exaggeration." He couldn't see Rake's face, but he could hear his smirk. "But you warm it adequately enough." A pause, his tone changing. "No. Not adequate. Incomparable. I wouldn't exchange you for any number of other bed partners."

"Oh. Well, good." It made Marius a bit breathless, knowing every word was pure truth.

Rake turned then, in a sweep of wings. He searched Marius's face. "How can you be sure?"

Marius reached for his hand. "I thought if I could just *avoid* loving you, then I wouldn't get hurt when you left. I don't think you're going to leave," he added in a rush when Rake's mouth opened to object. "I was just... afraid. But then, with the wyrbark, I realised there was no avoiding it." Some of the emotion from that night twisted in his throat, making his voice hoarse. "If you'd died, my heart would have been broken worse than John ever managed it. I'm already in too deep. It terrifies me, but I *want* to risk it for you. With you." He swallowed. "How are you sure?"

Rake curved a hand to his cheek. "Because I do not know how to love in some measured, rational fashion, to keep back some part of myself for safety. I can only love with everything in me. The world is less whenever you are absent. I want to gloat about your choosing me and wax lyrical about your virtues to anyone who will listen, human cultural niceties be damned. I want to make you happy." He sighed. "I have no doubt we will continue to argue over anything and everything, but I will never leave you, starling."

Something in Marius's heart shifted, a piece of certainty slotting into place, and all he could do was open his mind and let free the long, pure note of emotion.

After a moment, he felt it reflected back at him: a warm wave that washed away doubt. He was so dizzied by the sensation it took him a moment to realise what it was: Rake had taken down his shields and was focusing his thoughts with all his dread-sorcerer skill.

It was too much, and Marius pulled in his telepathy at the same moment as Rake's shields returned. They stared at each other, wide-eyed.

Rake being Rake, it was not long before his dazed expression shifted towards smug satisfaction. "Well," he said, swallowing. "Perhaps I ought to have done that sooner and saved us a great deal of miscommunication on the subject." He smiled. His eyes were soft as he cupped Marius's face. "A Valstar of my own."

AUTHOR'S NOTE

If you want to follow along with my next projects, you can sign up to my newsletter on my website ajlancaster.com. I include writing updates, snippets of what I'm working on, discounted book sales, and pictures of my cats. I tend to send out a news-letter every month or so, and you can unsubscribe at any time.

If you enjoyed *A Rake of His Own*, please consider leaving a review. Reviews help get the word out to new readers, and as an indie author without the support of a publishing house, I rely hugely on word of mouth.

ACKNOWLEDGEMENTS

From the bottom of my heart, thank you:

Marie & Mel, for troubleshooting walk-and-talks and your continued sympathy for my deeply unsympathetic whines.

Toni, for complaining that I couldn't leave these two without a resolution when you read book four. Rem, for your endless enthusiasm for this ship. Cilla, for coming round to this ship despite originally supporting a different one.

Steph, for generally helping to keep this writer sane.

Carla, for the continuing supply of amazing cakes.

To everyone who read this manuscript pre-publication and gave me feedback and support in equal measure: Mel, Cilla, Rem, Priscilla, Colleen, Lisette, Steph, and Caitlin. Every bit helped!

My wee Mastermind for Australasian Gaslamp Indie Authors aka Romy & Tansy; our zoom catch-ups have been a delight.

My fans who came up with all kinds of fabulous suggestions when I was stuck on naming Thistlefel (with special mention for Kate, who wrote me the loveliest emails and also came up with "helichaun")

Ross and Ria, for answering occasional PhD-related questions.

Any mistakes are my own (or deliberate hand-waving; what's the point of writing fantasy if you can't make stuff up to suit, right?)

And most of all thank you, my readers. Indie authors live or die on word of mouth, and your ongoing support for my books means the world to me.

ABOUT THE AUTHOR

Growing up in rural Aotearoa New Zealand, AJ Lancaster escaped chores by hiding up trees reading books. AJ wrote in the same way as breathing—constantly and without thinking much of it—so it took many years and accumulating a pile of manuscripts to connect this activity to 'being a writer'. Along the way, AJ collected a degree in science, worked in environmental planning, and became an editor.

Now living the urban NZ life with two cats and a wide variety of houseplants, AJ writes and indie publishes romantic, whimsical fantasy books.

In 2021, AJ Lancaster received the Sir Julius Vogel Award for Best New Talent, New Zealand's preeminent awards for science fiction, fantasy, and horror.

You can find AJ on the interwebs at:

- instagram.com/a.j.lancaster
- facebook.com/lancasterwrites
- twitter.com/lancasterwrites

Made in the USA
Coppell, TX
02 December 2024

41487557R00270